AUTHORS LOVE HIM

"Amazing."
—Michael Connelly

"Thrilling."
—Louise Penny

"Brilliant."
—Jeffery Deaver

"Watch for those twists—
they'll get you every time."
—Ian Rankin

"Edge-of-your-seat,
heart-in-your-throat suspense."
—Tess Gerritsen

"The novels of Peter Robinson are chilling,
evocative, deeply nuanced works of art."
—Dennis Lehane

CRITICS LOVE HIM

"Devilishly good."
—*New York Times Book Review*

"Superb."
—*Wall Street Journal*

"First-rate."
—*Washington Post*

"Atmospheric."
—*Los Angeles Times*

"Exquisite."
—*USA Today*

"Rewarding."
—*Seattle Times*

"The equal of . . . P. D. James."
—*St. Louis Post-Dispatch*

YOU'LL LOVE HIM

One of the world's most popular and acclaimed writers, **PETER ROBINSON** grew up in the United Kingdom, and now divides his time between Toronto and England. The bestselling, award-winning author of the Inspector Banks series, he has also written two short-story collections and three standalone novels, which combined have sold more than ten million copies around the world. Among his many honors and prizes are the Edgar Award, the CWA (UK) Dagger in the Library Award, and Sweden's Martin Beck Award.

CHILDREN OF THE REVOLUTION

CHILDREN OF THE REVOLUTION

AN INSPECTOR BANKS NOVEL

Peter Robinson

WILLIAM MORROW
An Imprint of *HarperCollins*Publishers

CHILDREN OF THE REVOLUTION. Copyright © 2014 by Eastvale Enterprises, Inc. All rights reserved. Printed in the United States of America. No part of this book may be used or reproduced in any manner whatsoever without written permission except in the case of brief quotations embodied in critical articles and reviews. For information address HarperCollins Publishers, 195 Broadway, New York, NY 10007.

HarperCollins books may be purchased for educational, business, or sales promotional use. For information please e-mail the Special Markets Department at SPsales @harpercollins.com.

A hardcover edition of this book was published in 2014 by William Morrow, an imprint of HarperCollins Publishers.

FIRST WILLIAM MORROW PAPERBACK EDITION PUBLISHED 2015.

The Library of Congress has catalogued the hardcover edition as follows:
Robinson, Peter, 1950–
   Children of the revolution : an Inspector Banks novel / Peter Robinson — First Edition.
      pages cm
   ISBN 978-0-06-224050-7 (hardback)
   1. Banks, Alan (Fictitious character)—Fiction. 2. Political activists—Fiction. 3. College campuses—Fiction. 4. Murder—Investigation—Fiction. 5. Police—England—Yorkshire—Fiction. 6. Yorkshire (England)—Fiction. I. Title.
      PR6068.01964C45   2014
      823'.914—dc23
                                                                        2013021320

ISBN 978-0-06-224051-4 (pbk.)

15 16 17 18 19   OV/RRD   10 9 8 7 6 5 4 3 2 1

For Sheila

The past lies like a nightmare upon the present.

—Karl Marx, *The Eighteenth Brumaire of Louis Bonaparte*

1

AS DETECTIVE CHIEF INSPECTOR ALAN BANKS WALKED along the disused railway track, he couldn't help but imagine two young lovers kissing on the footbridge ahead, shrouded in smoke from a steam engine. All very *Brief Encounter*. But the age of steam was long gone, and it wasn't love he was walking towards; it was a suspicious death.

Banks made his way towards the group of white-suited crime scene investigators standing outside a tent lit from inside, just beyond the bridge. Other CSIs were working on the bridge itself; its rusted metal sides were so high that Banks could see only their heads and shoulders.

The crime scene lay half a mile south of the village of Coverton, which stood at the very limits of the North Yorkshire county line, at the tip of the Yorkshire Dales National Park, across the A66 from Barnard Castle. The only way to get to the body, Banks had been told over the phone, was to walk along the old railway tracks or through the woods that ran parallel to them about fifty yards to the east.

The railway ran dead straight along a narrow, shallow, U-shaped valley cut into the landscape. The embankments were steep and grassy on both sides, and while there were plenty of weeds growing in the unkempt grass, no one had dumped prams, bicycle frames or refrigerators there, as people did in the more urban areas. The rails and sleepers had been taken up long ago, and the track had been paved over, though many of the flagstones were broken or uneven, and hardy weeds insinuated their way through the cracks. It seemed a long half mile to Banks, especially with the rain and wind whipping right at him down the man-made valley. The only human dwelling Banks saw on his journey stood to his right, just before he got to the bridge: a small, square cottage at the top of the embankment.

When Banks got to the outer cordon, he showed his warrant card to the officer on duty, who lifted the tape for him and handed him a protective hooded overall and shoe covers. Awkwardly, he took off his raincoat and put them on over his clothes. This area was where the CSIs and other officers not required at the immediate scene waited until they were needed. Only essential personnel were allowed through to the inner cordon, inside the tent itself, and as few people as possible at a time.

Already the CSIs were busy fixing up extra lights, as the early November morning was overcast and dull. Banks poked his head inside the canvas flap and saw the crime scene manager, Stefan Nowak, as immaculate as ever and dry, along with Dr. Burns, the police surgeon, and Detective Sergeant Winsome Jackman, all in their white coveralls. Peter Darby, the crime scene photographer, crouched by the body taking photographs with his beat-up old Pentax, his state-of-the-art Handycam in its waterproof case hanging over his shoulder. They all turned to greet Banks, except Darby. Suddenly, the tent seemed crowded, and its humid interior smelled like a wet dog.

Banks saw the crumpled body of an emaciated old man wearing a gray anorak and blue jeans, lying on his back. His neck lay at an impossible angle, one arm was bent in the opposite way to which it should have been, and a sharp knife of bone protruded through the denim on his inner right thigh. His clothes were wet with rain and Banks wondered how long he had been there.

"OK," Banks said to Winsome. "What happened? Run me through it."

"Dog walker found the body," Winsome said, without referring to her notebook. "Or rather, her dog did. Eight thirty-seven, to be precise."

Banks checked his watch. It was five past ten. "That's very precise."

"She's a retired schoolteacher. Probably used to checking her watch every now and then to see when the lesson's due to end."

Banks laughed. "I never realized how the teachers might have hated classes as much as we did. I used to believe they existed just to bore us and terrorize us."

"Children often take a very self-centered view of the world."

"Her name's Margery Halton, sir," came a voice from just beyond the tent's entrance flap. "Sorry for interrupting, but I'm PC Barry Kirwan, Coverton beat manager. I was first officer on the scene. Margery knows me. She came straight to my house, and I followed her up here and saw who it was, then I called it in."

Banks walked back and ducked under the flap into the open. "Where is she now?"

"One of the community support officers took her home, sir. Bit of a state."

"I'm not surprised," said Banks. "Who was he?"

"Name's Gavin Miller, sir."

"Local, then?"

PC Kirwan pointed. "Lived in that old signalman's cottage just up there, other side of the bridge. You must have noticed it on your way here."

Banks turned and looked at the squat cottage he had just passed. "Bijou" would be a kind description. "What do you know about him? What did he do for a living?"

"Don't know much about him at all, sir. Not much of a mixer. Kept himself to himself. Bit of an odd duck, or so the locals thought. Reclusive. Didn't get out much. I don't know how he made his living."

"Next of kin?"

"No idea, sir. I mean, he lived alone. I suppose there might be someone . . ."

"How long had he been living there?"

"He bought the place three or four years ago. It had been up for sale for quite a while. The market was very sluggish, and I think he got a good price. As you'll see, though, it's not very big."

Banks glanced at the embankment and the paved track. "So what's the story of this place, PC Kirwan? What's the lie of the land? How frequently is it used? What's access like?"

"We used to have a branch line here until Dr. Beeching closed it in the early sixties. That was before my time, of course. Anyway, since then, it's just fallen into . . . well, you can see for yourself. We get a few walkers in season, when the weather's good—we're not too far from the Coast to Coast—and maybe a few railway buffs, but not so many in these sort of weather conditions. It's a pretty secluded spot, as you can see, and it doesn't really lead anywhere." He pointed beyond the tent. "Keep going south, and you'll end up at a collapsed viaduct about a mile or so further on. Lark Woods are to the east, above the embankment, and there's a woodland footpath that winds through the woods by the river to the back of the village car park. You can't get a car within half a mile of here unless you really know the area. There are unsurfaced tracks and lanes, access to the signalman's cottage, for example, but they're not generally known, and none of them lead directly to or from Coverton, or anywhere else, for that matter."

"So he could have been lying there undiscovered for a while?"

"I suppose so, sir. But not for days, I wouldn't say."

"All night, though?"

"Easily."

Banks thanked PC Kirwan, went back into the tent and turned to Winsome. "What's the story here?"

"PC Kirwan phoned in to report a suspicious death and suggested we get some cover out here quickly, just in case there was any evidence left that needed preserving. When I got to the scene, it was pretty obvious that our man hadn't just dropped dead from a heart attack while he was out jogging, so . . . well, guv, you can see for yourself."

Peter Darby stood up. "Done for now," he said, and left the tent.

Banks turned to Dr. Burns. "Any idea what we're dealing with, Doc?"

Burns pointed beyond the open tent flap to the bridge. "It would seem from his injuries and the position of the body that he fell off the bridge. I don't think he's been moved, but I haven't had a chance to examine him fully for postmortem lividity yet. Dr. Glendenning will be able to give you a more accurate answer later, when he performs the postmortem. As you can see, the sides of the bridge are quite steep, most likely for the benefit of the farm animals that cross, or used to cross, so an accidental fall is extremely doubtful. It's about a thirty-foot drop, quite enough to cause the kind of injuries his body has sustained on the paved track. Broke his neck and several other bones. He'd also lost a lot of blood from a head wound, too, by the time I got here. And from the leg fracture, of course."

"All caused by the fall?"

Dr. Burns paused. "Possibly. Most."

"Aha," said Banks. "Not committing yourself?"

"Not yet."

"Is there any reason to suppose that someone pushed him?" Banks asked. "Maybe hit him over the head first? Or are you leaning towards suicide?"

"You mean, in which case why did I bring you all the way out here on such a miserable Monday morning?"

"Something like that."

"Well, there's nothing definite yet," Burns admitted. "All I'm saying is that I doubt it was an accident. If he didn't jump, then someone had to have thrown him over the edge."

"Would it be a far enough drop for him, or someone else, to be sure that it would kill him?"

"No," said Burns. "He could have got off lucky and simply broken a few minor bones. Falls are difficult to predict. We've all heard of someone who survived a long drop. But he landed in a very unfortunate manner. As I said, it was the broken neck and the fractured thigh that did for him. The femur severed the femoral artery. Very nasty. He bled out. It would have been quick, and in all likelihood, with the broken neck, he would have been unconscious, maybe even paralyzed, by then. He probably wouldn't have felt any pain, just a sort of growing numbness."

Banks raised his voice so that PC Kirwan outside the tent could hear. "Is there any way to get down from the bridge to the tracks without jumping?"

"Yes, sir," said Kirwan. "It's a bit steep, but you can just scramble down the embankment on either side. In this weather you'd probably end up sliding most of the way on your arse, sir. And there's a slightly better path to the cottage, a few steps cut into the earth."

"So, if it was deliberate, our killer probably knew that he could get down and finish off his victim if the fall didn't do it for him? Even if he had to slide down on his arse?"

"Yes, sir," said Kirwan.

"Any sign of a suicide note?" Banks asked the doctor.

"Nothing."

"Anyone checked out the cottage?"

"Not yet, sir," said Winsome. "We were waiting for you."

Banks glanced towards Nowak. "What do you make of it, Stefan?"

"I don't know," Nowak said in his impeccable and slightly pedantic English, the trace of a Polish accent discernible only now and then in certain cadences. "This weather makes it rather difficult for us. We're working on it, but we've found no fingerprints or footprints on the bridge so far, as one might expect if he'd hauled himself over the side and jumped, but the rain could easily have washed them away. It was quite heavy at times overnight. But the sides are rusted metal, while the base is wooden planks, so we'd be lucky to find anything anyway after a night's rain."

"How much do you reckon he weighs?" Banks asked.

"About a hundred and twenty pounds at a guess," Burns answered.

Banks thought for a moment, then asked Nowak, "Any chance of collecting much trace evidence from the scene?"

"There's always a chance," Nowak answered, "even in this weather. But I'd say no to finger- or footprints, unless someone came by the woodland path. The trees might offer some protection from the rain there."

"Tire tracks?"

"Same. The rain would soften the ground, and some impression might remain, but it's been coming down pretty heavily all night, and the odds are that it will probably have washed away anything laid down from before. We'll be doing our best, though."

"I don't doubt it. Blood? DNA?"

"Possibly. Diluted, difficult, but perhaps not washed away entirely."

"I see you've already bagged his hands," Banks said to the doctor. "Anything there? Skin under a nail, perhaps?"

"Hard to say from a cursory glance," said Dr. Burns. "He was a nail biter."

Banks stood for a moment taking it all in, listening to the thrumming of rain on the canvas. The tent was leaking. A few drops of water trickled down the back of his neck. He should have put his hood up, he realized too late.

The man *could* have jumped, of course. Murders were rare in this isolated part of the county. On the other hand, if he had been intent on suicide, why choose a method that, according to Dr. Burns, could in no way guarantee success and might very well involve a great deal of pain, even paralysis?

"Any idea how long he's been lying here?" Banks asked. "How long he's been dead?"

"It was a chilly night," said Dr. Burns, "and that would have slowed down the processes of rigor mortis and postmortem decay in general. But from what I can see, the paving stones are quite dry under the body. And there are no obvious signs of animal activity. I'd estimate overnight, somewhere around twelve hours, give or take."

"When did it start raining here?"

"Yesterday? About midnight, sir," said PC Kirwan from outside.

"Let's say for the sake of argument that he died between ten and midnight last night," Banks said. "If he didn't come here to kill himself, what was he doing here on a lonely footbridge not so far from his front door with someone who wanted to kill him?"

"Maybe he didn't know the person wanted to kill him, sir," Winsome said. "They could have just had a disagreement and started fighting spontaneously. Or maybe he got waylaid. He had his anorak on. He was prepared for going out."

"Good point. But, the bridge is *south* of his cottage. Not far, admittedly, but why would he walk even just a few yards south to the bridge if he was going to the village? PC Kirwan said there was a definite path from the cottage down the embankment. That would obviously have been the route he'd use, unless he fancied a walk through the woods. And where might he have been going if he hadn't been heading for Coverton?" Banks turned to PC Kirwan. "You said there's nothing further south except a ruined viaduct. Any ideas?"

"No, sir," said Kirwan. "It doesn't make sense. He should have no need to walk south and cross the bridge just to go north. And there's nothing but miles of open country. A few farms, of course."

"What was he carrying in his pockets?" Banks asked.

"I was wondering when you'd get around to asking that," Winsome answered. She picked up a plastic evidence bag from the bin beside her. "Mostly just the usual. It's all nicely bagged, sealed and signed. Wallet containing one credit card and driving license, expired, in the name of Gavin Miller, along with one five-pound note and some receipts from the Spar grocery in Coverton and Bargain Booze in Eastvale, mobile phone, keys, a small penknife, loose change, a packet of Silk Cut and a cheap butane lighter. Then there's this." With a slight touch of theatricality, she pulled out a bulky envelope and showed its contents to Banks. From what he could see, they were fifty-pound notes, the new ones, with Boulton and Watt on the back. "Cash," Winsome went on. "There's five thousand pounds here. I counted it. Not something you'd need for a walk in the woods, I'd say. And that's why we dragged you out here on a miserable Monday morning, sir."

Banks whistled. "Indeed. I suppose we can rule out a mugging, then?"

THERE WAS no garage attached to Gavin Miller's cottage, though there was a paved space beside it the right size and shape for a small car. But there was no car. Banks made a mental note to check whether Miller owned one. The bridge was too narrow for even the slimmest of sports cars to pass over, but the rough laneway widened in front of the cottage, and Banks assumed it probably joined up eventually with one of the local unfenced roads, as PC Kirwan had suggested. It was the closest thing to a road out of there, at any rate. Anyone who used it to get to Gavin Miller's house would probably have had to know of its existence in advance, though, which would indicate that if it had been used, there was a chance the assailant had known Miller and had visited him there before. But such speculation was for the future, when the CSIs had given Banks more to work on, and when he knew for certain one way or another whether Miller had committed suicide. At a quick glance, Banks could see no signs of a vehicle having traveled the track recently.

The postage stamp garden had been given over to the growing of herbs. Banks had been cultivating a similar patch himself over the summer, and he recognized thyme, dill, parsley, rosemary and chives. The key turned easily in the lock, and it was a relief to get inside out of the rain. Banks and Winsome were still wearing their protective suits and gloves so they could make a quick search of Gavin Miller's house without contaminating the scene before the CSIs came to turn the place over.

Banks fumbled for the light switch and found it to the right of the door. A shaded bulb in a ceiling fixture illuminated a small living room, with just enough space for a couple of well-worn maroon armchairs, a small bookcase, fireplace complete with tiled hearth and mantelpiece, and a desk by the window, which looked out through grubby, moth-eaten lace curtains over the footpath and the fields to the south, with the railway embankment, woods and bridge just visible to the left. The cream wall-to-wall carpet was marked by two large wine or coffee stains the shape of Australia and Africa, the wallpaper was peeling in places, where it reached the ceiling, and a few cheap framed abstract prints hung on the rose-patterned walls. No family photographs stood on the mantel or on the desk. The chilly room also smelled of stale smoke, as if it hadn't been aired or vacuumed in a while, and the layer of dust on the mantelpiece and desk bore this out. Banks remembered that Miller had a packet of Silk Cut in his pocket.

The desk had clearly been used recently, as the dust had been disturbed, and the computer that sat there wasn't dusty at all. The power light was on, screen saver showing a swirling pattern of psychedelic designs, and a squat black Wi-Fi hub stood on the window ledge, its blue lights steady. Beside it sat a green tin ashtray advertising John Smith's Bitter, in which lay a number of stubbed-out cigarettes, the ends of the filters stained brown. Banks eyed the computer greedily. It might contain information that would help him find out what happened to Gavin Miller, but he knew better than to touch anything. When you find a computer at any scene connected with a possible crime, you don't check the user's browsing habits; you leave it for the experts.

Banks and Winsome searched through the desk drawers and found stationery, mini USB drives, old backup CDs, chargers and various connecting wires. In one of the side drawers Banks found an envelope full of old photos: a pop festival of some kind, the stage way in the distance; a picket line scuffle, with police in riot gear; a student demo; a city Banks didn't recognize, tall buildings glinting in the sun; a group of people standing outside a modern building; more groups at restaurants and on beaches; mountains and a sheltered bay; a deep blue lake reflecting the fir trees on the hills that surrounded it, snow-capped mountains in the distance. That was it: some black and white, some color, no portraits, no dates, no names, no indication whether Miller had taken them.

The books were mostly paperback British and European literary classics, from *Robinson Crusoe* to *L'Etranger*. There was also a shelf of literary criticism and general nonfiction: Sartre's *Being and Nothingness*, Kierkegaard's *The Sickness unto Death*, F. R. Leavis's *The Great Tradition*. Heavy reading, Banks thought.

A door with a broken handle led into the kitchen, beyond which was a tiny downstairs toilet and washbasin. The kitchen was surprisingly tidy, dishes washed and standing in the rack beside the sink, all surfaces wiped clean. There wasn't much food in the fridge except for some wilted broccoli and leftover chicken tikka masala in a plastic container. Still, Banks wasn't one to speak; anyone who took the trouble to look would find the same in his fridge, as often as not, except he didn't bother with the plastic container. The green box by the door was full of empty wine bottles—cheap wine, Banks noticed—mixed in with a few whisky bottles, also cheap brands often on sale at Bargain Booze. It looked as if Miller preferred to stop in to do his drinking. If he was as reclusive as PC Kirwan had suggested, he probably did it alone.

Up a flight of narrow, uncarpeted stairs were two bedrooms and a bathroom, complete with small walk-in shower. A cursory inspection of the bathroom cabinet showed only the usual: razor, shaving cream, Elastoplast, and a selection of over-the-counter medications such as paracetamol, Alka-Seltzer and acid reducers. There were also two prescription medications: an old bottle of heavy-duty painkillers, still half full, and a more recent one of Ativan, sublingual. Banks could see no signs of a toothbrush, toothpaste or deodorant.

One bedroom was large enough to hold a double bed, wardrobe and dresser, and it was clearly where Miller had slept. The bed was unmade, strewn with discarded underwear, socks and shirts, and an MP3 player lay on the bedside table next to a glass of water, in which a dead fly floated, and a digital clock radio. Banks turned on the radio. It was tuned to Radio Two.

Winsome shivered. "A bit parky in here, isn't it?"

"The radiator's not turned on," said Banks. "He must have been counting his pennies."

"With five grand in his pocket?"

Banks shrugged.

The second bedroom seemed to be Miller's den, similar in a way to Banks's entertainment room at Newhope Cottage. There was a cheap laptop computer and the obligatory flat-screen TV hooked up to a fine surround-sound system, which was also connected to a turntable. Most of the equipment was fairly old, Banks noticed, at least three or four years, which is old for electronics. Gavin Miller's music collection began and ended with the sixties and very early seventies, and most of it was on vinyl. There was plenty of Soft Machine, Pink Floyd and Jimi Hendrix, and a lot of Grateful Dead, some of the LPs still plastic wrapped.

"A Dead head," Banks muttered.

"Pardon?" said Winsome.

Banks pointed to the rows of albums, CDs, DVDs and the blowups of the *American Beauty* and *Live/Dead* album covers on the wall. "It's what they call people who are fanatical about the Grateful Dead. It used to refer to people who followed the band around from gig to gig. How old was Miller? Did you check?"

"Fifty-nine," Winsome said.

"Jesus Christ!" said Banks, shocked that Miller had turned out to be close to his own age. "He looked to be in his seventies."

"That's what a hard life will do to you, sir."

Banks gazed at her curiously, wondering if that was one of her cryptic warnings. "He's about the right age, then," he said finally. "For the Grateful Dead and all that."

"Are you one, too, sir? A Dead head?"

Banks laughed. "Me? No. I just like to listen to them sometimes. And don't be cheeky. I'm not fifty-nine, either. It certainly doesn't seem as if anyone has broken in here, does it? There wasn't any damage to the door, and the electronic stuff is all intact. It's old, mind you, but it might fetch a few quid at a car boot sale. Some of these records are probably worth a bob or two to a collector."

"How many burglars have you met who'd know a valuable LP from a hole in the ground?" said Winsome.

"Maybe they get a better class of burglar around Coverton?"

Winsome gave him a look. "More likely, if anyone did break in, they were after something specific and not interested in a stack of old vinyl and posters. And they were clever enough to enter and leave the place intact."

Banks glanced at the DVDs and saw that Miller was a serious film buff. His shelves housed an extensive collection of foreign art house films from such directors as Tarkovsky, Almodóvar, Fellini, Kuro-sawa, Truffaut, Ozu and Godard, along with a stack of *Sight & Sound* magazines, right up to the previous month's issue.

Winsome gestured towards the film collection. "You know any of these, sir? You've watched them?"

"I've watched some of them, yes," said Banks. "I'm quite partial to a bit of Mizoguchi and Chabrol every now and then. Can't say I know them all, though."

"But does any of it mean anything?" Winsome asked. "I mean, as far as the investigation is concerned?"

"The films? I don't know," said Banks. "But I doubt it very much. They just happen to be the sort of thing that Gavin Miller liked, along with the books. He was clearly a bit of an artsy type. I suppose they could just as easily have been Rodgers and Hammerstein musicals or

Disney cartoons. I'm just trying to get a feel for him, really, Winsome, work out what sort of bloke he was, whether he was the type to commit suicide, if there is a type, where he might have got five thousand quid, what he might be intending to do with it. Now the sixties vinyl, that might mean something. There could be a drug connection. The Grateful Dead were involved in the early acid tests, and their followers are well known for taking psychedelics. LSD especially."

"Maybe it was all about drugs, then," Winsome said. "The money in his pocket and all. I mean, there's no suicide note or anything."

"Not every suicide leaves a note. And if he was doing a drug deal, and if someone robbed him of his stash, why didn't the killer go down the embankment to the track and take back his money? Five grand's a fair whack of cash to just leave behind. I can't imagine any dealer, or buyer, doing that."

"Dunno, sir. Maybe he thought he heard someone coming and scarpered? Or he saw that Miller was dead and didn't want to risk leaving any more forensic evidence?"

"Possible. Though PC Kirwan says the track is hardly ever used, especially at this time of year, and at night. Anyway, it's just an angle to consider."

Banks poked through some of the drawers and found, behind a pile of cassette tapes, an old Golden Virginia tobacco tin. When he opened it, he saw inside a packet of red Rizla cigarette papers some silver paper wrapped around about a quarter of an ounce of a sandy-colored, crumbly substance, which smelled suspiciously like hash. Also, in a plastic bag, were two small blue tablets, unmarked.

"It looks as if we've found the drugs," Winsome said.

"OK," Banks said, handing her the tin. "I'm heading back to the station. Madame Gervaise will be wanting an update. You stick with Stefan and his mob while they do a proper search of this place. Give them this to get analyzed and let them know that drugs may be on the agenda. There may be more hidden away. They'll know the usual places to search. I'll set Gerry Masterson on finding out all she can about Mr. Gavin Miller. I want his life story. Cradle to grave."

"SO LET me get this straight," Area Commander Catherine Gervaise said. "You don't know whether Gavin Miller was a suicide, a perpetrator who ended up being a victim, or the intended victim from the start?"

"No," Banks admitted. "How could we? We need to know a lot more about him, his background, what made him tick, any reasons he might have had for wanting to end it all. DC Masterson's working on it now."

"But you don't even know whether he was buying or selling drugs, whether any transaction had been carried out or not?"

"That's right. All we know is that he's dead under suspicious circumstances, there were drugs in his house, and he had five thousand pounds in his pocket."

"And you don't know whether he was deliberately killed or died as the result of a fight? Whether it was murder or manslaughter, in fact."

"The side of the bridge was too high for him to fall over without being lifted or jumping."

"Well, that's something, I suppose. Let's keep the five thousand pounds out of the media for the time being, if we can. I'll take a press conference at the end of the day, if anybody's interested, that is."

"Even with the possibility of suicide, there's bound to be a few vultures already, surely? Anyway, we'll keep the money under wraps. It shouldn't be a problem." Banks scratched his temple. "I'd be the first to admit that we need a lot more to go on before we can even get started, but if drugs are involved, I'm sure it'll be quickly and easily settled once we get a list of his mobile calls and the contents of his computers."

"I hope so. A quick result would go down nicely in these penny-pinching days. How's DI Cabbot doing?"

"Annie? She's fine. She's wrapping up another case. I'll bring her in if it turns out I need her on this." But Banks didn't think Annie was fine. She had changed since she had been shot over a year ago, become more reckless, more secretive, harder, even. She was more difficult to talk to, and their conversations ended up as arguments, or at least minor quarrels, far more often than was healthy. He was worried about her, but she wouldn't let him close.

"DC Masterson working out all right?"

DC Geraldine Masterson was their latest detective constable, who had just come out of her probationary period. "Gerry? Yes. She's doing well. She could do with a bit more confidence, but that often comes with experience. She's got a damn useful set of skills, but I don't think we let her out often enough to build her confidence. No problems to report, though."

"Good."

Enjoying the coffee from Gervaise's espresso machine, Banks figured that the penny-pinching hadn't yet reached as high as the chief super's budget for little luxuries. He felt a subtle shift of gear during one of Gervaise's lengthy pauses.

"Have you ever thought about retirement at all, Alan?" she asked after a few beats had passed.

Banks was taken aback. "Retirement? Surely I've got a couple of years left yet, haven't I?"

"Yes, yes. Of course you have. But the way things are going, with budget cuts and all, who knows? It's something that's being encouraged in a lot of cases."

"Including me?"

"Not specifically, no. Not yet. But I'm just letting you know that it's an option. You've done your thirty. Plus. You'd have a decent pension."

"It's not a matter of pensions," said Banks. "You know that. What would I do?"

Gervaise smiled. "Oh, I'm sure you'd find something, Alan. Bit of gardening, perhaps? Maybe take up a musical instrument? You like music, don't you? Learn to play the piano. Some charity work, helping out in a care home or a hospital, feeding the poor in a church basement, something like that? Get a life?"

Banks shifted in his chair. "Am I missing something? You're starting to make me nervous. Is this a roundabout way of telling me something I don't want to hear?"

Gervaise's smile was inscrutable. "Is that what you think? Does the subject of retirement make you uncomfortable, Alan?"

"As a matter of fact, it does. It makes me cringe."

Gervaise paused again. "More coffee?"

"No, thanks. I'm jittery enough as it is. All this talk about retirement."

"That's just one option. Have you ever thought about promotion?"

"You must be joking? Me? Surely I'm unpromotable?"

"You'd be surprised. You've made a few mistakes over the years, a few enemies, true enough, though many of them have moved on. You've also got a lot of influential and powerful people on your side, too."

"Even since that business with MI5?"

"Even since then. When did we ever dance to MI5's tune?"

"I didn't exactly notice the cavalry hurrying around the bend to my rescue when they had me over a barrel."

"Well, you have only yourself to blame for that. You didn't tell anyone what you were up to, did you? That's your greatest failing. But despite your maverick tendencies, you've still got a lot of support where it counts."

"What exactly *are* you trying to say?"

"It's simple, really." Gervaise spread her hands in a gesture of openness. "Nature abhors a vacuum. Since I was made chief superintendent, there's been a vacuum. It needs filling. Homicide and Major Crimes really needs a detective superintendent to run it. I can't think of a better person than you for the job." Gervaise had recently been promoted, and had also taken on the role of area commander for the Eastvale Local Policing Area.

"*Detective Superintendent!* Hang on. Wait a minute. You flatter me, but . . ."

"It's not flattery. Think about it, Alan. That's all I ask. Yes, there'll be more paperwork, more responsibility, more meetings, more crime stats and budgets to fret over, more of the sort of stuff you hate. And you're going to have to tread a bit more carefully, avoid stepping on too many toes. But on the other hand, there'll be more money and more holidays, and nobody's going to stop you working the way you do, even if it means getting your hands dirty now and then. This wouldn't be a move designed to stop you from doing your job the way you do it best. Some very high-up people have spent a lot of time discussing this."

"I thought my ears were burning a lot lately. You're saying I would still be able to handle cases as I see fit?"

"Within reason, same as always. If you mean can you get out there and work in the field, then the answer's yes. It'll just mean more unpaid overtime catching up with budgeting and reports and the rest of the paperwork."

Banks thought for a moment. He had never been greedy, but more money meant more CDs and DVDs, maybe even a better sound system, and a good turntable like Miller's to play the old vinyl he had brought up from his parents' house in Peterborough recently. More money meant getting central heating installed in the cottage, maybe even a lick of paint here and there. More holidays would mean the occasional bargain weekend in Paris, Rome or Barcelona. But he knew better than to get carried away with himself. Nothing came without a price tag. He had a vision of himself so consumed by paperwork and budget meetings that he simply had no time left to get out and do the job he was best at.

"What do you think?" Gervaise asked.

"I honestly don't know what to say."

Gervaise stood up and leaned forward, resting her palms flat on the desk. "You don't have to make up your mind right at this very moment. Give it a few days. Remember, though, that as a superintendent, you wouldn't have to retire until age sixty-five."

"I'll think about it, I promise," said Banks.

"Good man," beamed Gervaise. "I knew you would. Let's give it until this Miller case is settled and take it from there, shall we? By then, with any luck, you'll have yet another feather in your cap, if you keep your nose clean, that is."

Banks put his espresso cup back in its saucer and stood up to leave. "Whatever you say, ma'am."

AS USUAL these days, it was dark by late afternoon. As there were no other developments, and Winsome and the CSIs were still working

out at the scene, Banks took the file Gerry Masterson had prepared on
Gavin Miller home with him shortly before six o'clock and picked up
some fish and chips from Helmthorpe High Street on his way. He
hung up his raincoat on the rack by the door and carried his briefcase
and dinner down the hall to the kitchen, where he made a pot of tea
and sat down to eat and watch the evening news on the TV above the
breakfast nook. It was the usual depressing mix of weather, politics
and financial doom.

After he had put the dishes in the dishwasher—in a few days he
would have enough to make it worthwhile running the damn
thing—he poured himself a glass of Layers, an Aussie red blend he had
come to enjoy lately, then went into the entertainment room to select
the music.

As he searched through his collection, he found himself drawn to
the Grateful Dead. He hadn't played any of their CDs in a long time.
He had listened to the Dead a lot more when he was younger, and had
even seen them live once at the Empire Pool, Wembley, in 1972. He
remembered being impressed by Jerry Garcia's guitar playing. More
recently, he had been enjoying Norma Waterson's version of "Black
Muddy River." No doubt their music would make an appropriate
soundtrack for his reading. He didn't have much to choose from, as it
turned out, so he picked *American Beauty*.

Banks liked the sound of rain on the conservatory roof, so he decided he would sit out there to read over Gerry Masterson's preliminary notes on Gavin Miller. She had been most embarrassed and
apologetic that she had so little to show him when he had dropped by
the squad room to see her. The whole business was going far too
slowly, she said, and the notes she had were very sketchy and rough.
Usually, she would have much more information by now. Banks told
her not to worry and to stick at it.

He took his wine and briefcase through and settled back in his
favorite wicker chair. With the reading light on, he couldn't see a
thing in the darkness beyond the windows, just his own reflection
and that of the spines of the books on the shelves behind him. The
rain was softer now, a gentle hiss rather than a heavy drumming. He
remembered reading or seeing in a film somewhere that W. C. Fields

couldn't sleep unless it was raining, and that he lay dying for some time, until the rain started. Then he died. Banks thought he might like to die to the sound of rain, not in the icy shackles of winter or the bright warmth of a summer's day, or with the colored autumn leaves drifting down, but in spring, perhaps, an April shower falling on the glass roof and windows of his conservatory. It wasn't a morbid thought, but quite a comforting one, as was the sound. He sipped some wine and, with "Box of Rain" playing softly in the background, began to read the few pages of the hastily written preliminary notes that DC Masterson had been kind enough to photocopy for him to take home.

DC Masterson's account was very bare bones, though it covered a lot of ground, Banks noticed, and as he read, his imagination filled in some of the blanks. Gavin Miller had been born near Banbury, Oxfordshire, on November 29, almost sixty years ago. His father had been a teacher at a local comprehensive school, which Miller had attended, and his mother a housewife. Miller was an only child and grew up in a cottage at the end of a long leafy lane on the edge of town, with no close neighbors.

Miller had shown some academic promise at school, though he didn't quite get the qualifications necessary for Oxford or Cambridge. He did well in his A-levels, however, and ended up reading English at the University of Essex, which he attended from 1971 to 1974, leaving with a second-class honors degree. After a period spent working to save up as much money as he could, Miller disappeared to Canada in 1977 to study film and literature at Simon Fraser University, near Vancouver. From what Gerry Masterson could work out, he seemed to have remained over there for the next six years. That would explain some of the photos of cityscapes and mountain landscapes they had found in Miller's drawer, Banks thought. He had seen images of Canada like that before.

Gerry admitted that she had lost track of his movements during the four-year period after he graduated from Simon Fraser, from 1979 to 1983—the "lost years"—and she needed to contact consulates and immigration sources, registrars and administrative assistants, a time-consuming job, even if you were looking for fresh information. Miller turned up again at home in Banbury in 1983. He would have been pushing thirty by then, Banks calculated, and this was not an era when the children stayed at home as long as they do these days.

So far, Gavin Miller seemed like so many others, a young man who had not quite fulfilled his potential, or hadn't had as much potential to fulfill as he thought he did. He also didn't seem to have grown up, in some ways, but remained stuck in the interests and tastes of his youth. Even though he was fifty-nine, his small cottage was full of existentialist philosophy books and shelves of psychedelic vinyl from an earlier time.

The rain had stopped now, though it still streaked the windows. A fine day was promised for tomorrow, but you could never trust the weather forecasts these days. The only thing you could be certain of was that rain would come again, sooner rather than later.

The Grateful Dead were singing "Ripple," which Banks thought might be the kind of song he would like to have played at his funeral. Its airy mysticism rather appealed to him, the idea of life as a ripple in still water, when no pebble has been tossed into it. And the melody and harmonies were beautiful. He sighed. Enough thoughts of death and rain and ripples in undisturbed water. What was it about today that had sent his mind spinning in such a direction?

He realized that it was probably something to do with the similarities between himself and Gavin Miller. But just how alike were they? True, they shared some tastes in music and films, much of it the same as they had enjoyed in their youth, but was that so strange? They were close to the same age, had grown up with the same pop culture—the Beatles, James Bond, *The Saint,* Bob Dylan, and so on. Banks's dad still listened to Henry Hall, Nat Gonella and Glenn Miller, music he had first heard during the war. There was nothing odd about a taste for the past. Some people still enjoyed Abba and the Bay City Rollers.

Banks also had to admit that he often preferred stopping in and drinking wine and listening to music alone to going down to the local on a Saturday night. So what did that make him?

Newhope Cottage might be bigger and better furnished than the signalman's cottage Miller had lived in, Banks thought, but it was just as isolated, and Banks had deliberately chosen to live there after his divorce from Sandra. Had Miller been running away from something, too, and had it caught up with him? He could have simply been running away from himself, of course, and when he found he couldn't, had committed suicide. But Banks doubted it. Something didn't sit right about his choice of method, not when there were more than enough pills in his bathroom cabinet to do the job, and five thousand pounds in his pocket when he died.

Banks returned to what little remained of DC Masterson's notes. Almost a year after he had returned from Canada, Miller had begun a series of jobs in local colleges, where he had toiled away in obscurity for twenty years or more, teaching general arts, media studies, film and English literature in such places as Exeter, Grantham and Barrow-in-Furness, never staying in any one place for any length of time, until he arrived at Eastvale College in 2006.

Miller left the college in 2009, gave up his rented flat in Eastvale and made a down payment on the signalman's cottage near Coverton. It didn't appear that he had attempted to find another job. Gerry had noted that the person she talked to on the telephone at the college, Trevor Lomax, head of the department in which Miller had taught, seemed a little cagey when he found out who she wanted to talk about. He made a mental note to get someone to go out there and talk to Lomax the following morning.

Miller had married only once, as far as Gerry could discover, and that had lasted six years and had ended in 1996. His wife had remarried two years later and gone to live in New Zealand. Gavin's father had died three years ago, and his mother had entered a private care home near Oxford, which took up the money from the sale of the cottage outside Banbury and more or less all the savings that the Millers had accumulated over the years. When Miller died, he had been unable to meet his last two mortgage payments, the utility companies had been hammering at his door and his credit card was maxed to the limit.

The desperate financial straits Gavin Miller had been in towards the end of his life also made Banks think there might be something more to the drugs angle. People often saw drugs as a quick way of

making a big return on an investment. Someone so desperate for
money might turn to crime. Five thousand pounds was a lot of money
to a man in Miller's position, and it would have got him out of the
immediate hole he was in, at the very least, with even a little left over.

Blackmail was another possibility, of course, but most victims don't
kill their blackmailers, who have usually set things up in such a way
that if anything happens to them, the cat gets let out of the bag
anyway. No one had broken into Miller's house, for example, to see if
there was anything incriminating left behind there. If Miller had been
blackmailing someone, it was hardly likely that he would hand over
all his evidence for five thousand pounds. Blackmailers always have
something in hand, and they always come back for more.

Putting the file aside, Banks massaged his temples and rubbed his
eyes. It was getting late. *American Beauty* had finished some time ago,
and the silence was all embracing. Once in a while, he heard a light
breeze sough through the trees, or a distant car on the Helmthorpe
road, but apart from that, nothing. He topped up his glass, went into
the entertainment room to put on *Live/Dead,* and went outside.
There was a little bulge in the wall beside the beck, and he enjoyed
standing there, or even sitting on the wall when it was dry, to contemplate the night and enjoy his last drink of the evening. In the old
days, he used to love having a smoke out there, too, but those days
were long gone.

Already there were stars showing between the gray rags of cloud,
and the air was full of that lovely fresh earth smell you get after a good
country rainfall. It was still a little chilly, but he wouldn't be staying
out for long. He walked over to the wall beside Gratly Beck and
leaned at his usual spot overlooking the terraced falls all the way down
the daleside to the slate roofs of Helmthorpe High Street and the
church tower below the old mill, the fields and the cemetery. The
water was high after the rains, and the beck had turned into quite a
torrent. The falls were fast and noisy, filling the air with a fine cool
spray. Banks often enjoyed falling asleep to the sound of the rushing
water as he lay in bed.

To his left stretched the dark woods, raindrops dropping from
leaves as the wind shook them, and tapping on the leaves below. The

River Swain was a silvery squiggle along the flat valley bottom about a mile away. The strains of Garcia's lyrical guitar playing on "Dark Star" wove into the sounds of the beck and the dripping leaves as Banks leaned there thinking how much he loved the place, and how retirement might not be such a bad idea after all.

He thought about Gavin Miller for a while longer, the haggard and broken body that looked like that of an old man, then tossed down the rest of his wine, shivered and went back inside.

2

THE BOARDROOM, WITH ITS POLISHED OVAL TABLE, whiteboards and fancy new glass board, already christened Red Ron's Folly, was ready for the morning meeting at nine o'clock, and the whole team was present, including Area Commander Catherine Gervaise, DI Annie Cabbot, PC Kirwan and Stefan Nowak. Black coffee in one hand and black marker in the other, Banks took to the front of the room and tried to bring some order out of the fragments of information the team had dug up so far, starting with Gerry Masterson's exploration of Miller's life. The problem still remained that they couldn't be certain Miller's death wasn't due to suicide. Dr. Glendenning was set to perform the postmortem later that afternoon, and Banks was hoping he would unearth something that might help them decide one way or the other. Even so, the death seemed suspicious enough that he believed it was vital to get at least the beginnings of an investigation going as quickly as possible.

Gerry Masterson looked very businesslike this morning, Banks thought, with her red wavy Pre-Raphaelite hair tied back, a crisp white blouse, and oval black-rimmed glasses perched on her nose. She shifted her papers in front of her and cleared her throat. "Well, sir," she began, then gave a shy glance towards Gervaise, "and . . . er . . . ma'am."

"Skip the formalities, Gerry," said Gervaise. "Or else we'll be here all day."

Gerry's pale skin blushed a pinkish red. "Yes, ma'am . . . I'm sorry. I mean, right." She studied her notes, seemed undecided whether she needed them or not, then pushed them aside a couple of inches and rested her hands on the table, looking over her audience. "I assume you've read my notes on Gavin Miller?"

They all nodded.

"Well, it's slow going," she said, "and I apologize for not having very much to give you, as Mr. Miller doesn't seem to have had much in the way of social intercourse over the past while, or any sort of family life. Anyway, I've narrowed what I do know down to three areas that might benefit from fruitful inquiry."

Banks raised his marker, ready to take down what she said.

"First of all, and probably hardest of all to investigate, is the period he was overseas after finishing his degree at the University of Essex. We know that he spent the years from 1977 to 1979 at Simon Fraser University, near Vancouver, pursuing a graduate diploma in film studies and literature, then . . . well, we don't really know where he was or what he was doing for the following four years. I call them the 'lost years.' We're pretty sure he wasn't back in the UK until late 1983, but other than that . . . I still have a number of inquiries outstanding on this, a few calls I'm waiting for, and I'll follow up on them later today, when the time difference isn't quite so awkward, but it doesn't look too hopeful. It was a long time ago."

"You're thinking something might have happened during that 'lost' period that led to Miller's death thirty years later?"

"I'm just saying it's possible, sir. It's unknown territory. He could have made dodgy contacts that came back to haunt him."

"I think," said Gervaise, "that before we commit to putting any resources into investigating that period thoroughly, we should hear what else you have to say, or the next thing we know we'll be sending a team out there. And you know what havoc that would play with the budget."

"Of course." Gerry went on, a little chastened. "Next is a little closer to the present. It's his three years at Eastvale College from 2006 to 2009." She leafed through her notes. "I believe I made a note of how his department head Trevor Lomax seemed reluctant to talk about him."

"Any idea why?" Banks asked.

"No, sir."

Banks looked at Annie. "Can you pay Mr. Lomax a visit at the college?"

"Be my pleasure. You never know, I might learn something."

Everyone groaned.

Banks turned back to Gerry. "And the third area? You said there were three."

"Yes, sir. We need to know what Miller has been doing recently, since he's been living at the signalman's cottage outside Coverton. Someone must know something, but all I've managed to gather so far is that he was a loner with no friends in the village, and had few or no visitors, as far as anyone can tell. Not that they would have known, anyway, as his cottage was so isolated. I mean, I suppose he could have been having wild parties there every night, and nobody would have been any the wiser."

"Possibly not," said Banks. "Though the villagers might have noticed an unusual number of cars or motorcycles on their streets, or in their car park late at night."

"If they parked in the village," said Gerry. "All I'm getting at is that everyone's pretty sure he lived a quiet life out there, but he *could* have had regular visitors—a girlfriend, say. Probably no one would have thought anything of just one car parked in the village occasionally, or perhaps his visitor knew the tracks and lanes to take to get to the cottage and drove straight there."

"True," Banks agreed. "But did he have a girlfriend? We're calling him a loner, saying he didn't mix. Would a girlfriend put up with the kind of life Miller led out there? Might she not want to go out occasionally? A club? The cinema? For a meal or a drink?"

"Unless she was like him, sir."

"An odd couple, indeed. OK, I take your point. We'll bear it in mind. *Cherchez la femme.*"

Gerry didn't seem quite sure whether to smile or not. In the end, she didn't. "Thank you, sir. We also know that Miller was short of money. Maybe he got mixed up with some sort of fraud, or a loan shark? They can be pretty nasty when it comes to getting their money back."

"They usually stop short of murder, though," said Banks. "After all, they *do* want their money back."

"Perhaps he wasn't meant to die? It could have got out of hand. Miller fought back and ended up going over the bridge. Or he was used as an example."

"Possible," Banks agreed. "We'll look into it. About the five thousand pounds in his pocket. Do you think perhaps he might have resorted to blackmail?"

"He could have done," said Gerry, "though I haven't found any evidence of it so far. I'm also checking into the drugs connection, possible involvement in rural crime rings, something of that sort. Poverty can push people into crime, sir, and that's a dangerous and unpredictable world."

Banks made more jottings on the board. "We'll be making a thorough examination of all Gavin Miller's recent comings and goings," he said. "We should also make inquiries at all the farms within, say, a five-mile radius. Can you arrange that, PC Kirwan?"

"I'll organize some of the local beat bobbies to get on it right away, sir."

"There has to be someone who knew him, or who saw something," Banks said. "Liam's working on Miller's phone and computers right now, and he should have something for us later today. Thanks, Gerry, you did a fine job. Stefan, anything on forensics yet?"

"It pains me to say it," Nowak said, "but the rain washed everything away, if anything was there in the first place. We have no prints, either foot, finger or tire. It doesn't look as if the road that runs from the cottage out into the moors has been used recently. It would at least appear churned up in places, even if we couldn't get any clear tire tracks, but the surface seems smooth enough, even in patches where it's muddy from the recent flooding."

"Someone must have used it," Banks said. "How did Miller get his post?"

"He had a box at the post office in the village, sir," answered Gerry.

"OK. We'd better check that out, too." Banks glanced back at Nowak. "Sorry, Stefan. Please go on."

Nowak spread his hands. "That's about it."

"Will the money lead us anywhere?" Banks asked.

"Up a garden path, most likely. The bills are relatively new, it's true, but they're still used. And fifties are fairly rare, but these are not sequential. We might be able to trace some back to specific banks, but I doubt very much that we'll be able to trace them to a specific person or transaction, if the owner had his wits about him. There are some prints which we can try to match against our database, but so far all I can say is that a number of different people handled the bills. Sorry."

"Anything on the drugs Winsome and I found at Miller's house?"

"Some hash and what appears to be two tablets of LSD," Nowak said. "We didn't find anything else. Thing is, the quantities are very small. Strictly personal consumption."

"But he had to get it from somewhere, didn't he?" said Winsome. "However tentative, it's still a drugs connection. That could link him with some dodgy people. Where there's drugs there's money, and where there's money there's always the possibility of violence."

"True," said Banks. "Maybe you should have a word with the drugs squad later today? See if they can suggest a possible source. Well done. Anything else?"

"Well," Winsome went on, "there was no diary, nothing to give us an account of his daily activities, or an address book. No land line, either. He did have a scratch pad in one of his drawers, and it has a few numbers and names scribbled on it. I passed it on to Liam, and he'll be trying to coordinate with the information he gets from Miller's mobile and computers. Then Gerry can try and track down the names and addresses. It's my guess he had so few appointments, and he knew so few people, that he didn't need an address book or appointment diary. Then there were the photos we found. That's it."

Banks turned to PC Kirwan. "Find out anything more around the village?"

Kirwan opened his notebook. "A little, sir. Nobody had seen Miller since Friday, when he'd been to the Spar, on the High Street, to buy a few provisions and some wine on sale. He'd also been drinking in the Star & Garter before heading home."

Banks gazed at the glass board. There was a lot more written on it now than there had been at the start of the meeting, but how much of it was of any use? He needed connections, not disparate facts and guesswork.

"There is just one more thing that might be of interest, sir," said Kirwan. "I talked to a Mrs. Stanshall, who says she's certain she saw someone come over the stile from the woodland path into the car park, then get in a car and drive off. She's another dog walker. It was dark, though, and she couldn't give any more details, either about the car or the person, but she's certain it was about half past ten on Sunday night, same time she always takes the dog for a walk, rain or shine. The timing's about right. If someone was coming out of the woods and getting into a car at that time, there's a good chance he may be connected with Miller's death, isn't there, sir?"

"If someone did kill Miller, yes, I suppose so. It was definitely a he?"

"That was all she could be certain of. Something to do with his size and shape."

"There are big women." Banks looked at Winsome, who was six foot two in her stocking feet.

"Are you saying you think someone might mistake me for a man, sir?" Winsome asked sweetly.

"Well, no . . . I mean, perhaps, in the dark . . ."

Everyone laughed. "Don't go on, sir," Winsome said, hardly able to keep back the laughter herself. "You'll only put your foot in deeper."

"She said it was the way he moved as well, sir," Kirwan rushed on. "And his shoulders. There are streetlights that cast a little illumination on the car park. Not much, mind you, and the car was in one of the darker areas near the back, but enough to see silhouettes and such, so she's probably being as accurate as she can be. There's no locked gate or anything."

"CCTV?"

"No, sir."

"Pay and display?"

"No, sir. It's free."

"Normally I'd rejoice at that," said Banks, "but a written record of the time our mystery man arrived would be nice right now."

"Sorry, sir. But at least we know when he left, for what it's worth.

Anyway, she said he was bareheaded, but with hair, not bald, wearing a raincoat and trousers, definitely a man. She saw him get into the car, and she said women get into cars differently. I don't know about that, but she seemed certain. Maybe someone should have a word."

"There's a few things to follow up in Coverton," Banks said. "This Mrs. Stanshall might be more perceptive than you think she is. Seeing as Stefan tells us that the track from the cottage probably hasn't been used by any cars recently, then it makes sense that our man parked in the village car park and perhaps walked through the woods or along the railway path. Anyway, I'll head out there later this morning. Winsome, you can come with me and talk to Mrs. Stanshall. Maybe check out the post office box, too." Banks turned to Nowak. "And Stefan, would you have your team go over the woodland path again. I suppose if anyone used it, there's always a chance of some fabric caught on a twig, or even, God help us, a preserved footprint."

Nowak nodded. "We've been over it once, but we'll do it again."

"Anything else?" Banks asked. Nobody spoke up. "Right, you've all got your tasks. Just one more thing to consider. You might bump into one or more members of the media on your travels. The AC has suggested, and I agree, that we should keep all knowledge of the five thousand pounds to ourselves for the moment. It gives us a card up our sleeves should we need it. All clear?"

Everyone muttered their assent, and the meeting broke up. When they had all gone, Banks stood and gazed at the pictures and writing on the glass board. He sensed Gervaise behind him. "No forensics," she said. "That's a bit of a disaster for us."

"We'll manage," said Banks. "I've often thought that solving a crime has far more to do with understanding people and their motives than it does with spectrographic analysis and DNA."

"Maybe so," said Gervaise. "But in the end it's forensics that will get a conviction any day over motive."

GOLD AND russet leaves were spiraling down from the trees that lined the street of large Victorian houses. Along with the chill in the air, they reminded Detective Inspector Annie Cabbot that winter was coming as she parked her car and got out. The weather was fine enough at the moment, and there were even a few patches of blue sky between the clouds drifting across the sky like balls of fluff accumulated in a vacuum cleaner.

Annie walked past groups of students carrying rucksacks and satchels, chatting and laughing as they came and went from the warren of bedsits and flats inside the houses. The Arts Department was housed in one of the sixties buildings at the heart of the old campus, all flat roofs, prefab concrete and glass, broad horizontal blinds. Most of the buildings were about three stories high, but built in sprawling L-shapes, or forming squares around quadrangles in some sort of grotesque parody of Oxford or Cambridge.

To get to Lomax's office, Annie had to walk through iron gates and across a square of scrappy lawn, then climb two flights of stairs. She tried to get plenty of exercise, including yoga and Pilates, but since the shooting and the time spent both in hospital and in convalescence, she found that she had less energy than before, and she was slightly out of breath when she knocked on the door. The doctors told her she would improve over time, but that it would be a long, hard haul. She already knew that. It had been a long, hard haul to crawl away from the bright white light that had beckoned as she lay bleeding on the floor of Banks's conservatory over a year ago. There were days when she sometimes wondered whether it had been worth the effort. Something had broken in her, and she wanted the old Annie back.

She had telephoned ahead to make an appointment, so Lomax was expecting her. His voice called out for her to enter when she knocked, and she was surprised to find herself not in a vestibule with a fearsome secretary on sentry duty, but standing in the office itself.

To say it was book lined would be both too generous and inaccurate; it was book crammed, book piled, book besotted. They were everywhere. They probably bred overnight. The room even smelled of books. Here was a man who had never heard of a Kindle. The books were on the wall-to-wall shelves, on the floor, on the windowsills, on the chairs, on every flat surface, and even balanced on some of the curved or angled ones. Oddly enough, Lomax didn't look in the least bit bookish, Annie thought when he stood up to greet her, at least in the way she understood the term. There were no unruly tufts of hair sticking out at odd angles, no tweed jacket with leather elbow patches, no pipe, no thick glasses, no flyaway eyebrows. He was about fifty, Annie guessed, tennis-playing trim, casually dressed in a black polo-neck jumper and jeans, gray hair neatly parted on the left. He was quite handsome, with an engaging dimpled smile, a twinkle in his eyes and a firm handshake.

"Do pardon the mess," said Lomax. "I've been fighting for a larger office for some years now, but it never seems to materialize. Sometimes I feel they'd like to get rid of the arts faculty altogether."

"I know the feeling," said Annie, sitting on a chair Lomax had cleared of books for her. "Perhaps we should just give up and hand the country over to the bankers?"

"I thought they already owned it? Anyway, you mustn't talk like that. Never give up. That way lie philistinism and totalitarianism. Rage against the dying of the light, as Dylan Thomas put it. He was talking about death, of course, not revolution or protest, but perhaps the loss of all we value most could be seen as death of a kind, too, don't you think? Kierkegaard said the loss of the self can occur very quietly, unnoticed, as it were. Anyway, just listen to me prattling on. You'd think I haven't talked to anyone in months. Would you like some tea or coffee? I can ring down for some. It won't take a minute."

"If it wouldn't be too much trouble. Coffee, just black, please, no sugar."

"Not at all." Lomax picked up the phone and asked for two black coffees, then smiled sheepishly. "It makes me seem more important than I am," he said. "Maria will only bring coffee when I have a guest in my office. When there's just me, I have to go down and fetch it myself."

Annie laughed. A few moments later, there was a soft tap at the door, followed by the appearance of a pale, plump woman in a peasant skirt, her mousy hair tied in a ponytail. She balanced her tray on one hand and handed Annie and Lomax cups of coffee without cracking a smile or saying a word. Then she was gone. "You must excuse Maria," Lomax said. "She's from Lithuania. Her English isn't very good. She's got two young children to bring up alone. She takes evening classes, and she also does a bit of office cleaning. She's a very hard worker, and she probably doesn't have a lot to smile about."

"I suppose not," said Annie. She remembered Krystyna, the Polish girl she had helped out of a jam earlier in the year. She still received letters or postcards from her every now and then. Krystyna's English was improving, and she seemed to be finding her feet in the restaurant business back home in Kraków. Her last letter had talked of trying to get into chef's school. Annie wished her well; Krystyna knew how hard life could be when you started out with so little.

"Was Gavin Miller a particularly good teacher?" she asked.

"No, not really. I'm not saying he didn't know his subjects, or that he wasn't passionate about them. Don't get me wrong. He knew his stuff, all right. But Gavin didn't suffer fools gladly, and as you can imagine, he often had quite a lot of fools in his classes, especially the film classes. He tended to be very sarcastic, and irony's not a good teaching tool. It tends to go over the students' heads and rub them the wrong way. They just feel as if they're being insulted."

"But you say he had a passion for his subject. Is that essential for a good teacher?"

"You need some sort of engagement, commitment, some sense of vocation, as with anything in life. Besides, why would you do it, otherwise? The pay's not very good, and you don't get much in the way of thanks."

"Sort of like my job," said Annie, pausing a moment before asking, "Why did he leave? It all seemed rather sudden. He'd only been here three years and he was, what, only about fifty-five?"

Lomax avoided her eyes. "Well, you know. It was time to part company. Move on. He . . . you know. These things happen."

"Actually, I don't know what you mean, Mr. Lomax. Was he fired? Made redundant?"

"I suppose you could say that, yes."

"Which is it? There's a difference, you know. Did you fire him for being a sarcastic teacher?"

"Look, this is all very awkward, I must say."

"Awkward? Why?"

"It was a most delicate situation."

"What did he do? Shag one of his students?" Lomax blushed, and Annie wasn't certain that it was entirely due to her language. "He did, didn't he? That's why you're so unwilling to talk about it."

"I'm not unwilling. It's just . . . well, the college would rather avoid any adverse publicity. It was an internal matter. We've put it behind us."

"Don't worry, I'm the soul of discretion. This could be a murder inquiry, Mr. Lomax. I think you'd better consider that seriously and weigh it against your concerns for the reputation of the college."

Lomax seemed to shrink in his chair. "Yes, all right then. His dismissal was due to a sexual indiscretion." He shot her a glance. "But it wasn't what you think. He didn't have sex with the girl, well, not with either of them, really."

Annie sighed and leaned back, notebook on her lap. "I think it would be best if you just told me about it, don't you? You're saying that Gavin Miller's passion got him into trouble, not his sarcasm?"

Lomax sipped some coffee and eyed Annie sadly over his mug. "I don't think there was a great deal of passion in what happened to Gavin," he said. "Not on his part, at least. That's what was so unfair about it all, I suppose."

"What do you mean?"

"Gavin had no interest in young girls, especially girls like Kayleigh Vernon and Beth Gallagher, his accusers. They were just gum-chewing airheads to him."

"Gum-chewing airheads with big tits?"

"Believe it or not, I doubt that really made a difference to Gavin," he said.

"Why not? It does to most men."

"I think in some ways he was more interested in ideas than in life, in the dream rather than the reality. That was probably at the root of his problems."

"What problems?"

Lomax paused. "Before I go on, you have to understand that I wasn't a member of the committee, or disciplinary board, that held the hearing and finally dismissed him. I was a mere outsider. As his friend and head of department, I was regarded as biased in his favor. If anything, I tried to defend him."

"What was his defense?"

Lomax slapped his desk. "That's the problem. Right there. With this sort of thing, there really is no defense. It's a when-did-you-stop-beating-your-wife situation."

"You're saying that any lecturer who gets accused of sexual misconduct loses his job?"

"Basically, yes. Pretty much. Sexual misconduct with a student, at any rate. That's how it works. You could probably get away with murder and keep . . ." He put his hand to his forehead. "Oh, I'm sorry. Bad taste. That was stupid of me."

"That's all right. Go on."

"Well, what I was meaning to say was that, in today's climate, it's the most heinous crime there is in the teaching environment. Next to plagiarism, perhaps. It not only has overtones of rape, but it also touches upon abuse of power and betrayal of trust. Put those things together and they can be a powerful combination. Very hard to forgive or forget."

"Or disprove?"

"Practically impossible. Yes. I'm not saying that Gavin was a complete innocent, and he was certainly foolhardy, but in all the time I knew him, which admittedly was only two or three years, I had never known him behave in any other way than as a gentleman towards the opposite sex. He was, in fact, rather shy."

"So what actually happened? What was his 'sexual indiscretion'?"

Lomax shrugged. "That's just the problem. Nobody knows. They haven't installed CCTV in all our offices. Not yet. Gavin said he put his arm around the Vernon girl to comfort her when she cried after failing an important test. She said he made a pass at her and indicated that if she slept with him, he would make sure her test result was modified accordingly."

"That's it? But where's the evidence?"

"That's all there is."

Annie felt her jaw drop. As a victim of serious sexual abuse herself, she was hardly sympathetic towards predatory males, but even she could hardly believe that a man could lose his livelihood based on such flimsy hearsay. "That's not evidence," she said. "It's her word against his."

"I know. That's my point. She could just as easily have been lying."

"Why would she lie?"

"Search me. But it's a possibility. Teenage girls, even when they're nineteen, as Kayleigh Vernon was at the time, can be very confused emotionally, and very vindictive."

"And Kayleigh was both?"

"I didn't know her well enough to answer that question. All I can tell you is that Gavin told me he got the impression she had been sort of flirting with him all term, you know, making innuendos, making eyes, leading him on, teasing, that sort of thing. He admits to putting his arm around her because she was distressed, which, whatever else you might say, was really his biggest mistake of all. Whether she took it as a sign of his affections and felt affronted when he rebuffed her . . ."

"Is that what you think happened?"

"I think it's more than likely, and I think Gavin should have been given the benefit of the doubt, but as I said before, in this present climate, there is no benefit of the doubt."

"But if he thought she was leading him on, might he not have responded, and might he not have misread the signals?"

Lomax nodded glumly. "That's also possible. But she didn't say he attempted to assault her, she said he tried to blackmail her into having sex."

"What was the girl like?"

"Ordinary enough, as far as I know. Unexceptional. No one ever claimed she was a slut or a trollop, or anything like that. And Gavin was certainly no Lothario."

"What happened to the girl?"

"Kayleigh? She graduated eventually. I don't know where she is now."

"And the other complainant?"

"Beth Gallagher? Gone, too. Now, she *was* a troublemaker. She was also Kayleigh's best friend. It was very likely she egged Kayleigh on in her pursuit of Gavin, if indeed such a pursuit did occur, perhaps with the goal of humiliating him, and that she came out in her friend's defense when the going got too rough."

"She lied, too?"

"That's not what the committee or the board believed."

"But is it what you think?"

Lomax stared down at his cluttered desk, as if mentally rearranging the objects on its surface. "Yes," he said finally. It was more of a sigh than anything else. "She said he let his hand 'accidentally' brush across her breast in his office when they were discussing an essay she had written."

"So again it was her word against Gavin's?"

"Her word and Kayleigh's. Two to one. He didn't stand a chance."

"Did either of them have any motive for hurting Gavin Miller?"

Lomax hesitated before answering, and Annie got the sense that he was quickly making a decision on just how much to tell her, that he was probably going to hold something back. She filed away the reaction for later. She often found it was good to have a little unexpected ammunition in your arsenal for a second meeting, should one be necessary. "No," he said finally. "As I said, I think it was just an adolescent game, a cruel game that got out of hand. Beyond a certain point, there was no turning back."

"They could have retracted, told the truth."

"It wasn't an option. Then they would have been disciplined. They might have lost everything they had been working towards."

"Did Mr. Miller try to get in touch with either of the girls later, to berate them, or ask them to come clean about what they did?"

"Not that I know of. If he did, they certainly didn't report it to the college, and he didn't tell me."

"Were their parents involved?"

"Well, I assume they knew about it, of course, but they played no official role."

"Any further incidents?"

"What sort of incidents?"

"Involving Gavin Miller and the parents, for example, or the girls' boyfriends, older brothers. Anything of a violent nature, threats made, that sort of thing?"

"I never heard of anything like that. Look, I'm not an expert on this. There's a lot I don't know."

"I'm aware of that," said Annie. "But I'd appreciate it if you'd just bear with me and answer the questions as best you can. Did Gavin complain officially about his treatment?"

"I believe he did put in a formal complaint and appeal after his sacking, but it went nowhere."

"Climate of the times?"

"Exactly."

"There was no publicity about the incident, or the dismissal. Why was that?"

"It was what everyone agreed to at the time," Lomax said.

"Even Gavin?"

"Especially Gavin. Some members of the board made it quite clear to him how his name would get dragged through the mud in full public view if it ever became public knowledge."

"So that's why he never went to the press?"

"Yes. Oh, there were rumors, of course. You can't keep something like that a complete secret. But they died down. Gavin's name and alleged offenses were never made generally known."

"And the girls?"

"They didn't want their private lives splashed all over the morning papers, did they?"

"Was there anything more to all this?"

"Well, I've always thought the college had a hidden agenda, that they wanted rid of Gavin anyway, and this was their golden opportunity."

"Why?"

Lomax struggled. "Gavin was a bit of an outsider. He didn't quite fit in. He marched to the beat of his own drummer, and he didn't always follow college guidelines in matters such as curriculum and set texts and so on. He often couldn't be bothered to attend departmental meetings. That sort of thing. The college is a pretty conservative institution, on the whole, and Gavin was a bit of a maverick, not to mention left of center politically."

"I thought all academics were lefties?"

"Not here."

Annie paused a beat. "Were either of the girls involved with drugs?"

"I never heard anything about drugs."

The answer had come too quickly and was too definitive, Annie thought. And Lomax didn't look surprised enough by the sudden change of direction in questioning. More ammunition for a later interview, perhaps. She made some notes and sipped some more coffee before it went cold. "Not much more to go, now, Mr. Lomax. I'm sorry to rake up all this unpleasantness, but we need to know."

Lomax managed a grim smile. "It's all right," he said. "You have your job to do. And if I can be any help at all. Poor Gavin."

"Did you know him well?"

"I wouldn't say 'well,' but I did know him, considered him a close acquaintance, if not exactly a friend. There was always something a bit distant, a bit private, about Gavin. As if he wouldn't, or couldn't, let you get really close to him. We invited him to dinner once or twice—Sally, that's my wife, and I—but he said he felt a bit awkward not having anyone to bring. We even fixed him up with one of Sally's work colleagues once. She's a physiotherapist."

"What happened?"

"They went out together for a while, I believe, then it fizzled out. I told you he wasn't very good with women. I should imagine he went on about the Grateful Dead, Fellini or existentialism a bit too much for her liking."

"Existentialism?"

"You know, Sartre, Camus? The idea that the universe is arbitrary, meaningless, absurd."

"I know what existentialism is. I'm just surprised to hear that it's a belief anyone subscribes to these days."

"Well, it wasn't so much of a belief. I'd say when it came to that, Gavin was probably an atheist. But it was a philosophy that appealed to him."

"Can you give me the girlfriend's name?"

"Really, it was nothing."

"I'd still like to talk to her."

"Very well. Her name's Dayle Snider. She works at the health center in town."

"I know it." Annie had been there on several occasions for physio, but she didn't know Dayle Snider. She made a note of the name. "Did Gavin have any other friends or acquaintances around here?"

"I suppose Jim Cooper was a mate of his. He's in Media Studies. He teaches some general courses and specializes in music, as Gavin did in literature and film. I have my doubts about someone who professes to like the Cure teaching music, but it's not my decision. Give me a bit of Beethoven any day."

"I'm rather partial to One Direction, myself. Did you ever visit Gavin at his home?"

"Where? You mean the Eastvale flat?"

"No, sorry. The signalman's cottage in Coverton."

"After he left? Yes. I dropped by now and then to make sure he was all right. Damn awkward place to get to."

"How *did* you get there?"

"There is a sort of road that runs up to the front, but you have to go miles out of your way to get there by a very circuitous route. To tell you the truth, I found it easier to park in the village, walk up the old railway line and climb the embankment path, if the weather was at all decent."

"And was he all right on those occasions you visited him?"

"Not really. I don't think he ever recovered from the shock of what happened. Sometimes he got depressed. I don't think it was clinical or chronic or anything, just sort of depressed, the way we all get sometimes. He was always short of money, too. I'm afraid the college didn't come up with much of anything in the way of a settlement or pension. He'd only been with us three years, for a start, and then there were the circumstances of his dismissal. I'd give him a tenner every now and then, but it was just a stopgap, really. Beer and ciggies money. It wouldn't pay his mortgage. I'm afraid, on my salary, I couldn't run to that."

"How did he feel about what was done to him?"

"How do you think he felt? He was angry, resentful, bitter."

"Even in a universe he believed to be absurd and without meaning? You'd think he'd be gratified at having his philosophy borne out by reality."

"Philosophy is one thing, Detective Inspector, but emotions are quite another."

"Did he ever talk of suicide?"

"Only in a philosophical way. I mean, he never said he was actually contemplating it *personally,* or anything like that, but he sometimes argued for it as a valid philosophical proposition. I mean, if you read Schopenhauer and Camus, you can't help but meditate upon the *idea* of suicide."

Annie had read a little philosophy at university, but mostly old stuff like Plato and Aristotle. She knew nothing of the modern philosophical ideas except what she had picked up growing up in the artists' colony with her father. That was where she had first heard of existentialism, and she had even read a Jean-Paul Sartre novel once to impress a boyfriend. It hadn't worked, so she never read another. "What do you mean by the *idea* of suicide?" she asked.

"The idea, not the reality. I mean that you might discuss the philosophical validity of murder, for example, or of incest, but that doesn't mean you're going to go out and murder someone or sleep with your mother. And anyway, isn't all this rather moot? I understand you said on the telephone you were investigating the *murder* of Gavin Miller. That indicates to me that he was killed by someone. There's no possibility of suicide, is there?"

Annie could have kicked herself. She should never have said *murder.* It was far from definite yet, not until after the postmortem. "We try to keep an open mind. Do you know of anybody who would want to kill him?"

"Surely you must be dealing with a gang of yobs, or someone who kills for the pleasure of it? Like a serial killer?"

"You've been watching too much telly, Mr. Lomax," she said. "For a start, you need at least three murders under your belt to be called a serial killer, and in the second place, the manner of Mr. Miller's death . . . well, let me just say it wasn't consistent with the psychology of that sort of crime."

"How do you know there aren't any others?"

"What do you mean?"

"How do you know that the person who killed Gavin hasn't killed others before him? Perhaps not around here, but elsewhere. Don't some of these people have jobs that take them all over the country? Isn't that how the Yorkshire Ripper slipped through your fingers?"

"I'm afraid my fingers were busy turning the pages of *Jackie* when the Yorkshire Ripper was caught," said Annie, "but you make a good point. I'll make sure I take it up with my boss."

"I'm sorry," said Lomax. "I don't mean to tell you your job."

"That's all right, sir. We're always grateful for as much help as we can get from members of the public." Annie put her notebook away and got up to leave. "Just for the record, where were you on Sunday night?"

"Me? At home. With Sally."

"All evening?"

"Yes. We were watching TV. *Downton Abbey*."

Annie smiled. "Ah, yes. Very good."

Lomax glanced at his watch. "It's almost lunchtime," he said, turning on the charm and smoothing his hair with one hand. "There's a decent pub around the corner. Perhaps you'd let me buy you a drink and a meal? We could discuss existentialism. Or something."

"Sorry, sir," said Annie, her hand on the doorknob. "I've got a nice rissole with my name on it waiting for me in the police canteen, and you've got a lovely wife called Sally at home."

THE COMPUTER lab was located in the annex, just down the corridor through the double doors from Banks's office, and it didn't seem to have been suffering too much from budget cuts. Their computer equipment was state of the art, and the spacious room in which it was housed was fitted with a machine that surreptitiously sucked the dust off your shoes and clothes when you went in. As far as Banks knew, it even sucked the dandruff out of your hair. When computers were first used in businesses, Banks remembered, they filled whole rooms with whirring tape machines—the kind you see in old James Bond movies—and dust was anathema. It didn't seem such a big deal today—his own computer got pretty dusty at times—but old habits die hard. Scientists, he had found, and CSIs in particular, were absolutely obsessed with contamination of evidence. He even had to wear a white lab coat over his suit, not to mention the ubiquitous latex gloves.

The turnover in CSI technical computer personnel was fast and frequent. Rumor had it that as soon as they reached puberty, they had to be replaced by a younger version. Liam Merchant, however, was at least forty, and Banks had known him for a couple of years. They even had a pint together occasionally after work, and sometimes Liam's partner Colin joined them. Liam was an opera buff and something of a wine expert, so they had those interests in common. Before working for the North Yorkshire police, he had been a software designer for a successful private company. He was still a civilian, not a police officer.

"Alan," he said, extending his gloved hand to shake. There was something rather perverted, Banks always felt, about the clasping of hands in latex, but he tried not to let it bother him. "Your timing is impeccable, as always."

"We aim to please. How's Colin?"

"Thriving, thank you."

"Tell him I said hello. So what have you got for me?"

"Where do you want to start?"

"Anything on the computers?"

Liam led Banks over to a workbench, on which sat Gavin Miller's laptop and desktop computers. "We're only just beginning, but first off," Liam said, "I have to tell you that there's nothing special about them. They're your common or garden, on sale at PC World every other week computers. At least they would have been about four years ago. Still using Windows Vista, for crying out loud. Of course, they're perfectly adequate for most people, if a bit slow and prone to seizing up every now and then for no reason, but cheap and . . . well, not exactly nasty, but hardly in the Rolls-Royce or BMW class, either. Not even a Ford Focus, to be honest."

Banks knew that Liam was as much a snob about computers as he was about wine and opera recordings, but it was worth putting up with an occasional outburst of snobbery for the useful tips that Liam tossed his way. "Anything interesting on them?" Banks asked.

"Depends what you mean by interesting. No modifications, just the bog standard factory presets. Not even a few extra modules of RAM, which the laptop could certainly use. On them? Well, the usual. Anti-virus and antispyware programs. Reasonable quality, so-so settings, but free software, thus limited." He waved his hand from side to side to demonstrate the precarious nature of Gavin Miller's computer protection. "Which is living dangerously when you visit some of the sites he did."

"Oh?" said Banks, interested at last.

Liam grinned. "Don't get your hopes up, old boy. There's nothing illegal or exciting. No kiddie porn, thank God, nor sheep shagging or what have you. Is sheep shagging illegal, by the way?"

"There are probably laws against it," said Banks. "Though I can't say as I've ever had to enforce any lately. The animal rights people might have a thing or two to say about it, mind you. I mean, how would you know if the sheep said yes or no?"

"'I thought "baaa" always meant yes, Your Honor'? Anyway, I'm all for Sheep Shaggers Liberation, if there is one. To move on . . . we have the usual free porn sites—boringly hetero, I'm afraid—and from what I can gather, his tastes run from the so-called normal to the slightly fetishistic."

"As in?"

"Nylons and lingerie. American cheerleader uniforms, or at least professional ladies dressed in said uniforms. Apart from a few milfs, he seems to like them young, teens and college girls, or what passes for young on these Web sites. He's not fussy about type or ethnic origin, quite happy with blondes, brunettes, blacks, Asians and Orientals, as long as they're young." Liam scratched his chin. "There seem to be a lot more Eastern Europeans on these sites these days."

"Some of the girls are forced or tricked into it," said Banks. "Trafficked. It goes in waves. These days most of them are trafficked from ex–Soviet bloc countries in Eastern Europe. It used to be Southeast Asia. Africa before that."

"Three cheers for good old capitalism, eh?" said Liam. "Opening up new markets all the time. Anyway, you'll be happy to hear that there are no dwarves or ladyboys. Doggy style, but not doggies. One-on-one, rather than threesomes or gang bangs. No fisting or machines of ass destruction."

"Ouch," said Banks.

"My apologies. I've been reading too many American magazines. I have to say, your Mr. Miller is disappointingly normal. No leads there. No Internet plots to murder anyone or buy drugs. Not even Viagra. He certainly didn't appear to buy any online medications."

"Who among us could stand such scrutiny of his computer?"

Liam narrowed his eyes. "I wouldn't mind an hour or two with your hard drive one day, old boy," he said. "I'll bet you've got a more interesting range of browsing than Mr. Miller."

"You'd be disappointed, I'm afraid," said Banks. "It's mostly music and e-mails. Sorry."

"So *you* say. Anyway, in my experience, it's where many people live their secret lives these days, no matter how public it all is. That's the irony, I suppose. People assume it's private, but in reality it's wide open. It's also easy to hide there, to take on other identities, become anyone you want. You can stalk and slander to your heart's content. You can praise your own work to the skies and piss on everyone else's. Perverts and cowards love it. Then there's Facebook and Twitter, the narcissist's Elysian Fields. Bloody baby pictures and bad restaurant reviews because the waiter didn't bow and scrape enough for your liking. It's worse than those dreadful people who start talking on their mobile phones the minute they take their seat on a train. 'I'm on the train, darling. We'll be leaving in a few minutes. It's still raining here.' I mean, who bloody cares?"

Banks laughed. "So why do you spend so much of your time working with computers then, Liam?"

"Because I love them! I love their purity, their simplicity. And because it's just about all I can do to make a living. It's not computers that's the problem, it's people. Not the machines, but the people who build them and run them. By the way, do you happen to be a connoisseur of fine champagne?"

"I wouldn't go that far, but I enjoy the odd glass now and then as much as the next man."

"The *odd glass*? The *next man*?"

"Stop being so arch, Liam. I like champagne. Yes. I just don't have anyone to share it with as often as I'd like."

"Ah   yes, I see. Well, short of introducing you to a friend of mine I think would like you *very* much, if you think you can find your way to polish off the *odd* bottle by yourself now and then, without any help from the *next* man, I have a reliable source of decently priced Pol Roger Cuvée Sir Winston Churchill. Various vintages. The 1979 will be well out of a policeman's price range, but there are less expensive alternatives, if no parallels. Interested?"

"I might be. Depends on the price."

"I'll send you an e-mail."

"Thanks. Did Gavin Miller have a Facebook page?"

"No. He did contribute occasional reviews and articles to a number of fanzines and movie fan sites. Unpaid, I should imagine. I suppose you've heard of the Grateful Dead, too?"

"Indeed I have. I was listening to them just last night. Great band."

"Well, there was a lot of Web activity connected with them, including set lists for all the concerts they've ever played along with quite a lot of downloads. I must say I was quite astounded when I saw how many there were. In fact, Mr. Miller seemed quite addicted to rock and roll in general, with a real passion for vinyl music sites."

The emphatic distaste with which Liam pronounced the words "rock and roll" was hard to miss. Music began and ended with opera, as far as he was concerned, and he and Banks had had a number of disagreements on the subject. Luckily, Colin was a bit more broad-minded and was at least fond of some jazz, just as long as it didn't get too adventurous or discordant. Early, not late, John Coltrane. Cool Miles, not funky. Bix and Louis even better. "What do you mean by Web activity?" Banks asked.

"The usual. Downloads, file sharing, discussion groups, blogs, tweets, chat rooms, threads, message boards, eBay, Craigslist, esoteric memorabilia sites, you name it. Nothing illegal, unless you count the file sharing and the occasional illegally downloaded bootleg recording." Liam passed him a print of the screen capture. "This was the page that was showing when he last closed the lid of the laptop. I don't know whether it means anything."

Banks took the photo from Liam. "Any idea what time?"

"He logged off the desktop at seven forty-five Sunday evening, but that doesn't mean he went out immediately to meet his death."

"Point taken," said Banks. "We think it was later than that, anyway, and someone was seen leaving the car park in Coverton around half past ten. It just helps us pinpoint the timing a bit more accurately."

"Ah, one of those detective thingies."

"That's right." Banks read the printed sheet. It was a simple Wikipedia article about the music of 1972, listing the albums released in that year. Banks remembered 1972. He had been living in Notting Hill and attending London Polytechnic, studying for his Higher National Diploma in business studies. Glancing down the page, he was surprised to find that Creedence, Them and the Velvet Underground had all split up that year, and that the first album to be released was *Jamming with Edward*. He handed the sheet back to Liam. "*Jamming with Edward*, indeed," he said.

"I assume you've heard of it?"

"Yes," said Banks. "It was something to do with the Rolling Stones."

"There's a lot of late 1971 and early 1972 in his recent memory. Top movies, current events, bestselling LPs, politics, what books were being read, that sort of thing. *Fear and Loathing in Las Vegas, Be Here Now, The Dice Man*. Specific searches on movies such as *A Clockwork Orange, Get Carter, 10 Rillington Place*. And vinyl LPs like *Rainbow Bridge, Harvest, Tupelo Honey*. Whatever they are."

"Music, Liam. Music."

"If you say so. And what does all this add up to, O great detective?"

"Wish I knew," said Banks. "That he was interested in 1972? I've had a quick look around his home and his vinyl and DVD collections, too. It's similar to what you found on his computer. I get the impression that our Mr. Miller lived in a bit of a fantasy world since he lost his job. Or in the past. He satisfied his needs with DVDs and online porn and chat rooms. Definite loner. Anorak."

"No wonder he was a loner if he was sitting around at home listening to rock and roll records and watching porn. Who'd want to share that with him?"

"Everyone needs a hobby, Liam. If he was searching all this 1972 stuff on his computer, maybe he was on a nostalgia fishing trip, searching for something from his past, reminding himself what happened back then? He certainly didn't seem to have much going for him in his life around the time he died. He would have been at university back then. He was at Essex from 1971 to 1974, so 1971 to 1972 would have coincided with his first year. Maybe it was his annus mirabilis? His first great love? Or he could have been doing research for something. A book, or an article, maybe? You said he wrote pieces for fanzines and what have you now and then?"

"Some film review sites and book reviews, yes."

"Were there any visits to suicide sites, assisted death, that sort of thing?"

"None."

"Any other recent searches?"

"Much of the same, really, music, current events, film, books, including a few for '73 and '74. Could they have any connection with his death?"

"If they do," said Banks, "I've no idea what it might be yet, but I'll make a note of it. As I said, those were the years he was at university."

"Perhaps he met an old friend who stirred it all up?"

"Perhaps."

"Or maybe he was meeting someone to buy or sell some sort of rare, forbidden Grateful Dead bootleg recording?"

"I doubt that there are any. The Grateful Dead have put out just about every concert they ever played in one format or another, mostly for free. It's a novel idea, though, Liam, someone murdered in a rare Grateful Dead bootleg deal gone wrong. I like it."

"Well, what would I know? I'm just a civilian."

"Let's leave the speculation behind for the time being. Have you had a chance to work on the mobile yet?"

"We're still processing the SIM card, but I wouldn't expect too much more. We did get a list of the recent calls made and received, along with the scratch-pad numbers. It's just a cheap phone, not a smartphone or anything fancy like that, so there's no e-mail or Web browsing. He didn't seem to do texts, and there aren't very many calls, which makes our job a lot easier." He passed Banks a sheet of paper. In the week before his murder Miller had made only three calls and received two. Before that, there were a few more to or from different numbers scattered about, but as Stefan Nowak had said, not very many.

"Not much to go on, is it?" Banks said.

"I guess you could say our Mr. Miller was definitely not a party animal. It's a pay-as-you-go mobile, and his last top-up was five months ago, for a tenner. He's still got four pounds sixty pence left. I know people would go through that in an hour."

"So he lived his life online?"

"So it appears. What there was of it. Sorry."

"And the photos?"

"Just photos. I can't say exactly how old they are, but they're not digital. Some of them look to be late sixties or early seventies to me, judging by the architecture and what people were wearing. As far as we can tell so far, they're all over twenty years old, anyway. The last ones were probably taken outside some college or other in the late eighties. Maybe where he got his first teaching job. Anyway, we're getting them scanned, and you'll have copies as soon as we can. We'll be checking the originals for prints, of course, like the envelope and the money, but I wouldn't expect too much."

"Too bad," said Banks. He held up the sheet. "Can I keep this?"

"It's your copy. Take this, too. We got it from the computer. It might come in useful."

It was a head and shoulders shot of Miller. From the background, it was clearly taken by the computer's built-in camera: straggly goatee; slightly hostile, lined face; deep-set eyes; thinning, longish hair. Banks thanked Liam and headed back to his office.

3

THERE WEREN'T MANY SHOPS ON COVERTON HIGH Street. On one side stood a row of detached houses set back behind low stone walls or fences and hedges, most with trees and well-tended gardens. Each house was unique; and one even had an octagonal clock tower attached. Banks guessed it was probably an old converted schoolhouse. All were built from local limestone, with the occasional dark seam of gritstone in a lintel or a cornice. Where the row of houses ended, across from the entrance to the car park, there was about six feet of grass before the narrow drive that led down to the Old Station. The station, empty for years, had recently been converted into a combination café and gift shop, the kind of place that smells of potpourri and scented candles, and some of its wall space had been given over to exhibitions of works by local artists. Behind the station, on the road that ran at a right angle to the High Street, stood the Star & Garter, a low-roofed, whitewashed building. No doubt, in spring and summer, hanging baskets of geraniums would festoon its facade, but in the grip of a wet and chilly November, it was noticeably bare and unwelcoming.

There was one TV van in the car park, Banks noticed, and a few media types sniffing about, but not very many. Gavin Miller's death wasn't especially sensational, and the only reason it had drawn any interest at all was that it had happened in such an out-of-the-way spot.

A press conference back in Eastvale later in the day should satisfy all their needs, at least for a while.

Before he had left Eastvale, Banks had given the list of Miller's mobile calls to Gerry Masterson and asked her to match names and addresses to the numbers. He had brought Winsome along with him to Coverton and dropped her off down the road to talk to Mrs. Stanshall, the woman who said she had seen someone get into a car at ten thirty Sunday evening. They would meet up later in the mobile unit, parked in the car park over the road.

A smattering of lunchtime drinkers clustered around the bar, and one or two of the tables were taken by out-of-season tourists, but other than that, the Star & Garter was a quiet enough place. Banks ordered bangers and mash and an orange juice and asked the landlord if he would come over and join him when he had a free moment.

"I suppose it's about Gavin, isn't it?" said the balding, broad-shouldered man who joined him a few minutes later, bringing Banks's lunch with him. "Mind if I talk to you while you eat?"

The use of the victim's first name didn't pass Banks by. "Not at all. Friend of yours, was he, Gavin Miller?"

The landlord, Bob Farrell, pulled out a chair, sat down and pushed forward until his belly touched the edge of the table. "I wouldn't exactly call him a friend," he said. "But I knew him. It's terrible, what happened. Someone said they thought he might have been murdered. Is that true, or did he jump?"

"We don't know for certain yet, Mr. Farrell. Did he ever give you any reason to think he might harm himself?"

"No. I'm just saying, like. Who knows what goes on in his fellow man's mind, when you get right down to it?"

"Who, indeed. Was he a regular here?"

"When he could afford to be. He was usually a bit strapped for cash."

"Did he ever pester anyone for a loan, for a drink?"

"Not that I've heard. He always paid his way."

"Gambling?"

"I don't hold by it. You might have noticed, we don't even have any one-armed bandits in here, no matter how much the brewery puts the pressure on. A man has to stand by his principles."

"Of course," said Banks. "I was just wondering if Gavin Miller ever mentioned a flutter on the ponies, fiver on a cup match, that sort of thing."

"I never heard him. I don't think Gavin was a gambler. If he ever had any money, he spent it on his record and DVD collection. The rest went on booze and fags."

"Did he drink a lot?"

Farrell considered the question for a moment, then said, "He wasn't what I'd call a real serious boozer. And I've seen a few of those in my time. Never caused any trouble, if that's what you mean. On the other hand, he could put it away when he wanted to. And I think he also drank a fair bit at home, too. A lot do, these days, you know. It's cheaper. Killing the local pub trade."

Banks was aware how many of the Dales pubs had closed down over the past few years, victims of recession, cheap canned lager and drink driving laws. "How much would he drink on an evening here? On average?"

"Five pints was his limit. I've rarely seen him have more than that. But he wasn't in here more than once every two weeks or so. And he'd always walk out as straight as he walked in."

"Did he usually drink alone?"

"Mostly. He did come with another bloke from time to time. Not very often, though. About the same age. Dressed a bit too young for his age, if you know what I mean. Earring. Hair over the collar. Probably thought he looked trendy."

"Did you catch his name?"

"Jim, I think."

Annie had told Banks that Trevor Lomax had mentioned someone called Jim Cooper, a friend of Miller's from Eastvale College. Perhaps it was him? It would be easy enough to find out. "What about your regulars? Did he mix with them?"

"Some of the other locals would join him every now and then. He wasn't exactly unsociable, you understand, but he didn't seek out company. You'd have to approach him, then he'd be happy enough to have a chat for a while. He wasn't standoffish, really, but he wasn't very good at small talk, at blethering, you know what I mean? People didn't usually like to spend very long talking to him. He wasn't interested in football or rugby, and he didn't seem to watch telly much, either, which I must say form the main topics of conversation in here of an evening. He was a bit of an egghead. He was more interested in those foreign films of his."

"So that's what he talked about?"

"Nobody here's interested in that stuff. People like things you can watch without having to read the bottom of the screen."

"But people tolerated him?"

"Oh, aye. He were harmless enough, were Gavin. I mean, they might have had a bit of a laugh at him, but he'd no side, Gavin hadn't, and he took it all in good humor. And he knew his stuff. Arts, really. Films, music, books, that sort of thing. If ever there was a trivia question needed answering, Gavin was your man. He could be funny, too, sometimes. He did a passable imitation of that old Monty Python philosophers song. Mind you, he'd have to be well in his cups before that. And then there were times he'd tell stories about traveling around in the States, too, hitchhiking and going to Grateful Dead concerts, and they were quite interesting, I must admit."

This must have happened during the "lost years" Gerry Masterson had referred to. It would be worth passing it on to her. "Did he ever mention drugs?"

Farrell's eyes narrowed. "Are you thinking that's what got him killed?"

"I'm not thinking anything yet, Mr. Farrell," said Banks. "As I told you, we don't know what happened. I'm just trying to keep an open mind and find out as much as I can."

"Aye, well, there's no drugs in here, I can tell you that. I wouldn't have it. I'm not saying there aren't some in town might indulge, you'd get that anywhere, wouldn't you, but I'll have none of it in here."

"So Gavin Miller never mentioned drugs?"

"Not in front of me."

Banks moved on. "Do you know of anyone who wished him any harm?"

"Not here, in the village, certainly."

"What about women? Did he ever come here with a girlfriend, try to chat up any of the regulars, tourists, whatever?"

"I never saw him try. Not that we get many in here worth picking up. He was quite pally with Josie, the barmaid over there."

Banks followed his glance towards the bar and saw a woman with bottle-blond hair, probably in her mid-forties, pulling a pint. "I understand that he was in here on Friday night. Did you see him then?"

"No. I wasn't working—had a Licensed Victuallers do—but Josie was on. She might remember something."

"Can you send her over?"

Banks finished his bangers and mash while Bob Farrell went to cover for Josie. She came and perched on the chair beside him, just as he had emptied his plate. "Josie. I'm DCI Banks. I wonder if I could have a quick word with you about Gavin Miller. I understand you knew him?"

Josie nodded. "I can't believe it. I just can't get my head around it. I was saying to Geoff over there at the bar that he was in here just the other night, Gavin, Friday it was, living and breathing, just like you and me."

"Was he any different from usual on Friday?"

"Come to think of it, he was. Quite chipper, really. For Gavin. He even managed to crack a smile or two."

"What time did he come in?"

"About half past five, with his shopping. Almost forgot it, and all, when he left about half nine."

"That's a long time to spend here, isn't it?"

"He did drink a bit more than usual, though I wouldn't say he was really drunk, if you know what I mean. He just seemed in a good mood right from the moment he came in. Not that he was a misery all the rest of the time, mind you, though, like I said, he often did seem a bit sad, depressed, you know, weighted down with burdens of the world. He seemed in a much lighter mood on Friday."

"You say he had more to drink than usual?"

Josie nodded. "I asked him if his boat had come in, and he just tapped the side of his nose, like, and said, 'Never you mind, Josie, my love, never you mind.' Then he asked if I wanted a drink, myself. First time he's ever done that."

Banks guessed that Miller had been less cautious about spending what little money he had because he was expecting a larger sum in a few days, which meant that he already knew by Friday that he was going to receive five thousand pounds on Sunday. It was just another little piece of evidence that seemed to indicate Miller might have arranged to meet someone at the bridge, and that meeting had ended in his death. Also, if he was in such good spirits on Friday, it was hardly likely that he committed suicide on Sunday, though circumstances could change drastically in two days. "Did he say why he was in such a good mood?"

"No. It were just general good spirits, I thought. And I know not to look a gift horse in the mouth."

"What did you think of him, in general? You said you knew him. Did he tell you his troubles?"

"No. Nothing like that. We just passed the time of day. He might tell me about a book he was reading—he was a great reader, was Gavin—or some music he'd listened to. You know, just chitchat."

"What about his friend? Apparently he sometimes came in with a chap called Jim. Did you ever meet him?"

"Yes. I think they used to work together or something," said Josie. "I can't say as I took to Jim at all. Far too full of himself."

"Did he try to chat you up?"

"Thought he was God's gift."

"And Gavin?"

"Gavin? That's a good one. If you'd known him you wouldn't be asking that. Gavin wouldn't know how to chat up a paid escort."

Banks laughed but said nothing.

"I suppose in a way he might have been interested, though," Josie went on, touching her hair.

"Oh?"

"Yes. Well, you know, a woman can tell these things."

"Indeed."

"But it wouldn't never have worked."

"No? Why not?" Banks sipped his orange juice. "Not your type?"

"I wonder if he was anybody's type," Josie said wistfully. She leaned forward and lowered her voice. "And just between you and me, he wasn't exactly number one in the personal hygiene chart, if you catch my drift."

Banks remembered the absence of toothbrush and deodorant at Miller's cottage.

"All in all," Josie concluded, "I felt sorry for him, and I quite liked him, he was a nice bloke, but frankly speaking, I thought he'd be too much work. Sorry, I'd better get back behind the bar now, Bob's giving me some funny looks. Ta-ta."

Banks thanked Josie for her time and told her there was an incident van in the car park in case she, or any of her customers, thought of anything else, then he left to pick up Winsome.

AFTER HE had dropped off Winsome back at the station, Banks had spent a good part of the afternoon watching Dr. Glendenning at work on the postmortem, which revealed that Miller's poor general state of health before his death was due partly to malnutrition and alcohol, and partly to personal neglect. The main thing as far as the investigation was concerned, though, was that Dr. Glendenning had been able to confirm time of death and that some of the contusions on Miller's body, along with internal injuries, a broken nose and a split lip, were antemortem and were indicative of some sort of violent struggle. According to the traces of postmortem lividity that remained, despite the blood loss, the body had also not been moved after it had hit the ground.

Dr. Glendenning was also able to establish that the violence was caused very shortly before death, certainly not hours or days, and as no one knew anything about Gavin Miller getting beaten up, they now had a probable killing on their hands. Given that it would have taken a bit of effort to lift Miller up and heave him off the bridge, Banks was leaning more towards murder than manslaughter, though a clever barrister might convince a jury that no killer could be certain that such a fall would have resulted in the death of his victim.

At half past five, Banks gathered the troops in the squad room for an informal end-of-the-day meeting. DC Doug Watson was still out manning the mobile unit in the car park off Coverton High Street, and PC Kirwan was making the rounds of the local farms, but Winsome, Annie and Gerry were all present, along with some of the civilian staff and CSIs. All Winsome had been able to discover from Mrs. Stanshall was that the car was dark, shiny and "ordinary-looking," by which she meant not a van or a people mover, and that she was positive the person who got in was a man, medium height and build. He had hair, but she couldn't say what color other than "darkish." There had been no interesting mail in Miller's post office box, either, only final demands for electricity and broadband bills.

What was it they used to say on the old quiz program? "Would the real Gavin Miller please stand up?" Where was the real Gavin Miller? Banks wondered. They still didn't know why he had been out on the bridge that Sunday night—probably some time between ten and half past, if Mrs. Stanshall was as right as she thought she was. They didn't know why a man who was, to all intents and purposes, broke had five thousand pounds in his pocket, or why he had got into a scuffle that might have resulted in his death. More than twenty-four hours had gone by since the discovery of the body on Monday morning, and they didn't seem to be much the wiser. The only other thing close to a lead they had was the list of calls, and Gerry Masterson was working on them.

"So what have we come up with today?" he asked the assembled team. "Gerry? Please tell me you've got some leads from the phone calls."

"Well, sir, there are one or two I still have to track down, but in addition to Trevor Lomax and Jim Cooper from the college, there's not much else." Gerry opened the file in front of her. "The most recent calls," she said, "were on Friday morning. He made three calls, which is very unusual in the light of his limited usage. One was to a dentist on Coverton High Street."

"What was that about?"

"I rang the dentist, and he was only too happy to tell me that Mr. Miller had made an appointment to come in for some bridgework, whitening, and possible implants. The dentist was quite chatty, really. Even asked if I'd ever thought of having any cosmetic work done myself."

"Cheeky bastard." Banks smiled and perched on the edge of Doug Watson's empty desk. "Dr. Glendenning remarked on the poor condition of his teeth at the PM," he said, feeling that terrible fear in the pit of his stomach because he had been avoiding a visit to the dentist's for too long now; he would have to make an appointment soon. "I must say, the timing is interesting. Isn't that kind of dental work expensive?"

"It can be," said Gerry. "Usually is. Anyway, the second person he spoke to that day was a fellow vinyl collector. There was some rare Japanese pressing of an early John Lennon LP on eBay, and they were discussing whether it was worth making an offer for it. The other chap—George Spalding he's called—said it was a pity neither of them would be able to afford it, but apparently Miller seemed to think he might be in with a chance if the price didn't go too high. Spalding checks out. He lives in Splott and he's got an alibi. It sounded legit to me, sir."

"Splott?" said Winsome. "Where on earth is that?"

Gerry Masterson smiled. "Cardiff," she said. "Lovely-sounding place, isn't it?"

"And the third phone call?" Banks asked.

"Interesting. An estate agent called Keith Orville. I've talked to him, too, and it seems that Gavin Miller was interested in renting a small storefront in Coverton High Street. Apparently, he was thinking of opening a specialist vinyl record shop."

"Interesting, indeed," said Banks. "So here we have a man who's so poor he can't pay his mortgage or his utility bills, is suffering from malnutrition, and can only afford a night at the pub every two weeks or so, and two days before he dies he's making appointments for expensive dental work, planning to bid for a pricey piece of vinyl on eBay, and inquiring about renting retail premises. Doesn't that tell us something?"

"Other than that he didn't have any business sense?" said Annie. "Well, let's see. No money had been reported missing, so he couldn't have just found it in the street, and he hadn't withdrawn it from his bank account, so obviously he had come into, or was soon expecting to come into, some money."

"Right." Banks told them about Miller's good mood in the Star &
Garter the Friday before his death. "He hadn't got it by then," he went
on, "but he seemed certain enough of getting it, and he already had
plans for using it. Which pretty much convinces me that the five
thousand pounds he was carrying was definitely his, wherever it came
from, whoever gave it to him, and that he was hardly likely to be
giving it away. In fact, it seems to indicate that he had been given it at
a meeting shortly before he was killed, either by the person who had
given him it—who for some or reason or other wasn't able to take it
back—or by someone who watched, or who knew about the transaction in advance, and planned to rob Miller afterwards. Again, he
didn't manage to get his hands on the five thousand pounds, either.
I've thought and thought about that, and apart from the obvious—that
the killer thought he heard someone approaching and ran off—I can
think of only two other reasons offhand why the money was still in
Gavin Miller's pocket when his body was found some ten or eleven
hours after his death. First, and most obvious, is that the killer didn't
know about it. And second, perhaps less obvious, is that the killer
didn't want it."

"What do you mean, sir?" Winsome asked.

"I mean, maybe money didn't mean anything to the killer. Maybe
that wasn't what it was all about. Maybe the killer already had enough
money. Maybe he could afford to leave five thousand pounds behind?"

"Nobody ever has enough money, sir," said Winsome. "With all
due respect, I don't believe anyone would leave five thousand pounds
behind just because he didn't need it. Certainly not anyone capable of
murder."

"Maybe you're right," said Banks. "I'm only putting it forward as a
vague possibility. Maybe he was worried it was marked with a special
dye or something? Anyway, I can't think of any other reasons than
those three. If one of you can, please let me know."

"I'll tell you something else," said Annie. "If he was planning on
getting his teeth fixed and renting a shop, he wouldn't get much
change out of five thousand pounds to bid for anything on eBay."

"That's true," said Banks. "So perhaps it was only the first install-
ment?"

"Blackmail?"

"Possibly. All we know is that it meant a lot to Gavin Miller, even if we don't know how he came by it. Meant enough for him to start making plans about turning his life around. Perhaps he had some valuable records to sell, to get the business started? Or could he simply have been selling drugs? Winsome? Is this all about a drug deal gone sour?"

"It could have been," Winsome answered, "but we've no evidence of that. Apart from the cannabis and two LSD tablets he had at his cottage, clearly for personal consumption, I've not been able to get a lead on any other activities in that area. I spoke with the drugs squad earlier this afternoon. They've never heard of Gavin Miller."

"Still," said Banks. "They don't know everything. Especially if he was just starting out."

"No, sir. But I think they'd know if he was dealing in any sort of quantity. Certainly five thousand pounds' worth."

"Fair enough."

"Anyway, I'm still liaising with them, like you suggested, and right now they're trying to track down anyone who might have sold him the stuff we found. Stefan's given them an accurate chemical analysis, so they've got plenty to go on. I understand that many of these illegal substances have various tags or markers that can link them to certain batches and shipments. Anyway, because it's not a great amount, just street level, and because Miller doesn't appear to have traveled any further than Eastvale or Coverton in the past while, they think they should be able to get a lead on his local supplier soon enough. There aren't that many in the area. If we lean on the supplier a bit, he should be able to tell us whether Miller was a player. Personally, though, I doubt it. I mean, look at the way he lived. If he was selling drugs, he certainly wasn't making much money at it, was he? And how would he get around to meet his contacts? He didn't even have a car."

"Good point," said Banks. "But maybe this was the first shipment? And maybe he wasn't working alone? Keep at it."

"I don't really know if this is worth mentioning," Annie said, "but Trevor Lomax at Eastvale College suggested that Miller's murder could be part of a series. Watching too much telly, I said, but I thought it was worth an hour or two on the computer."

"And?"

"Nothing so far. I've been checking national records for the past three years. No mysterious deaths under similar circumstances—victims thrown from high places—and no vinyl collecting connections or anything as far as I can tell."

"So Lomax thought there was some homicidal Dead head running around killing vinyl collectors?"

Annie smiled. "Something like that. I suppose it must be hard for him to accept that Miller killed himself or that he was killed by someone close to him. He was a bit full of himself, but he's the closest we've found to a friend of Miller's so far, and he did give me a couple more names to check out."

"We know about Cooper," said Banks. "Who else did he mention?"

"A woman called Dayle Snider, old girlfriend of Miller's."

"Excellent," said Banks. "Keep working the college angle. Talk to Cooper. Talk to the Snider woman. There could be something there. I'm far from convinced that we know all there is to know about this sexual misconduct business, too."

"It's ludicrous," said Annie. "The word of two 'gum-chewing airheads,' as Lomax put it. There has to be more to it."

"If there is," said Banks, "I'm counting on you to find out what. OK, that's it for today."

BANKS HAD picked up a Chinese takeaway on the road out of Eastvale and was warming it up in the microwave. The drive to Helmthorpe and Gratly hadn't been too bad when he made it around seven o'clock, but if the rain continued to fall all night, as the forecasters predicted, then there was a good chance that the area by the bridge at the Relton turnoff in Fortford would be closed by morning. That would mean a two-mile diversion via the Lyndgarth road, if the Leas weren't flooded, and three if they were. Still, he was getting used to it now. The same areas had flooded every time it had rained that summer, and there was no reason for them not to flood now. Neither the county nor the local councils had done a thing to change the situation, as far as Banks knew. People just learned to avoid the affected areas and wait for the water to go away, the same way they did with the snow and ice.

Still, he was home now, in his cozy cottage, with the prospect of music, perhaps a little Patrick Hamilton to read, and maybe even a DVD later—something from the new noir collection that the post-man had left around the back that day. It was a long time since he'd seen *Kiss Me Deadly* or *In a Lonely Place,* for example.

As he poured himself some wine and checked the chicken fried rice and Szechuan beef, which weren't quite ready, he thought about the postmortem he had attended earlier in the afternoon. He still felt slightly shaken by it. Some people said the more autopsies you at-tended, the more you got used to them, but for Banks it was the op-posite. Each one was worse than the one before. It wasn't the blood and guts, intestines and fat layers exposed; he thought, perhaps in a fanciful way, that it was just the presence of death in the room, the aura of a violent end. He was starting to feel the same at murder scenes, too. This was no beautiful young woman raped and strangled, no innocent child killed to satisfy some pedophile's fear of discovery; it was an emaciated, out-of-shape, unattractive man in late middle age. Nor was it a friend or acquaintance. Banks hadn't known Miller, despite feeling some sense of kinship with him due to their closeness in age and musical interests. But the older he got, the more he felt that when a man's body is lying there twisted and abandoned on some remote railway track, or naked on the pathologist's slab, and someone is pulling out his internal organs, it doesn't have to be personal; it be-comes somehow universal. Death with a capital *D*. The Reaper is in the building. He felt vaguely sick thinking about it; a healthy slug of Aussie red helped. Maybe retirement wasn't such a bad idea. Could he really handle the extra years on the job if he got promoted? Did he really want to?

That evening, he ate in the kitchen again, this time listening to an old episode of *I'm Sorry I'll Read That Again* on Radio 4 Extra and halfheartedly working on a half-finished crossword from the *Sunday Times* on the table in front of him. He hadn't realized before that "in crime scene" was an anagram for "reminiscence." Maybe the clue was trying to tell him something?

When he had finished his meal, he filled up his glass, went into the entertainment room and put on Miles Davis's film score from *L'ascenseur pour l'échafaud*. He loved the atmospheric music, though he had never seen the film, and he thought he might check online later to see if it was available on DVD. He carried his wine and book into the conservatory and settled down to read. The wind rattled the flimsy structure, and the rain poured down the windows and roof as if someone were throwing bucketfuls at them. Sometimes it felt as if the little island, and Banks's little part of it in particular, had been under assault for months. He wondered how much more the old place could take. He had thought it was a solid enough conservatory, but there had been two leaks there already that summer, in addition to one in the main roof. If the wind got much worse, it could blow the whole damn structure away. Still, not much he could do about it now.

As he listened to Miles's haunting, muted trumpet on "Générique," he thought again about his experience in the mortuary. Was it his own approaching mortality that made him feel that way? He had never really thought about it much, but Madame Gervaise's remarks about retirement the other day had made him feel his age, as had seeing Miller's body on the abandoned railway. It was hard to believe they were almost the same age. He had always been reasonably healthy, even though he could have taken better care of himself. His blood pressure was a bit high, but his weight was fine, and his doctor had recently lowered the dosage of statins he took to control cholesterol, remarking that his "good" cholesterol was getting much better. A bit less cheese and fewer takeaways would probably solve the problem altogether, but he would miss them too much, and would rather take a little pill every night and avoid grapefruit.

So why was it that he found himself becoming so morbid? True, friends had died recently, including Paul Major, one of his old classmates, of lung cancer just last month. They hadn't been in touch often over the years, weren't really close, but he remembered when he and his friends used to gather around Paul's Dansette on summer after-

noons in the mid-sixties and listen to the Who, Bob Dylan and the
Rolling Stones.

Luckily, his elderly parents were both still alive, despite his father's
angina and his mother's brush with cancer. They were still active, off
on cruises all over the world since they had inherited his brother Roy's
fortune. Right now, while he was sitting in his rickety conservatory,
they were somewhere in Southeast Asia—Vietnam or Thailand, he
wasn't quite sure—spending his inheritance. And this was a couple
who had thought Blackpool was a long way to go for their summer
holidays when Banks was young. Banks sipped some wine. It must be
his job, he thought. The homicide rate in North Yorkshire was hardly
comparable to New York's, or even London's, but one or two a year
were quite enough, he found. Each death was a story, pathetic, tragic,
even comic on occasion, but they accumulated and weighed him
down like the snow on a rolling snowball. He became encrusted with
death, heavy with it.

Enough morbid thoughts, he decided. Maybe it was time to crack
out the Chicken Dance CD, open the bubbly and invite a few friends
over. As if.

Miles played "Florence sur les Champs-Élysées" and Banks opened
his Patrick Hamilton. He had hardly finished a paragraph when his
mobile rang. He picked it up from the matching table beside his
wicker chair and slid his thumb across the bottom.

"Banks."

"Sir," came the familiar voice. "It's me. DC Masterson. I'm sorry to
bother you at home."

Banks thought he could hear crowd noise and the overexcited
voices of football commentators in the background. Gerry must be
watching the game on TV. He had forgotten about the European Cup
match tonight. Not that he really gave a toss about Manchester United.
"It's all right, Gerry. I'm open all hours. What is it? Something important?"

"It could be, sir. I've traced the other numbers Gavin Miller called."

"Anything interesting?"

"I think so. One of them was ex-directory. That's why it took me a
bit more time."

"And?"

"Veronica Chalmers, sir."

"As in *Lady* Veronica Chalmers?"

"Er, yes, sir. Gavin Miller rang her up a week ago yesterday just before two o'clock in the afternoon. They talked for close to seven minutes."

"There's no mistake?"

"No, sir. Seven minutes, less a few seconds."

"That's quite a long time."

"Yes, sir."

"Just a week before his death. And he was the one who rang her?"

"Yes. I don't think anyone else used his mobile. Her number was also scribbled on his scratch pad, sir, along with the others he called. No names. She lives up on the Heights."

"Yes, I know. Right. Thanks again, Gerry. You've done a terrific job. Maybe you can do a bit of digging tomorrow morning, if you can spare a bit of time from HOLMES, and find out all you can about Lady Veronica Chalmers. But tread softly. We don't want to set off any alarms. And it might be best if we keep her name to ourselves, just for the time being."

"Yes, sir."

4

BRIERLEY HOUSE STOOD IN THE AREA OF EASTVALE called the Heights, or what the locals knew as Millionaires' Row, a short stretch of ten grand houses widely spaced along the hilltop that crested the town to the north, above the bend in the river. All built of local limestone, though in varying styles, most of them had high stone walls and wrought-iron gates. Most of the gates stood permanently open, though some were locked and linked by intercom with the houses themselves.

The gates to Lady Veronica Chalmers's house stood open, and as Banks drove down the winding gravel drive, past manicured lawns, flower beds and an ancient copper beech, he felt like Philip Marlowe going to visit Colonel Sternwood, though he doubted that he would find Lady Chalmers sitting in a hothouse. He parked next to a beautifully maintained old MG sports car. A red one.

It was ten thirty in the morning. As yet, neither Banks nor Gerry Masterson had told anyone about Gavin Miller's phone call. Banks had considered ringing Lady Chalmers after he had heard the news from Gerry the previous evening, but had decided against it. Though he couldn't imagine that she was involved in any way with Gavin Miller's death, he didn't want to give her too much time to think, or worry, before his visit. Those first impressions could be so important.

There was a brass bell push beside the paneled yellow door, and when Banks pressed it, he heard the chimes ring inside. Nothing happened for a few moments, then he thought he heard a muffled voice followed by the click-clack of high heels across an uncarpeted area. When the door opened, a beautiful young woman with straight dark hair down to her shoulders, a flawless olive complexion, full lips and big loam-brown eyes smiled and asked him who he was and what he wanted. She had the merest hint of an accent, which Banks thought might be Greek or Italian, but he could have been wrong. In her early thirties, Banks guessed, she was casually but smartly dressed in a navy skirt and a buttoned white blouse, tucked into the waistband.

Banks showed her his warrant card and said that he would like to see Lady Chalmers on a private matter. The young woman invited him to step into a spacious reception area with a marbled chessboard floor, a high ceiling and a large fireplace, and bade him wait there while she went into one of the rooms, taking his warrant card with her. As she walked away, he noticed not only her fine figure, but that she wasn't wearing high heels, just shoes that made a lot of noise on the floor. She returned a moment later and led Banks through another door. "Please make yourself comfortable," she said. "Lady Chalmers is on the telephone at the moment, but she will be with you in a short while." Then she turned and closed the door behind her.

He was standing in a light and airy room with a number of interesting paintings on the walls, most of them abstract or impressionist in style. One interested him in particular, a striking contemporary portrait of a man and a woman standing some distance apart in a room not entirely unlike the one he was in. He thought he recognized the style, though not the actual painting, and when he walked closer to examine the signature and saw he was right, he swallowed, stepped back and stared at the painting again.

He turned his attention next to the large sliding glass doors and saw once again why these houses commanded the high prices they did. The doors led out to a flagged patio area, complete with white garden furniture, an expensive barbecue and an outdoor dining setup. They wouldn't have got much use out of that this summer, he thought. Stone steps led down to a lower garden, a lawn edged with shrubs and flowers, and more garden furniture. Bay trees, rosebushes and fuchsia

stood against the drystone walls of the neighboring houses, giving the
garden a private, cozy feeling. The only flora showing any color were
the teardrop flowers of the fuchsia, still reddish purple like a fresh
bruise.

The view, of course, was stunning. Looking directly ahead to the
south, Banks took in the vista of the town center cupped in its hollow,
the Norman church, the cobbled market square, the Swainsdale
Centre and bus station, and the castle ruins up on their hill. Beyond,
Hindswell Woods straggled up the slope on the other side of the valley
and thinned out towards the summit, above whose ridge spread the
ever-changing sky, dark and threatening where it seemed to rest on
the line of the ridge itself, but lightening and showing gaps of blue
higher up. Below the castle, the terraced gardens stepped down to the
river and its waterfalls, which these days were running at full capacity.
Banks could hear their deep rumbling even through the double glaz-
ing. Across the river, slightly to the left, lay the Green, another desirable, if not quite as expensive, residential area of Eastvale, with its old
trees, green space and ordered streets of Georgian semis.

Banks sensed rather than heard someone enter the room and turned
to see a woman standing there, smiling and holding out his warrant
card. He took it and shook her hand. It felt warm and delicate in his.
"Veronica Chalmers," she said with the slightly challenging smile of
someone obviously aware of both her position and her effect on men.
"My friends call me Ronnie."

Banks felt tongue-tied for a moment. He didn't feel that he could
call her Ronnie, but Lady Chalmers was a bit of a mouthful. He resolved to try not to use her name at all.

Lady Veronica Chalmers was a remarkably beautiful woman. Banks
put her age at mid-forties, only because of crinkling crow's-feet
around her eyes, which he thought added to, rather than detracted
from, her beauty. She was simply dressed in thigh-hugging designer
jeans and a pale blue scallop-necked top. Her tousled blond hair fell
down over her shoulders in lustrous waves, and a shaggy fringe covered most of her forehead. She had a heart-shaped face and unusual
green eyes flecked with amber. Her teardrop pendant and matching
earrings, which he could just see in the shadows of her hair, echoed

their colors. So here he was, in a house up on the Heights, surrounded by beautiful women. A man might think he had died and gone to heaven.

Lady Chalmers gestured to a winged armchair, which sat at an angle to its partner in front of a low glass table. Facing the view, of course. "Do sit down. I've asked Oriana to bring us tea. I hope that's all right?" Her voice was naturally posh, educated, but not in any way patronizing or arrogant. When she sat down opposite him and relaxed, crossing her legs, he noticed how smooth and pale her skin was. Alabaster came to mind.

"Perfect," said Banks. "It's an unusual name, Oriana."

"Yes. Oriana Serroni. It's Italian, of course." Lady Chalmers looked towards the sliding doors. "Normally, I'd take tea outside," she said. "Even at this time of the year. But . . . well . . . you know what it's been like lately."

"The deluge," said Banks.

"Indeed."

"It's a beautiful house."

"Thank you. We're very lucky. Of course, it's far too big for us, but Jem does do a lot of entertaining here."

"I take it that Jem would be Sir Jeremy, your husband?"

"Yes. I'm afraid he's away in New York at the moment, working on yet another new production. He's away a lot."

"I should imagine so," said Banks. He knew that Sir Jeremy Chalmers was a theatrical producer of international reputation, and a man with influential friends, including the chief constable and the local member of Parliament, who also happened to be a cabinet minister, which made Banks more than a little nervous about his visit. What a theatrical producer actually did, though, and who he did it for, Banks had no idea. He had always assumed it was a euphemism for a wheeler and dealer, the moneyman, what they used to call an impresario, but he was willing to admit there might be more to it than that. Sir Jeremy was known for his multimillion-dollar musical productions, along the lines of *Les Mis* and the Andrew Lloyd Webber spectacles. He had a reputation for taking on odd choices of source material— even odder than *Sweeney Todd* or *The Phantom of the Opera*—so much so that the joke was that his next production was likely to be *The Texas Chainsaw Massacre III—The Musical* or the rather more highbrow *Remembrance of Things Past, Part I*. It hadn't happened yet, but Banks wouldn't be surprised if it did. Whatever Sir Jeremy did, it had made him a lot of money, which had bought him a beautiful wife and home, not to mention a knighthood.

Banks nodded towards the painting that had engaged his attention. "I couldn't help but notice, but is that really what I think it is?"

Lady Chalmers's eyes widened. "Why, surely you don't think we'd allow any forgeries in our house, do you? Yes, it is. A genuine Hockney. It was a wedding present, actually."

"You *know* Hockney?"

She gave an enigmatic smile. "Our paths crossed briefly in Los Angeles, many years ago. My first husband was an artist. Now Hockney's come back home again, of course. Bridlington." Her expression took on a note of sadness. "It is such a beautiful painting, though, don't you think? The positions of their bodies, the sense of space, the expressions on their faces. It says it all. The distance, the yearning."

She sounded wistful, and Banks had the strangest feeling, as he glanced over at the painting again, that the woman in the couple was *her,* perhaps with her first husband. It wasn't an exact likeness, of course, but there was just something about it, the features, the bearing. He quickly dismissed the idea. "Absolutely stunning," he said. "It reminds me of a story I read about Joan Collins, I think it was, or maybe Jackie. Anyway, she said she loved one of Hockney's paintings of a swimming pool, but she couldn't afford the painting, so she bought the swimming pool instead."

Lady Chalmers laughed. "I haven't heard that." She gestured towards the painting. "Of course, I would never have been able to afford the painting." She paused, then went on, head tilted to one side as she observed Banks closely. "I must say, you intrigue me. A policeman who knows something about art."

"I don't know very much, I'm afraid. It's not my main area of interest, I have to confess. You'd have to meet my DI for that. I'm more of a music aficionado."

"Of course." She clapped her hands together. "Alan Banks. I should have known. The policeman with the rock musician son. I've read about you in the local newspaper. Samantha, my youngest, absolutely adores the Blue Lamps."

"My fame precedes me, clearly," said Banks. "I'm Brian Banks's father, yes, for my sins." Though he liked to complain about it to his son, Banks was secretly proud to be the father of such a popular and accomplished musician. And the Blue Lamps were doing well. They'd had songs on *CSI, Grey's Anatomy* and *House,* the lineup had settled down, and Brian was doing most of the songwriting. They had also been nominated for, though not won, a Mercury Prize, there was a gig on *Later . . . with Jools Holland* coming up, and their third CD had made the charts. With any luck, Brian would be keeping Banks in his old age.

At that moment Oriana came in with the silver tea service, all poise and smiles.

"This is Alan Banks, Oriana," said Lady Chalmers. "Brian Banks's father."

Oriana's loam-brown eyes widened. "I'm very pleased to meet you."

"Oriana's a big fan, too," Lady Chalmers explained as Oriana walked away. "But she's probably too embarrassed to say so. I don't know what I'd do without her," she whispered when Oriana had left the room. "She takes care of everything."

It must be nice to have someone who takes care of *everything* for you, Banks thought, especially someone as lovely as Oriana.

"By the way," Lady Chalmers went on, "Jem and I are attending a function in Harrogate with your chief constable next weekend."

"Be sure to give him my regards." Banks picked up his cup and saucer carefully. "I'm afraid I wasn't invited."

Lady Chalmers didn't bat an eyelid. "Must have been an oversight."

"It's all right, anyway," said Banks. "I have a previous engagement." They looked at each other and started to laugh.

"I suppose I should let you get around to business and ask you why you're here, shouldn't I?" said Lady Chalmers into the silence after the laughter had subsided.

"It's a minor matter, really," said Banks, "and I was hoping we could clear it up quickly and easily."

"I suppose I should get nervous when a policeman says it's a minor matter. Like when a doctor says it. It's usually the prelude to something cataclysmic."

"Hardly, in this case. I don't know if you've heard, but a man was found dead on the disused railway line up around Coverton early Monday morning."

Lady Chalmers frowned. "I do believe I heard something about it on the news. But how can I possibly help?"

"Does the name Gavin Miller mean anything to you?"

"It sounds vaguely familiar. Is that the name of the person you just mentioned . . . the dead man?"

"Yes. Naturally, we've been trying to find out all we can about him, and one of the things we discovered was that he telephoned this house a week ago Monday, just before two o'clock in the afternoon. Do you remember that call?"

Lady Chalmers put her hand to her chest. "Here? Are you sure?"

"Yes."

"Someone did ring that Monday afternoon, just after lunch, asking for money. Something to do with the alumni society. Said he was from the university. His name may have been Miller. I must confess, I wasn't paying much attention. I already give quite generously to my alma mater. I try to maintain close connections."

"Which university was that?"

"Essex."

"What did he want to talk about?"

"What do alumni people usually talk about? Donations, scholarships, that sort of thing. He was very chatty. I must say, it was hard to get him off the line."

"But you didn't know him? He hadn't called you before?"

"No, never."

"You see, the phone call went on for nearly seven minutes. That seems rather a long time to deal with a request for alumni donations, especially when you've already given at the office, so to speak."

"I suppose it does, when you put it like that. But I assure you that's all it was. Seven minutes? Are you sure?"

"Was Oriana here?"

"No, she has Mondays off. She visits her grandfather in a care home near Malton. I'm afraid I was quite alone. Is that a problem?"

"I shouldn't worry about it. I'm sure there's a simple explanation. How did Gavin Miller get your number? It's ex-directory, isn't it?"

"Yes. I have no idea. I should imagine it's easy enough if anyone really wanted it. The university might even have it on file, I suppose."

"They probably do." Banks made a mental note to check with Gerry. He took the photograph of the old, haggard Gavin Miller that Liam had given him and showed it to Lady Chalmers. "Do you recognize this man? Have you ever seen him?"

She studied the picture. "Is that him? Your victim?"

"Yes."

She shook her head. "I don't recognize him at all. He's not familiar." She paused. "He looks so . . . old."

The front door opened, and Banks heard footsteps in the hall. Not Oriana's. Then a voice called out. "Mummy? Mummy? Are you home?"

"In here, darling," Lady Chalmers called back.

The door opened and a woman in her early twenties stood there. She bore a striking resemblance to Lady Chalmers. Blond, sporty and healthy—though perhaps just a little horsey around the large mouth and jaw—was the first description that came to Banks's mind. She was wearing a riding jacket, boots and breeches.

When she saw Banks, she slowed down, her eyes shifting from one to the other. "Is something wrong, Mummy? You look like you've seen a ghost. Has something happened to Daddy?"

"Don't be silly, dear. Of course nothing is wrong." She turned back to Banks. "DCI Banks, this is my elder daughter, Angelina. She's just back from Middleham. We keep some horses with a trainer there. I don't know why, but Angelina likes to go out on the gallops early in the morning. She's been living with us here ever since she finished university."

"And you can't wait to get rid of me, can you? To marry me off." Angelina walked over to Banks. Her handshake was firm and dry. "I'm very pleased to meet you, DCI Banks. Wait a minute? Aren't you . . . ? The Blue Lamps? My little sister listens to them all the time.

She wants to be a rock star, too. But what are you doing here? I mean what are the police doing here?"

"It's nothing, really," Banks said, sitting down again. "I was just talking with your mother about a case I'm working on." He got the distinct impression that Lady Chalmers had expected him to leave when her daughter came home, and that she was disappointed he hadn't taken the hint. But he thought he might as well see if Angelina knew anything. He asked her about the phone call and showed her the photograph, which she also didn't recognize. "You say his name's Gavin Miller? I've never heard of any Gavin Miller. And I wouldn't have known about any phone call. I was at an auction in York a week ago Monday, all day, so I wouldn't have been here, anyway."

"An auction?" said Banks.

"Yes, a horse sale."

"Oh, I see." He paused. "I don't suppose either of you collects vinyl records, do you?"

"Vinyl? You are joking, of course?" said Lady Chalmers.

"Just a thought. By the way," he asked. "I was admiring the MG when I came in. Whose is it?"

"It's mine," said Lady Chalmers. "I always wanted one."

"A bit damp in this weather, I should think?"

"You'd be surprised."

There was an awkward silence, and Banks felt it would be best not to overstay his welcome by too long. However vague the description they had got of the car in the Coverton car park, it was nothing like a red MG, and the witness was certain it was a man she saw getting into it. He got to his feet again and walked over to the door. The ladies followed suit, and Angelina opened the sitting room door for him. "Well, thank you very much, Lady Chalmers, Angelina," Banks said, then, at the risk of inviting their wrath, he couldn't help but ask one more question, Columbo style, before he left. "What were you doing on Sunday evening, around ten o'clock?"

"Why, we were here," said Lady Chalmers, a puzzled expression on her face.

"All of you?"

"Yes. Except for Jem, of course. He left for New York from Heathrow on Friday. And Sam. She's up at St. Andrew's, just started her final year. Oriana made dinner for about eight o'clock. In addition to everything else, she is a wonderful gourmet cook. Then she and I attended to some business in the study, and I think after that the three of us watched a DVD."

"That's right," Angelina said to Banks. "I remember. It was an old one. *Night of the Iguana*. Richard Burton."

"I know it," said Banks. "Excellent."

Lady Chalmers smiled at Banks, moved closer to her daughter and put her arm around Angelina's shoulder. "We love watching old movies together."

Banks handed Lady Chalmers his card and asked her to call if she remembered anything useful. Oriana, who didn't seem to have been too far away, walked him back across the checkered hall to the front door and opened it for him.

"I'm sorry we couldn't be of any more help," Lady Chalmers called after him from the door to the sitting room. Her voice echoed slightly in the high reception hall.

"That's all right," Banks said. "I told you it was a minor matter. Now you've cleared it up for us. Nothing to it."

But when he sat behind the wheel of his car, feeling a little punch-drunk from the conversation, his mind echoing with conflicting thoughts and feelings, he began to wonder. That phone call still bothered him. There might be nothing to it, and possibly, just possibly, Gavin Miller *had* been calling about alumni business, but seven minutes was a long time, and he wasn't convinced that Lady Chalmers had been telling the whole truth. Besides, from what he knew of Miller, he was hardly likely to be the kind of person collecting for the university alumni society. He didn't even have enough money to feed himself. There had been something brittle about Lady Chalmers's responses when Banks had questioned her, like a fragile eggshell that would crack if you prodded it too hard. But what was inside? What was the shell protecting?

NORMALLY, WHEN Annie walked into a physiotherapy department, she was there for treatment, but today, when she and Winsome called by the medical center attached to the Swainsdale Centre, she was there on other business entirely. The center was a modern brick building, two stories high, and the physio department was on the ground floor. The foyer smelled of menthol and embrocation. When they asked for Dayle Snider, the receptionist pointed them in the direction of a corridor to the right.

"She should be in her office," the receptionist said, glancing at the clock on the wall and checking the computer screen. "Her next appointment isn't until after lunch."

Annie knew that. She had called ahead and timed their visit for a gap in Dayle Snider's calendar. She saw the name on the door and knocked.

"Come in."

Annie and Winsome walked into a small office with a window looking out on the river at the back of the center and across to the Green. There were the usual filing cabinets and rows of box files, a bookshelf full of medical texts, laptop computer on the desk, small printer on the window ledge. The room smelled of some sort of aromatherapy mixture.

"I'm sorry," said Dayle, standing up to greet them. "I'm afraid my office wasn't built for consultations between more than two people. Let me get another chair."

"Its all right," Winsome said. "I can stand."

"Nonsense." She disappeared next door for a moment and came back carrying another chair. "Gary's not in today, anyway, so he won't mind. Now, please, sit." Dayle Snider was rather severe, Annie thought, with her cropped and streaked dark hair, white coat, and glasses on a cord around her neck, though she was attractive in an angled, chiseled sort of way, and she had the sort of body you only get from regular and strenuous exercise—taut, perhaps a little sharp on the curves, but not without a certain feline grace. She was also used to giving the orders, it seemed; though her manner was polite, there was a commanding tone underneath it. She was also, Annie noticed, perhaps tall and strong enough to tip the emaciated Gavin Miller over the edge of the bridge. And the massages and physio she gave would increase her strength and keep her in shape. Annie hadn't really considered Dayle as a suspect, but she realized that, at this point, everyone connected with Miller had to be viewed with suspicion.

"Haven't I seen you somewhere before?" she said to Annie.

"Probably. I've been here for treatment a few times. Terry Feldman."

"Yes, of course. One of Terry's. I hope everything's satisfactory?"

"Just hunky-dory."

They sat. Winsome took out her notebook and pen.

"What can I do for you?" asked Dayle. You didn't tell me very much on the telephone."

"Did you know a man called Gavin Miller?" Annie asked.

"Gavin? Yes. Why?"

"I suppose you've heard the news?"

"What news?"

"The news of his death."

Dayle remained silent for a few seconds, then she blinked and whispered, "No. No, as a matter of fact I hadn't heard. I'm afraid I haven't been paying a great deal of attention to the news lately. Too busy. I'm very sorry to hear it. How did he die?"

"He died as the result of a fall," Winsome said, leaning forward in her chair. "We think he might have been pushed."

Dayle patted her chest. "Good lord. Killed? But who would want to murder Gavin?"

"That's what we're trying to find out," Annie said. "We were hoping you could help us. We understand you knew him? Dated him?"

"Well, yes . . . I suppose I did. For a while. But that was a long time ago."

"How long?"

"About four years. We didn't go out together for very long."

"Oh? Why was that?"

Dayle seemed affronted by the question; a frown appeared between her eyebrows and her lips tightened, but she stiffened her back and said, "We just weren't compatible, that's all. Hasn't that ever happened to you? I'm sorry if I seem a bit distracted. This is just very hard to take in. I'm not saying that Gavin was a close friend or anything, I haven't seen him for years, but when it's someone you know who dies, no matter how little you knew them, well, it gets to you, doesn't it?"

"I understand," said Annie. "And I'm sorry if I gave you the bad news in a brutal way. We're not here to interrogate you or upset you at all. We just thought you might be able to tell us a bit about Gavin. He seemed to be something of an enigma."

Dayle let out a harsh laugh. "Enigma? You can say that again. I mean, that's putting it mildly. Gavin had all the social graces and people skills of a Trappist monk. And you ask me why we didn't go out for long."

"But he was a teacher, wasn't he? That's what I can't understand. Surely he had to deal with people all the time in his job? He must have had some social skills."

"Yes, but that was his work. It's like an actor being onstage, then being shy and retiring in real life. Gavin was like that. He came alive in front of a class."

"You attended his classes?"

"He invited me to a lecture he gave at the local film society once. Something about Ozu. Anyway, he was a good public speaker. What I mean is that he was socially inept in the real world, and especially one on one," Dayle said. "He was fine with groups, on his favorite subjects, and more than competent at his job, but for Gavin, well, I suppose you could say Sartre's maxim was true; 'L'enfer, c'est les autres.'"

"'Hell is other people,'" said Annie.

"Yes. A bit melodramatic, I suspect, but there you are. He didn't know what to talk about, how to engage people, how to have a simple conversation."

"So he could have offended someone by his manner?"

"He could have. Certainly. Very easily. But it wasn't especially his nature to be offensive. If he was, it would have been because he didn't realize it."

"Insensitive, perhaps?"

"More like it. But even that indicates a certain amount of self-awareness. Gavin was sort of absorbed in his own world. It was a bit of a fantasy world."

"We know about his interests and his online life."

"Yes. They took up a lot of his time, and even more of his energy, even then, when he had a full-time job. Apart from being fairly well informed on literature and world affairs and politics in general, he couldn't relate to much else that people talked about. He'd be the kind to interject some doom-laden quotation from Nietzsche or Camus at an inappropriate moment in a dinner conversation. It could be quite charmingly gauche, but more often it was not. It ended a few conversations, that's for sure."

"I understand you met him at Trevor Lomax's house?" Annie said.

"Yes. A dinner party. It was one of Sally's little attempts at matchmaking. I'm a physiotherapist by training, but I also studied philosophy as a subsidiary subject at university, and I like to read. Booker nominees, that sort of thing. Sally thought we might have something in common."

"But you didn't?"

"I'm not saying that. I actually quite enjoyed Gavin's company at first. He was bright, and passionate about his own interests, and he could be quite witty when the spirit took him. It was OK as long as you were willing to do all the listening."

"Do you know if he had any enemies?" Annie asked. "Can you think of anyone who might want to harm him?"

"Not that I know of."

"Do you remember the problems he had at the college?"

"Do I remember? That was one of the things that hastened the end of our relationship, such as we had. He even came around to the house one night in a terrible state wanting to talk to me all about it."

"What state? Was he drunk?"

"Yes."

"Did you listen to him?"

"I didn't have much choice. You never did with Gavin. He'd just barge in and start talking, especially when he'd had a few. Oh, I could have sent him away, I suppose, thrown him out physically, even, but I have to admit that I was intrigued."

"What did he say about it all?"

"That it was all pure fabrication, of course. That the girls were lazy lying sluts. Oh, all sorts of things. He was venting his feelings and his frustrations. What you'd expect, I suppose, from someone who claims he's being wrongfully persecuted."

"And was he, do you think?"

Dayle paused and put a finger to her lips for a few moments before answering. "I'm not so sure," she said finally. "I mean, I probably shouldn't be saying this, but Gavin *was* sexually insecure. He could actually appear quite an attractive man, in his way, but he had very low self-esteem in that department, something to do with his failed marriage, I think, and he . . . well, he wasn't good at seizing the moment, shall we say."

"I'm sorry to be indelicate," said Annie, "but did you have a sexual relationship?"

"We didn't have intercourse, if that's what you mean. Gavin was nervous and inexperienced. Not that I'm any great expert myself. I didn't sleep around. Don't. But you could tell."

"Was he impotent?" Annie asked.

"I think he probably suffered from erectile dysfunction. Yes."

"How did he react to that?"

"What do you mean?"

"Did he get angry, tearful, apologetic?"

"Not angry. Sort of resigned. He didn't say anything, really, just withdrew into himself. We only tried the once. I always thought it was perhaps because I was too overconfident for him. A strong-minded, independent career woman. I suppose I can be a bit overbearing at times. Maybe I come on too strong."

"Do you think he would have preferred a more subservient woman?"

"I'm sure he would have done."

"Was he angry when you split up with him?"

"Perhaps more disappointed, hurt, but it came out as anger. He called me a few choice names."

"Did he harm you or threaten to harm you in any way?"

"No. Nothing like that. He simply disappeared from my life. I never saw him again."

"After the trouble with the college?"

"Yes. After he lost his job. He was desperate for someone to believe in him. He thought that someone was me. I probably let him down."

"Did you bear a grudge against him?"

"Good Lord, no. What are you getting at? It was me who dumped him, you know."

"Did you ever visit him in Coverton?"

"No. I haven't seen him since that time he came over to see me. He was still living in a poky flat in Eastvale then."

"Did he ever ask you for money?"

"No. Never."

"The girl who accused Gavin Miller of sexual misconduct said that he told her he would fix a test result for her if she had sex with him. Does that sound right to you? Do you think he would do something like that?"

"How can you expect me to answer a question like that?"

"I'm only asking whether you think it's likely. Do you think he might resort to coercion, given the opportunity? Do you think that perhaps exerting power in that way over a woman might arouse him, or that he might even behave in a mercenary way and see the situation as one to be exploited?"

"I really can't . . . I mean, perhaps if she seemed vulnerable, if he thought he couldn't possibly fail, then . . . yes. Perhaps he might. Perhaps it might excite him."

Annie and Winsome stood up to leave, then Annie asked, "Can you tell us where you were last Sunday evening, around ten o'clock?"

"Is that when it . . . ? When Gavin . . . ?"

Annie just nodded.

Dayle twisted the diamond ring Annie had noticed on the third finger of her left hand. She had twisted it a lot during the interview. "I was with Derek," she said. "My fiancé. We went out for dinner to the Blue Lion in East Witton, then we went back to his place in Ripon."

Annie thanked her and they left.

GERRY MASTERSON waited for Banks at a copper-topped table in the Queen's Arms that lunchtime, sipping her slimline tonic, quite relieved that Banks had asked her to continue her research and DS Jackman had gone with DI Cabbot to talk to the Snider woman, instead of her. DI Cabbot scared her. She looked around and saw there was no one else from the station in the lounge at the moment. Not that it mattered. This was not an assignation. Discretion was all Banks wanted, along with his lunch, of course, and Gerry thought she knew why.

He had been to see the Chalmers woman that morning. Lady Veronica Chalmers. What he had found out, or concluded, Gerry had no idea yet—he hadn't been very forthcoming over the telephone—but she bet that that was what the hastily called meeting was about.

She felt nervous. She was still the new girl, and Banks was the boss. There was Area Commander Gervaise, too, she supposed, but AC Gervaise was too remote to think about most of the time. Gerry hardly ever saw her except at some of the briefings, but Banks was right there, on the case, all the time. There was no escaping him. She liked him, but he still terrified her. There was an intensity and focus about him that made her feel nervous around him, a weight and depth of feeling that made her feel shallow. And she wasn't. Sure, she liked playing football with the local women's team, liked sport in general, but she read books, too, and she thought about things, important things; she worried about the environment, climate change, the polar ice caps, polluted oceans, the lot. Starving children, too. And war. She hadn't joined any organizations, but that didn't mean she didn't care. But Banks always made her feel as if her caring was superficial. And the damnedest thing about it was that she knew he didn't do it on purpose, that he would be mortified if he thought she felt that way. And she also knew that, when it came right down to it, he didn't really feel anything more deeply or more powerfully than she did. Damn it, he never even mentioned climate change, pollution, war or starving children. It was all down to her own stupid feelings, her imagination, her lack of confidence. Annie Cabbot scared her because she was quick and fierce, with an abrasive tongue to match sometimes; and Winsome Jackman was tall and silent, mostly, and Gerry never felt that she was satisfying Winsome's exacting standards. But only Banks made her feel shallow. And she wasn't, dammit, she wasn't.

She saw him walk through the door and glance around the room. He caught her eye, raised his eyebrows in greeting and walked over. Gerry touched her hair, tucking a stray wave behind her ear. She was proud of her flowing red hair; it was perhaps her only true vanity. She hated her freckles, though some boyfriends had said they found them sexy. The rest of her she thought was OK. She hoped she looked presentable. She guessed that Banks must have come from his office because he wasn't wearing an overcoat, and it was chilly outside. He wore a navy blue suit, white shirt and purple tie. When he sat down, she noticed that the top button of his shirt was undone and the knot in the tie was quite a loose one.

"What did Lady Chalmers say, sir?" she asked.

"She admitted that Gavin Miller called her a week ago last Monday. Something to do with alumni affairs. She was very vague about it, and very surprised when I told her the call lasted seven minutes. Nobody else was around when she took it."

"Do you believe her story?"

"No. But I can't think why she might be lying, or what she might have to do with the case. On the other hand, I just can't see a seven-minute call about a donation to the alumni society, or Miller being involved in such a thing. She also seemed shocked when I showed her the photo, mentioned how old he looked."

"As if she remembered him when he didn't look like that?"

"Maybe. But I couldn't say for certain. It was just a feeling I got. I may have been imagining things I'd like to be true. Anyway, can you check and find out whether he was involved in alumni affairs in any way?"

"Of course. One of the numbers on his scratch pad was a University of Essex number. It may help."

"And maybe you can find out something about Lady Chalmers's secretary, too, or whatever she is. Her name's Oriana Serroni. Hungry?"

"Ravenous, sir."

"Had a chance to look at the menu? I'm buying."

"Thank you, sir. The steak sandwich on a baguette sounds perfect."

"Steak it is." Banks got up and walked over to the bar, where Gerry watched him share a few words and a laugh with Cyril, the landlord. He came back carrying a pint in one hand and another slimline tonic in the other. Gerry thanked him for the drink.

"No problem. Cheers." He took a sip of his beer. "Anyway. Lady
Veronica Chalmers. What did you find out about her?"

"Probably nothing you don't already know, sir." Gerry opened the
file in front of her, though she knew most of it by heart. "She comes
from a good old wealthy Buckinghamshire family, the Bellamys.
Raised in the old family manor house outside Aylesbury. Very la-
di-da. Trust funds and all the rest. Family made their fortune in the
colonies originally, mostly South Africa and India. Luckily, they in-
vested wisely and were able to get their money out and carry on with
their privileged existence after partition. Her father was a bigwig at
the National Gallery and a pretty well known art expert and collector.
Not exactly Sir Anthony Blunt, but . . . well, I'm sure you get the idea.
All the best schools for Veronica, of course. Jolly hockey sticks, ponies
and what have you. But apparently she got a bit wayward when she hit
her teens. The family wanted her to go to Oxbridge, and she could
probably just have squeaked in, but she chose to go to the University
of Essex instead."

"So she said. From debutante to Essex girl? Bit of an odd choice,
isn't it?"

"Teenage rebellion. Making a statement. It happens often enough."

"OK. Carry on."

"Not much more to say, sir. She did do some postgraduate research
work later at Cambridge, then decided against an academic life. She'd
written a historical novel, which she got published. It did quite well.
Then she wrote a couple of brief literary biographies of rather neglected figures in quick succession—Rumer Godden and Rosamond
Lehmann. Then she started a series of Regency romances under a
pseudonym, Charlotte Summers, which she still writes. There's been
a spate of recent articles in the national press and the local papers. No
doubt carefully orchestrated by her publicist."

"Cynic," said Banks. "What are they? Bodice rippers?"

"I suppose you could call them that."

"Read any?"

Gerry felt herself blush. There came that shallow feeling again. "I
must admit that I have, sir."

"Any good?"

"I think so. They're very well written, and the research seems convincing. To me, at any rate. But I'm no expert. They keep me turning the pages, anyway."

"Go on." Banks drank some more beer. Gerry thought he seemed to be enjoying her discomfort, but she realized that he probably didn't even know she was uncomfortable.

"She met her future husband, Jeremy Chalmers, in 1985, when he was working for the National Theatre, and they were married the following year. Both were living in London then. In Fitzrovia. Their first daughter, Angelina, was born in 1988, and a second daughter, Samantha, followed in 1992. Her husband was knighted in 2003. They've been living at Brierley House, in Eastvale, ever since Angelina was born. He's from Yorkshire, the East Riding, and she said in one of the interviews that they had always dreamed of a place in the Dales. Her parents are deceased. One sister, Francesca, five years older, who lived in Derbyshire, a few miles outside Buxton. She died two years ago of an inoperable brain tumor. She was married to Anthony Litton, semiretired Harley Street specialist. Gynecologist, I believe, and very much one for the upper crust. He still commutes between London and Derbyshire on occasion. They have one son, Oliver."

"Oliver Litton?"

"Yes."

"The Oliver Litton so hotly tipped to be our future home secretary?'

"One and the same."

Banks whistled. "Some family. A knighthood and a future home secretary. Curiouser and curiouser. Any hint of a juicy scandal in Lady Chalmers's life?"

"None, either juicy or otherwise. There was one previous marriage, however, in 1981, after her postgraduate thesis, to an American artist called Chad Bueller, much against her parents' wishes. It must have been the tail end of her rebellious phase. He was far from being a penniless artist, however, being both very successful and highly collectible. She went to live with him in Los Angeles, in Beverly Hills, believe it or not, but it didn't last. It took her two years to find out that he preferred the company of members of his own sex, and she came back to England after the divorce. Published her first book shortly thereafter. It concerned Edward II. I remember doing it at school, sir. Christopher Marlowe. You know what happened to Edward II?"

Banks flinched. "That red hot poker business, wasn't it? Go on."

"She met Jeremy Chalmers at a book signing, then started to settle down, and the rest is history."

Banks thought about the painting in the Chalmerses' living room, the way the couple were standing apart, the palpable sense of distance and tension between them. Was that Lady Chalmers and her gay husband? Perhaps just after she'd discovered the truth? No, he decided; he was being fanciful. She wouldn't want to live with something like that on the wall, reminding her of what happened every time she walked into the room. On the other hand, it *was* a Hockney, and 1983 was a long time ago. "If she was in California from 1981 to 1983, there's an overlap with Gavin Miller's time over there, isn't there?" he asked.

"Yes," said Gerry, "but as far as I can work out, there are no missing years in Veronica Chalmers's life. It seems doubtful that their paths would have crossed, with him doing his *On the Road* imitation and her living the life of Riley in Beverly Hills."

"True." Banks had driven a rented Cadillac convertible around Beverly Hills just last year, sometimes marveling and sometimes gagging at the mishmash of imitated styles—Rhenish castles, English stately homes and Tudor mansions, Tuscan villas, French châteaux, all rubbing shoulders. Well, not quite, as there were often quite large spaces between them and acres of manicured lawn surrounding them. The place made the Heights look like a rundown council estate. Or "social housing," as they were calling such places now.

Their sandwiches came, and both said nothing for a few moments while they ate. Then Banks washed his third bite down with a draft of beer. "There's something I don't quite understand," he said. "You told me that Lady Chalmers married this Chad Bueller person in 1981 and lived in L.A. for two more years, right?"

"Yes, sir. Until late 1983."

"Then she came home, met Jeremy Chalmers and married him in 1985, right?"

"Yes, sir," Gerry said again, aware that her mouth was full and trying to cover it as inconspicuously as possible while she spoke. She passed her folder to Banks. "I made a copy for you, sir. It's all in here, dates, details, places, everything. I've just given you the bare bones."

Banks tapped the folder. "Thank you. I appreciate that. But wouldn't she have been only about seventeen in 1985? And that would mean she was far too young to get married in 1981? By my calculation, she'd have been about thirteen. Jerry Lee Lewis might have got away with it in Tennessee in the fifties, but I doubt that Chad Bueller did in California in the eighties."

"Sir?"

"Well, how old is she? I'd say not more than mid-forties."

Gerry checked her notes. "Mid-forties? Sir, Veronica Chalmers is fifty-nine. She was thirty when she got married to Chad Bueller."

Banks reran the images of Lady Veronica Chalmers in his mind: the lithe, trim body in tight jeans, the attractive crow's-feet around her startling eyes, the alabaster skin, natural long blond hair tumbling over her shoulders. No extensions, as far as he could make out. No signs of the surgeon's knife. "That's hard to believe," he said. "She certainly doesn't look it. I suppose I never was any good at guessing women's ages."

Gerry smiled. "She must be remarkably well preserved, sir, if you thought she was in her forties. I suppose she can afford to stay young."

Banks glanced at her, and she thought she could see humor in his twinkling eyes. "Lady Chalmers is a very attractive woman, Gerry, and I don't think it's down to cosmetic surgery, though I suppose I could be wrong about that, too. No doubt the money does help to buy the right potions and creams."

"No doubt, sir. But does it mean anything? Her age?"

"Other than that I was wrong? As a matter of fact," Banks said slowly, "I think it might mean a great deal. Here's what I'd like you to do next."

5

WHAT DID YOU MAKE OF MS. SNIDER, THEN?" ANNIE
asked Winsome as they sat in the cafeteria of Eastvale College
drinking Coke Zero with their vegetarian curries, which to Annie
tasted more like vegetable soup with a teaspoon of curry powder
stirred in at the last minute. Jim Cooper had said over the telephone
that he would join them there after his class, and they had seized the
opportunity to take a break and get something to eat. The students
bustled around them, occasionally casting curious glances in their direction. Annie didn't blame them. For once, though, it wasn't because
Winsome happened to be a six-foot-two-inch Jamaican woman. The
college was the only place in Eastvale—a town of close to twenty
thousand people—where you saw any kind of racial mix. There were
Orientals, blacks, Asians, all sorts, in addition to plenty of Europeans.
Of course, you would see overseas students in town occasionally,
shopping or having a night out at one of the pubs or clubs on the
market square, but mostly they hung around the campus area, where
most of them lived in bedsits or residences. There was plenty to do out
there, on the southeastern edge of town, quite a few pubs and even a
nightclub or two, plus the Union got bands every Saturday night. It
wasn't exactly *The Who Live at Leeds,* but they prided themselves on
bringing in popular up-and-coming bands, and the students were an
enthusiastic audience, the ticket sales good.

But this time people were staring at them because she and Winsome were by far the oldest people in the refectory.

Winsome swallowed a mouthful of curry and pulled a face. "I must say, I felt a bit sorry for Gavin Miller," she said.

"Why?"

"Oh, I don't know. I can see what she meant about them being ill suited. It doesn't sound as if he would have been at all comfortable with a woman like her."

"It just goes to show you, Winsome, it's not always just a matter of having interests in common."

"I think I already knew that. I had a boyfriend once, back in Jamaica. Met him at church. Everyone said he was a nice boy and came from a good family. We both enjoyed Bible studies and cricket."

"You?" said Annie, almost choking on her curry. "Cricket?"

Winsome smiled. "And why not? It's practically a religion where I come from. If you can't beat them, join them. And I was a pretty good off-spinner, if I say so myself."

"You played, too? Wonders never cease."

"I got Brian Lara out first ball in a charity game."

"He must have been knocking on a bit by then."

"No, he wasn't."

"Just teasing. Anyway, this boy?"

"William, his name was. His father was a minister, too."

"So what was the problem?"

"Well, we did have a lot in common and everything, but . . . well. He picked his nose."

"He what?"

"I told you. He picked his nose."

"And for that you dumped him?"

"Would you go out with a boy who picked his nose? It's a sign of poor hygiene, and poor hygiene means bad character, which in turn hints at moral bankruptcy."

Annie thought of some of the boys, and men, she'd been out with and shook her head slowly. If all they'd done wrong was pick their noses she would have had a much easier time of things. "Winsome, I'm certainly glad I don't have to worry about coming up to your standards."

Winsome gave her a puzzled glance. "Anyway, he tried to put his hand up my dress, too. So there. I was right about him." She pushed her tray away and folded her arms. A few seconds passed, then she looked at her plate. "That was terrible," she said, and started laughing.

Annie laughed, too. "I heartily agree. But let's get back to Dayle Snider. She was pretty quick to condemn Gavin Miller, don't you think?"

"Clearly Gavin Miller had problems with women," said Winsome. "I don't like to pass judgment without full knowledge of the facts, but from what I've heard, I would have to agree that a man like him, timid, weak, frustrated, but lustful, might well have tried to get his own way with a girl by devious means. It wouldn't be the first time a man's done something like that."

"Well, it lost him his job," said Annie.

"Quite rightly. You can't have people like that in contact with the young and vulnerable."

Annie felt a presence hovering over them and turned to see a man in an open-neck checked shirt and baggy chinos. He was in his mid-fifties, she guessed, hair thinning at the front and far too long at the back, plastered down by some sort of gel. He was wearing a Celtic cross on a heavy silver chain around his neck, and a gold earring dangled from his left ear. On the whole, Annie was usually suspicious of men who wore jewelry, and she hated men with earrings on sight. She didn't know why; she just did.

"Jim Cooper," he said, sitting down in the free plastic orange chair and offering his hand. Annie shook it first, then Winsome. "I didn't think you were students," he went on. "Not that we don't accept mature students here, of course."

Well, thought Annie, here's a man who knows how to ingratiate himself with you right off the bat. She imagined he and Gavin Miller might have been comparable in their lack of social graces and general appeal to the opposite sex. Maybe Cooper didn't pick his nose, though Annie wouldn't have been surprised if he did, but she bet he was the sort who would stick his hand up your dress on a first date. It was a snap judgment, of course, the kind that got her into trouble far too often, but sometimes a woman just knew. So far, Eastvale College wasn't doing terribly well in the "best place to find a man in Eastvale" stakes. And then there was the earring. She would have to work hard at maintaining a polite front throughout the interview.

Along with Cooper had come a new influx of students anxious to sample the vegetarian curry, and the noise level was making it difficult to hear. "Do you have an office or somewhere quieter we could go?" Annie asked Cooper.

He glanced around the refectory. "Yes, I suppose it is a bit of a racket, isn't it? Funny how you get used to such things. My office is about the size of an airing cupboard, but if you're not up for a game of sardines, there's a staff coffee lounge where we should be able to get a bit of peace and quiet. And a decent cup of coffee."

"The lounge will do nicely," said Annie.

They walked out of the canteen and across a busy square into another three-story concrete monstrosity. Towards the back was the staff lounge, and Cooper turned out to be right. It was practically deserted, decorated in soft, muted colors, with vertical fabric blinds and padded sofas and armchairs. They each got a coffee from the machine and took a corner table. Annie's armchair was lumpy and badly angled, however, and nowhere near as comfortable as it had appeared. She had been far more comfortable in the molded plastic orange chair.

"I'm afraid I don't have very long," said Cooper, checking the time. "I have another class at two. Communications."

"What's that?" asked Winsome.

"Mostly it's a matter of teaching parts of speech and sentence structure to people who don't speak English," Cooper said, "but it's actually meant to cover the whole gamut of human communication, how we think, and what it all means. Trouble is, most of the students *don't* think."

"All of them?" Winsome asked.

"No. Not all," Cooper conceded. "You do get the occasional one who stands out."

"Was Kayleigh Vernon one of them?" Annie asked.

Cooper's eyes narrowed. "You go straight for the jugular, don't you? As a matter of fact there were only two things about Kayleigh Vernon that stood out, and I'm sure you can guess what they were."

Annie gritted her teeth. "So she was no genius," she managed to grind out.

"You could say that. Average. Uninspired and uninspiring, except to thoughts of idle lust on a summer's afternoon. Definitely second-rate material, intellectually speaking."

"And this test that she failed?"

"Wasn't the first, or the last. Oh, she managed to scrape through in the end with a good enough diploma to get her a job as a tea girl in a film studio, or some such job, if she was lucky."

"Is that what she's doing?"

"No idea. I've no more interest in them from the moment they leave."

"Doesn't sound as if you have an awful lot of interest in them while they're here," Winsome commented.

Cooper gave her a surprised glance. "It's a job," he said. "What can I say? They come and go. I remain."

"You were a friend of Gavin Miller's both before and after the incident," Annie went on. "What did you make of it all?"

Cooper's rumpled face took on a more serious expression, and he ran his hand over his hair. "Poor Gavin," he said. "I really am very upset about what happened to him. I still get angry when I think about it. I suppose I try to cover up my feelings with flippancy, but it's a real loss."

"Not many people seem to agree."

Annie was aware of Winsome giving her a puzzled look and realized that she might have been just a bit too harsh. Fortunately, Cooper didn't notice, or he simply ignored it. "Gavin was a good mate," he went on. "I'll admit he was a bit eccentric, not to everyone's taste, but I think the college could have treated him with a bit more respect."

"What did he say to you about what happened?"

"You're asking me if he confessed in private?"

"If he did, I'd be grateful if you'd tell me, but I'd prefer the simple truth. Believe me, all we want to know is whether the sexual misconduct incident could be in any way connected with Gavin Miller's death. We're not after blackening his character."

"Just as well. You'd have to join the queue. And you'd be a bit late.

The simple truth, eh? Now there's an oxymoron if ever there was one. Surely even in your job you must be aware that the truth is rarely simple?"

"Stop pissing us around, Mr. Cooper. Did Gavin Miller maintain his innocence?"

Cooper swallowed and glared at her. "Always."

"And did you believe him?"

"He was my friend."

"That's not an answer."

"Does it really matter what happened in the Marabar Caves?"

Annie and Winsome gave one another puzzled looks. "What are you talking about?" Annie said.

"*A Passage to India*. David Lean or E. M. Forster, depending on your point of view. An Indian man is accused of raping an English girl in a cave. The viewer, or reader, doesn't really know what happened. It's the consequences that are important."

Annie smiled at Winsome. "Well, don't you just love intellectual show-offs?" She leaned forward and stared hard at Cooper. "We didn't do that one at school. We did *Howards End,* and I bloody well wished it would. End, that is. The consequences here were that Gavin Miller lost his job, and now he seems to have been murdered, so what went on in his office that day *does* happen to be important."

"I told you, the truth is never simple."

"Bollocks," said Annie. "It's only complicated when people like you complicate it with literary allusions."

"Then, yes, as it happens. I did believe him."

"Alle-bloody-luia. Thank you. Now why would Kayleigh Vernon lie about something like that?"

"Kayleigh? How would I know her motives? I'd guess it was probably her idea of a joke, a bit of fun. But I'd guess that Beth Gallagher probably put her up to it."

"You knew them both?"

"I taught them media studies. It's not the same thing as knowing them. They were both cheats and teases. Gavin's first big mistake was letting himself be alone in his office with one of them. Kayleigh Vernon was failing. Half the time she didn't turn up for his classes, and when she did she was too busy admiring herself in her mirror or touching up her nails to do any work. Failing the test would mean failing the course, and she'd have to repeat the whole thing the following year. She needed to pass that course in order to graduate."

"But why would he put his arm around her?"

"To console her. For all his brains, he was soft, was Gavin. Not quite as cynical as me."

"And Beth?"

"I'd say Beth was more of an opportunist. They often go far."

"Are you suggesting that Gavin Miller didn't touch either of them?"

"I'm saying we don't know for certain that he did, but that it doesn't matter. The whole thing was a joke, a farce. There was no evidence, no case."

These were Annie's feelings exactly, but she kept quiet. She didn't want to show Cooper that she agreed with him on anything.

"I told him he should go to the press with the story," Cooper went on, "but he wouldn't. I should have known. Gav was shy of all the attention bad publicity like that would bring. He couldn't have handled it."

"But weren't the girls risking a lot by lying?" Annie asked.

"What were they risking? You can see what happened for yourselves. The deck was stacked in their favor. It could have been any one of us."

"But it was Gavin Miller."

"Yes. And I'm not sure he ever got over it. Gav wasn't the sociopath some make him out to be; underneath it all, he was soft and sensitive. True, he was awkward with women. He was shy, yes, but even when they laid it on a plate for him, he wouldn't take the bait. Hopeless."

"Are you sure he wasn't gay?"

"If he was, he never tried it on with me. No, he fancied women. There's no doubt about that. I mean, sometimes we'd get pissed and watch a bit of porn together, and . . ."

Winsome held her hand up. "Whoa. Too much information."

Cooper frowned at her. "What? Oh. It wasn't anything illegal. Just . . . Anyway, Gav wasn't gay."

"I take it you're not married, then, Mr. Cooper?" Annie said.

Cooper grinned. "Never found the right woman."

Annie could see why it might take a bit of searching, but she just nodded and went on. "What did you think of Dayle Snider?"

"That ball-busting bitch. God knows why Lomax thought she was even a remote possibility for Gav. I wouldn't be surprised if she turned out to be a dyke."

"Why don't you tell us what you really think, Jim?" said Annie.

He caught her tone and gave a sheepish smile. "It was just another humiliation for Gav, that's all. So I have no reason to like her. I don't know the details, but Gav probably felt so intimidated he couldn't get it up or something, and no doubt she made her dissatisfaction known and humiliated him further. He didn't talk about it. And she dropped him the minute his troubles started."

"What was she supposed to do? According to Dayle, he came over to her place drunk one night and started raving. Maybe she had good reason to think he was guilty?"

"Why?"

"Maybe he'd tried something similar with her?"

"No way. Besides, he wouldn't need to. She'd have spread her legs at the drop of a hat."

Annie rolled her eyes. "What did the two of you talk about when you were together?"

"Well, with Gav it wasn't as easy as most blokes around here—you know, football, telly, complain about the students and the administration. He liked a drink, though, as do I, so we'd get in a bottle of Johnnie Walker or a box of wine, or even go out to the pub sometimes. The Star and Garter in Coverton."

"Who paid?"

"Well, I usually paid the lion's share. Gav was broke most of the time after he got the sack. They didn't give him a nice pension, you know, and he spent all he had on the down payment for that bloody cottage. Wanted somewhere isolated, away from it all."

"Did he talk about the old days a lot?"

"Sometimes. We'd listen to old sixties stuff. Dreadful, some of it. I'm more into punk, myself. He'd ramble on about escapades on the road in his American days, going to Grateful Dead concerts and what have you."

"Did he give you any details, like where he was at what time, names of people he knew, that sort of thing? Anything specific?"

"Nah. It was years ago. I mostly tuned out, anyway. He just seemed to ramble on. Probably tall tales, too, toking up with Jerry and the lads backstage."

"Drugs?" said Winsome.

"That was back in the early eighties," said Cooper. "There must be a statute of limitations. Besides, he's dead."

"Did he ever take or mention drugs when the two of you were together?" Annie asked. "I mean other than old escapades. Anything more current?"

"No, not really. He got a bit nostalgic about the old scene once in a while, said he wouldn't mind traveling back in time. But nothing serious, no."

"So as far as you know, Gavin Miller wasn't involved with drugs, either as a user or a seller?"

"That's right. Not when I knew him, anyway. I daresay we all committed a few indiscretions in our youth. It's what youth's about, isn't it?"

"Let's get a bit more up to date, Jim," Annie went on. "Sunday evening, around ten o'clock. Where were you?"

"Me? At home, marking papers, most likely."

"Most likely?"

"Well, I went down to the George and Dragon for a couple of pints at some point in the evening. I don't remember exactly when."

"People saw you?"

"Sure. I'm a regular there."

"Do you know of anyone who harbored a grudge against Gavin?"

"Not that I can think of."

"What about Kayleigh and Beth?"

"Nah. They got what they wanted. They won, didn't they?"

"Parents? Big brothers? Boyfriends?"

"For crying out loud, it was over four years ago."

"Some say revenge is a dish best served cold," said Winsome.

Cooper stared at her. "Out of the mouths of babes."

"Enough of that," Annie snapped. "What about Dayle Snider? Might she have harbored a grudge?"

"I suppose she could have done. You know, taken it as a personal insult to her sexual allure if Gav couldn't come up with the goods. And she's certainly got the muscles for it, especially in the last while. Gav's been losing weight terribly. Poor sod hardly got a square meal every day. He was just flesh and bone."

"When did you last talk to him?"

"Middle of last week."

"And how was he?"

"Remarkably cheerful, actually."

"Did he say why?"

"No. He just said the lean times might be coming to an end." Cooper snorted. "Well, they certainly did, didn't they, but not in the way he meant it."

"He didn't elaborate?"

"No. Just that. Like, watch this space. He'd been going on about opening a record shop in the village for some time, vinyl only. A collectors' paradise. He said it would bring in punters from all over the country. The Chamber of Commerce would be on their knees thanking him."

"And he was in a position to do this?"

"You must be joking. It was a dream. Gav was nothing if he wasn't a dreamer. But I must say he seemed remarkably optimistic about it the last time we talked. I told him he must be crazy, in this day and age. Everyone buys online now. The market for collectors must be a pretty small one."

"Was he worried about anything?"

"No. I just told you, he was quite cheerful."

"Before that?"

"He was always worried about money, and he sometimes got a bit depressed and angry when he talked about his ex-wife. She left him for a plumber, apparently. I don't think he ever got over her. And sometimes his resentment over what happened at the college would burst up to the surface, and he'd relive it all over again."

"Might he have wanted revenge on Kayleigh and Beth?"

"I would if I'd been him, but I think he just saw it as the system being against him. Mostly when he got angry it was the board and the committee he insulted. The ones that actually fired him. The ones he thought were supposed to support him."

"So he felt betrayed by the college authorities?"

"Very much so."

"What about Trevor Lomax? How did Gavin feel about him?"

"OK. They got on all right. He didn't place Trevor in the enemy camp. Trevor didn't sit on the committee, called it a kangaroo court and tried to defend Gav. He got into trouble over that himself. Gav respected him. He's just a bit wishy-washy, that's all. No balls. I think it's the wife who wears the trousers in that house, as they used to say."

"Sally Lomax?"

"Right. And she's a good friend of that Dayle Snider woman. Makes sense to me."

"Did Gavin have any other close friends?"

"I wouldn't say anyone was close to him, really, except me. He didn't seem to have any old friends from school or university days. Still, I can't say I have myself. You lose touch, don't you?"

"Might Gavin have arranged to meet one of the girls on Sunday for some reason? Kayleigh or Beth?"

"I can't think why. Unless she'd promised to give him a blow job or something, which I very much doubt. Besides, they're not around here anymore."

"Where are they?"

"I told you, I neither know nor care. I'm sure the college authorities will be able to tell you. Due to some fault in the stars, no doubt, they both graduated."

Annie realized that the sooner they tracked the girls down and talked to them, the better. She didn't think they'd get much from Kayleigh or Beth, especially if they were liars and expert manipulators, but it had to be done. At least Annie would get the chance to decide for herself whether she thought they were lying or whether Gavin Miller really was guilty as charged. A police interview can be a bit more challenging than a committee already weighing in your

favor. She could ask a few more awkward questions than an academic panel. Her back was hurting like hell from the chair she was sitting in, and she didn't think there was much more to be gained from continuing their conversation with the obnoxious Mr. Cooper, so she gave Winsome the nod and stood up to leave.

"Is that all?" Cooper said, remaining seated.

"For the moment," Annie said.

He grinned in what he probably thought was a charming, lopsided way. "But don't leave town, right?"

"As a matter of fact, you can go where the hell you like, Jimmy," said Annie, and walked out with a shocked Winsome following in her wake.

"THIS IS police harassment, this is," complained Lisa Gray when Winsome approached her as she left the converted Victorian terraced house near the college where she rented a flat.

Winsome opened the passenger door. "You saved me from having to climb the stairs. Thanks. Get in. And that's enough of the attitude."

It was pouring down again, naturally, and the street, with its tall dark brick houses and dripping trees, seemed very bleak. The trees weren't quite bare yet, and soggy leaves lined the gutters and stuck to the potholed tarmac surface of the road.

Head hidden inside her hoodie, Lisa slid onto the front seat and hunched down. "I'm clean, you know. I don't know what your drugs squad buddies told you, but you won't find anything on me." The rain was hammering on the roof of the car and streaming down the windows.

"Fasten your seat belt," Winsome said, turning on the ignition and setting off.

Lisa did so. "Where we going?"

"That's up to you. We can go for a nice cup of coffee in the Swainsdale Centre, or to a cold, smelly interview room at the nick. Your choice."

Lisa looked at her with clear, bright eyes, the hood slipping back

just a little to reveal a fringe of damp hair and a pale complexion. "What's the catch?"

"No catch. If you're willing to talk to me, it's the coffee shop, just you and me, nice and easy. If it's going to be like pulling teeth, it's the nick."

Lisa appeared to mull this over for a few moments. "You buying?"

Winsome sighed. "I'm buying."

"Grande latte?"

"You drive a hard bargain, Lisa, but a grande latte it is."

"And one of those big chocolate chip cookies."

"Enough," said Winsome. A few moments later, she pulled into the shopping center car park and found a spot on the fourth level. From there, they could walk straight through to the floor they wanted. The coffee shop at the far end was busy inside, but there was a table free out front, where they could watch the crowds of shoppers come and go to Next, Argos, Boots and Currys Digital. She told Lisa to sit down and went inside to buy the coffees, keeping an eye on her as she waited. She didn't expect Lisa to make a run for it, but she didn't want to seem like a fool if that did happen. She had brought down a runner with a rugby tackle in Marks & Spencer once and never lived it down back at the station. It was almost as notorious as the so-called dropkick she had used to knock a troublesome drug dealer off a third-floor balcony on the East Side Estate.

When she saw the cookies, she decided that she might as well have one herself. A treat for doing a miserable job on a miserable day. There were umbrellas and wet coats all over the place, but the smell of hot coffee and fresh ground beans overwhelmed it all, for which Winsome was truly thankful.

"Service with a smile. And from a copper, no less," said Lisa, who seemed a small, shrunken figure huddled at the table. Conversations and children's cries buzzed around them, and the hissing and sputtering of the espresso machine vied with the grinder in the background to make conversation almost impossible. Eventually, Lisa pulled her hood back and Winsome got a full view of the pretty pixieish young face with the large gray-blue eyes. Lisa's dyed blond hair was cropped short and streaked pink and yellow here and there, which somehow

made her appear even younger than her twenty-three years. She also looked odd enough, with the various piercings on display, that one or two people glanced over at them, the big black woman and the skinny punk, and turned away quickly. Winsome wondered who frightened them the most.

"I know you, don't I?" said Lisa. "You're not DS."

"I'm sure we've seen one another around town from time to time. Actually I am DS. Detective Sergeant, that is, not drugs squad. DS Jackman."

"Yeah. I've seen your picture in the papers, too. I know you. You're the one who drop-kicked the Bull over the balcony of Hague House, on the East Side Estate, aren't you?"

Winsome sipped her coffee and smiled at the memory. "Yeah, well, he did ask for it. But it wasn't a dropkick."

"Awesome," said Lisa. "He was a real mean bastard. Used to beat up the girls. But what do you want with me?"

"Your name came up," said Winsome. She wasn't here to persecute Lisa. Her name was on the list of people Gavin Miller had called over the past month, and the drugs squad had picked her as the most likely person to be supplying Miller with small amounts of cannabis, even though she wasn't a dealer herself. She knew people, they said; she could get her hands on small amounts, act as the middleman, put people in contact with those who had what they needed. A facilitator. The drugs squad kept an eye on her in case she led them to any of the bigger players, but they had no particular interest in her themselves. What also caused them to pick Lisa was that she had a connection with Eastvale College and had taken courses with Gavin Miller four years ago, the academic year of his humiliation and dismissal. "I need information," said Winsome. "I want to talk to you about Gavin Miller."

Lisa sipped some latte. It left a line of froth on her upper lip that almost covered the ring that was stuck through it. She wiped the foam off with the back of her hand. Winsome noticed a tattoo of an angel on her pale, thin wrist. "Poor bastard," said Lisa. "I heard what happened to him."

"Did you know him?"

"Of course I did. You already know that, or you wouldn't have brought me here, would you?"

"That's the way I like things to be," said Winsome. "I ask questions and you answer them. That way we don't need to go down the nick."

"No skin off my nose. I told you, I'm clean. And anything incriminating you claim I told you, I'll deny it."

"Nobody's interested in arresting you, Lisa. Not even the drugs squad. We know what you do. You're not a big enough fish."

"Yeah, right . . . well, just so's you know. How did you find me?"

"You talked to Gavin Miller on the phone recently, and the drugs squad have heard of you." She paused. "Let's get this straight before we begin, Lisa. They say you're not exactly a dealer. You say you're not a dealer. I'm not interested in what your business is. I'm only interested in Gavin Miller. Not only did you supply drugs to him, which, by the way, makes you technically a dealer, but he was your teacher at Eastvale College four years ago, and if you find it hard to be frank about all this, then we'll go to the nick right now."

Lisa held her hand up. "OK. OK. I get it. Fine. I've got nothing to hide. But if you know all that already, what do you need me for?"

"What happened?"

"What do you mean, 'What happened?'"

"You were in college, doing well, as I heard it. What happened?"

"Oh, you mean why am I wearing a hoodie and mixed up with drugs, not to mention covered in tattoos and piercings?"

Winsome couldn't help but smile. She might be a moralist and a bit of a prude at heart, but she admired true spirit and individualism. Lisa could be a challenge. She bit into her chocolate chip cookie. It was good. An elderly lady passed them on her way to the toilet and cast a look of unmistakable hatred at them both. Neither could fail to notice.

Lisa turned to Winsome. "Tarred with the same brush, huh? Sorry, I didn't mean anything racist by that."

"I know what you meant. I've been getting that sort of treatment all my life." She looked Lisa up and down. "It seems as if you've had to work a bit harder for it."

Lisa seemed surprised for a moment, not sure whether to be insulted or not, then she burst out laughing and reddened. "Yeah," she said. "Yeah, you got that right. I suppose you could say that." When she laughed and blushed she looked like an innocent teenager, but the hard expression quickly returned.

"So what happened?" Winsome asked again.

"Nothing happened. Not in the way you mean it. I didn't suddenly get abused by my uncle or raped by a gang of retards or anything. Things changed in my life, that's all. For the worse. And that fucking place was full of phonies. I suddenly saw through them, is all."

"A revelation?"

"Yeah. Like Saul on the road to Damascus. A blinding light."

"Did you graduate?"

"No."

"You chose to get involved with the fast crowd instead? Was that another sudden conversion?"

"Something like that. Anyway, what's it to you? I don't deal drugs, but if I did, I'd argue they're a commodity like anything else. I'd argue that I was supplying a need that would only be supplied elsewhere if I didn't do it. It's one of the basic functions of capitalism, an open market, a choice of products and suppliers. I'd also argue that what I'm selling, or facilitating, is pretty harmless, probably less so than alcohol and cigarettes."

"But it's still illegal."

"So was booze in America during Prohibition, and Coca-Cola used to have cocaine in it, and you could buy laudanum at the local chemist's. I could go on. Anyway, who are you? Eliot Ness or something? Are you on some sort of moral crusade?"

Winsome shook her head. "No, I'm not on any sort of crusade. Just curious what sends someone with so much potential as you obviously have down a wrong turn, that's all. What can you tell me about Gavin Miller?"

"He was one of the good ones."

"You liked him?"

"As a teacher. Yes."

"Did you ever meet with him one-on-one?"

"Sure. We had to discuss essays and stuff. He liked my work. He said my grammar and spelling weren't too good, but I thought for myself and didn't just regurgitate what I'd read in books or what he said in class. We talked about life and stuff sometimes."

"In his office?"

"Mostly. A couple of times we went for a drink or a coffee. That's all."

"Trevor Lomax said Gavin Miller wasn't a particularly good teacher because he insulted the students."

"He could be sarcastic sometimes, but most of them deserved insulting. And he loved his subjects, literature and film studies, which were my passion, too, and if he found the slightest grain of interest in anyone, he'd cultivate it. The problem was that he rarely did. Find a grain of interest."

"Is that what he did with you? Cultivate your grain of interest?"

Lisa turned away. "I suppose so. Tried. I could have been a better student."

"Didn't you find him odd?"

"A total fucking weirdo, but so what? So was I. We were both outsiders. And he was cool without trying. It was natural. We could talk about anything. He didn't judge me. He respected my intelligence for what it was."

Lisa was the first person who had ever said that about Gavin Miller, at least to Winsome, and most likely to anyone else involved in the investigation of his death, or so she believed. "Did you sell him drugs?" Winsome asked, sensing a mood of candor and pushing the envelope a bit. "And you can put all this 'hypothetical' business aside. It doesn't fool anyone, except yourself, maybe. As I said, I'm not interested." She held her arms out. "No wires."

"I wouldn't know where to look." Lisa paused a moment to enjoy some coffee and cookie, then she said, "Sell Mr. Miller drugs? You must be fucking joking. If you must know, I scored for him. Yes. I know people. He didn't. Sell? Most of the time I had to pay for them myself."

"You *bought* him drugs?"

"Just cannabis, right." Lisa leaned forward and lowered her voice. "Mr. Miller never had much money. I do, OK—and not from drugs dealing, if that's what you were thinking. So what if he enjoyed a little weed now and then? The man was a throwback to the sixties, politically and artistically. Spreading the wealth around."

"So you gave him drugs because you shared his Marxist philosophy?"

"I'm no more a Marxist than I'm a drug dealer. Not in the way you see it. Sure, I put people in touch with one another sometimes, or as in Mr. Miller's case, yes, I got him what he wanted. But I didn't profit from it. Like I said, it cost me more often than not. Drugs aren't how I make my living."

"How do you do that?"

"Well, I'm sort of unemployed at the moment, but I've published a few short stories and poems, and I'm working on a graphic novel and a movie script at the moment."

"What are they about?"

"They're dark fantasy. Sort of an alternate world thing."

"Like Harry Potter?"

"Darker, but just as successful, I hope. I also do a bit of busking. And I make jewelry. Sell it down the market."

"Do you have a studio?"

"Hah! You must be joking. But I have a friend who does."

"Well, good luck with all that. Let's get back to Gavin Miller and the drugs."

"Oh, for fuck's sake, it wasn't much. Can't you just leave it alone?"

"Were you supplying him with drugs when you were his student?"

"No way! I never even knew he was interested until a few months ago. Besides, I didn't have access to any of that stuff at college."

"When did you last talk to him?"

"About three weeks ago?"

"Was there anything different about him?"

"Different? No."

"What did you talk about?"

"We didn't talk. I was in a hurry so we just . . . you know . . . did the deal."

"Did he pay that time?"

"No. He said he'd catch up with me later. I was used to it by then."

"Where did you get the drugs you sold, or gave, him?"

"You don't think I'm going to tell you that, do you? I know people, that's all. I grew up on the East Side Estate. You never really leave it."

"I take it you didn't have anything to do with Gavin Miller's murder?"

"What do you expect me to say to that? No, I didn't. I hadn't seen him for a couple of weeks."

"Where were you on Sunday night?"

"At home in the flat. I had some mates around. We were watching telly."

"*Downton Abbey*?"

"You must be fucking joking. We had a DVD. The new Shane Meadows."

"Would they vouch for you?"

"Course they would. Would you believe them?"

"Do you own a car?"

"What? Yeah. A Peugeot. It's about ready for the knacker's yard, but it gets me around."

"Have you ever been to Coverton?"

"Why would I go there?"

"It's where he lived."

"He never told me where he lived. Why would he? We always met in town."

"Was Gavin Miller a dealer? Was he in the business, on the money-making side, or trying to get in?"

"Mr. Miller? No way. Mr. Miller a dealer? He wouldn't have had the bottle for it, for a start. And he wouldn't have had to come to me, would he? Besides, there was no way he could have financed himself."

"No matter how you dress it up," Winsome said, "what you do is illegal. You know that. And you might think that cannabis is a harmless enough pastime that should be legalized, but LSD is a Class A drug. There's a reason for that. It can do really bad things to a person's mind. Gavin Miller had two hits of LSD in his possession at the time of his death. I suppose he got that from you, too? We can check. You can go to jail for that. How long do you think you could survive there?"

"Well, thanks for your concern, and all, but to tell you the truth, I don't really think about it. I live one day at a time. And Mr. Miller only ever wanted a couple of tabs of acid, once. He said he wanted to try it again. Relive the experience. I knew someone who had a source, that's all. Reliable quality."

They had found only two tabs of acid among Miller's stash, it was true, so he clearly hadn't even got around to taking the LSD before he died. Winsome had promised herself not to shift into reformist gear with Lisa, but it was difficult. Here was another bright, promising young girl perhaps on the verge of throwing her life away, as Winsome saw it. Once again, she admonished herself to focus on the task at hand and not to stray into the muddier avenues of rehabilitation. Maybe selling a bit of cannabis wasn't such a terrible thing, after all. Plenty of the people had smoked it where Winsome came from, and they hadn't all been drug-crazed criminals. "OK," she went on. "So you don't think Gavin Miller was a dealer, and he wasn't likely to become one?"

"Right. He just liked to get off his face every now and then. What's wrong with that?"

Winsome could think of a few things, but she didn't want to sound even more prudish, so she sipped some coffee, then wiped her mouth with her serviette. "We're trying to find out who killed him, Lisa. You say you liked him. He was an oddball, OK, but there's nothing illegal in that. Everyone says he was harmless, so who would want to harm him? Why?"

"I don't know," said Lisa. "I really don't. But I'll bet you it's got nothing to do with drugs. Maybe he owed someone money or something?"

"A moneylender? What makes you think that?"

"I dunno. Just that he was always broke. Whenever I talked to him, anyway, which wasn't that much or that often."

Winsome knew that she couldn't mention the five thousand pounds yet. The public still didn't know about the money. If Gavin Miller wasn't involved in dealing drugs, as she was coming to believe was the case, then the money probably had nothing to do with that, or with Lisa Gray. Lisa certainly wasn't at a level to deal in numbers that high, and it wasn't a price that Miller could afford to pay. "Just out of interest," she said, "you were around when Mr. Miller had his spot of trouble at the college, weren't you?"

"Spot of trouble? They fucking crucified him."

"Were you in his class at the time?"

"It's not like school. You have classes with different lecturers. I was in his film history course, yes. There were a lot of slackers there because they thought it was a doddle and all you had to do was sit and watch movies week after week, but it was really quite tough, and lots of people dropped out early on. Quite a few failed, as well."

"What about Beth Gallagher and Kayleigh Vernon."

"The Bitches of Eastvale? Actually, they were prize cunts."

"Do you think Gavin Miller did what they said he did?"

"No way."

"How do you know?"

"He told me. He was clearing his desk, and there was no one around. All his so-called mates who shared the office space were too embarrassed to be there to say good-bye when he left. I was walking by the office. His door was open. I said good-bye and that I was sorry to see him go. And he told me."

"Why you?"

Lisa shrugged. "I told you. We got along OK. I listened to him. Maybe he liked me and my good opinion mattered to him. Or maybe I just happened to be there at the right time. I don't know. I like to think he felt he could trust me."

"Was there any—"

"No, I wasn't fucking him, if that's what you're after. There was nothing like that. He never even tried it on. Was always a real gentleman. A bit shy about all that, really."

"What did he actually say to you that day in his office?"

"He said he'd been accused of making an improper suggestion to Kayleigh Vernon and letting his hand brush over Beth Gallagher's tits, and he'd been asked to leave. He swore to me that he didn't do it. He said that he was innocent, and he didn't know why the two girls would want to do something so cruel to him. That he wanted me to know that, whatever anyone else believed. That it was important I should believe him."

"And what did you say?"

"I told him that I believed him."

"Were you sure?"

"If I wasn't then—which I was, pretty much—then I certainly was later."

"Why?"

"Because I overheard the two cunts talking in the toilet when they thought there was no one else around."

"When was this?"

"Later. Two or three weeks after he told me."

"What were they saying?"

"That they'd got away with it, got rid of him, and how easy it was. They hadn't expected everyone to just believe them, but it was so easy they couldn't believe it. They were laughing at the way the members of the examining tribunal, or whatever they called themselves, had simply believed them, especially when Kayleigh put on the water-works."

"But why did they want rid of him?"

"It was Beth, really. She was the ringleader. She put Kayleigh up to it, then she weighed in herself when they thought another voice would do it."

"Was it some sort of practical joke?"

"Fuck, no. Sorry. But no. If you're searching for a drugs connec-tion, perhaps this is it. They said how pleased Kyle would be. That's another thing I didn't find out until later, and something Mr. Miller obviously didn't know about, either. Kyle McClusky hung out with Beth and Kayleigh, and he was starting to deal a bit. Quite a lot, actu-ally. I'm surprised your lot weren't on to him. And Kyle dealt the really bad stuff, stuff I'd never touch with a barge pole."

"Such as?"

"Crystal meth, coke, oxycodone, even heroin. He sold roofies as well."

"Are you saying . . . ?"

"Kyle McClusky was a piece of shit."

"So what did Gavin Miller have to do with all this?"

"He found out about it. Or someone told him. He knew McClusky from one of his classes and gave him a chance, told him he'd better leave while he could, or he'd report him to the college authorities and the cops. If you'd known Mr. Miller, you'd know how much effort it cost him just to do that. And I don't know if he was smoking spliffs himself then, or anything, but I very much doubt it. There was never any talk, anyway. If you ask me, it was just something he got back into after he lost his job. He always seemed pretty straight at college. Weird, but straight, if you know what I mean. I think when he lost his job, he started drifting back into the past, trying to relive his favorite years. I can understand that. Sometimes the future doesn't seem worth facing."

"You're too young to be talking like that, Lisa."

"How old do you have to be to know that life sucks sometimes?"

"What happened to Kyle McClusky?"

"Fuck knows. Or cares. He just disappeared, eventually. I think he's in Manchester or Birmingham or somewhere. Ask your drugs squad. Even they'll probably have him on their books by now. Course, he was really pissed off with Mr. Miller for ruining all his dreams, though from what I knew of him he didn't have a hope in hell of realizing them to start with. If truth be told, he was probably more pissed at the thought of losing his nice little drugs business, and those cunts Beth Gallagher and Kayleigh Vernon came up with a plan to help him get his own back."

"Didn't Gavin Miller try to explain all this to the college authorities? It would have given the girls a motive for getting him sacked, for lying about what happened."

Lisa snorted. "That's a laugh, that is. What could he prove? Nothing against Kyle McClusky, that's for sure. Remember, he had known what Kyle was up to ages before he got hauled up before the board, but he *hadn't* reported him. That wouldn't look so good to a committee of stuck-up prigs, would it? It was the girls' word against his, and the college believed the girls. End of story."

"Did Gavin Miller *know* that Kyle hung out with Beth and Kayleigh?"

"I don't think so. Not till later. Kyle was only in one of his classes, and not the same one as Beth and Kayleigh. No one made the connection until too late."

"But you found out later?"

"Yes. I saw the three of them cozying up together and giggling at a party, totally stoned, sharing a joint. But that was a few weeks after Mr. Miller got kicked out. Again, far too late, it seems."

"So Miller ruined McClusky's dreams, and McClusky, with the girls' help, lost Miller his job," said Winsome, "but at the time he had no way of linking the two incidents: what he'd done to Kyle, and what Beth and Kayleigh were doing to him. But what about you? You say you were his friend. You knew. Or you found out later. What did you do with your knowledge? Why didn't *you* help him? Why do you say it was too late?"

Lisa stared into the remains of her foamy coffee. "I was having problems of my own then. I wasn't very clear about things."

"Drugs?"

"No, it wasn't drugs," Lisa snapped. "For crying out loud, you lot seem to think everyone's problems are down to drugs. If you looked a bit closer, you'd see that some lives are actually improved by them, but that's too much to expect of you, I suppose. It was . . . just life. That's all. I was going through a bad time. A rough patch. You don't need to know the details."

Winsome held her hand up. "Sorry, Lisa. I have to ask these questions."

"Yeah, I suppose you do . . . but it just makes me so . . . If you want to know the truth, I don't do drugs. Well, except for a little dope now and then. But no speed, no E, no crystal meth, no downers, coke or heroin. Never have. Not even acid. Don't touch them. I was drinking and smoking too much, sure, but no other illegal drugs. And, no, I don't care to explain or justify myself. So just move on, will you."

"OK. Did you ever tell Gavin Miller about what you'd overheard?"

"No."

"Why not?"

"What was the point? It was too late, like I said. They weren't going to reopen the inquiry. It would only make him more bitter. Besides, it was after he left, moved away, and we'd lost touch. We didn't see each other again, not until quite a while later when . . . you know, he phoned and asked me about the weed and all. I mean, we

weren't mates, we didn't socialize or anything. I didn't even know
where he was living. And I was away a lot of the time."

"He sought you out?"

"Yes."

"How did he get in touch?"

"He phoned me on my mobile. This was ages after he got the sack,
like, maybe three years or more. I'd left Eastvale for two years and
come back and all that."

"Why you?"

"When I was at college, when we had our little chats, he once
talked about the old days and how they all used to smoke up and listen
to the Grateful Dead or whoever and talk about enlightenment and
The Tibetan Book of the Dead—like getting wasted wasn't just a bit of
fun for them, but part of some sort of deep spiritual search, and how
all that had changed—and I laughed and told him, damn right, the
people I smoked up with wouldn't be caught dead doing anything like
that. They just wanted to get stoned. He laughed with me. He wasn't
judgmental, and he obviously remembered that I was someone who
might know where he could get hold of some hash or grass when he
wanted it."

"How long ago was this?"

"Less than a year. Spring."

"Did he say why he wanted it all of a sudden?"

"No. We met in a coffee shop. Not this one. He told me he had a
lot of time on his hands, and he'd been doing a lot of thinking about
those old times he told me about, remembering, you know, what it
was like back then, the music, the Eastern religions and tarot cards and
stuff. He sounded like he'd done it all before, but not for a long time.
He said it had been years since he'd done anything like that. He
wanted to try smoking a joint again and maybe dropping a tab of acid,
and he asked if I could help him out."

"How did he seem?"

"I don't know. He seemed sort of defeated, a bit sad. Like his life
didn't have much meaning, and he was trying to lose himself in the
past."

"Were you surprised by his request?"

"Of course."

"Didn't you suspect it was some kind of entrapment?"

"No. Why should I? He was always good to me. He wouldn't do that. He wasn't a snitch. To be honest, he was also a bit of a deadbeat when we met, a bum, with the old clothes and straggly beard and all. Not that some of your undercover colleagues don't do a pretty good job of looking like deadbeats, but there's always the tell. Their shoes are too clean, or their teeth, or something. But Mr. Miller was genuinely down on his luck. I honestly thought he just wanted to recapture something from his lost youth, or something like that."

"Like what?"

"I don't know. Maybe he'd had visions of angels and heavenly light or something. There was just something sort of . . . haunted . . . about him."

"Let's get back to what you were saying before. What did you do to help Gavin Miller after you'd overheard Beth and Kayleigh admit they'd set him up?"

"Best thing I could think of when I was together enough. I talked to his mate, didn't I? Told *him* the whole story."

"Who? Jim Cooper?"

"No. Not that useless pillock. Mr. Lomax, the head of the department. He'd stuck up for Mr. Miller before, at the hearing, or so Mr. Miller told me. He said he'd see what he could do."

"And what happened?"

"You know as well as I do. Fuck all happened. Kyle McClusky was gone. Mr. Miller was gone. Beth and Kayleigh were graduating. The boat wasn't rocking anymore, and that's the way everyone wanted to keep it. Including, I should imagine, Mr. Trevor fucking Lomax."

"SO IT appears that the college disciplinary board sold Gavin Miller down the river," Winsome said in the Queen's Arms that evening, after she had finished telling Banks and Annie about her meeting with Lisa Gray.

"According to Lisa Gray," said Annie.

"She'd no reason to lie."

"Everybody lies," said Banks.

"More so if you cozy up to them," said Annie. "Then they think you're their mate."

"But they also tell you far more than they ever would if you kept your distance," Banks argued. He had long been a proponent of the casual, chatty interview, leading the interviewee slowly through shared interests, opinions and small talk towards more pointed questions. True, it gave him more chaff and wheat to sort out, and it posed a few challenges when it came to discerning the truth, but in his experience people tended to clam up, or lie outright, when he came at them with a stiff and official approach. Not everyone agreed, of course, and Banks was also quite willing and able to use the harder method when he felt it was justified. The only thing you had to remember was that people lied no matter which approach you took.

"I'm not saying that Lisa didn't lie," Winsome said. "I think there's a lot she didn't tell me, and a lot she evaded. But I also think there's a good deal of truth in what she said, that's all. Remember, Trevor Lomax also seemed to think Gavin Miller had been ill treated."

"Fair enough," said Banks. "No wonder the poor sod was bitter. This Lisa have an alibi?"

"At home watching telly with her mates."

"Check it out, will you?"

"Lomax didn't do much to help the situation, though, did he?" said Annie. "Not according to your Lisa. And he certainly didn't tell me about her coming to see him."

They sipped their drinks. Even Winsome was having a gin and tonic. She said she needed it after her meeting with Lisa Gray. "But it's still the sort of break we've been looking for, isn't it?" she said. "Now we've got another possible suspect in Kyle McClusky. I know it's a long time after the events at the college went down, but something could have put him and Gavin Miller in touch again—drugs, for example—and something could have flared up. McClusky shouldn't be too hard to find. We're going to have to talk to the girls, too."

"There was no record of calls to any of them on Miller's mobile," Banks pointed out. "Not Kyle McClusky, not Beth, not Kayleigh."

"Maybe they were too careful for that."

"And as Annie said, there's still Trevor Lomax," Winsome went on. "Lisa said she told him what she knew about Gavin Miller warning Kyle off, and what she overheard the girls talking about in the toilets, but he didn't do anything. Maybe he was involved, too. Maybe he didn't try to help Miller as much as he professed to do because something would come out about him?"

"I suppose it's possible," said Banks. "Maybe if Miller had actually reported Kyle McClusky—you know, officially—then things might have turned out differently. But the incident was well over by the time Lisa Gray knew and told Lomax about it, and I doubt very much that he wanted it all raked up again on the say-so of some young junkie student friend of Miller's. Imagine how well that would go down. They'd probably try and prove he was having it off with her, too."

"Lisa wasn't a junkie," said Winsome. "And she wasn't 'having it off' with Miller. I believe her on that score. She's full of attitude, swears a lot, likes to sound tough, but she wasn't a junkie. She just said she had some personal problems. Besides, Lomax might have had other reasons for not doing anything."

"Like what?" Annie asked.

"I don't know. Maybe something came up between Trevor Lomax and Gavin Miller? Maybe Miller only just found out that Lisa had been to see Lomax back then, that she had told him the truth and he had done nothing. Lisa said she didn't tell Miller what she'd done, but maybe she's not telling the complete truth about that. Maybe she told him shortly before he was killed. I don't know for sure. All I know is that it's given us a lot more to think about."

Banks turned to Annie. "Maybe it's time you and Winsome started to ruffle a few feathers at Eastvale College. Cooper. Lomax. Even that Dayle Snider woman. She might not work there, but she's connected. Talk to the girls. Track down Kyle McClusky. Find out what Lisa Gray's problems were. And someone should try to get in touch with the ex-wife in New Zealand. She might be able to tell us something."

Annie made a note. "Where's Gerry?" she asked.

Banks glanced at his watch. "She should be here soon. The poor lass has been on the telephone and the Internet most of the day. She's running down a few things for me."

"For you? What things?" Annie asked. "Personal? Or is it something we should all know about?"

"I honestly don't know yet. Somebody else who might be lying. It
depends on the answers."

"And then?"

"Well, then," said Banks, "we're either all back where we started,
or we begin a new journey into the heart of darkness."

"You're being a bit cryptic, aren't you?" Annie said. "Even for
you."

"There's something you're not telling us, sir?" Winsome prodded.

Banks sighed. "It might be nothing," he said, but he knew he had
to tell them his concerns about Lady Veronica Chalmers.

IT WAS after nine o'clock, and Banks was into his second glass of
wine and Jesse Winchester's first album when the doorbell rang. He
put down the report on Lady Chalmers's life he had been reading and
went through to the front to answer it. When he got there, he found a
very nervous Gerry Masterson standing on his doorstep in her jeans
and woolly jumper, a scarf wrapped around her neck.

"I'm sorry it's so late, sir," she said. "But I thought I should come
and report in person."

Curious, Banks invited her to hang up the scarf by the door and led
her through the little den and the kitchen into the conservatory.
"Wine?" he offered, brandishing the half-full bottle.

"No, sir. Thanks, but I'm driving. A cup of tea would go down
nicely, though. This is a nice place you've got, sir."

"I like it," said Banks. "Tea it is." He disappeared into the kitchen.
The kettle boiled in no time, and he carried the teapot, mug and milk
and sugar on a tray back to the conservatory. He also grabbed the
packet of chocolate digestives on his way. Jesse Winchester was singing "Biloxi," which Banks thought was such a beautiful song that it
made you want to go there.

"That's lovely music, sir," Gerry said, leaning forward in her wicker
chair. She had the CD jewel case in her hand. "I can't say I've ever
heard of Jesse Winchester."

"Before your time," said Banks. "He was an American draft dodger who ended up in Canada. But I'm glad you like it. Now what brings you here at such an hour?"

"The reason I'm so late is that I was waiting for a phone call from western Canada. They're eight hours behind us."

"I never could get those time zones right," said Banks. "I always seem to get them the wrong way around and upset people. So what did you find out?"

"Well, it wasn't easy, sir. I mean, it was about thirty years ago, for a start. It's hard to find the right people to talk to."

"But you managed, I gather? Milk? Sugar? Biscuit?"

Gerry accepted the tea and biscuit Banks handed her. "To cut a long story short, I managed to find out that Gavin Miller spent the years between 1979 and the end of 1982 teaching at a small college in a place called Nelson, British Columbia. It's in the 'interior,' apparently, or I think that's what they called it. I assume that means it's not on the coast. Anyway, the problem was that the college closed down in 1983, and the lecturers scattered to the four winds. That's around the time Miller went back home to Banbury."

"So what about his travels around the U.S.? Hanging out with the Grateful Dead, following Jack Kerouac's trail?"

"Tall stories," said Gerry. "He was teaching at the college year round. I'm sure he got a few weeks off now and then, though, and he may have traveled in the States if he made enough money—I really can't seem to get anywhere with U.S. Immigration on that—but most of the time he was working in the interior of British Columbia, Canada."

"I see," said Banks. "So I also assume it's unlikely that he mixed with Lady Chalmers and her crowd in Beverly Hills?"

"Extremely doubtful. Their time in North America overlapped, yes, but they would have moved in very different social circles, and so far there's no evidence of his ever visiting California. It's quite a long way. The thing is, though, and the real reason I came to see you in person rather than just phoning, is that I found out something else. Something that might be much more important." She put her mug down on the table and clasped her hands on her knees. Banks could see the excitement in her flushed face and glittering eyes. "Remember when I told you Veronica Chalmers's age, and you were shocked because you thought she was much younger?"

Banks nodded.

"And then you said it might be important. Well, it is. You were right in your suspicions. Gavin Miller and Veronica Chalmers were exact contemporaries at the University of Essex."

"Bingo," said Banks.

"I got one of the admin assistants to dig back through the records. We've struck it lucky. Both Veronica Bellamy, as she was then, and Gavin Miller were students at the University of Essex between 1971 and 1974."

"How many students were there at that time?"

"Around two thousand."

"That's not very many. She said she didn't know him, that she'd never talked to him before, but if they were exact contemporaries . . . Miller was visiting a lot of Web sites tracking down old early seventies stuff—albums, movies, books and so on. On a nostalgia fishing trip. What if Veronica Bellamy was part of that? Part of that lost time he wanted to recapture? He even started smoking cannabis again. Did they know one another?"

Gerry seemed disappointed. "That I can't say, sir. I'm going to have to dig a bit deeper for that. The admin assistant wasn't around back then. I do know that Veronica studied history and politics, and Gavin took English literature, so they probably weren't in the same classes, though they may have had subsidiary subjects that overlapped. And uni is as much about social life and clubs and stuff as it is about learning. At least that's my recollection of it. It's certainly possible their paths crossed."

"You're right. But we need more than that. Is there any way you can check whether they did meet? You know, whether they were members of the same clubs, societies, that sort of thing? I still don't believe she's telling us the full story."

"I should be able to get class lists easily enough. Maybe even society membership details."

"It's a start."

"From there, I might be able to track down somebody who actually knew Veronica Bellamy or Gavin Miller back then, or knows someone who did. But remember, sir, it was forty years ago. Is it worth it? I mean, do we take Lady Veronica Chalmers seriously as a suspect? Might we not be just wasting our time? And looking for trouble?"

"We won't know that until we've followed all the leads, Gerry," said Banks. "At the moment I'm curious to know where she stands in all this. I certainly think there's more of a connection between her and Gavin Miller than she's saying. That phone call explanation doesn't ring true at all. Or the alumni business. What did you find out about Miller's links with alumni affairs?"

"He didn't have any, sir. I spoke to the director of the Alumni and Development Team, and she's never heard of him. He wasn't on any of the lists they had, either of donors or fund-raisers. And Lady Chalmers, as she told you, is already a generous donor."

"Interesting," said Banks. "Why should she want to lie about it?"

"I don't know, sir, but I did find out one thing. They have Lady Chalmers's ex-directory number at Essex, and one of the junior people in the alumni office gave it to Miller. He sounded legit. Said they were old friends and he'd lost touch and needed to contact her about an informal reunion of some kind. Sounds a bit thin to me, but she took pity on him. I suppose some people just want to be helpful, like that nurse who told the press about Kate Middleton's condition and then committed suicide. She was thorough, though, the woman in the alumni office. She checked out his connection with the university and everything, discovered the two of them were there at the same time before she rang back to give him the number."

"Well, that's one mystery solved," said Banks.

"But what possible involvement could Lady Chalmers have, sir?"

"None that I can think of. But that doesn't make her much different from any of the other suspects we might have in this case. The same goes for alibis. They're all flimsy." Banks sipped some wine and let the music wander in his mind for a few moments while he thought things over. Gerry seemed on edge, anxious to leave now that she had delivered her news. "Look," said Banks finally, "I understand your concerns, and I'm honestly not sure myself how, or how far, we should proceed with this. But putting aside the fact that we're talking about a 'Lady' who lives in the Heights and knows the chief constable, Veronica Chalmers is clearly lying about the reason for that telephone call. She went to the same university at exactly the same time as Miller. That's three years they had to make one another's acquaintance, among a student population of around two thousand. I can't believe they weren't aware of one another. Their times in the States overlapped, even though we think it unlikely they met there, and they both lived in Eastvale for three years when Miller was teaching at the college, even though their social circles would have been worlds apart. I don't know about you, but that's too many coincidences for me. Lady Chalmers certainly merits another visit." Banks paused. "Have you entered all this into the system?"

"The telephone numbers on Gavin Miller's mobile, the university details. I had to, sir. It's—"

Banks waved her down. "It's all right. I'm not criticizing. You're absolutely right to do so. In fact, I'm the one in serious breach for not writing up the visit I paid her this morning. But let me worry about that. The next visit will be a lot more official, and I'll take DI Cabbot with me. That's not a reflection on you at all, Gerry, in case you're wondering. Your work on this so far has been sterling, but . . . well, let's just say there might be repercussions. What I'd like you to do, as discreetly as possible, but with full openness in terms of gathering and entering information—in other words, by the book, under my instructions—is to continue your investigation into Lady Chalmers in general, and the Essex years in particular. If there is a connection, find it. Let's not forget, Liam told me that Gavin Miller had been doing a lot of computer research into the early seventies in the days or weeks before he died. Winsome also said that Lisa Gray told her Miller was nostalgic about old times, haunted, as if he were searching for his lost youth. Maybe Veronica Bellamy was a part of that. It's a line of inquiry we can't afford to overlook. But it's delicate. Tread carefully."

"What if I have to go to Colchester?"

"Go where you need, within reason. Just keep me posted where you are and what you find out."

"Of course, sir."

"Gavin Miller is turning into a far more interesting and complicated person than I ever imagined when this business started," Banks said. "By the way, does Lady Chalmers have anything to do with Eastvale College?"

"I don't know, sir, but I'll check into it."

"And have any of the people we've talked to already, or even Miller himself, ever had anything to do with Sir Jeremy Chalmers? After all, there are plenty of artsy types involved, and he's in the theater world. It's not beyond belief."

"Again, I'll see if I can find anything."

Banks saw Gerry to the door, then settled down with his wine again. Jesse Winchester was singing "Yankee Lady," and the case was beginning to get very interesting.

6

S O LET ME GET THIS STRAIGHT. YOU'RE ALL CON-
cerned about protecting poor little Miss Masterson, but you're
quite happy to drag me down in the shit with you. Is that the way it
is?"

Banks laughed. "Well, since you put it like that . . . I suppose so.
But look at it another way, Annie. Would you be really happy spending the whole day at your desk on the phone and computer instead?
Would you like to enter the data into HOLMES? Do you want to be
crime analyst on this?"

"You've got a point. How do we approach Lady Chalmers?"

Banks pulled into the drive and stopped outside the front door.
"Softly, softly. Leave her to me. But we know more than she knows
we know this time, so let's see if we can't corner her somewhere she
can't scramble out of so easily."

"How did she sound on the phone?"

This time, Banks had telephoned ahead to set up an appointment in
the interest of making the visit more official. Perhaps it wasn't a full
official interview, but it was more than just a social chat, and he
wanted Lady Chalmers to know that. "Fine," he said. "A little puzzled, even anxious, perhaps, but fine on the whole. At least she didn't
try to wriggle out of it."

Oriana answered the door, though she wasn't smiling this time.

Loyalty to her mistress no doubt dictated that she disapprove of police interest, even when it came from Brian Banks's father. Banks hoped he wasn't losing his son a fan in the process of the investigation. Two, if you counted Samantha Chalmers.

Lady Chalmers was waiting in the same room as before, and she had two people with her. A young man in an expensive pin-striped suit sat beside her. Banks thought he had seen him before, around the courts. The other man leaned against the fireplace. He was wearing a tan V-neck jumper over a cream shirt, and he looked as if he might have just come from the golf course. He was probably a few years older than Banks, with a fine head of gray hair and a reddish complexion. There was an air of authority about him, as well as anger, and Banks's first thought was that he must be Lady Chalmers's husband Sir Jeremy, hurriedly returned from New York. He tried to run any photographs he might have seen of Sir Jeremy through his mind, but he couldn't remember paying attention to any.

"This is Mr. Ralph Nathan, our family solicitor," Lady Chalmers said, pointing to the younger man first. "And this is my brother-in-law, Anthony Litton." Nobody made a move to smile or shake hands. The two men just nodded curtly at Banks and Annie.

"Hardly necessary, I'd have thought," muttered Banks. The presence of the solicitor and the doctor raised his hackles; it would change the whole tenor of the interview. So this was what it was going to be like from now on, he thought. War. Whether she knew it or not, Lady Chalmers had raised the stakes.

"I'm simply here as an observer, Mr. Banks," said Nathan, with a smarmy grin. "Please don't pay me the slightest bit of attention." Anthony Litton just cast his cold eye over them all from his spot by the hearth.

"Easily enough done," said Banks. When they were all seated, and Annie had her notebook out, he glanced through the rain-streaked windows at the town below, noting the shafts of sunlight on the river and the castle keep, the faint beginnings of a rainbow over the hill. "Lady Chalmers," he began, "is it true that you attended the University of Essex between the years 1971 and 1974?"

"Why, yes," said Lady Chalmers, apparently surprised by the question. "Didn't I tell you before that was where I went? I studied history and politics. Why?"

"Just out of interest, why did you choose Essex?"

"Why does one choose any one thing over another? It was a new university. Progressive. I was young. Progressive. I really didn't want to go to one of those old fuddy-duddy establishments where people like me were expected to go."

"Like Oxford or Cambridge?"

"That's right."

"Though you went to Cambridge later to do postgraduate work."

"Maybe I'd grown up a bit by then. I was a rebellious young woman, Mr. Banks, as many people were at that time. Though why it should be of any interest to you is beyond me." She cocked her head. "Tell me, weren't you also just the teeniest bit rebellious when you were young?"

"I still am. Did you know Gavin Miller?"

Her expression hardened, and the air around her seemed to chill. Banks noticed she was twisting her hands on her lap. "I told you yesterday. No."

"But he was also at the University of Essex between the years 1971 and 1974, studying English literature."

"Then there's no reason we would have met. It's a big university."

"Not that big. Not then. Around two thousand students, I believe. And both departments were on the Wivenhoe Park campus, just outside Colchester. You were both students. You'd have shared certain facilities, the student pub, residences, the refectory, perhaps gone to the same concerts? Lou Reed? Slade? King Crimson?"

"You've got me there," said Lady Chalmers. "And you've done your homework. I went to two of those. I can't say I was ever a Slade fan."

"And yet you maintain that you never met this man?" Banks showed her the photo again.

"She's already answered that," said Anthony Litton. It was the first time he had spoken, and his voice had an impatient edge. He sounded like a man who was used to being listened to. Obeyed, even, without having to explain himself.

Lady Chalmers glanced at her brother-in-law, then turned back to Banks and went on. "No. At least, I certainly don't recognize him from that photograph. I suppose he must have looked much younger back then."

Banks made a mental note to try to get Liam to put a rush on copies of the older photos of Miller they had got from the search of his house. The only photo they had at the moment, from the camera in his computer, made him appear more like a tramp than anything else. "But he hadn't changed his name," he said.

"Then, no. I don't remember him. But I'm not very good with names."

That sounded a bit disingenuous to Banks. Someone in her position, with a heavy social calendar, had to be good with names. He looked out of the window again. Two magpies landed high in a tree below the garden, frightening away a flock of sparrows. Mr. Nathan was starting to fidget, straightening the creases in his trousers and brushing imaginary hairs from his lapels, as if he were eager for an opportunity to break into the conversation. Banks turned back to Lady Chalmers. "Yesterday you told me you received a telephone call from Gavin Miller at two P.M. a week ago last Monday."

"That's right. Around that time. And I think that's what he said his name was."

"It was him. The call that lasted for almost seven minutes, as I told you yesterday. You said it was something to do with alumni donations, but that hardly takes seven minutes, especially if you weren't interested. Can you tell me what else the two of you talked about during that time?"

"My client doesn't have to tell you anything," interjected Nathan. "Her word should be enough."

Anthony Litton beamed down on the lawyer.

"Of course," said Banks. "But I'm sure you understand, Mr. Nathan, that we need all the information we can get on Gavin Miller and his state of mind in the period leading up to his death. If Lady Chalmers could help us in any way—"

"But I can't," protested Lady Chalmers. "It was exactly as I told you. Some chat about how the university was doing in tough economic times and so on. New building projects, residences. I wasn't really paying attention."

"You've heard what Lady Chalmers has to say," said Litton. "Is there really any point in continuing with this?"

Banks ignored Litton and kept his eyes on Lady Chalmers. "As far as we can ascertain," he said, "Gavin Miller had no connection whatsoever with the Alumni and Development Team at the University of Essex. He had nothing to do with the place since he graduated in 1974."

"Then he was lying," said Lady Chalmers. "But that's what he told me. I don't know what else I'm supposed to say."

"The man was clearly trying to con my sister-in-law out of some money," said Litton. "He was nothing but a common criminal. These things happen all the time, in case you didn't know. Telephone fraud. Perhaps if you devoted a bit more of your time to protecting honest, law-abiding citizens instead of interrogating them . . . ?"

"How long have you lived in Eastvale?" Banks asked Lady Chalmers. He could see Litton in his peripheral vision, clearly irritated by the lack of response to his sarcasm.

"Since Angelina was born, in 1988."

"Did you know that Gavin Miller worked as a lecturer at Eastvale College from 2006 until he was dismissed four years ago?"

"How would I know that?"

"He was dismissed for sexual misconduct. You might remember the case? It was pretty well hushed up, though you can't keep a scandal like that completely under wraps."

"I don't remember it. But then I usually don't pay much attention to such scandals."

"Do you know Kayleigh Vernon or Beth Gallagher?"

"No. Who are they?"

A sudden idea came to Banks. Winsome had mentioned that Lisa Gray was working on a dark fantasy script. Lady Chalmers wrote historical fiction under a pseudonym, but everyone knew it was her, and Sir Jeremy was in theater production. Perhaps Lisa had approached them, asked for their advice on how to get published or produced. "What about Lisa Gray?"

Lady Chalmers didn't waver. "No."

"Mr. Banks. Please stop badgering my client."

"I'm sorry. I wasn't aware that I was badgering her. Pardon me if it seemed that way, Lady Chalmers. I'm just confused, that's all."

"That makes two of us," said Lady Chalmers, smiling, clearly emboldened by Nathan's interruption. "I'm confused as to why you're here questioning me for the second day in a row when I've already told you everything I know."

"You haven't told me anything. Consider it from my perspective. You were at the same university as the victim during exactly the same time period, yet you say you never met him. You lived in the same town as him for three years, yet you say you never met him. You were both in North America between 1979 and 1983. He made a seven-minute telephone call to your number a week before he was murdered, which you admit you took, yet you say you never knew him. Don't you know how suspicious that all seems?"

"Suspicious?" said Litton. "In what way? This has gone far enough. What you're implying is absurd. Thousands of people live in this town, and my sister-in-law doesn't know all of them. And as for the population of North America—well, I suggest you work out the odds on that one yourself. Besides, why should she know a bloody college teacher who was fired for, what did you say, sexual misconduct? It's ridiculous. Are you suggesting that my sister-in-law is lying? That she was somehow responsible for this man's death?"

"Not at all, sir," said Banks. He turned back to Lady Chalmers. "I'd just like to know why you're not telling me the whole truth."

"That's enough," said Nathan, getting authoritatively to his feet. "This is nothing but a mass of coincidences and circumstance. I don't know how you dare suggest such things." He glanced at Lady Chalmers and Sir Anthony, then back to Banks and Annie. "And now, Mr. Banks, Ms. Cabbot, I think it's time for you to go. I'm sure you can find your own way out."

Not inclined to give Nathan any kind of concession, Banks ignored him and asked Lady Chalmers, "What are you hiding? Why don't you want to admit to knowing Gavin Miller? Was he blackmailing you?"

"Because I *don't* know him! Didn't know him. Why can't you just believe me and leave me alone?" Her eyes were pleading. She turned away. "I've got nothing more to say on the matter. If you want to talk to me any further, you'll have to arrest me and take me down to the station, or whatever it is you people do."

"I don't think we've quite got to that point yet," said Annie.

Lady Chalmers shot her a glance. "Then perhaps you should leave."

Anthony Litton walked over to Lady Chalmers and rested his hand on her shoulder. "I think my sister-in-law is right," he said. "You're bullying her, and you've got no proof of anything. She's had enough. She's upset. It's time for you to leave. She clearly had nothing to do with this man."

There was no Oriana to lead them back across the broad checkered floor this time. They had definitely gone down in the world, Banks thought as they got back in the car.

WINSOME HAD decided to take Gerry Masterson with her to interview Beth Gallagher because the young DC needed the experience, and Gerry had located both Beth and Kayleigh for her. Kayleigh Vernon was a researcher at the new BBC studio complex on Salford Quays. They would talk to her later. Beth Gallagher, whom they were on their way to see at the moment, had moved to London to work for a TV production company, but she was presently assigned to a TV police drama near Thornfield Reservoir. Gerry had told her that Beth was a floor runner, which Winsome guessed was a sort of gofer or general dogsbody.

The flooding wasn't too bad on the road out of Harrogate towards Thornfield Reservoir, apart from a deceptively deep puddle every now and then, when the car sent sheets of water whooshing up on either side. Luckily, there was never anyone walking by the roadside so far from civilization. Gerry had got good directions over the phone, and she seemed to be a decent enough driver, even if she did go too fast on occasion, Winsome thought as they followed the makeshift signs to the base unit.

The reservoir appeared below them, beyond the woods that straggled down the hillside. It was full almost to the brim. Winsome vaguely remembered Banks telling her once about an old case there, before her time, when the water had dried up one summer and revealed the remains of an old village, including a body that dated back to the Second World War. Not much chance of it drying up these days, she thought.

Just past the eastern end of the reservoir, the road dipped down into a vale and a sign on a tree showing an arrow pointing left directed them to the farm gate. The gate was closed, and a rent-a-guard asked them their business and examined their identification before opening it for them. The field the TV people were using as their base camp was filled with caravans, trailers, vans and cars, people wandering everywhere, like an encampment of Travellers. At the center of it all stood a blue double-decker bus, which seemed to have been converted into a canteen.

Winsome suggested that they park close to the gate to avoid getting the car too bogged down in the mud, which was churned up and glistening everywhere. There had not been enough heat recently to allow the water to evaporate from the rain-soaked earth. Anticipating the lie of the land, Gerry had put their wellies in the back of the car, and they struggled to get them on before stepping out. Winsome's felt half a size too small. The mud squelched unpleasantly beneath her feet, like the slippery innards of some slaughtered farmyard animal.

They walked towards the first group of caravans and saw a row of several trailers with the actors' names on the doors. The star's was the largest, of course; it seemed quite luxurious from the outside, big enough for an *en suite*, Winsome thought. The people they passed paid them no attention, as if they were used to strangers wandering around their camp. Winsome accosted a bearded young man in torn jeans and a woolly jumper and asked him where they could find the floor runner.

"Probably running somewhere," he said. When Winsome didn't respond to his attempt at humor, he pointed to a white caravan not far from the bus. "That's the office," he said, and went on his way.

Winsome and Gerry squelched on towards the caravan and knocked on the door. Though they had talked to the line producer, they hadn't called Beth Gallagher to let her know they were coming because Winsome stressed the need for the element of surprise. If Beth had lied or was keeping something back, then they didn't want to give her time to fabricate a story or bolster it up or, worse, run away. There was no answer.

"If you're looking for Beth," said a young woman passing by, "she's just gone out to the shooting location to deliver some script revisions to the AD."

"AD?"

"Sorry. Assistant director. Anyway, it's open. You can wait inside for her if you want. She shouldn't be long."

Winsome thanked her, and they scraped the mud off their boots as best they could on the metal steps and went inside. Someone had placed a sheet of cardboard just inside the door, and it was covered with muddy footprints. The office was heated by a small electric fire, turned off at the moment. There were two desks, both of them rather messy, and the walls were plastered with schedules, notes and photos of the cast. There was a battered sofa against the only free wall, and they both sat down.

It was only about ten minutes before the door opened, during which time Gerry had played a game of Solitaire on her smartphone and Winsome had gone over her notes for the interview. It was her. She seemed surprised to see them waiting, and then nervous when she found out who they were. She was taller than Winsome had expected, long legged, with her jeans tucked into her wellies, and full breasted under the tight sweater, with an oval face framed in curly chestnut hair. She positively radiated youth and health.

"What is it?" she asked. "Has something happened? Is my dad all right?"

"Your dad's fine, as far as we know," said Winsome. "No, it's about something else entirely."

Beth sat down on the swivel chair at the desk and swung it around so she was facing them, stretching out her legs and crossing them. The chair squealed. "What is it?"

"Did you hear about Gavin Miller?"

"Gavin Miller? No. What . . . ?"

"He's dead," Gerry said. "We think he was killed, in fact."

"Oh . . . I . . . I don't know what you expect me to say."

"As long as you don't say you're glad he's dead," said Winsome, smiling.

"Oh, I would never say that. I wouldn't wish that on anyone. But why come to me?"

"We're talking to everyone we can find who was ever connected with him. He didn't seem to have a lot of friends, so we're mostly talking to his enemies."

"We weren't enemies," said Beth. "He abused me, yes. But we weren't enemies."

"You forgave him?" Winsome asked.

Beth twirled one of her curls around her long tapered index finger. "I suppose so. It was a long time ago. I don't think about it anymore."

"Four years, give or take a bit."

"Yes."

"You're doing all right?"

"I know it doesn't seem like much," Beth said, "but it's what I want. It's a rung on the ladder. Lots of ADs, even line producers, start as floor runners. You do a bit of everything, get to learn all about the business from the ground up."

"Is that what you want to be?" Winsome asked. "A director?"

"I wouldn't necessarily aim that high—I'm not really that artistic—but I'd like to get into production at some level."

Winsome, who had never been clear about the difference between directors and producers, let alone assistant directors and line producers, let that go. "Well, good luck, then."

"Thank you. Er . . . I really am very busy. I'm still the junior around here. We've got the author coming in this afternoon—the author of the books the series is based on—and I have to take care of him. We like to keep the authors happy. That way they won't complain too much about what we do to their books."

"We shouldn't keep you very long," Winsome said, and nodded towards Gerry, who took out her notebook. "We'd like to talk to you about Gavin Miller."

"I really thought I'd put all that behind me. I don't know anything about him."

"Things have a way of coming back to haunt us. Were you telling the truth about what happened in his office?"

"What do you mean? Of course I was. Are you suggesting that I was lying?"

"Well, were you?"

"No."

Someone opened the door to the caravan, another woman, a few years older than Beth. "Oh, sorry," she said, glancing at Winsome and Gerry. "Didn't know you had company. I'll come back later, shall I?"

"Sure, fine," said Beth. She glanced at her watch. "Give us fifteen minutes."

The door closed again and Winsome carried on. "Can you tell us exactly what happened that day?"

Beth slouched sulkily in her chair. "I've been over it hundreds of times with the board and the committee and whatever. Do I have to go through it all again?"

"Humor me," said Winsome.

Beth scowled and twisted her lips about a bit, then said, "I was in his office. Professor Miller's. He wasn't really a professor, but we called them that. We were going over an essay I'd done on the production problems in *Heaven's Gate*. I don't know if you've heard of it, but—"

"If you want this to be quick, Beth, you'd better skip the movie précis."

Beth glared at Winsome briefly, then went on. "It was an important project. Twenty percent of my final marks. And part of it was that you had to be able to discuss it, defend it, to the prof. So, anyway, there I was, sitting on the other side of his desk, reading out a particular section, when he got up, walked behind me and reached down to point out something on the page over my shoulder, and as he did so, his fingers brushed . . . you know . . . by my breast."

"Was there any possibility this was accidental?"

"No, I don't think so. I mean, I'd seen him taking surreptitious glances at them before, when he thought I didn't know about it. Even in class sometimes. It wasn't as if I wore low-cut tops or tight sweaters or anything. I can't help having large breasts."

"Did he grasp it or squeeze it?"

"No."

"Just brushed his fingers lightly against it?"

"Hard enough that I could feel it. Isn't that enough?"

"And what did you do?"

"I told him to geroff, and he scuttled off back to his chair a bit red-faced. He wrapped things up pretty quickly after that, told me the essay was fine, and I left."

"What did you do then?"

"Nothing."

"Why not."

Beth chewed her lower lip. "I know it doesn't look good, but I was worried that if I said anything, if I reported him before the end of term, then he'd fail me. I was doing quite well, and I didn't want to screw things up."

"Did he have that much power? Enough to derail your academic chances?"

"I don't know. I wasn't thinking it through logically. All I know is that he still hadn't marked me on the essay or the final exam, and I didn't want to jeopardize my chances of passing."

"That makes sense," said Winsome.

"Weren't you concerned about other students, though, Beth?" Gerry asked. "If it had happened to you, it could happen to others, couldn't it? And it could have gone further with some. I mean, what if he'd asked you to have sex with him in order to get a good mark. Would you have done that?"

Beth seemed flustered. "But he didn't, did he? He touched my breast."

"Even so, you can't have felt very secure with someone like that working in the department."

"I didn't really think it through, I told you. I just . . . you know . . . I tried to forget about it. I didn't want to make a fuss."

"But you didn't succeed in forgetting about it, did you?" Winsome said. "When your friend Kayleigh Vernon complained about Gavin Miller, you came forward and added your complaint to the list. That was also before your final marks were in, I believe."

"If there were two of us, then they would have to listen to what we said, wouldn't they? They wouldn't just be able to ignore us. He wouldn't be able to get revenge by failing us."

"Is that really what you thought?"

"Of course. Wouldn't you?"

Winsome didn't know. If there had been any such behavior going on at her school, everyone in the community would have known about it, and it wouldn't have been tolerated. Her father was always complaining about how people took the law into their own hands, but he was a part of the community, too; he understood the people, and he turned a blind eye on many occasions. Later, when Winsome was at university in Manchester, she had thought she was more than capable of taking care of herself in such a situation, though it had never occurred. "I suppose it's true that there's strength in numbers," she said. "Could that have been why you added your story to Kayleigh's?"

"I told you. That's what happened. Why don't you believe me?"

"Because it's come to our attention that the two of you were hanging out with a drug dealer called Kyle McClusky. Kyle dealt bad stuff, like methamphetamines, oxycodone, cocaine and Rohypnol, or roofies, used for slipping into unsuspecting girls' drinks and making them compliant for sex. What we heard was that Gavin Miller warned Kyle to leave or he'd report him. Kyle left, but he was angry, he wanted revenge, and for that he enlisted you and Kayleigh. You probably thought it was a great lark. Isn't that what really happened?"

Beth had gone quiet and very pale during Winsome's interpretation of events. For a while, she said nothing, then she muttered, "I can't speak for Kayleigh, but I know what happened to me."

"That doesn't sound very convincing," said Winsome. "Listen to yourself, Beth. Strength in numbers. You made it all up, didn't you, both of you, partly to get revenge for Kyle, and partly—well, for fun, or out of cruelty? It was a lark."

"No!"

"Someone overheard you boasting about what you'd succeeded in doing when you thought there was no one listening."

"Who? Who said that? When? Where?"

"It doesn't matter who, when or where," said Winsome. "The point is that it's true, isn't it?"

"I don't know. How could I remember something like that? It's probably a lie. I don't remember doing anything like that. But it doesn't matter now, anyway, does it? Professor Miller's dead and we've all moved on."

"You did terrible damage to his career, to his life," Winsome said. "Doesn't that bother you?"

"He was always staring at my breasts."

"But he didn't touch them, did he?"

Beth's lips drew tight together. She said nothing, but Winsome could see it in her eyes, that mixture of fear and defiance; Beth was working out what they could do to her, how brazen she could be. In the end she whispered, "No."

"And Kayleigh?"

"We were talking. She said he was always ogling her, too. He was a creep. We thought we'd get our own back and give him one for forcing Kyle out of college at the same time."

"Don't you realize that he probably did Kyle a big favor by not reporting him to the authorities immediately?"

"We didn't see it that way at the time."

Winsome nodded to show her understanding, and that she was being nonjudgmental. In fact, she was thinking what an utter worthless soul this girl and her friend were, and how they deserved some sort of punishment for what they had done to Gavin Miller. But she wasn't going to express any of that. It would only put Beth on the defensive when they needed to get her to relax her guard. "OK," she said. "That's better. I'm interested in the drugs. Did Kyle supply Mr. Miller with drugs while he was at Eastvale?"

"Mr. Miller? No way," said Beth incredulously. "Mr. Miller was a prof. He . . . I mean, he wouldn't be taking drugs, would he?"

"Might Kyle have wanted to take his own revenge on Gavin Miller? I mean, he felt that Miller robbed him of his education, of a chance to make something of his life."

"How would I know? Kyle was pissed off, sure. Who wouldn't be?"

"Which one of you was going out with him?"

"Kyle? Neither of us, really. I mean, we just hung out and partied. I suppose him and Kayleigh used to fuck sometimes when they were high. Kayleigh liked coke, and Kyle usually had some."

"And you?"

"I never touched any of it."

And the moon is made of green cheese, thought Winsome, but

again she nodded sagely, and with understanding. Kyle and Kayleigh, what a funny combination it sounded. As if they should be on a reality TV show.

"Do you still see one another?" Gerry asked, glancing up from her notebook. "You and Kayleigh."

"What?" Beth looked as if she had almost forgotten Gerry was there. "Oh, no. We went our separate ways. It's four years ago. A lifetime. We've both moved on."

Right, thought Winsome, and Banks is still chasing the connection between Gavin Miller and Lady Chalmers that, if it existed at all, goes back forty years. Four didn't seem so long by comparison; it was all relative. "So you don't see one another, you never meet up for a drink, anything like that, talk about old times, have a laugh?" she asked.

"Nope."

"And Kyle?"

"I've no idea where he is or what he's doing, and I don't care."

"So it was all just a bit of a lark to you?"

"I suppose it was, yeah. What of it? There's nothing you can do. Not now. Why don't you just let sleeping dogs lie? Too much time has gone by. Nobody at the college would thank you for raking it up. And Professor Miller's dead, so he doesn't care, does he?"

"I suppose not," said Winsome. "Can you think of anything in any of this mess that could possibly be linked with Gavin Miller's murder?"

"Well, I certainly didn't do it!"

"Did he ever come to you and ask for money?"

"No. Why would he do that?"

"Where were you last Sunday night around ten o'clock?" Gerry asked.

"Here. Ask anyone. We work Sundays, and we don't finish till midnight or one o'clock."

"Did you ever see Gavin Miller again after he was dismissed and you graduated?"

"No. Why would I? It was just something I wanted to forget, put behind me."

"But why? It was fun, wasn't it? Didn't you want to carry on torturing the poor man?"

Beth rubbed at an imaginary patch on her jeans. When she looked up again, Winsome thought her eyes were glistening a little, as if brimming with tears, though none came. "It was fun at first, yes. Just to have *something* actually happening around that bloody mausoleum was fun. It was fun to see just how pompous they all got, all pompous and holier than thou. But then . . . I mean, I just wanted it to stop, wanted to say let's put an end to it, let it go."

"Why didn't you?"

"It was too late. I couldn't. It seemed to have a momentum all of its own by then. Everything was in motion. If we'd retracted then, we'd have been the ones out on our ears. I mean Kayleigh and me. Kyle was already out."

"So you went on with the farce right to the bitter end?"

"Yes. I mean, it's not as if he didn't ogle us or anything."

Ogling's one thing, Winsome wanted to say, and touching is quite another, but she kept quiet.

"Beth, have you ever heard of Lady Veronica Chalmers?" Gerry asked. "Did Gavin Miller ever mention her to you?"

"Who?"

"Lady Veronica Chalmers. She writes as Charlotte Summers."

Beth shook her head slowly in incomprehension. "I've heard of her, of course, read about her—isn't she the one who writes bodice rippers, whose husband produces those big Broadway spectaculars?—but just from the entertainment sections in the papers. Not from Professor Miller or anyone else."

"From Kyle or Kayleigh?"

"No. Why?"

"It doesn't matter," said Gerry.

"Is there anything more you can tell us?" Winsome, asked, standing up to leave.

"No," said Beth. "It was a stupid thing to do, I know, but it's over. I've got my life to live now. There's no point dwelling on the past, is there?"

WHEN BANKS and Annie returned to the station from Brierley House, after a brief stop for coffee and a postmortem of the interview on their way, there was a message for Banks at reception, asking him to go up to Area Commander Gervaise's office as soon as he was available. Annie raised her eyebrows, grinned and said, "Good luck," then hurried up to the squad room.

Banks took a deep breath and began following her up the stairs. When he reached Gervaise's office door, he knocked and was immediately asked to come in. He shouldn't have been surprised to see Assistant Chief Constable Ron McLaughlin sitting opposite AC Gervaise, but he was. Lady Chalmers must have been very quick off the mark, indeed, he thought. Unless it was that smarmy lawyer, Ralph Nathan.

McLaughlin grunted a greeting, and Gervaise told Banks to sit down. There was no offer of coffee. "I assume you know what this is about?" she began.

"No idea," said Banks.

"Cut the crap, Alan," McLaughlin cut in. "I've had the bloody chief constable bellowing fire in my ear for half an hour already this morning, and I'm in no mood for flippancy."

"Sir."

"As I understand it, you've paid two visits to Lady Veronica Chalmers in the last two days. Is that correct?"

"Yes, sir."

"What was the reason for these visits?"

"A man called Gavin Miller was found dead on a disused railway track near Coverton. Dr. Glendenning's postmortem revealed that he had been involved in a scuffle before going over the side of a bridge. We checked his mobile phone records and found out that he had called Lady Chalmers a week ago. Her number is ex-directory, so he had gone to a bit of trouble to get it from their old university, Essex, and the whole thing smelled very suspicious."

"How?"

"The phone call lasted almost seven minutes. Yesterday, Lady Chalmers told me it was something to do with the University of Essex alumni donations."

"And the problem is?"

"We've discovered that Gavin Miller had no connection whatsoever with the alumni team at Essex, or anywhere else. Lady Chalmers was extremely vague about the whole thing. I don't believe her version, sir."

"Why would she lie to you?"

"That's what I'd like to know. I can't think of any good reason, unless she's hiding something."

"Isn't it more likely that Miller was lying to her, trying to pull some sort of a scam?" said Gervaise. "You already know he was short of money and not averse to criminal activity, a drug addict, if the drugs found in his cottage are anything to go by. He was clearly trying to con her out of some money."

"That's what Anthony Litton suggested," said Banks. "And that's the most logical explanation."

"Well?"

"Why didn't she say so? All she had to tell us was that Miller was trying to con her and we'd have believed her. Instead she gives us some bollocks about alumni donations. And how did Miller know she was an Essex alumna?"

"Surely that's a matter of public record? Anyway, it can't have been that difficult to find out."

"It was dead simple, actually," said Banks. "He was at Essex at exactly the same time as she was. They probably knew one another. But Lady Chalmers never mentioned anything about that. And Miller wasn't a drug addict or a dealer. His drugs were for personal use."

"So that makes it all right, does it?" McLaughlin butted in. "Come off it, Alan. You surely don't think Lady Veronica Chalmers had anything to do with this man's death, do you? A drug user, a sex offender and a loser like Miller?"

"I don't know, sir. All he did was smoke a bit of marijuana from time to time. I'm just saying that I don't think that makes him a junkie. I doubt that Lady Chalmers was strong enough to throw him over the railway bridge, but she was rich enough to pay someone to do it."

"Don't be absurd. What evidence do you have?"

Banks glanced from McLaughlin to Gervaise and back again. He shifted in his chair. It wasn't the comfortable one he usually got. McLaughlin had that one. "I'll admit that at the moment it's pure conjecture, but it's logical conjecture, if we can find a motive." He told them what he knew about the points at which Lady Chalmers's and Miller's paths coincided.

"And you believe that all these things are connected and might make her a murderer?" said Gervaise.

"I'm saying that it's possible, that's all. If it were anyone else, we'd investigate it without question."

"And you have actual evidence that they knew each other at Essex, in America, in Eastvale?"

"Not yet. Nothing concrete."

"These 'connections' are preposterous," said Gervaise. "Circumstantial. So they lived in Eastvale at the same time. Lots of people do. I should imagine they moved in very different circles."

Banks glanced at McLaughlin. "Obviously."

"Enough of that, Alan," McLaughlin said, reddening.

"And the same in America," a tight-lipped Gervaise went on. "Besides, as I understand it, Miller was in Western Canada, not America—or at least not the United States of America—which is some distance from Beverly Hills, isn't it?"

"He could have traveled there, or she could have gone to Canada."

"But why? Do you have any evidence to suggest that?"

"No," said Banks. "And it's beginning to seem like I'll never get the chance to dig up any."

"Is this some sort of witch hunt?" McLaughlin said. "Have you got something against the woman?"

"I don't like being lied to, sir. Not by anyone."

"Then you're in the wrong line of work."

Banks half rose from his chair. "Is that some sort of threat?"

"Alan, sit down," Gervaise intervened, and he noticed she also gave McLaughlin a chastising glance. The ACC looked uncomfortable, but he didn't pull rank, as a lesser man might have done. "As far as I can see," Gervaise went on, "all you have against Lady Chalmers is nothing but vague suspicions and coincidence. You have no evidence that she knew this Miller character at all. You ought to know you need a lot more than that before you go around challenging or accusing people."

"Challenging titled people, you mean. And I haven't accused

anyone of anything except perhaps not telling the full truth. What did Anthony Litton and Ralph Nathan tell you?"

"Oh, come off it, Alan," Gervaise said. "Get real, as they say. Yes, *Lady* Chalmers is a respected and honored member of the community, as is her brother-in-law in his. This isn't some street-corner drugs dealer you're questioning. A bit of decorum, a bit of respect, wouldn't go amiss."

"I was respectful," Banks said. "They just didn't like what I was saying."

"Insinuating, more like it. And I can't say I blame them," said Gervaise. "As I understand it, you even suggested that Lady Chalmers was being blackmailed by Miller. I'm not sure I'd like it if someone came around to me suggesting that sort of thing." Her tone softened, and she seemed to relax in her chair. "Don't you think you're letting yourself get a bit carried away by this, Alan?" she went on. "There's nothing sinister about any of it as far as I can see. I'm sure ACC McLaughlin agrees." McLaughlin nodded to show that he did. "Haven't you heard of Occam's razor? The simplest explanation is usually the best one. Yet you choose to go for the complicated conspiracy theory stretching back forty years. Take this business of going to university together. It turns out that I was at the same university as Liam in the lab, and at the same time. I didn't know him. I was doing sociology, and he was in computer studies. I wouldn't have known if I hadn't read over his CV when he started working here. For crying out loud, Alan, this was forty years ago you're talking about. How could any of that possibly have any impact on the murder of an antisocial, disreputable character in the here and now?"

"So I gather you're asking me to lay off?" Banks said.

"Not asking," said McLaughlin. "I don't want you visiting Lady Chalmers and her family again, or even talking to her on the telephone. Do I make myself clear?"

"Yes, sir."

"We can count ourselves damn lucky the press haven't found out about it. Let's keep it that way. Is there any media interest, by the way?"

"In Miller's murder?"

"Yes."

"Minimal," said Banks. "It's not as if he was rich or famous or any-thing." He was about to add, "Or played golf with the chief consta-ble," but thought better of it and bit his tongue.

"Any chance of a leak?"

"I can't see how. Nobody's approached me, at any rate."

"So we should be able to keep all this under wraps, if you stay away from the Heights from now on. We don't want some keen young re-porter spotting you going in or coming out of Brierley House."

Banks shrugged.

"Let me and the press office handle all media requests to do with the Miller case in future."

"No problem," said Banks. He hated dealing with the media, anyway.

"Surely you've got other promising lines of inquiry to pursue?" Gervaise added. "I've read all the statements and reports that have come in. I'm up to speed. What about that drug dealer Miller got kicked out of Eastvale College? Kyle McClusky. He sounds like a nasty piece of work. Or the girls who accused Miller of sexual harass-ment? Or Lisa Gray, another drug dealer? Who's working on all that?"

"DS Jackman, mostly, ma'am, and DI Cabbot and DCs Masterson and Watson. We also have some of the local Coverton officers helping out. As you know, we're short staffed."

"You'd be able to manage perfectly well if you didn't go around tilting at windmills," added McLaughlin.

Gervaise went on, reading from her copy of the file. "Then there's a woman called Dayle Snider, who clearly had no time for Miller. There could be some sort of sexual angle involved. Not to mention his two lecturer colleagues, Trevor Lomax and Jim Cooper. There could be something there, too, going back to his dismissal. Yet you choose to spend your time sniffing around one of Eastvale's most prominent citizens who just happened to go to the same university as the victim forty years ago."

"Is that what it is, Alan?" said McLaughlin. "That working-class chip on your shoulder again? Can't you accept that anyone who comes from a background of wealth and privilege can be any good? Do they always have to be crooks and liars? Is that what it's all about?"

Banks struggled to remain calm. He knew that the ACC had a point. "We'll investigate all those avenues," he said. "And any others we may come across. It's still something of a scattershot approach."

"Well, just keep Lady Chalmers out of your sights," McLaughlin said. "That's all." He got up, dusted off his trousers and stalked out of the office.

"Ma'am, I—"

"I don't want to hear it," Gervaise said. "You know the lie of the land, Alan. Remember what we talked about the other day. Concentrate on the drugs angle. You're on a very short leash. Now get back to work and find us a killer."

IN THE car heading back to Eastvale, Winsome seemed unusually quiet. Gerry concentrated on the driving, enjoying snatches of countryside every now and then, the lemon and red leaves still clinging to the trees, and replaying the interview in her mind. After a while, she risked a sideways glance. "Anything wrong, boss?"

"No."

"You sure? You're awfully quiet."

There was a longish pause, then Winsome said, "I just wish you hadn't mentioned Lady Chalmers to Beth Gallagher. That's all."

"But I wanted to see her reaction."

"I can understand that, but by mentioning her, you've put the idea in Beth's head that Lady Chalmers might have something to do with the Gavin Miller case."

"Well, she might."

"Yes, but do you really trust someone like Beth Gallagher to keep her mouth shut, especially after what she just told us? How do you know she won't go blabbing to the press?"

"She only told us because she thinks she's safe now, that we can't touch her."

"We can't."

"I was thinking about that, boss," said Gerry after a few moments. "Maybe there's a way we can."

"Oh. How?"

"Well, we can't prosecute her, right, and we can't get Gavin Miller his job or his life back, but we could blacken her character with her employers, make sure she suffers for what she's done by losing her job, like he did, her prospects."

"That would be revenge."

"But look at what she did. She colluded with her friend to ruin a man's life because of a worthless drug dealer, and because she thought it would be fun."

"It doesn't matter," Winsome said. "That's not part of our job. Revenge isn't for us to mete out. If she's meant to suffer for her sins, it'll happen without our interference."

"What? Like karma?"

"Something like that."

"But isn't that rather like the story of the drowning man who refused all the help that was offered to him because he believed God would save him, then cried about being abandoned?"

"And God told him he had been given every opportunity to escape but that he had turned them all down? I don't really think so. Honestly, Gerry, I've thought about it. Believe it or not, I have the same impulse to revenge as you. Those girls deserve to suffer for what they did to Gavin Miller. But we're not the instruments of that kind of justice. If we could build up some sort of case against her, fair enough, but it's not our job to go around and tell her employer that we think she once did a bad thing. Beth Gallagher confessed to something we suspected anyway. She only did so because she thought it didn't matter anymore. From now on, it's between her and her conscience. I'd say she has at least the beginnings of one. She's certainly not entirely comfortable with what she's done. Maybe a few sleepless nights is the best punishment we can expect for her."

"Are you religious, boss?"

Winsome thought for a moment. "No, not really. I mean, I had a religious upbringing, Sunday school and all that, but I don't go to church or anything. Only weddings, christenings and funerals. Why?"

"But do you believe in God."

"Yeah," said Winsome. "Yeah, I suppose I do. You?"

"I don't know. I try to be a good person."

Winsome turned and smiled at her. "Well, that's a start."

"I wish I shared your certainty about Beth Gallagher having a con-science."

Winsome glanced at her. "I don't have any more certainty about that than you do," she said. "Just hope. But I'll save my anger for the one person who probably could have done something about Miller's predicament when he was offered the chance."

"Trevor Lomax?"

"Indeed. Left here."

They sat in silence for a while, and Gerry digested what Winsome had said. "There's probably not much we can do about Lomax, either, you know," she said, "except try to make him feel guilty, too."

"Well, if we can manage that, at least it's a start, isn't it." Winsome paused. "You know what really disappoints me about our trip this af-ternoon?"

"No," said Gerry. "What?"

"We didn't see any stars."

BANKS SUPPOSED he was sulking, though he preferred to think of it as nursing his wounds. Either way, he had driven off in a huff after his session with Red Ron and Madame Gervaise. After splashing around some of the more remote dales roads, by fields half submerged in water tinged reddish with mud, he decided that he was hungry. It was after two thirty, so he didn't expect much in the way of pub grub, but a sandwich would fill the gap nicely, and if he couldn't get any food, then a pint and a packet of crisps would do.

Turning a tight bend at a dip in an unfenced moorland road run-ning northwest out of Lyndgarth, he came to a pub he had never seen before. At least he thought it was a pub. It didn't have the most wel-coming of facades, only large blocks of weathered limestone darkened by the morning's showers. Banks could imagine that the walls were probably about three feet thick to survive the wind and cold up here in winter. The swinging sign was so cracked and weather-beaten that he could hardly read it, though he thought it said "Low Moor Inn." The wind was howling around the moors, but though the ground was boggy, it had the advantage of being high, and much of the moisture had drained off into the system of becks and streams that crisscrossed the lower pastures and fed eventually into the Swain, now close to bursting its banks and flooding the Leas, just outside Eastvale. Up here, there were only the tangled roots of gorse and heather under a huge iron-gray sky; a few sheep wandered, bleating as they searched for anything they could find to eat in the woody undergrowth.

There were three cars outside the pub, which Banks took as a good sign. He parked beside a mud-spattered Range Rover and walked into the arched entrance. A handwritten sign said "Walkers Welcome" with an arrow pointing towards an old boot scraper beside a wooden bench and a rack for muddy boots. The creaky door opened inward. He had to stoop as he went in, but he found himself in a cozy, stone-walled room with a huge fireplace blazing away, its flames reflected in the polished horse brasses on the walls and around the bar, in the dark varnished wood and rows of colored bottles in front of the long mirror. What little lighting there was in the bar was dim, and the stone walls were decorated with gilt-framed paintings, the horse brasses and what Banks assumed to be old-fashioned farming implements. The handful of customers looked up as he entered, then seeing nothing of interest, returned to their conversations and their drinks. The barman, wearing a scuffed leather waistcoat over a collarless shirt, gave a brisk nod of greeting.

Banks hadn't known that places such as this existed anymore, as if untouched by modern times. So many pubs in the dales had closed over the past few years, or fallen into the hands of London landlords and breweries who wanted to modernize them, turn them into chain family-style pubs, and get the young crowd back in at night with large-screen football broadcasts and cheap beer. But this place was a throwback. Banks could be happy here. There was no television blaring, no music playing, only the muffled conversations around him and the fire crackling and spitting sparks in the broad stone hearth. A bundle of gray fur that was probably the landlord's dog lay curled up in front of it. The dog made no investigation of the newcomer. Banks had to look carefully to see that it was breathing.

"I'll have a pint of Sneck Lifter, please," Banks said, glancing towards the hand pump. He didn't usually drink the stronger beers and ales, but he felt that his sneck needed a bit of lifting after the session with Red Ron and Madame Gervaise. As the man poured, Banks asked if there was any chance of food.

"Hot pie in t'oven" was all the answer he got.

"What sort of pie?"

The landlord looked at him as if he were gormless. "Game pie."

"I'll have a slice of that, too, then," Banks said.

"Tha'll have to wait till it's ready."

"No problem."

"Aye." The landlord handed him his pint. Beer and foam dribbled down the glass.

"By the way," Banks asked before going to take his pick of the empty tables. "This is the Low Moor Inn, right?"

The landlord scratched his whiskers. "That's what t'sign says."

"Where's the High Moor Inn?"

Again, he got the look reserved for the village idiot as the landlord gestured behind him with his gnarled thumb. "Up there, o' course."

"Of course," said Banks and went to sit down. He decided on a small round wooden table not far from the fire. The floor was unevenly flagged, and his chair legs scraped on the stones as he pulled it out. The table was a bit wobbly, but the slip of paper summoning him to Gervaise's office, folded and stuck under one of the legs, soon took care of that. He had the latest copy of *Gramophone* magazine in his briefcase, along with a folder of Gerry Masterson's notes, so he decided he would just take a long leisurely late lunch away from it all. He also had his mobile, so if there were any developments or emergencies, he could be easily reached. Or so he thought until he checked it for messages and found out there was no reception. Maybe it was the thick stone walls.

For the moment, though, he didn't care. He was warm, he had a pint in front of him, *Gramophone* open at the review section on the table, and a piece of hot game pie was on its way. He was also a long way from the office. Despite his rebellious ways, Banks rarely found himself on the carpet. It had happened a lot with Jimmy Riddle, who had been a very hands-on chief constable a few years ago and had taken against him for some reason, but since then most of the CCs had

kept their distance and stayed out at county HQ, where they belonged, sending out press releases, opening village fetes and giving out
sound bites, leaving their assistants, like Red Ron, to do most of the
real work. He had run afoul of ACC McLaughlin once or twice, but
only in minor ways. He liked the man and had never seen him as
angry as he had been earlier. It must have been a hell of a bollocking
he had got from the CC, who, he remembered, was a good friend of
Sir Jeremy and Lady Veronica Chalmers. No doubt he called them
Jem and Ronnie.

What rankled most of all was being told to lay off, especially when
he thought he was on to something. Madame Gervaise and Red Ron
probably thought they had explained away all his suspicions and convinced him that what he thought was evidence was nothing more
than a tangle of circumstance, contradiction and coincidence, but a
real copper thrives on circumstance, contradiction and coincidence;
they are the warning signals he keeps a lookout for. OK, perhaps there
was nothing he could prove yet, but that wasn't the point. The point
was that the possible link between Lady Veronica Chalmers and Gavin
Miller was a line of inquiry worth pursuing, and Red Ron had closed
it off, like Dr. Beeching did to the old railway track where Miller's
body had been found.

Banks and his team could take as many easy shots as they liked at
the drug dealers and the college crowd, it seemed, as long as they
didn't disturb the landed gentry. But the real truth lay beyond Eastvale
College, Banks felt. In his experience, no drug dealer would leave five
thousand pounds in a dead man's pocket, even if he did think he heard
someone coming. And nobody talked for seven minutes on the telephone to someone they professed not to know, about a matter he
wasn't even connected with. Not if they had been at the same university at the same time, even if it was forty years ago. Gavin Miller had
been more cheerful the week before his death than he had in a long
time, so the few witnesses who knew him—such as the Star & Garter
staff—had said. And the phone call to Lady Chalmers had been made
almost a week before his death. Coincidence? Banks didn't think so.

So what was the connection? What was the Chalmers family holding back? And more to the point, how could Banks find out? If the

matter went back forty years, there wasn't a lot of hope, and he certainly couldn't expect any help from Lady Chalmers, even if he was allowed to talk to her. If he were to continue investigating against orders, he would have to rely on Gerry Masterson's research abilities and risk damaging her career. On the other hand, she was only following the instructions of her SIO. He had given her more or less free rein and saw no reason to curtail that since his warning. It wasn't as if she were planning on talking either to Lady Chalmers, Anthony Litton, Sir Jeremy, or to any other members of the family. If she could somehow come up with just one bona fide connection between Lady Chalmers and Gavin Miller from the Essex days, then perhaps Gervaise would reconsider and give Banks a bit more leeway. After all, he wasn't insisting that Veronica Chalmers had killed Miller, only that she knew something and might be able to help.

In the meantime, there was something he could do. The beautiful Oriana Serroni. Gerry had already dug up a bit of background on her. There was nothing incriminating, nothing to link her with Miller, though her history was certainly interesting and colorful. Her grandfather had spent most of the war as POW in a camp near Malton, in North Yorkshire. Like most of the prisoners there, he hadn't tried to escape. Life was soft and relatively safe there. Most of the POWs worked on the land, and many of them formed friendships with the local farmers—and the local farmers' daughters. After the war, like many others, Giuseppe Serroni had remained in the UK and married a local girl, Betty Garfield. They lived on her parents' farm and soon took over most of the work. They had two sons, the youngest born in 1953. Young Stefano was a restless soul, and in 1974 he left for Italy, where he wanted to explore his roots in Umbria. Time passed, and four years later, he married a local girl called Maria. The couple had several children, including a daughter they named Oriana, born in 1980. Maria wanted to escape the poverty and rural isolation of the place, so Stefano was persuaded to take her back to England with him in 1986, and his parents took them in. They visited Umbria often, though, as Maria missed her family there, and Oriana enjoyed a truly international upbringing.

As it happened, Sir Jeremy Chalmers's family was also from North

Yorkshire and had known the Serronis for years. When Veronica came into the fold, of course, Oriana was only five or six, but she was a beautiful, bright child. Ronnie and Jem soon became very fond of her, and she became a big sister, and later babysitter, to Angelina and Samantha. As she grew up, Oriana also showed remarkable academic skills, in addition to becoming a very organized and efficient researcher. After university, she drifted a little, uncertain about her career path, and that was when Veronica stepped in and suggested she work as her researcher, and perhaps also take on a few household duties, things she had already done with ease at her own family's home, such as cooking the occasional meal, organizing appointment calendars, keeping the books, and so on. Thus, Oriana became Lady Chalmers's amanuensis. As far as Gerry Masterson could ascertain, Oriana was still single and didn't appear to have a steady boyfriend.

Oriana seemed to be close to Lady Chalmers, Banks thought. He had noticed how her attitude had changed between visits, how the smile had disappeared and the frozen demeanor took its place. She was loyal to her mistress, however old-fashioned that might seem, and that was surely a good thing, but perhaps she was also *concerned* about Lady Chalmers, and perhaps Banks could exploit that concern. He thought he knew how he could go about contacting her with minimum fuss and little chance of official reprisal, though there was always the risk that Oriana might go running to Lady Chalmers, Nathan or Anthony Litton.

Interrupting his chain of thought, a short, plump red-faced woman in an apron came over and deposited a knife and fork on his table, along with an assemblage of chutneys and bottled sauces, some of the bottles without labels, indicating that they were probably homemade. There was no sign of a serviette. Moments later she returned with a plate, on which rested the largest slice of pie Banks had ever seen, surrounded by mounds of vegetables covered in steaming gravy. "Watch out for t'shot" was all she said before she waddled away. As he watched her go, Banks was reminded of the line from the old folk song, the one about "the cheeks of her arse going chuff, chuff, chuff."

Most of the game pies he had ever eaten had been cold, but this was fresh from the oven, and he had to wait a few minutes for it to cool. It was delicious, however, and he soon found out what she meant about the shot, luckily just sensing a piece of buckshot before it broke one of his teeth. He ate even more slowly and carefully after that, not wishing to precipitate a visit to the dentist. The pie was gamey, of course, but not too much so, and the pastry was light and flaky. Banks ate and drank, reading the reviews in *Gramophone* and making mental notes for his next shopping trip. He would try to talk privately with Oriana, he decided, but before then, he would try to put Lady Chalmers out of his mind and try to wrap up the Eastvale College angle.

So what next? Banks wondered when he had finished his pie. He certainly didn't feel like going back to the station. He was too full, for a start, and if he sat in his office chair he would probably doze off. He would finish his pint, he decided, then head out to Coverton, see what was happening with Doug Watson at the mobile unit, maybe have another quick stroll up to the crime scene, see if anything leaped out at him. Then home. It was a plan.

7

So what happened to you yesterday afternoon?" Annie asked Banks on their way to see Trevor Lomax. "I tried to call you."

"I was out at the crime scene. No reception," Banks said. "You didn't call back or leave a message, so it can't have been important."

"It wasn't. And there is reception at the crime scene, at least at the top of the embankment there is. I assumed you weren't answering because you didn't want to talk about it."

"Talk about what?"

"What happened with Red Ron and Madame Gervaise."

"Oh, that. What do you think happened? They warned us off."

"Off Lady Chalmers?"

Banks looked around with mock concern. "Who else has a title around here?"

Annie squinted at him from the passenger seat. "So they gave you a bollocking?"

"It wasn't a bollocking."

"Whatever. You were off sulking, weren't you? Drinking and listening to some weird music, I'll bet. Licking your wounds."

"You've got imagination, I'll give you that."

"Well? Tell me I'm wrong."

"Here we are." Banks pulled up behind the college building. "Sure he's in?"

"Sure as I can be," said Annie. "I checked with the department. He doesn't have any classes on a Friday morning. He might be seeing a student or working on Monday's lecture, but he's usually in his office."

"Right. Lead on."

Annie led Banks into the squat concrete and glass building and up the stairs to Trevor Lomax's office. The door was slightly ajar, and they heard voices from inside. Banks tapped softly and pushed the door open. Lomax was sitting at his cluttered desk; a girl sat opposite him with a clipboard resting on her lap.

"Who the hell are . . . Oh, Ms. Cabbot?" he said, smiling when he saw Annie.

"We're sorry to bother you, Trevor," Annie said. "This is my boss, DCI Banks. We'd like a quick word, if possible."

"I was just—"

"We're very busy," said Banks. Then he looked at the puzzled girl, bowed and gestured with his arm towards the open door. "If you don't mind."

Flustered, she gathered up her things and left without a backward glance.

"Was that really necessary?" Lomax asked.

"Like I said, we're busy." Banks proffered the empty chair to Annie and leaned against the wall beside the window.

"Cast your mind back to four years ago," Annie said. "Several weeks after Gavin Miller's hearing and dismissal."

"I don't—"

"Did a young woman pay you a visit and tell you she had evidence that Miller didn't do what he was accused of?"

"Why should anyone—"

"Cut the bullshit, Mr. Lomax," said Banks. "We know the whole story. It's just a technique we use. You know, feeding it out bit by bit as questions, see if you slip up anywhere. We don't ask questions to which we don't already know the answer. With you, I think we can just cut to the chase, can't we?"

"Your boss is a bit full of himself, isn't he, Ms. Cabbot?" said Lomax, smiling at Annie.

Annie didn't return his smile. "You might as well tell us the truth, Trevor. When he gets like this he's unpredictable, not to mention impossible to call off."

"Are you threatening me?"

"Not at all. I'll jog your memory a bit, see if it helps. Lisa Gray. Remember that name?"

"I remember a young woman coming to me with some cock-and-bull story."

"Now we're getting somewhere," said Annie. "How do you know it was a cock-and-bull story?"

"The board had made its decision, implemented it. It was over and done with. If anyone had any information, they should have come forward earlier, before or during the hearing. They had every chance."

"But Lisa Gray didn't know about it during the hearing," said Annie. "She only found out afterwards. Don't you remember what she told you? She overheard a conversation between Beth Gallagher and Kayleigh Vernon in the ladies' and came to tell you about it. She also told you about Gavin Miller warning Kyle McClusky off selling drugs on campus, and that was the reason Beth and Kayleigh ganged up to discredit him. The three of them were mates. Surely you remember that?"

"So she said. But it was nothing but hearsay. Pure invention. There was no proof."

"And there was proof of Miller's guilt in the first place?" Annie shook her head. "Did you question the girls again after you received this new information, ask them if it was true?"

"No. As I said, there would have been no point. I'd done everything I could for Gavin. The hearing was over, the decision had been made. The girls had already been through enough. Why put them through the trauma all over again?"

"Gee, Trevor, I don't know," said Annie. "Because a man's reputation and livelihood were at stake? A friend of yours."

"And if Beth and Kayleigh had been lying," Banks said, "as Lisa Gray claimed they were, then surely it was your duty to investigate that and find out?"

"You mistake my job for your own, Mr. Banks. It wasn't my duty to do anything of the kind. It was over and done with. I'd already done my best to stick up for Gavin, but to no avail."

"What was it your duty to do?" Annie asked. "Brush it under the carpet?"

"I resent that. Gavin Miller was a friend of mine."

Banks scratched his head. "That's what puzzles me. He was supposed to be your mate. I'd love to know how you treat your enemies."

"That was uncalled for."

"Was it?" Banks moved away from the wall, leaned forward and rested his palms on the desk. "A girl comes to you and tells you she overheard two girls who've accused a fellow employee, a friend of yours, of sexual misconduct, having a giggle about how they pulled the wool over everyone's eyes, including yours, and you do nothing. I have to ask myself why."

Lomax leaned back in his chair. "And what brilliant conclusion do you come to?"

"There are a number of possibilities," Banks said slowly. "The first one that comes to mind is that Kyle McClusky also supplied you with drugs. Perhaps you bought some roofies from him and had your way with some leggy eighteen-year-old student. Or maybe you scored a bit of speed so you could stay up all night marking essays. Maybe you were shagging Beth or Kayleigh. Obviously, Kyle knew about this, and if he went down he would make sure as hell you went with him, so it was in your best interests to keep him out of the whole affair. Gavin Miller didn't know Kyle was a pal of Beth's and Kayleigh's. As far as he was concerned, there was no connection between his warning Kyle off selling drugs, which had taken place some time before, and the accusations the girls made of sexual misconduct. But you knew, didn't you? And as only you and the Gray girl knew that she'd been to see you—or so you thought—it was a simple matter of sitting on it."

"That's absurd. You're accusing me of buying drugs from Kyle McClusky and having sex with a student? This is bordering on slander. Maybe I should call my solicitor."

"I didn't hear him say anything about sex and drugs," said Annie.

"I'm simply suggesting it as a possibility," Banks went on, "a reason why you didn't do anything with the information Lisa Gray brought to you."

"I told you. It was too late. The decision had already been made. It would have done no good to . . . to . . ."

"To what? Rake it all up again and risk the publicity? Wouldn't be good for who? For you? For the college?"

"Of course it wouldn't have been good for the college. What's wrong with that? Don't you lot all close ranks and pull together when someone attacks one of you?" He glanced sharply at Annie. "Didn't you do exactly that just now?"

"You're comparing what you did to us closing ranks?" Banks leaned back against the wall again. "Now I've heard it all. Annie, I've had enough. Perhaps you can take it from here?"

"What DCI Banks means is that the information was entrusted to you, a friend of the accused, by perhaps the only other person around here who seemed to give a damn what happened to him."

"But nobody would have listened to her," said Lomax. "To Lisa Gray. I wanted to avoid getting personal about it, but she was neurotic, a delusional, drunken trollop. She started out as an outstanding student, but she was failing her courses and going downhill fast in every way."

"What was wrong with her? Why did she change?"

Lomax shrugged. "It happens. She was probably on drugs."

"Why do you say that?"

"It's true. The girl was on the verge of expulsion herself. She was behind in her work, she'd been abusive to members of staff, she'd missed more than half of her classes and attended at least one of them while intoxicated. Imagine how well it would have gone down if we had publicized an exoneration of Miller by such a person. Not that I'm saying it *was* an exoneration. All Beth and Kayleigh would have had to do was stick to their guns."

"Beth Gallagher admitted to us that she fabricated her story."

Lomax swallowed. "She did? When?"

"Yesterday," said Annie.

"And you believe her?"

"My DS believes her," Banks said. "And that's good enough for me."

Lomax spread his hands. "Well, what can I say? If she'd admitted that at the time, maybe I could have done something, but it was too little, too late."

"Couldn't you somehow have reinstated Gavin Miller after you found out the truth?" Annie asked.

"What truth? Lisa Gray's say-so? Weeks after he'd been dismissed? I can't imagine any precedent for that sort of action. Can you? Who'd believe her? Don't forget, it's ultimately down to the government. They provide our money. We're not a private institution, you know. Besides, I thought you were investigating Gavin's murder, not his dismissal."

"Oh, we are," said Annie. She glanced towards Banks, who gave her a nod. "We just think they might be connected. How many people did you tell about Lisa's story?"

"What do you mean? Nobody. Why?"

"Not Jim Cooper, or anyone else on the board or the committee?"

"No. Why would I? Jim Cooper wasn't on the committee. Besides, I don't particularly like him, to be honest, and the board . . . well, it wasn't their concern."

"Did you tell your wife?"

"Sally and I share everything. It was she who advised me that it would be foolish to go to the board with the girl's story, that I'd be laughed off campus."

"Might your wife have told someone else? Dayle Snider, perhaps?"

"I very much doubt it. Besides, Dayle and Gavin weren't together then."

"What about Kyle McClusky dealing drugs on campus?"

"We didn't know about that, either, if he was. And he'd gone by then."

"Thanks to Gavin Miller warning him off."

"Yes, well . . . as I said, we didn't know about that. Gavin didn't see fit to tell us. What Gavin did was tantamount to a tip-off more than anything else."

"Does Jim Cooper use drugs? Did he buy from Kyle?"

"How on earth would I know? It wouldn't surprise me, the way he goes about trying to be so hip and cool all the time, but really I have no idea."

"Imagine this, Trevor," said Annie. "You reminded me that we're investigating the murder, not the dismissal. Well, consider this scenario. Somehow, four years after the events that lost him his job, Gavin Miller finds out that Lisa Gray came to you with information that might have exonerated him, and that you did nothing. Maybe she told him, or maybe he found out some other way. It doesn't matter. He confronts you about this. He's broke, and he wants money, compensation, perhaps, so he blackmails you. If you don't pay, he'll denounce you to the college authorities for some indiscretion or other that he knows about. You arrange to meet at the old railway bridge south of Coverton. It's a nice, secluded spot. Something goes wrong. Maybe he decides he'd rather have a public apology and his old job back. Whatever. You struggle and end up pushing him over the bridge. Maybe it's an accident. Maybe you didn't mean to kill him. Or maybe you couldn't afford to pay a blackmailer, so you went there intending to kill him. What kind of car do you drive?"

"This is outrageous!"

"What kind?"

"An Audi."

"What color?"

"Black."

"Someone saw you getting into your car around ten o'clock last Sunday night in Coverton car park. How does that sound, Trevor?"

"Preposterous," said Lomax. "You'll never convince anyone of that."

"Oh, we might," said Annie. "And it might just be true, mightn't it?"

"I already told you. I was at home with my wife."

"Watching *Downton Abbey*. Yes, we know. But alibis can be very fragile things, Trevor. In our experience, wives especially don't make very convincing alibis."

Annie stood up and walked toward the door. Banks followed, while Lomax remained at his desk, red-faced and spluttering.

"Cooper next?" Banks asked when they got down the stairs.

"I suppose so," sighed Annie. "But I've had enough of this place for the moment. Lunch first?"

"Good—" Banks's mobile went off. He stopped on the stairs and listened for a while, as Annie waited impatiently.

"Who was it?" she asked, when he'd finished.

"Doug Watson."

"And?"

"He's located Kyle McClusky. Seems he's a guest in HM Prison Leeds."

"MR. COOPER," called Annie. "I'm so glad I caught you before you left for the weekend." She was crossing the grassy square when she saw Cooper leaving his department with his battered briefcase in his hand and a silk scarf wrapped artistically around his neck, longish hair hanging over at the back. He looked exactly as Lomax had described him, someone pathetically trying to appear younger and more hip than he really was. He probably liked to hang out in the student bar, too, Annie thought, pretend he was one of them, and maybe, just maybe, to appear extra cool, he might like to score some coke or speed once in a while, or smoke a joint.

Banks had gone back to the station after lunch to follow up on the call they'd got about Kyle McClusky, so Annie was on her own for this one. She didn't mind. It would be a pleasure to puncture Cooper's sense of self-importance and arrogance.

"I like to get away early on a Friday," said Cooper as Annie fell into step beside him. "I don't have any classes in the afternoon, so I usually manage to get the paperwork done and slip away before three. What is it this time?"

"Oh, you know. Just a few more questions."

"I thought I'd already answered all your questions."

"We keep coming up with new ones. It's the funny thing about this job. One piece of new information comes in, and it changes the whole picture."

"And this time?"

"Well, perhaps there's somewhere we could have a quick chat?"

"Would my car do?" Cooper pointed his key ring at a red Toyota, and it beeped as the door locks opened. Annie didn't particularly fancy the idea of being enclosed in a car with Cooper, but it was a bit nippy outside, and what could happen, anyway? She was sure she could still take care of herself, despite the odd aches and pains she still suffered since the shooting. Besides, she didn't think he had the bottle to try anything.

Once they had got seated, the heater on, Annie half turned to face him and said, "It's about the Gavin Miller case."

"I thought so. Still not caught your man?"

"Or woman."

"Oh, yes. Mustn't forget. Equal opportunity murders these days. Well, how can I help you this time?"

"That's assuming you helped us last time."

"Didn't I? I'm mortified. Well, I must try to do better, mustn't I? Ask away." The faint mocking smile never left his face. It was the kind of smile that made Annie want to slap it off. Hard. "What is this new piece of information? You have me intrigued."

"We think that Gavin Miller's murder may be linked to the events of four years ago."

"That's a bit of a stretch, isn't it?"

"It was very traumatic for him. He lost his job, his living, his self-respect. It was the start of a long downward spiral."

"You don't have to tell me what it did to him. I was there, listening, lending a shoulder, not to mention a tenner or two."

"But it wasn't enough, was it?"

"Nothing ever is. I couldn't turn the clock back."

"He wanted more money, didn't he?"

"Don't we all?"

"Don't try to be clever. You know what I'm talking about. Gavin Miller was desperate for a change in his fortunes. Desperate enough to take things in his own hands and seek it. By blackmail, perhaps?"

"Gavin? You obviously didn't know him. Never. He might have been a bit of an oddball, but he wasn't a crook. Gavin was a gentle soul, angry and bitter though he was. He would no more have blackmailed someone than he would have hurt them."

"People change," said Annie. "Sometimes circumstances drive them to it. What do you think of Trevor Lomax?"

"Lomax. He's a competent enough department head, but there's not a great deal of energy or sense of innovation about him. He's about as exciting as a wet Sunday in November."

"Shortly after Gavin Miller was fired, a student overheard Beth and Kayleigh boasting in the ladies' about how they'd pulled the wool over everyone's eyes about Miller. What do you think about that?"

"First I've heard of it. Did she tell anyone?"

"Trevor Lomax."

"And?"

"That's as far as it went."

"The bastard."

"Why do you say that?"

"Well, it could have helped Gavin, couldn't it? Lomax was also supposed to be his friend. I didn't know anything about this."

"Trevor Lomax said it was too late, and he didn't believe the source."

"Who was it?"

"I can't tell you that."

"Then I can't really help you. Why didn't Gavin tell me about it, or make a fuss himself at the time?"

"He never knew about it."

"Trevor didn't tell him?"

"No. He thought it would only upset him more, as it clearly wasn't going to go towards getting him his job back."

"It all sounds like a bit of a mess, doesn't it?"

"It does. I think a lot of the people involved were going through hard times. Drugs were involved, and we still think they may be involved with Gavin Miller's death. Did you know anyone called Kyle McClusky?"

"Kyle McClusky? The name is vaguely familiar. Is he a student?"

"Was. He hung around with Beth and Kayleigh. Gavin Miller warned him off selling drugs around campus, and he dropped out. He blamed Gavin for all his woes."

"That's right. Gavin did mention someone called Kyle dealing drugs. One of his students. I suggested he have a quiet word, and maybe he'd disappear before we had to bring in the authorities. Is that what happened?"

"Yes."

"But? I can see a 'but' coming."

"But he enlisted Beth and Kayleigh to help him get his revenge. They thought it sounded like fun."

"So that's why they . . . ?"

"Yes. There's no evidence either way, of course, but there never was in the first place."

"But this means that Gavin was telling the truth, doesn't it? That he didn't do it." Cooper surprised Annie by putting his face in his hands and sighing deeply. "My God, poor Gavin. I'm so sorry. I should have done more."

"You really didn't know about any of this?"

"No. On my word. Do you think I would ever have advised him just to give that dealer a warning if I'd known how it would all turn out? I'd have said to bring in the police right away."

"Life is full of what-ifs," said Annie. "There's no point dwelling on them. You never bought any drugs from Kyle McClusky?"

"I didn't even know him. And me? Drugs? What do you take me for?"

Despite herself, Annie actually found herself inclined to believe him. "You didn't know it was a setup. Gavin didn't know. As far as we can gather, apart from the girls themselves, and Kyle, of course, the only people who knew were Trevor Lomax and the person who told him."

"And this person who told Lomax was the one who overheard Beth and Kayleigh talking about what they'd done?"

"Yes. Three weeks or so after Gavin Miller was fired."

"God, this is awful. But why would they be talking about it so long afterwards?"

"I have no idea. That's a good point."

"Neither Lomax nor his informant told anyone else?"

"Lomax told his wife. That's all. Lomax said it was too late, and that the source was untrustworthy."

"But he didn't even try." Cooper shook his head slowly. His earring dangled. "That's Lomax all over. Why shake things up when every-thing's running on an even keel? The bastard. I'll bet that wife of his helped him make up his mind. The Snider woman, too, I wouldn't be surprised."

"Why do you say that?"

"It's obvious, isn't it? Sally Lomax only thought about her husband's career, and Dayle Snider had history with Gav. Bad history."

"Point taken. Look, I'm sorry this all came as such a shock to you," Annie said. She handed him her card. "But if you do think of any-thing that might help us, you'll let me know, won't you?"

Cooper held her gaze with his and nodded. His eyes were damp. "I will," he said. "I certainly will."

AFTER MAKING arrangements to go to Armley Jail, as HM Prison Leeds was commonly known, to talk to Kyle McClusky on Monday, Banks had picked up the disk of scanned photos from the lab towards the end of Friday afternoon and got Gerry Masterson to print them off for him. She and Winsome had just got back from talking to Kayleigh Vernon in Salford, and they had found out nothing. Unlike Beth, Kayleigh still vehemently denied making up her accusations against Gavin Miller, said she had nothing to do with drugs and had not been in touch with anyone from the old college days in years. She said she had been working at the time of Miller's murder, and her alibi checked out, as had Beth's. Winsome had also taken a little time to check up on Lisa Gray's alibi, and that checked out, too, providing that her friends were telling the truth, which was always a caveat in such mat-ters. If they found any other evidence pointing to Lisa, they'd bring in the friends and give them a more comprehensive grilling. For the moment, though, it appeared that Beth, Kayleigh and Lisa could be ruled out as suspects based on their alibis.

Now he sat in his conservatory, sipping red wine, listening to Van Morrison's *Saint Dominic's Preview* and examining the photos for the second time. It was the weekend, and the investigation would scale down a bit over the next couple of days. The rain had stopped, and the weather seemed to have settled down to a sort of dull uniform gray, with occasional periods of drizzle. The remains of the pizza he had picked up on his way home still sat on the glass-topped table.

After separating out the pure landscapes and cityscapes, Banks pored over the group shots, some of which clearly featured a younger Miller, without beard and with a thicker head of fair hair, still worn long, fuller in the face. He had already asked Gerry to crop and print enhanced versions showing Miller alone, then to make several copies and distribute them among the team. Though the photographs had been taken in the late eighties, by the looks of them, outside a college of some description, they might come in useful when Gerry was trying to refresh people's memories about Essex in the early seventies. Certainly no one from back then would recognize Gavin Miller from the more recent photograph.

The earliest photographs had clearly been taken at the Isle of Wight pop festival in 1970. Some of them showed the stage below, to the left, and the vast crowd stretching as far as the lens could see. It was impossible to make out who was playing, of course, but Banks recognized that the photos had been taken from the tent city that sprang up on "Desolation Hill," where he had spent part of the festival with his girlfriend of the time, Kay Summerville. The rest of the time at the Isle of Wight they had been in the thick of the crowd, closer to the stage. The Who, the Doors, Miles Davis, Joan Baez, Joni Mitchell, Leonard Cohen, Jimi Hendrix. They hadn't slept for three nights. After the festival, they had pitched their tent on a clifftop near Ventnor for a few days and done nothing but make love, stare out to sea and go to the pub.

The early seventies had been Banks's own brief period of freedom between school and the police, then marriage and children. He sometimes regretted that he hadn't simply flown the coop and gone on the road for a while after his time at London Polytechnic. It wasn't so much that he regretted what he *had* done with his life, but he sometimes regretted what he *hadn't* done. Sometimes it seemed that one life wasn't enough. He wanted to live parallel lives. Do it all. The brief taste of freedom he had enjoyed in the Powys Terrace flat hadn't amounted to a great deal, but it had been a lot of fun. He'd had no interest in drugs, but he went to a lot of gigs and met plenty of girls. He remembered the excitement of the music. Some of Banks's favorite albums were from this period: Van Morrison's *Moondance, The Who Live at Leeds,* Neil Young's *After the Gold Rush.* Then came the new crowd, with Bowie, Roxy Music, King Crimson and T. Rex leading the way. Heady times, indeed.

It was almost ten thirty when his mobile rang. Thinking it might be Brian, on the road, he answered quickly. At first he heard only a faint voice on the other end, sounding more like a whisper.

"Hello," he said. "Can you speak up a bit? I can't hear you very well." Perhaps the music was a bit too loud, but Banks didn't want to go to the entertainment room and turn it down.

"It's me, Ronnie," the voice said.

"Ronnie?" For a moment, Banks was puzzled. He didn't know any Ronnies. Then it dawned on him. "Lady Chalmers?"

"Please. Just Ronnie. Forget about the lady."

But that was as difficult as before; her voice was still posh, even though she sounded the slightest bit tipsy. "Where are you?" he asked.

"In London. In a hotel. Jem's out with his luvvie pals at the Ivy, no doubt downing cognac and telling stories about Larry and Dickie. I'm watching TV and having a little drink, myself. Drinking alone. Isn't that terrible of me?"

Banks looked at the glass in his hand. "Why didn't you go with him?"

"Those evenings bore me. Besides, I'm not feeling very sociable tonight."

"You shouldn't be calling," Banks said. "I'm not supposed to be talking to you."

"Is that Van Morrison I can hear in the background? 'Listen to the Lion'?"

"Yes," said Banks.

There was a pause. "I love Van Morrison. That was always one of my favorites, *Saint Dominic's Preview.* And *Veedon Fleece.* I always wondered what a veedon fleece was, didn't you?"

"Why are you calling me, Lady Chalmers? Has something happened I should know about?"

"I told you, it's Ronnie. No, nothing's happened. I'm just calling to apologize. I feel bad about it."

"For what?"

"Did you get into trouble? You did, didn't you?"

"When?"

"After you came to see me with your colleague. Annie, isn't it? When Ralph and Tony were there."

Banks was still smarting from the unpleasant half hour he had spent with Red Ron and Madame Gervaise. "Maybe a little," he said. "Probably no more than I deserved. It's not your fault."

"But I feel responsible. You didn't deserve it. I mean, I'm sorry. I didn't mean for anything like that to happen."

"You don't have to apologize to me. If you think I was out of line—"

"No. It's not that. It wasn't me."

"What do you mean?"

The silence on the other end lasted just long enough to make him think Lady Chalmers had fallen asleep or dropped the phone on the bed, but then she came back on the line again. Van Morrison was still singing about the lion inside him. Banks was wondering where she had got his number, but then he remembered he had given her his card. "It was Tony," she said. "My brother-in-law. Jem was away, so I rang Tony and told him you'd been to talk to me and were coming back again. I told him I needed some support. Tony drove straight up from Derbyshire and said it would be a good idea to have our solicitor there, too. After you'd left the second time, Tony rang your chief constable and reported the conversation. I just want to say that I'm sorry. I didn't mean for all that to happen. I'm not really that sort of person. You were only doing your job. But I haven't done anything wrong. I don't know why you're picking on me. Is there some reason you don't like me?"

"I'm not picking on you, and I don't dislike you. And I appreciate the apology, but there's really no need for it. These things happen."

"Especially when you're still a little bit of a rebel? I know. But even so . . . I don't tell tales out of school. I just wanted you to know that. I just wanted someone on my side, that's all. I'm not a tattle-tittle."

"Tittle-tattle."

"Whatever."

"Well, I appreciate it," said Banks. "But don't worry. You won't have to deal with me again."

"I'm sorry to hear that. I thought we might actually have quite a bit in common. You like Van Morrison, for a start. In another time, under different circumstances, perhaps we could be friends."

"Good night, Lady Chalmers. And thanks for calling."

"Ronnie, please. Good night. Enjoy the rest of the music."

And the line went dead.

Banks reached for his glass and took another sip of wine. What the hell was all that about, he wondered? Was she flirting? It sounded like it. She was certainly apologizing when she didn't need to. Maybe she was trying to ingratiate herself to him. He had thought she had been lying to him when he questioned her about Gavin Miller, and he had been just as sure that it was her who had set the brass on him. Perhaps he was wrong. Anthony Litton seemed like the sort of man who was used to exerting influence where it counted. After all, there was a cabinet reshuffle coming in just under a week, and his son Oliver's name was on everyone's lips as the possible new home secretary. On the other hand, maybe Lady Chalmers had just had a few drinks too many, her husband had left her alone, or they'd had a row or something, so she'd phoned out of boredom or annoyance. But why him? It still didn't make sense. Was she trying to tell him something? There had been something in her tone that could have been fear, or anxiety. Was she worried about something? In danger, even? Had he been rude? He thought he had.

For one mad moment, he thought of calling her back, the phone in his hand, then he decided against it. If any word of this got back to Gervaise, he would be in serious trouble. That wouldn't necessarily bother him if he thought it was worth it, but in this case he wasn't at all sure. Perhaps there was more to Miller's phone call than she had admitted, for reasons he didn't understand, but perhaps also the call had nothing to do with Miller's murder. Perhaps, as Red Ron and Madame Gervaise had suggested, the murder was more to do with drugs or the college scandal.

And why had Anthony Litton dashed all the way up from Derbyshire? To intimidate the police? A family closing ranks? Lady Chalmers was his sister-in-law, of course, and she had told him she needed his support, but it all seemed a bit melodramatic. Why had

Litton insisted on the lawyer's presence, and why had he complained about Banks to the chief constable afterwards? It was tale telling of the worst kind.

The more Banks thought about the last interview with Lady Chalmers, the more he felt that neither he nor Annie had crossed any lines. It had all been polite and aboveboard, trying to clear up some confusing contradictions. So why the overreaction?

Sir Jeremy had been in New York when the murder occurred, but, like Lady Chalmers, he was resourceful, and he wouldn't necessarily dirty his own hands with such a distasteful act. Could he have had something to do with it? Would a theatrical producer know where to find a hired killer? Maybe in New York he would. And was Lady Chalmers unsuspecting, worried, perhaps even a little frightened by the events going on around her?

Well, he might never know the answers, he realized, as he stood up to refill his glass in the kitchen and put on another CD in the entertainment room. This time he chose *Veedon Fleece*. Like Lady Chalmers—Ronnie—Banks had always wondered what a veedon fleece was, too.

8

I DON'T LIKE ALL THIS SNEAKING AROUND, SIR," SAID Gerry Masterson over tea and toasted tea cakes in the Golden Grill. "It makes me nervous."

"Gerry, you don't have to do it if it makes you uncomfortable. Honestly. You can bow out anytime you like, and there'll be nothing said."

Then Gerry smiled. "I don't dislike it all *that* much," she said. "I just worry sometimes what'll happen if we get caught. It's bound to happen."

"We'll cross that bridge when we get to it," said Banks. "For now, what did you find out over the weekend?"

"You asked me to check whether Lady Chalmers was involved with Eastvale College at all, and the answer's no. Also, I can't find any connections between Gavin, or anyone else involved in the case, and Sir Jeremy. It doesn't mean there's nothing there, of course, but nothing leaps out."

"It was a long shot, anyway," said Banks. "It vaguely crossed my mind the other day that Sir Jeremy might have something to do with it, but I doubt it very much. Anything else?"

"I managed to get in touch with Gavin Miller's ex-wife. She's called Roxanne Oulton now, and she lives in Christchurch."

"Have anything to say?"

"Not much. She hasn't been back over here since she married her second husband."

"The plumber?"

"Yes. She admits that her marriage to Gavin came to a nasty end, and Gavin felt betrayed. She felt guilty about having the affair, but she said it was the only way she could get free of him."

"I can understand that," said Banks. "Sometimes people need someone else to go to when a relationship ends, to help get them out of it. It doesn't always last, though."

"Well, this one seems to be lasting. Anyway, Gavin and Roxanne didn't exactly part on the best of terms, and she spent most of the phone call telling me how useless and self-centered Gavin was."

"Sounds like a typical ex-wife's complaint," said Banks. "Did she know anything about his university days? Canada? Lady Chalmers?"

"No. They didn't meet until later, when he was teaching in Exeter, and apparently he wasn't so obsessed with the past back then."

"What about the university? Get anything from them?"

"It wasn't easy. Most of the staff aren't there, of course. Some people still have the concept of weekends off, you know."

"I vaguely remember," said Banks, smiling in sympathy.

"Anyway, I managed to get the class lists before end of play on Friday, and I've been going through them, trying to contact anyone who might have had classes with Veronica Bellamy or Gavin Miller back then."

"Any luck?"

"It's a long job. First you've got to track them down, then you've got to catch them in. Remember, it was forty years ago, and there are quite a few people on the lists. Some are dead, some have moved away, left the country. Someone did tell me that he thought that Ronnie Bellamy was a mover and shaker in the Marxist Society."

"Do we know if Gavin Miller was involved in that, too?"

"Nothing so far."

"Pity. I was thinking maybe they were both recruited by Moscow as sleepers, and that's why Lady Chalmers was so disturbed by Miller's phone call and his murder."

Gerry laughed. "Really, sir?"

"Yes. He gave her the password that was deeply implanted in her brain, the one that activated her." Banks shrugged. "It was worth a try."

"Well, I did also manage to get through to someone who was sure that Veronica Bellamy lived in one of the student residences, a place called Rayleigh Tower, at least during her first year. I should be able to get through to student accommodation, and perhaps get copies of the old Marxist Society lists today, and they might have some records. After all, it's not a very old university, and you'd think they'd want to keep a record right from the start. I should be able to find someone who was in the same residence at the same time as her."

"It's possible. How will that help us?"

"If Veronica Bellamy lived in a student residence, which it appears she did, then I can also check Gavin Miller and see if he was in the same building, or nearby, for a start. Then I can find out who else was living there and get in touch with them to see if they remember anything and are willing to talk about it. A neighbor might remember more about her than someone who merely went to lectures with her. Same with the Marxist Society, if there still is one, and if its members don't see giving out any information to the police as consorting with the capitalist oppressors. But the written records won't tell us much. They're just the bare bones. The real story has to come from people who knew Ronnie Bellamy or Gavin Miller, preferably their friends. It's all a matter of memory. We need to find someone who can place Veronica and Miller together back then in one way or another."

"Can you do all this on the quiet?"

"I can do my best, sir, as long as the AC doesn't come poking around in the squad room. I think DI Cabbot and DS Jackman are going to be out of the office questioning people most of the day."

"OK," said Banks, finishing off his tea cake. "Do your best, and keep your head down. I'll be out all day, but get in touch if you find out anything interesting."

"WHAT DO you want this time?" asked Dayle Snider, when she opened her front door to Annie and Winsome later that morning. "It's supposed to be my day off."

"So they told us at the center," said Annie. "Mind if we come in?"

"Do I have a choice?"

"There's always a choice," said Annie, following her into the hall.

Dayle was wearing a close-fitting tracksuit with a white stripe down the trouser legs and trainers with blue markings. Her brow seemed a little clammy, as if she had been working out. Almost as if she had intuited Annie's line of thought, she said, "Yes, you did disturb me, actually. I was on the treadmill."

"Never understood the point of those things," said Annie. "Not when you've got such beautiful countryside all around you, in all directions."

"Have you checked the weather lately, Detective Inspector Cabbot?"

"It's a fine morning for a long walk."

"For once." She led them into a bright, compact kitchen that looked over the dale to the west, its steeply rising valley sides crisscrossed with drystone walls, slopes deep green from the summer's rains rising to rocky outcrops and long scars of limestone, silver-gray in the pale November sun. The Leaview Estate, at the bottom of King Street, southwest of the town center, had been built just after the war and was starting to show it a little around the edges. Nonetheless, its elegant mix of Georgian semis, terraces and detached houses, built of limestone and gritstone, in harmony with much of the rest of Eastvale, was still one of the most desirable middle-class residential areas in town. All the streets were named after flowers, and Dayle Snider lived on Laburnum Close. The neighborhood was certainly posh enough that it was attractive to burglars, but the police patrolled regularly and discreetly, and didn't consign it to the same rubbish heap as they had the East Side Estate, on the other side of town, where PCSOs often feared to tread, and Crime Reduction teams spent their time telling parents how to lock their doors properly while their children were out burgling houses down the street.

"I suppose you'd like some tea?" Dayle asked.

"That would be nice," said Annie.

Winsome nodded. "Me, too, please."

Dayle made a show of reluctantly filling the kettle and plugging it in, then emptying the teapot and searching for another teabag. York-shire Gold, Annie noticed. Her favorite. Dayle leaned against the counter while the kettle came to a boil. The tracksuit flattered her figure, Annie thought, showing her firm thighs and flat stomach to advantage. It made her realize that she needed to step up her exercise regime herself, if she hoped to get beyond all the aches and pains of her residual injuries and lose those few pounds she had gained over the past year or so. It was a matter of striking a balance between rest and exercise, and she hadn't quite got it right yet.

While the tea was brewing, Dayle got down three bright yellow mugs from the cupboard over the counter area and set them in a row, a little jug of milk and bowl of sugar next to them. Annie and Win-some sat at the breakfast table by the window, gazing out at the view, Annie wondering whether the massing of gray clouds in the far west meant more rain later. If their silence made Dayle nervous, she wasn't showing it.

"OK, so what is it this time?" Dayle said as she delivered the mugs of tea and took her seat at the table.

"It's really just a little point you might be able to help us clear up," said Annie.

Dayle blew on the surface of her tea. "I'll do my best."

"You're a friend of Sally Lomax's, right?"

"Yes. We work together."

"How close are you?"

"Sally's a very good friend. I mean, we socialize outside work, go for a drink now and then, and so on, as friends do."

"And she brought you together with Gavin Miller for dinner at her house. Am I right?"

"Yes. But you already know that."

"And though you and Miller got on OK for a while, the relation-ship didn't take?"

"No."

"So you ditched him."

"What is this? I've already told you all about that."

"Please bear with us, Dayle."

Dayle frowned. Whether it was at the use of her first name or at

being asked to bear with them, Annie wasn't certain. "Now, around
the time Gavin Miller had been accused of sexual misconduct, he
came to see you here, drunk, you said, and started to pour out his feelings of being an innocent person victimized and demonized."

"Right."

"But you didn't believe him."

"There's no smoke without fire."

"And you also had firsthand examples of his awkward sexuality and
his apparent inability to handle normal relationships."

"You could say that."

Annie sipped some tea. It was a bit weak. She liked to use two tea-
bags steeped in the pot for seven minutes. A blackbird perched on the
wall at the back and sang. Such a beautiful song for such a common
and underappreciated bird, she thought. "In fact, you considered it
quite believable that he might try to bully or blackmail some poor
defenseless young student into having sex with him."

Dayle paused. "Well, I wouldn't put it quite like that, but it certainly wouldn't have surprised me, no."

"Did Gavin Miller know you felt that way about him?"

"Of course not. Why would I tell him that?"

"Even when he came to see you?"

"No. I tried to listen patiently. I made all the right noises and got
rid of him as quickly as I could."

"He wasn't angry with you?"

"He had no reason to be."

"And you never saw him again?"

"No."

Winsome turned a page in her notebook, and Dayle glanced over at
her. "What's this all about? Would you please get to the point?"

Winsome glanced at Annie, who went on, "Did you have a conversation, or a series of conversations, with Sally Lomax several weeks
after Gavin Miller came to see you?"

"I've had many conversations with Sally. I told you. We're friends."

"Yes, but this one was specifically to do with Gavin Miller and his
problems. Someone had been to see Trevor Lomax at the college.
Someone who told him that she had overheard the two girls who ac-

cused Gavin Miller talking in the ladies', and that they had admitted they set him up. Do you remember that?"

Dayle averted her eyes. "Vaguely. Why? What does it matter now?"

"Did Sally Lomax seek your opinion on the subject?"

"She may have done. We often discussed things. It's what friends do."

"Personal things?"

"All sorts of things."

"Did she tell you that her husband was in a bit of a quandary? He was a friend of Gavin Miller's, and he wanted to help him, but he didn't trust the girl who came to see him with the information, and he thought she might be making the whole thing up."

"That's more or less what Sally said, yes."

"And that it was also too late to do anything, anyway, and that trying to do something might cause a hell of a stink and drag the college into some nasty publicity, something they had managed to avoid thus far?"

"She may have mentioned that. Sally is very committed to Trevor's career."

"Is Trevor ambitious?"

"I suppose you could say he is."

"And Sally?"

Dayle thought for a moment, cradling her mug. "She likes her job, but I wouldn't say she was ambitious. She's more than happy to follow along behind Trevor's coattails, be the belle of the department Christmas party. Sally's a very attractive woman."

"So her ambitions are for her husband?"

"Sally's no Lady Macbeth."

"Sorry, that's not what I meant. Interesting point, though. Look at all the bodies in that play."

"Are you suggesting that Gavin's murder four years later has anything to do with some misguided plot of Trevor's to take power?"

"Not at all. How could it have? Gavin Miller had no power. Trevor Lomax was his boss. Besides, what would be the next step for him? Dean? Vice-chancellor? I don't know much about the college hierarchy."

"Clearly. Then . . . ?"

"Well, whatever it is, he hasn't got there. He's in exactly the same position as he was four years ago. Department head. What I'm asking is what you advised Sally Lomax to tell him."

"I don't know what you mean."

"A woman whose ambitions are mostly for her husband's success tends to have a great deal more power and influence over him than we'd imagine. She has to, in order to maneuver him into making the right decisions, the ones that benefit his career, and therefore her, the most."

"This is all a bit too Machiavellian for me."

"Did Sally seek your advice?"

"She asked me what I thought about it all, yes."

"And what did you tell her?"

"That Gavin probably put the girl up to it, making up some story about overhearing them."

"Would it surprise you to hear that Gavin had never heard anything about the matter, or at least so we believe? That it never went any further than Trevor Lomax's office?"

"I can't say as I've ever really given it much thought."

"You should," Annie said. "You see, based on your experience with Gavin, you told Sally to ignore what the girl said, that he'd most likely done it, and that no good would be served by trying to open another inquiry on the basis of one student's say-so. That it would only cause problems for Trevor, and possibly harm his future career prospects. Am I at all close?"

Dayle's lips drew tight, and her expression darkened a little. She put her mug down and folded her arms. "So what if I did? It's true, isn't it? No one ever comes out of these things smelling of roses."

"Well, Gavin Miller certainly didn't."

"Gavin, Gavin, Gavin. I'm sick of hearing about poor bloody Gavin. Other people have worked hard for what they've got, you know. I don't see why we should all waste our time helping some bloody loser to get reinstated for something he probably did anyway. Making him out to be some sort of victim we should all feel sorry for. Believe me, coercing a student was probably the only way Gavin Miller could have got laid."

"Except with you," said Annie. "And he'd already failed that test, hadn't he? Did that make you feel angry and rejected, Dayle, that he didn't fancy you enough to shag you? What did you do wrong? Come on a bit too strong with him? A touch of the *Fifty Shades*, was it? Bring out the whips and chains?"

Dayle stood up abruptly. "That's it, you nasty little bitch. I've had enough. I let you into my home, and you sit there and insult me. I don't have to listen to any more of this. You can get out now. Both of you. Go on. Get out!"

"Oh, sit down, Dayle," said Annie. She could see that Winsome was on the verge of leaving but gestured for her to remain seated. "We're not going anywhere until we've got what we want."

"I'll make an official complaint to your boss."

"Go ahead. It wouldn't be the first time."

Slowly, Dayle subsided back into her chair like a deflating doll. "You can't talk to me like that."

"Sorry," said Annie. "Really. It's just that shock tactics sometimes get us where we want to go much faster than being nice. Save a lot of time."

"And where is it you want to go?"

"I want to establish that when someone went to tell Trevor Lomax what she had overheard in the ladies', Lomax was close to believing her and close to trying to find some way of exonerating Gavin Miller. But that you persuaded Sally Lomax that Miller was not worth her husband's putting his career on the line for and that Miller probably did what he was accused of, anyway."

"OK, so that's what I thought. That's what I said. What of it? I'm entitled to my opinion, aren't I?"

"And Sally Lomax, fortified with your agreement to what she was already inclined towards thinking herself, managed to persuade her husband to do nothing."

"Most likely. But what does it matter now?"

The blackbird had stopped singing and moved on, Annie noticed. The rain clouds had moved closer, and their shadows were hastening over the green valley sides. "Well, it only matters," she said slowly, "if Gavin Miller somehow found out about it all a couple of weeks ago."

The silence stretched as Dayle took in the implications of Annie's statement and worked out what they meant. Annie could watch the process in her expression, the shadows flitting across her features like the clouds over the hills. "Are you saying you think this is why he was murdered?" she said finally.

"I'm saying it's a possibility. Think about it, Dayle. Four years ago you manage to help talk a man's friend out of possibly saving that man's career, or at least his name. I'd say there could be enough anger and recrimination in all that to supply a pretty strong motive, wouldn't you? Perhaps even blackmail was involved. We don't know. But say Gavin Miller *did* find out that you were instrumental in Lomax's decision not to help, and that he blamed you just as much, if not more than, Lomax himself."

"But that's ridiculous. That would make *him* want to murder *me*. He was the one who got killed."

"Maybe he arranged to meet you on the bridge. Maybe he'd asked you for money, and maybe he did intend to kill you, but when things got out of hand, and you lost your temper first, you got the better of him, chucked him over the bridge. He was pretty skinny and weak. Malnutrition will do that. You're strong enough to have lifted him over the edge. But it could have been self-defense. Manslaughter at the most. Probably was."

Dayle stood up again and her chair fell over. "Right. That's it. No more messing about." She pointed towards the door. "Out! Both of you. And don't come back. If you do, I promise you I'll have my solicitor here before you can even sit down."

"We'd better make sure it's not a Friday afternoon, hadn't we then, Winsome?" Annie said, standing to leave. "Odds are he won't appreciate being called off the golf course. TTFN."

BANKS HAD arranged his chat with Kyle McClusky for late Monday afternoon, after which he was having dinner with Ken Blackstone in Leeds. Before that, he had other plans, about which he had told no one. He knew that he had been warned off Lady Chalmers and her family, but Oriana Serroni wasn't exactly a family member. Technically, of course, he would be on the carpet again if anyone found he had talked to her, so he was depending very much on her discretion, as well as her concern for her mistress. Of course, it might all blow up in his face, but nothing happened if you just sat on your arse and waited for it. Sometimes you had to stir things up, *make* things happen.

He found the care home outside Malton easily enough. It was a grand old mansion converted into individual suites. Expensive, no doubt, but with her connections, Oriana could afford it. The dull weather that had started on the weekend seemed to have settled in, Banks thought as he parked across the street and read the morning paper while he waited. At least the rain had stopped, and the temperature was comfortably into double figures.

He had waited a little more than an hour and was struggling to finish the crossword when Oriana walked out, bade farewell to a white-uniformed nurse and headed towards her cream Mini. Quickly, Banks stepped out of his Porsche and headed across the street. He got to her before she could open the door, and said simply, "Oriana. I wonder if we could talk?"

A range of emotions seemed to cross her face in quick succession, most of them negative. Finally, she seemed confused and uncertain how to respond, then her whole body seemed to relax, and she nodded. "You're checking up on me, are you? Very well. But I'll talk to you for her, not for you. And I'll divulge no family secrets."

"Understood," said Banks. "Can I buy you lunch?"

Oriana managed a little smile. "There's a nice pub about two miles away," she said. "Follow me."

She drove fast, and Banks wondered whether she was trying to lose him or just impress him. Two miles of winding road later, she turned into a pub car park, and Banks followed her.

The dining area was fairly full, and they raised a few eyebrows walking in, the young exotic beauty and the slightly graying detective. They found a table by the window and sat. Banks had to credit Oriana with good taste. It wasn't a chain pub, the tables had no little brass plates with numbers on them or oversized laminated menus stuck between the salt and pepper and the ketchup bottle. This was a class place. In moments, a waiter was at their side with tasteful menus bound in imitation leather, printed in italics. Banks had to take out his cheap Boots glasses to read it. Oriana didn't. Her big brown eyes were just fine by themselves. Banks examined her surreptitiously as they both made their decisions. He wondered if she had ever worked as a model, or onstage; she certainly had the carriage and the figure for it, and she dressed well, even casually, soft kid's leather jacket, simple white top, jeans. Her hair hung dark and straight, its natural luster catching the light when she moved. As she concentrated on the menu she nipped her lower lip between her teeth.

Banks expected her to go for a salad, but she chose the confit of duck with dauphinoise potatoes. Banks decided on steak frites, the steak medium rare.

"Drinks?" asked the waiter, after he had taken their orders.

Normally, in a pub, Banks would have ordered beer, but this place seemed more like a posh restaurant, and he was having steak, so he asked about red wine by the glass and settled for a Rioja recommended by the waiter. Oriana asked for the same, so the waiter brought a half carafe. "We shouldn't be over the limit if this is all we have," said Banks.

Oriana smiled. "You're the policeman. I am in your hands entirely."

"I noticed you didn't seem too pleased the other day when I turned up at Brierley for the second time," Banks said.

Oriana frowned. "There was a bad feeling around the place. I don't like that. Ronnie was worried. It makes for a bad atmosphere. Perhaps I blamed you a little bit. But I . . ."

"What?"

"Nothing."

"You call her Ronnie? I noticed that the other day."

"Of course. Why not?"

"I thought you worked for her, that's all."

"I do. But our families are old friends. We don't stand on formality."

"I know a little bit about your history," Banks said.

She cocked her head to one side. "You *have* been checking up on me."

"No, nothing as serious as that. Just a little background research. How is your grandfather, by the way?"

Her brow furrowed. "It can't be long now," she said. "Have you ever wished for something to happen, yet hoped that it never would, with every fiber of your being? That's how I feel about him. Mostly he's not my grandfather anymore, but sometimes he is. Mostly he remembers no one, and he is so frightened by everything, then sometimes he'll smile and say my name, and it makes my heart melt." Tears came to her eyes. "I'm sorry."

"No, not at all. Alzheimer's?"

She gave a little shudder. "I hope that never happens to me. I hope someone would kill me first."

"Maybe that's not the sort of thing you should be saying to me," said Banks.

They both laughed; it broke the tension and dispelled some of her sadness.

The waiter appeared with their drinks and a plate of crusty bread with olive oil and balsamic vinegar for dipping. Banks didn't like either, so he left it well alone. The waiter then poured the wine from the carafe into their glasses and slipped away.

"I understand that your families have had a very long relationship," Banks said. "And, believe me, I really haven't been spying on you, and I wouldn't want you to betray any confidences in any way. I just got the impression that you were perhaps as concerned about Lady Chalmers as you were angry at my reappearance."

"Any anger was because of the upset it caused. I mean, it wasn't you. And that man Nathan. I don't like him."

Like a fool, Banks asked why, and the look she gave him told him everything he needed to know about Nathan. It should have been obvious; Oriana was young and beautiful, Nathan was young and full of himself. Blushing a little at his lack of insight, he picked up his wineglass. They clinked and made a quick toast, then he moved on.

"And Anthony Litton?"

"Oh, Tony's all right, I suppose," she said. "I've known him for a long time. I don't think I'm giving away any family secrets when I say I think he's a bit of a pompous arse, not to mention a bit of a bully. He's used to giving the orders and getting his own way. But you'd expect that of a Harley Street specialist, wouldn't you? I'm certainly glad I'm not one of his patients, though I understand he's a very good doctor."

"I gather he's still practicing."

"Only part of the time. He keeps his surgery, and he has other doctors who work with him. He goes down to London regularly and, of course, he keeps the most prestigious, wealthy and famous patients for himself."

Banks laughed. "How long have you worked for Lady Chalmers?"

Oriana arched an exquisitely plucked eyebrow. "You don't know? I thought you knew everything about me."

Banks smiled. "I'm sure it's in the file somewhere."

"Just over ten years," Oriana answered. "Since shortly after I left university."

"And you live at Brierley House?"

"Yes. I didn't always. I had a flat in York for a while. But I do for the moment. It suits us all very well."

"You're mainly a researcher, am I right?"

"Yes. I do the research for Ronnie's books. I enjoy it, and she doesn't. I also organize her schedule, drive her to book signings and other promotional events. And I accompany her on overseas book tours. Australia. South Africa. The USA. Canada. Also various cities around Europe, places where there are book fairs and festivals and so on. She's translated into nearly thirty languages, you know."

"A busy life. It's a wonder she gets any time to write."

"It can be. But I enjoy it. I find travel very stimulating."

"Do you also act as her literary agent?"

"No. That would be too much. Her agent is in London."

"What about the housekeeping?"

Oriana laughed. It was a charming, musical sound. "I'm not a housemaid, if that's what you're thinking," she said. "Can you picture me on my knees scrubbing the kitchen floor?"

"Not exactly, no."

"I answer the door if I'm at home and not otherwise occupied. Ronnie doesn't like to be disturbed when she's working. It breaks her rhythm. I do some of the cooking because I love to cook. It's a passion of mine. That's all. My mother was an excellent cook, and she taught me all she knew."

"In Italy?"

"Yes. In Umbria. You know the region?"

"Just a little. I've been to Perugia and Assisi. It's a very beautiful area."

"Yes."

"Why did your family leave Umbria?"

"There wasn't much for them there. My father was not a natural man of the soil, like my grandfather, and he wasn't interested in wine making. He tried for some years, when I was still a child, but he wanted a city career, so he came back here to go to university. In Hull. And my mother wanted more from life, too. She had grown up country poor, and she saw her chance, I think, in my father's connections with England. Also, I think my father had found his roots in Italy, and he decided he preferred the ones he had in England, but in a way my mother never left home. Living in the countryside is very beautiful, and easy to remember through rose-colored glasses, but it is also very hard work to make ends meet. I was only about six when we came here. I don't really remember it very well. My father studied hard, and in the end he became a land surveyor, and now he travels all over the place. He'll be retiring soon. Something he's not looking forward to. But it's not me and my family you want to talk about, is it?"

Banks was actually more than happy to sit there and listen to her talk about herself and her life all day, but he realized he should get down to business. Their food appeared. Banks's steak was perfectly cooked, the frites crisp and skinny. Oriana said her duck was perfect, too.

"It's about Lady Chalmers," he said. "I'm sorry that my talks with her seem to have upset the household so much. As you probably know, I've been warned off by my bosses, so I'd be grateful if you would keep this little meeting secret."

"You want me to keep secrets for you now?" She raised her eyebrows. "A secret tryst? How exciting." Then she turned coquettish, casting her eyes down and smiling shyly. "But are you sure you can trust me?"

"I don't know," said Banks. "It seems that if I want to know anything more about what's going on at Brierley, I have no choice."

"There's nothing I can tell you, so I'm afraid there won't be very much to keep secret."

"I'd just rather no one know we've met, that's all."

"Including Ronnie?"

"Not Lady Chalmers so much. I'll leave that up to you. I'm more worried about Anthony Litton and Ralph Nathan than about her."

"In that case, you needn't worry. I certainly won't tell either of them."

They ate in silence for a while. It certainly beat Banks's usual lunchtime fare at the Queen's Arms or the Indian takeaways that often passed for dinner, though any meal would have to go a long way to beat the game pie at the Low Moor Inn. Perhaps Oriana would enjoy that, too. What a stupid thought, he realized, and got back to business. "Do you know anything about this telephone call I asked Lady Chalmers about?"

"No. As you know, I was out. I visit my grandfather every Monday. I often come here for lunch afterwards, too. Usually alone. I like to sit and read a book while I eat sometimes."

"Me, too," said Banks, "when I get the chance." He paused, trying to find a way of getting around to hinting that Lady Chalmers was lying without offending Oriana. "Only, it seems like a long telephone call about something she wasn't interested in. Does Lady Chalmers often spend a long time talking to strangers on the telephone?"

"I wouldn't say that. Ronnie is always polite on the telephone, even to those people who pester her trying to sell things. I tell her she should tell them to go away and hang up, but she tells me they have a job to do, and it's not her place to be rude to them. What can I say?"

"You don't usually answer the telephone for her?"

"Sometimes I answer it, if she's busy. Not always."

"So you don't find it odd that she spent seven minutes talking to Gavin Miller?"

"No, not really. If they were both at the same university, they might have had some memories in common they chatted about. Remembering their professors, other students, funny things that happened. It wouldn't have to mean they knew each other at the time."

"It's possible, I suppose." Banks showed her the two pictures of Gavin Miller, old and new. "Do you recognize this man? Have you ever seen him? Has he ever been to Brierley House?"

Oriana squinted as she stared, her dark glossy hair framing her oval face. "No," she said finally, pushing them back towards Banks. "I have never seen him. Is it the person who phoned?"

"Yes."

"He was quite handsome when he was younger."

Banks reexamined the image, taken from the group photo outside a college building twenty-five years ago. She was right. Miller had been quite good-looking as a young man. Again, that set his mind wandering back to the University of Essex in the early seventies, when Miller and the lovely young Ronnie Bellamy had been students at the same time. "Did Lady Chalmers ever talk about her student days?" he asked.

Oriana thought for moment, then said, "Just sometimes, years ago, when I was still at university myself."

"What did she say?"

Oriana was silent for a few moments, then she said, "Mostly she used to complain what a drab and self-centered lot we students were these days, only interested in getting our degrees so we could get good jobs and earn a lot of money. She talked about the 'old days' like you people do, as if they were some sort of golden age. The revolution. You were children of the revolution. Always fighting for the cause. Always altruistic, never self-interested." She laughed at Banks's expression. "What? Am I not telling the truth?"

"I suppose there is a certain amount of nostalgia for the old days," Banks admitted. "But it did seem real enough at the time. It seemed within our power to change things. Make a better world."

"Is that what you wanted to do? Is that why you joined the police?"

"I suppose it is, in an odd sort of way. It seemed better than throwing ball bearings under the feet of police horses in Grosvenor Square."

"Then you grew older, yes, and you no longer wanted to change things. And just look at the world now."

"Well, someone said that if you're not a communist when you're twenty, you've got no heart, and if you're not a conservative when you're forty, you've got no brain."

Oriana laughed at that. "So true."

"So Lady Chalmers was a left-wing firebrand at university, was she?"

"So it seems. She went on demonstrations against the government, against wars and dictatorships, that sort of thing. Yes. And I don't think I'm giving away any secrets to say that I think she also needed to rebel against her family, against the privilege in which she had been brought up. The grand mansion. The servants. And there was the way they earned their fortune. I'm not entirely clear about it, but I think much of the family fortune came from colonialism, perhaps even the slave trade, or at least from the exploitation of native populations. That wouldn't sit well with Ronnie's Marxist ideals at the time. She made none of the choices her parents would have wanted her to make. She is very independent minded and strong willed. Stubborn and hardheaded, too, sometimes, Jem says. I had to confess that I wasn't very political at university. Perhaps I spent too much time on my studies and not enough out on the picket lines, though I don't remember any picket lines."

"Margaret Thatcher got rid of them all. How do you get along with Sir Jeremy?"

"Jem? Fine," said Oriana. "He's kind, considerate, funny, intelligent. And he knows so much about theater, its history, characters. He has such wonderful stories to tell. Funny, too. It's just a pity he's away so much."

"His work demands it?"

"Yes. If he's not abroad somewhere, he's down in London at the offices. Mind you, Ronnie's away a fair bit, too, especially when there's a new book out. Me, too."

"How do he and Lady Chalmers get along?"

Oriana narrowed her eyes. "I told you. No family tales. They get along fine."

Was there a hidden message there, Banks wondered, or was Oriana merely being discreet? So what if there was a little turbulence. Most marriages suffer turbulence every now and then, as Banks well remembered. "The girls?"

"Hardly girls anymore. Well, Sam's still at university—St. Andrews, studying drama. She likes to come down for the weekend when she can get away. She hasn't decided yet whether she wants to be a rock star like your son or a famous actress. Those are the best times, when the family's all at Brierley. Angelina's 'in between' at the moment. She got a decent-enough degree at St. Hilda's, in Oxford, and I'm sure she'll find a job eventually, but right now she's enjoying her horses."

"What line of work is she interested in?"

"Well, her degree is in history, but she's horse crazy. Who knows which direction she'll go in. Right now, it wouldn't surprise me if she took a job as a stable 'lad' just to get a foot on the rung. They're wonderful girls. My 'little sisters.'"

Banks took another photograph out of his briefcase, one he had examined in great detail, through a magnifying glass, the previous evening. It showed a large group of students marching, carrying banners in favor of the miners. Banks pointed to one blurry figure, clearly a young blond woman, her head just visible between two other burlier figures. "Is that her?" he asked. "Is that Lady Chalmers?"

Oriana peered at the photograph, then gave a dismissive pout. "It could be," she said. "But perhaps not. It is hard to tell."

"Lady Chalmers went to the same university at the same time as the man who got killed, you know, the man who phoned her."

"That doesn't mean she knew him. He's not in the photograph, too, is he?"

"Not that one, no," said Banks. "But if he did know her, and if he was in trouble or something, and for some reason he called her . . ."

"Then she would be lying about the reason for the telephone call."

"About its content, yes." Banks didn't like the way this was going; he thought he was losing Oriana. At that moment, the waiter came by to take away their plates and ask if they wanted anything else. They both ordered coffee, Oriana's an espresso. She swirled what was left of her wine in the glass, then set it aside. Banks finished his off.

When they had their coffees, Oriana leaned forward towards Banks, resting her hands on the white tablecloth. Her fingers were long and tapered; she wore no rings. He could just see the tempting line of olive cleavage below the neckline of her top. "Look," she said, "you probably know this already, but the only reason I'm talking to you is because I've been worried about Ronnie. She's been distracted since that day. Very jumpy. I didn't know it was the telephone call that upset her because I didn't know about it until you came, but now I think it is. The timing is right, and I can think of nothing else to explain her behavior. Now, all this week, she has seemed distant and has been very quiet. Whether this has anything to do with what you've been asking questions about, I don't know, only that she hasn't been herself, and I've been worried about her."

"So you're willing to admit that she might be lying about the call?"

"If she is, it's for a good reason."

"I'm afraid that doesn't help me. Have you tried talking to her?"

"I've asked her several times if there's anything wrong, but she won't say. Something is bothering her, though. I can tell."

"But you couldn't even make a wild guess at what it is?"

"No. I do know that she can't have harmed anyone. Ronnie is a kind and gentle person. She wouldn't hurt a soul."

"In what way was she distracted? Would you say she was anxious, sad, angry, or upset?"

Oriana considered this for a moment, then said, "Mostly depressed and worried, I would say. Perhaps anxious, also. It's as if she has a great weight on her mind. Not angry or sad or upset or anything."

"Guilt?"

"I don't think so."

"But you've no idea what she's depressed or worried about?"

"No."

"And she was like this even before Gavin Miller was murdered?"

"Yes. All week since the phone call."

"And after the murder?"

"The same, perhaps even more so after you came."

"OK," said Banks. "Thank you for being so frank."

"I'm not saying all this for you," she said. "I'm telling you for her sake. For Ronnie's sake. Because I'm worried about her. And because

I know she could never have hurt that man. It's true that we were all at home that night. I made dinner, and we watched a movie the way we usually do on Sunday nights, exactly as she told you. She was here all the time. All three of us were."

"I understand."

Oriana sat back in her chair and finished her espresso. "Now I must go," she said. "Thank you for a nice lunch."

Banks made a motion to the waiter, who brought over the bill. He seemed to be smirking as he ran Banks's credit card through his machine, as if he had decided they were lovers on their way to some hotel bed for a bit of afternoon delight. "What's your problem?" Banks said, glancing up at him. "Can't an uncle treat his niece to lunch once in a while?"

The waiter blushed, Oriana could hardly hold back her laughter, and Banks felt rather pleased with himself.

9

BANKS HAD ALWAYS HATED PRISONS. COME TO THINK of it, he realized, he probably wasn't alone in that. Everybody hated prisons. The people who worked in them probably got used to them, and the prisoners had no choice, but to the casual and occasional visitor, they were sordid and cruel places where bad things happened. Men got raped by other men, or stabbed by filed-down toothbrushes in the showers. Over his years in the force, Banks had helped put plenty of people away, but it wasn't something he ever got used to, and he tried not to think of their lives after they had been sentenced. His job usually ended with giving evidence in court, then it was up to the judge and jury. He also realized that the odds were he might have helped convict more than one innocent person, too, but those thoughts were reserved for waking at 4:24 in the morning and being unable to get back to sleep. Mostly he lived with it, grateful only that there was no longer capital punishment and that he had no deaths on his conscience. Misery aplenty, certainly, probably some blood on his hands, too, if truth be told, but not death. Grateful also that when he saw the inside of a prison it was as a visitor.

Armley Jail, built in 1847, of dark gritstone, resembled the medieval castle of some evil dark lord. No doubt it had been built that way on purpose. The Victorians had very strict and religious ideas about punishment. Since then, a couple of blockish redbrick wings had been added, rather like Lego buildings, which broke up the facade some-what, but they didn't really take much away from the overall image.

Formalities done, mobile left at the reception area, Banks followed Tim Grainger, whom he had met before, inside across the cobbled yard of the old section. He knew from previous visits that just ahead to the right, up on the first floor, there used to be an apartment where the hangman, as often as not Pierrepoint, spent the night before an execution. From his window, he was able to see across the courtyard to the execution shed below. That was an office now, as was the flat, but the old condemned cell was still there, with its small bunk and scratches on the dank wall, just down some steps next to the grate in the floor where they used to sluice off the bodies after they had hung for an hour to ensure death. Banks had been there once with Grainger, and he still had nightmares about it. But that barbarism was done with now, at least in Britain, though it had been done away with in practice only a few years before Banks had started on the force.

They went inside. Perhaps the thing Banks noticed most, and hated most, about jails was the constant sound of the locking and unlocking of doors. There seemed so many of them, and they all seemed so heavy that the place constantly resounded with the echoes of banging doors, jangling keys and tumbling locks. He found himself forever stopping while Tim inserted yet another large key, then waiting while he very carefully made sure he locked up again behind him after they had passed through. Various warders said hello as they crossed the office area towards the cells. Most prisons had been built on the same model, an X shape, so that guards could stand at the center and see all the way down every wing. When Banks and Grainger passed the hub, it was methadone time on one of the wings, and the queue of prison-ers stretched down the corridor.

Tim had arranged for Banks to conduct the interview in his own office, rather than a cell, as Kyle McClusky wasn't considered a dan-gerous prisoner or any kind of flight risk. They were also served with coffee and chocolate biscuits before McClusky was brought up. Once Banks and McClusky were settled, Tim left them to it. There was, of course, a guard on the door, just in case. Banks poured McClusky some coffee, added milk and sugar and waited for him to settle down.

He seemed nervous, but not too jittery. One leg was jumping, and he bit his nails, but that was all. He seemed healthy enough, though there was nothing he could do about that prison pallor. His hair was cut short, and his face was bony. He hadn't shaved for a couple of days.

"OK," said Banks. "We might as well start. Any idea what this is about, Kyle?"

"They didn't tell me. They don't tell you anything in here. Do you think you can get me a reduction in my sentence if I talk to you?"

"Come on, Kyle. You know I would if I could, but you only got six months, and you've served nearly three already. You'll be out in weeks, maybe days the way things are going these days."

"Yeah, I know. But every little bit helps, man. I mean, you scratch my back, I'll scratch yours. You know, like, if I talk to you, what's in it for me?"

The back-scratching image repelled Banks, but he had given some thought to what might be in it for Kyle. The question hadn't been entirely unexpected. "I was rather hoping that you'd want to talk to me, anyway, Kyle. You see, Beth and Kayleigh are in a bit of trouble, and you might be able to help them out."

"Those bitches! I wouldn't cross the road to piss on them if they were on fire. It's fucking Beth's fault I'm in here in the first place."

"How do you work that out?"

"She wouldn't help me, right? Too fucking high and mighty, now she's got an important job in telly, and a nice new flat and that poncy boyfriend. Too good for the likes of me."

"What do you mean?"

"I was down on my luck, wasn't I? I needed a place to crash, a little cash, you know, just to get back on my feet. I went round to her flat. She sent me packing. Wouldn't even let me in the front door. Talk about helping an old friend. So don't talk to me about that bitch."

This was, in a way, even better than Banks had hoped. Beth certainly hadn't told Winsome and Gerry about this. He had needed a way to get McClusky talking about what Lisa Gray had said Beth and Kayleigh had done, without having anything on the table to offer him. The chance to help Beth and Kayleigh had been his opening gambit, but now that he knew Kyle hated Beth so much, he could use that to even better advantage, and probably get him to tell the truth about what happened at Eastvale College, as long as it reflected badly on the girls. But he would have to be careful; drug dealers and users lied.

"That is a bit mean," he said sympathetically. "I can see where you're coming from. But she didn't tell us about that."

"She wouldn't, would she? But it's true."

"I'm sure it is. Do you remember her friend, Kayleigh Vernon?"

"She's just as bad. You'd think, you know, after all the freebies I gave her, that she might lend me a little of the readies when I was in need."

"You went to her, too?"

"I was running out of options."

"But she didn't help?"

"No way. Same story as the other one. I'm all right, Jack, fuck you. They think they're better than me, but they're nothing but a pair of lying bitches."

"Why's that, Kyle?"

Kyle seemed to need a break from his anger. There was a dribble of spittle on his chin, and he wiped it with the back of his hand. He rubbed his face, drank some coffee, scratched his crotch and slumped back in his chair. His attention appeared to have wandered, as if he had lost track of the conversation. Banks wondered if he had just taken his methadone. "Man, I don't know."

"You said they were lying bitches. You must have had a reason for saying that."

"I don't remember."

"Come on, Kyle. It was only four years ago. Eastvale College. Do you remember Gavin Miller?"

"That the teacher who kicked me out?"

"That's the one."

"Ruined my future, man. I was going places."

"What were you doing?"

Kyle just gave him a sideways glance. "Nothing, man. I wasn't doing nothing. Just minding my own business."

"What did he think you were doing?"

"Some dumb cunt must have told him I was dealing drugs. I mean, all I did was help a few people out from time to time. You know, people who needed stuff. It was just fun, man."

"Like roofies or methamphetamine?"

"Whatever."

"Was it Beth or Kayleigh who told on you?"

"No. They were too into it. They were then, like, before they got all successful. Not the roofies, just the speed and spliffs. Probably snort coke through fifty-quid notes these days, or lick it off the end of some banker's dick." He seemed to like that image, and it set off a fit of laughter that ended in coughing. Banks gave him a few moments to recover.

"Why do you say someone must have told Gavin Miller that you were selling drugs?"

Again, Kyle seemed to have lost the thread. "I can't remember, man. It's a long time ago. It was just something he said. I remember thinking, like, this is down to some dumb cunt who got slipped a roofie and got fucked. This was, like, her revenge."

"But you don't know who?"

"No."

"Did you ever wonder about the girls who were given the Rohypnol, Kyle, about what happened to them?"

"Nah, not really. Never thought much about it. Why?" He scratched himself again.

"No reason. Why didn't any of them come forward?"

"They probably enjoyed it. I mean, it's what they want, isn't it, man? Even if they don't admit it. Either that or they didn't remember."

"But someone must have remembered something."

"So it seems. Who cares?"

"Do you think it was a girl who'd been raped getting her own back on the person who sold her rapist the drug?"

"Could be. I don't know."

"Why not take her revenge on the person who raped her?"

"How should I know? Maybe she did, and you don't know about it. Maybe she already cut his balls off, and he's lying dead in a ditch somewhere. Didn't think about that, did you?"

Well, well, Banks thought. Maybe Kyle had a point there. It was another avenue worth investigating. Not the castration so much as someone else hurt, killed or hospitalized around that time. If the person who had administered the drug had been punished already by his victim, there might be good reasons why the rapist hadn't wanted the sordid incident to be public knowledge. And if the girl who had been raped remembered who did it, she might well have worked out some sort of private revenge on her assailant that wouldn't be attributable to her. Shame and guilt were normal reactions to being drugged and raped, no matter how much you tried to tell the victims it wasn't their fault. And she had used Miller as a tool to get revenge on Kyle, the dealer. Unless . . .

"Was it you, Kyle?" Banks asked.

"Was what me?"

"Did you use the Rohypnol on someone yourself?"

"Why would I do that, man? I didn't need no Rohypnol."

Banks filed the possibility away and moved on. "Do you remember later, after you'd left Eastvale, Gavin Miller was sacked for sexual misconduct? Both Beth and Kayleigh said he touched them and made inappropriate suggestions."

"I remember. I was still crashing at Kayleigh's place off and on back then. It was that motherfucker Miller, the one who got me kicked out."

"That's right."

"So justice was done after all."

"Well, Gavin Miller lost his job and a good deal else."

"Like I said. Justice."

"He was murdered last week, Kyle."

"Miller?"

"That's right."

"Well, fuck me. Who did it?"

"That's what we're trying to find out."

Kyle looked around, over his shoulder. "There are murderers in here, man. You have to be careful. Know what I mean?"

Banks nodded. "Do you know who might have wanted to harm Gavin Miller?"

"Well, I didn't do it. I was in here."

"Did you ever see Gavin Miller after then? Say in the past year or so?"

"Why?"

"Maybe he wanted to buy drugs from you? Maybe he wanted to go into business?"

"Miller? You must be joking, man. No, I never seen him since that day in his office he put it on the line."

"Do you think Beth or Kayleigh might be lying about not having seen him?"

"How do I know? I can't see why they would lie about it, though, if that's what they said." Kyle paused, clearly thinking about the way the two girls had let him down in his hour of need. "You know what? I'm gonna tell you something about those bitches? You ready?"

"I'm ready," said Banks.

"After Miller told me to stop doing what I was doing or leave town, I don't know how long after, but we were sitting around in Kayleigh's flat getting high and—"

"Who was sitting around?"

"Us. Beth, Kayleigh and me."

"Right. And what happened?"

"We were talking, like, you know, about what happened, and about what a nerve that guy had and all that. And they were, like, saying how he was always staring at their tits and their arses all the time, like some perv. I mean, that's wrong, man. Like, a teacher shouldn't do stuff like that."

"It's not very professional."

"That's the word. Unprofessional. Not that you can blame him. I mean, Kayleigh had a lovely arse, and Beth's tits . . . juicy, man, know what I mean?"

"So you were sitting around, the three of you."

"Yeah, just, like, chillin', listening to music, smoking some weed, and they were all like pissed off about this Miller telling me to leave or he'll call the pigs, and ogling their tits and just dying to cop a feel, so I just said, like, what if he did. They didn't know what I meant at first, but I told them, you know, it wouldn't be too hard if one of them sort of offered herself and then yelled rape. Wouldn't be the first time, man."

"So you suggested that one of them should seduce Miller, have sex with him, and then cry rape?"

"Was that a great plan, or was it not?"

"What did they say?"

"Well, we talked about it for a while, you know, had another spliff, and they said they thought that would be too much, like, neither of them *really* did want to *actually* fuck the guy. I could dig that. I mean, he was old, man."

"So what did you decide?"

"We talked about it some more, and then we came up with another idea, one where they wouldn't have to get fucked by him."

"And that was?"

"Exactly what happened. We decided the plan would work best if Kayleigh made a complaint that this Miller had, like, touched her, in his office or something, and come on to her and all, then Beth would come out and say, yeah, he'd done that to her, too, a while ago, but she hadn't dared talk, but now Kayleigh's courage had, like, powered her. It was great, man. That's how much they cared about me then. Not like now."

"So that's what they did?"

"That's what they did. And the fucker got booted out on his arse."

"And he never did anything to either of them."

"That's the beauty of it. And they never had to fuck him. But he certainly ogled their arses and their tits, didn't he? I mean, he would have fucked them if he'd had half a chance. Teachers shouldn't do that, man. We were teaching him a lesson." He laughed at his own weak joke. Banks was amazed he got it, so fried by drugs did his brains seem.

"So, first Kayleigh went to the college authorities with her story, then Beth put her hand up and said, 'Me, too.'"

"That's right. You got it."

"And where were you through all this?"

"Gone. Hit the road. Couldn't see me for dust."

"Did you follow the story?"

"What for?"

"To find out what happened to Miller, to Beth and Kayleigh."

"Nah. What's the point? I had places to go, things to do."

"So you never looked back?"

"That's right."

"Jesus Christ." Banks shook his head slowly.

"What's wrong?"

"Nothing," Banks said. "You wouldn't understand. I'd like to thank you for your time, Kyle." Banks pressed the button beside the desk, as Tim Grainger had told him, and Grainger appeared a few seconds later, along with a warder. "Done?" he said. "Everything all right?"

"Everything's fine," said Banks. "We're done."

"You'll remember about my time off for cooperating, won't you, man?" Kyle said as the warder led him away. "You can't say I wasn't cooperative."

"No," said Banks. "I sure as hell can't say that."

"OH, IT'S you again. Come in," said Lisa Gray, managing a weak smile, when Winsome and Annie turned up at her door. It was marginally more welcoming than the greeting Dayle Snider had given them earlier, but not much. Lisa gave Annie a suspicious glance, and Winsome introduced them.

"Not interrupting anything, are we?" Winsome asked. Annie had agreed that her partner should do most of the questioning, as she already seemed to have created some sort of bond with Lisa. Annie would jump in as and when she felt like it.

"Not at all. I was just reading."

It was a small flat just off the western edge of the campus. Close enough, but not part of it. You could see the concrete and glass lowrises through her second-floor window, the students wandering about with their backpacks or briefcases. A knobby cactus stood in a pot on the windowsill. The room was painted a sort of creamy orange, the lighting was dim, from shaded lamps, and framed movie, exhibition and concert posters and art prints hung on the walls: *Cat People,* Salvador Dalí, Joy Division. One showed a beautiful but decadent- and dangerous-looking young man, long wavy hair, shirtless, wearing leather trousers, holding on to a microphone stand as if it were the only thing keeping him on his feet. "The Doors" was written aslant across the top.

The room was thinly carpeted and furnished with a charity-shop three-piece suite, whose frayed arms and faded red rose pattern had seen better days. There was an old black-leaded fireplace, or imitation lead, Winsome sincerely hoped, complete with hob and andirons. Lisa had a wood fire burning, and it took the chill off the air nicely. There was a hint of sandalwood incense mixed with the slightly damp, musty smell of the room. Winsome didn't recognize the music that was playing, repetitive strings spiraling on and on, reaching a crescendo, then shifting abruptly, changing key. It was hypnotic. She saw the name "Glass" on a CD cover. Banks would probably know them. He knew all sorts of trivia; he ought to be on *Pointless*. Lisa's book, *A Tale for the Time Being,* by Ruth Ozeki, lay open facedown on the coffee table.

"I suppose you'd like some tea?" Lisa said.

"As a matter of fact, we're just about all tea'd out," said Winsome.

"I think I'd like some. Mind if I put the kettle on?"

"Fine. Go ahead."

Lisa disappeared into the kitchen. The music continued, quietly insistent, in the background. Winsome heard a tap running and a gas ring flare, then Lisa returned and sat, lifting up her legs and wrapping her arms around her knees. "What can I help you with this time?"

The pink and yellow streaks were gone from her blond hair, which fell in a ragged fringe over her forehead. Winsome wanted to lean forward and brush away a lock that covered one eye. Lisa was wearing loose-fit jeans and a baggy sweatshirt, so that it was still impossible to see what sort of a figure she had, except that she was frail and slender, certainly not capable of throwing Gavin Miller over the side of the railway bridge without help. Her face was clean of makeup, and there was a sort of innocence about it that belied her experience.

"Same as before, really," Winsome said. "We just want to clarify one or two points."

"If I can."

"The last time I talked to you," Winsome said, "you were a bit vague about a few things. One of them being what problems you were going through at the time, what it was that made Trevor Lomax disbelieve you when you came forward. He told us you were neurotic, abusive, delusional, behind in your work, on drugs, and a trollop."

To Winsome's surprise, Lisa laughed. "Well, he's just about got all the exits covered, hasn't he? What about alcoholic? Didn't he mention that?"

Winsome grinned. "He might have done. Something about turning up for a class while intoxicated."

"Thought so. He's a prick. He believed me. He just didn't want to get involved."

"But he got involved before, at first, when the charges were brought against Gavin. He was one of the few people to defend him. Why the sudden change of heart?"

"Do you actually know for a fact how much he did for Mr. Miller? Or exactly what he did? I shouldn't think the change of heart was all that sudden. I imagine he got his fingers burned the first time, and he wasn't inclined to put them in the fire again. The powers that be wouldn't have taken kindly to anyone stirring up the past all over again. And I was well aware that I'd probably make a less than satisfactory witness."

"But you still thought there was a chance?"

"Hoped. You have to try, don't you?" A shrill whistling came from the kitchen. Lisa excused herself and disappeared for a moment. Winsome and Annie exchanged glances. When Lisa came back she was carrying a steaming mug.

"So Trevor Lomax never said exactly what it was he did to try to help Gavin in the first place?" Winsome asked.

"Not to me. Maybe you should ask him."

"And you take that to mean that he didn't do very much at all?"

"Well, given that he wasn't present when the alleged incident occurred," Lisa said, "I should imagine his defense consisted of a character reference, and perhaps a slur against Beth and Kayleigh."

"But he couldn't have known anything else at the time."

"What do you mean?"

"He didn't know about Kyle. The connection. The reason why Beth and Kayleigh conspired to frame Gavin Miller. Neither did you."

"That's right."

"So this was really all between you and Gavin Miller?"

"I don't know what you're getting at."

"It's simple, really," Annie chipped in. "What DS Jackman really wants to know is how did Gavin Miller find out about Kyle Mc-Clusky's illegal activities?"

"Someone must have told him."

"Was that someone you?" Winsome asked.

Lisa pointed her thumb at her chest. "Me?"

"That's what I said. You seem to be unusually involved in the whole business, and when I ask myself why, I find myself thinking it was because you started it. You tipped Gavin Miller off about Kyle McClusky's illegal activities in the first place, so when you saw him in trouble, and you found out it was related to what he did to Kyle, you felt a responsibility. That's fair enough. Am I right?"

There was a long pause. Lisa blew on the surface of her tea and took a sip. The scent of chamomile drifted towards Winsome. Immediately it reminded her of home, though chamomile didn't grow there. Perhaps all exotic scents reminded her of home. She liked chamomile tea, wished she'd said yes when it was on offer. "What if I did?" Lisa said, lifting her eyes from the mug to look directly at Winsome, rather than Annie.

"Did you?" Winsome asked.

Lisa held her gaze for several seconds. It felt like minutes to Winsome. "Yes," she said finally. "I'd seen what Kyle was doing, what was going on. One or two people had told me about the effects of the stuff he sold. A friend of mine nearly OD'd, and one girl thought she'd been raped, but she couldn't remember anything. I didn't like to do it, but it was the right thing to do, wasn't it? Tell on him?"

"It was a brave decision," said Winsome. "But why did you tell Gavin Miller?"

"Because he was the only adult who took me seriously about anything. The only person in authority I trusted. And he knew Kyle from one of his classes. He could have a private word with him."

"Why not go to the college authorities, or to us?" Annie asked. "I mean, here's someone who's selling drugs—very nasty drugs, not that nice hippy-trippy stuff you got for Gavin Miller—and you know about it, you see the results for yourself. Why not go to the police instead of some ineffectual lecturer?"

"Gavin wasn't ineffectual. I . . . I just couldn't."

"Why not, Lisa?" Winsome asked gently to offset what she thought of as Annie's aggressiveness. Not that it couldn't be effective—she could be hard on interviewees herself—but she felt unusually protective of Lisa, perhaps because she seemed so vulnerable. But there was something she wasn't telling them.

Lisa chewed on her lip. "They'd never have believed me. I just wasn't in great shape. I couldn't have handled all the questions, the lawyers, court."

"What was wrong with you?" Winsome pressed.

"Nothing, for fuck's sake. I just couldn't do it. All right?"

"So you went to Gavin Miller?"

"Yes. He dealt with the problem, didn't he?"

"But he didn't put Kyle McClusky in jail, where he belonged," said Annie.

"Jail's not the answer to everything."

"No, but it's a bloody good start for some people."

"He'd only have become more of a criminal in there, learn more tricks, let his hatred of society curdle."

"Very poetic," Annie said, "but not our business. We're in the business of putting away villains, not babysitting them or making excuses for them. You don't get rid of rats by catching them in a cage then taking them next door and letting them out. Thanks to you, Kyle McClusky's stayed out there, on the streets, helping more boys dose girls with roofies so they could have their evil way. And I've got news for you. He's in jail now learning more tricks and letting his hatred curdle. Pity it's too late for some."

Lisa stared down into her lap. Winsome could tell she was crying. She gave Annie a warning glance. Her harsh approach wasn't helping matters; it was pushing Lisa to clam up. Annie slid her finger across her lips in a sealing gesture.

"So Gavin Miller told Kyle to get out of Dodge?" Winsome said, trying to break the tension.

Lisa paused for a while, sniffed, then she looked up. "Something like that. An ultimatum. Drugs dealing or college."

"So because you initiated this, when Gavin was later charged with sexually intimidating Kayleigh, then Beth came forward, you wanted to help him, right?"

"I didn't realize the connection then. I just wanted to help him because he was good to me, but there was nothing I could do at first. Then when I heard them talking about it in the toilets later, boasting and laughing, I went to Mr. Lomax. He was the head of department, after all, and he was supposed to be Mr. Miller's fucking friend."

"How much later?" Annie asked.

"I told you, I don't know exactly. A few weeks. Three weeks, a month, maybe, at the most. Before the end of term, anyway."

"So why would Beth and Kayleigh be crowing over what they'd done to Gavin Miller in the ladies' toilets a month after they'd done it?" Annie butted in. "It doesn't make sense."

Lisa turned to Winsome, as if expecting her to leap to the defense. She didn't. "I don't know, do I? All I know is what I heard."

"Why didn't you tell the committee the truth at the time?" Annie went on.

"What do you mean? How could I know the truth then? I've told you. It was only later when I heard them."

"But you knew that Beth and Kayleigh were friends with Kyle."

"No, I didn't. Not from the start, I didn't. I didn't see any connection between Mr. Miller's problems and Kyle's activities until later, when I overheard Beth and Kayleigh in the ladies'. They said something about what he'd done to their friend Kyle. It was only then that I found out and realized what it meant. Besides, what difference would it have made?"

"Oh, come on, Lisa," said Annie, "you can't have known what the committee did and didn't know. And isn't it funny that all of a sudden you remember a very important part of Beth and Kayleigh's conversation you neglected to mention earlier? You're making it up as you go along, aren't you? You can't expect us to believe you were so out of it you couldn't even get the committee to put two and two together, to have another go at the girls. They probably couldn't have stood up to a proper interrogation. Beth Gallagher came clean pretty quickly when we talked to her."

"Only because it happened so long ago. Only because she knows there's nothing you can do to her. Only because Mr. Miller is dead. Only because it doesn't fucking matter anymore. And because you're . . . you're . . . you bullied her."

Winsome saw the tears form in Lisa's eyes again and start to make tracks down her cheeks. "But it *does* matter, Lisa," she said. "It matters precisely *because* he's dead."

"But surely you can't think I had anything to do with that?" Lisa pleaded. "Why won't you just leave me alone?" The tough streetwise chick Winsome had met only days ago was gone now, replaced by a confused and frightened young girl.

"But it may all be connected," Winsome said. "And there may be something you can tell us that might not seem important or relevant to you but that will help us. Can't you see that? We don't always travel by direct routes."

"I still don't see how I can help you."

Winsome had a definite sensation that the channels of communication were closing down.

"This is getting us nowhere," Annie said, standing to leave. "We're going round in circles."

Sadly, Winsome agreed. When she looked at Lisa, she still felt for her, and she also still felt that she was missing something. Lisa was stubborn and secretive and private. It would take more than what they had right now to pry the truth out of her.

BANKS HAD got to Leeds early, parked the car near the Merrion Center and walked down to Browns, on the corner of the Headrow and Cookridge Street, where he was supposed to meet Ken Blackstone. Ken was usually a curry man, but he had pleaded a dodgy stomach and suggested something a bit less spicy this time. It was an overcast evening, but warm enough. Banks was standing outside talking to Annie on his mobile, and as he talked, his eyes scanned the crowds of city workers going home, mingled in with legal types from the nearby courts and law chambers on Park Square, most carrying rolled-up umbrellas and briefcases, waiting for buses that came in clusters of two and three, in all colors—cream, purple, maroon, green—double-deckers or long bendy-buses, bound for the suburbs and beyond, to such exotic destinations as Huddersfield, Halifax, Bradford, Cleckheaton and Heckmondwike.

Down the Headrow towards Westgate, Banks could see past the art gallery, set back behind its paved forecourt, to the great columns, lions and dome of the Victorian town hall, where the clock said it was twenty to six. Still ten minutes to wait. He had heard Annie talk about the frustrating interview with Lisa Gray, and her sense that there had to be more to the story, but he still felt more focused on Lady Veronica Chalmers and her interesting past in the warm after-glow of his lunch with Oriana. In turn, he told Annie about his inter-view with Kyle McClusky, and how it had confirmed that the charges against Miller were a sham.

Gerry Masterson had gone to Stockton to talk to someone who remembered Veronica Bellamy from the old University of Essex days, so she might be able to pick up a connection with Gavin Miller. The Gray girl certainly hadn't killed him, thought Banks. Neither had Ve-ronica Chalmers. The connections still felt just beyond his grasp, like the networks of veins and arteries in the human body that needed special dyes to bring their problems to light. He felt the need of more information, of a special dye. Each new fact changed the whole pat-tern, and he knew from experience that somewhere out there was one as yet unforeseen change that would finally make it all make sense.

He ended the call with Annie and decided to go and wait for Ken inside the brasserie. The place was already bustling, but it was large enough, and he got a table by the Cookridge Street side, from where he could see the same scene through the window that he had just been watching from outside. He got menus and ordered a glass of Rioja. He would be driving back to Eastvale tonight, so that would have to be his only drink of the evening. Browns was a chain, but a relatively good one as these things went. Banks glanced over the menu. What-ever he ordered, it would be his second full meal of the day. Most days, all he got was a cup of coffee, a sandwich or a Greggs pasty and

a warmed-up takeaway. This was living high on the hog by comparison.

DCI Ken Blackstone arrived five minutes late. He didn't offer an
apology, any more than Banks expected him to. A copper's life was
unpredictable, and being late was part of the burden. Only five minutes late was pretty damn good, actually. Ever the snappy dresser,
under his raincoat he wore a light wool suit, shirt and tie. The shirt
was crisp white linen, and the tie was rather flamboyant for Banks's
taste. Banks felt shabby, in contrast, in his old Marks & Spencer suit
and open-neck shirt. He had worn a tie with it for lunch with Oriana
but had taken it off as soon as he got in his car to set off for Armley
Jail. With the tufts of hair over his ears and his wire-rimmed glasses,
Blackstone had always reminded Banks more of an academic than a
copper. In fact, the older he got, the more he came to resemble some
of the photos Banks had seen of the poet Philip Larkin.

Banks had known Ken Blackstone for years and considered him
perhaps his closest friend, as well as a trusted colleague and a police
officer he respected. He had spent many a drunken night on Blackstone's sofa after his split from Sandra, working his way through the
massive collection of torch songs on vinyl—Billie Holiday, Dinah
Washington, Sarah Vaughan, Blossom Dearie, Keely Smith, Thelma
Grayson—usually waking up with a massive hangover and somebody
or other singing "It's De-Lovely." It was a lost half year, more or less,
but he had come through it in the end.

A while later, he had found Annie—or rather, she had come to
work with him on a case that started near her home village of
Harkside—and they had become lovers for a while, until work got in
the way and Annie felt that it was no longer appropriate to be sleeping
with her boss. She was ambitious but cautious, and he didn't blame
her, but he did miss their intimate times together. No matter how well
they worked together, and how well they got along off duty, there was
always a hint of awkwardness about their relationship after that. As
people do, Banks and Blackstone had drifted apart a little over the
years, and he hadn't done any crying on his friend's shoulder over his
recent split with Sophia, had hardly told him anything about her. He
also realized that he knew nothing of Blackstone's love life since the

divorce years ago. Still, it was good to have dinner with an old friend, do some catching up and cover a bit of work ground at the same time. He had always found Blackstone good to bounce ideas off; he could listen and help Banks articulate half-formed notions, bring them to light. He was the dye.

"This is the life, eh, Alan?" said Blackstone, sipping a gin and tonic. "Sometimes I wonder why we bother with the rest of it. We've both done our thirty, and more. Why don't we just retire and keep bees or something?"

"Because we'd get bored?"

"Mm. Sometimes I think I could handle that," Blackstone said seriously, crossing his legs after pulling at the creases in his suit trousers. "Especially when I look in the eyes of another dead teenage junkie, or a butchered prostitute, a seventy-year-old rape victim, another stab victim, or some unlucky passerby caught in gang crossfire."

"The joys of city life. But seriously, Ken, what would you do? Wouldn't you miss it all? Retirement terrifies me. I'm frightened I'd drop dead within a year."

"I'd find plenty to do. So would you. Maybe I'd get an allotment, for a start, take up growing marrows. Win prizes. You've got your music, books, travel, long country walks. Learn an instrument, a foreign language. Maybe you could work on your memoirs?"

"About the only positive thing I can see in retirement is not having to write any more bloody reports," he said. "I'd never write another word as long as I live if I didn't have to."

"Well, it'll happen eventually, old mate. Bound to. I suppose if you think you'll miss it so much, you could always get a job as a security guard."

"Sure. Lots of detection skills required for that."

"In a few years we'll have no choice."

The waiter came and took their orders. Banks went for the chicken, leek and mushroom pie, and Blackstone ordered the baked salmon, no sauce, and a salad.

"Health kick?" Banks asked.

"Blood pressure and cholesterol."

"Take the statins. You can eat anything then. Except grapefruit."

"I'd rather stay off the pills. Doc says I can control it with exercise and diet."

"Good luck."

"Try not to sound so positive."

"Maybe I'll go on a world cruise when they kick me out," Banks said. "Meet a rich widow. Just keep on sailing, round and round the world."

"There's nobody in your affections right now?"

Banks immediately saw an image of Oriana in his mind, but he banished it at once. "Not at the moment. You?"

"I've been seeing an admin assistant from the uni for a couple of months. We met online. I don't know how serious it is."

"The kids must be all grown up now."

"I knew there was something I meant to tell you. Jackie's pregnant. I'm going to be a grandfather. Can you believe it? Kevin's still a waste of space, 'looking for his place in the world' he calls it, but sponging off his dad and narrowly avoiding nick is about all it amounts to, really. But Jackie's going great guns. Marriage, career, now kids."

Banks clinked glasses. "Congratulations. But don't be too hard on Kevin. We all need to find our place in the world. I don't know whether to be grateful or not, but neither of mine is showing any signs of marriage yet, let alone child rearing." Banks's son, Brian, was touring in France, Holland and Germany with the Blue Lamps, and his daughter, Tracy, had recently moved to Newcastle, where she was working at the university and doing a part-time postgraduate degree in history, with a view of becoming a teacher or a university lecturer.

"I'll let you know what it's like."

"How's Audrey?" Audrey was Blackstone's ex-wife.

"Don't know. I never hear from her. Jackie tells me she's buggered off to the Dordogne with some retired chartered accountant."

"That's one place to avoid when you do retire, then. It must be full of boring English émigrés. It's funny you should bring up retirement," Banks went on. "Madame Gervaise mentioned it just the other day. Said if I keep my nose clean over the next while I might make super and not have to retire until I'm sixty-five."

"And can you?"

"What?"

"Keep your nose clean for a while?"

"I'm not too sure about that. Something nasty's brewing. I can feel it in my water."

Their food arrived, and both paused while the waiter rearranged the cutlery and fussed about filling glasses from the bottled water they had ordered. When the flurry of activity had settled down, Blackstone took another sip of gin and tonic and said, "Do tell."

"I was just talking to Annie before you arrived," Banks said, "and she and Winsome reinterviewed a witness this afternoon. You know about the Gavin Miller case? A disgraced college lecturer chucked over the side of a railway bridge?"

"I've read something about it, but you'd better fill me in on the details."

Banks told him in as concise detail as possible about Gavin Miller's death and their investigation into its circumstances, including his and Gerry Masterson's foray into the life and times of Lady Veronica Chalmers and family. By the time he had finished, they had almost done with their main courses and Blackstone was halfway through a second drink. When the waiter asked if they wanted dessert, both declined and ordered coffees.

"So what's your problem?" Blackstone asked when the waiter had gone.

"Too many suspects, but none that really stand out. Flimsy alibis, no forensics, one or two of our favorites not physically capable of chucking the victim over the bridge—the sides were quite high—too little in his life to help us track down useful connections. It's all a bit of a jumble. I was telling Gerry Masterson just the other day that I'm beginning to wonder if they weren't both Russian sleeper agents called back to action and something went wrong."

"That bad, is it? But you seem to have narrowed it down to two lines of inquiry," Blackstone pointed out. "The Lady and the college crowd."

"That's true. But there are too many suspects in the college crowd, and the Lady's been ruled off limits."

"Since when did that stop you?"

"It doesn't. Usually." Banks grinned. "You're right. It hasn't."

"And that's why you can't see yourself keeping your nose clean for a while?"

Banks leaned forward. "She's got something to do with it, I'm certain of it, Ken. Maybe she didn't kill him, in fact I'm almost certain she didn't kill him, but there's a connection beyond all the things we've learned already, and I just can't seem to grasp it."

"That's usually because there are vital pieces missing. This is what you have your DC Masterson running around after?"

"She's keen."

"She won't be so keen if your chief constable finds out. Or even AC Gervaise."

"Let me worry about that."

"Fair enough. And what exactly do you expect her to find out?"

"Primarily, some connection between Veronica Bellamy, as she then was, and Gavin Miller from their university days."

"And if there isn't one?"

"Back to the drawing board. Drugs are still a possibility. But I'm certain there is."

"OK. Let's say, for the sake of argument, that there is. So what? What could it possibly have to do with his murder forty years later?"

"You know how these things go, Ken. A buried secret, perhaps? A shared crime? I won't know until Gerry comes up with something solid, will I?"

"By which time you'll have pissed off the bosses so badly that you might as well start applying for that security guard's job right now. And take your DC with you, for what career she'll have left."

"I knew I could always depend on you to cheer me up, Ken."

Blackstone sipped some coffee and grinned. "You wouldn't want it any other way."

"But if I'm right, then nobody's career is damaged, and we've caught a criminal. A rich one, perhaps, but a criminal nonetheless."

"But you said she couldn't possibly have done it."

"She could afford to have it done."

"Aha, the old hired assassin trick."

"Why not? It beats the passing tramp trick. Come on, Ken, you know it happens."

"And just how is Lady Veronica Chalmers going to find a hired assassin to do her bidding? In the local pub?"

"If I knew the answer to that, I'd have her in custody. I'm not saying the whole thing makes sense yet."

"You're telling me it doesn't. Honestly, Alan, you've met her, talked to her a couple of times, poked into her past. Do you really see her as the kind of woman who would hire someone to kill someone?"

"How do I know?"

"Trust your judgment. You used to."

"Then, no, I don't. But maybe her husband was involved?"

"You said he was away in New York."

"I mean in finding someone to do the job. Theatrical producer. He must know some pretty dodgy types, surely?"

"Maybe. I'm sure there are a lot of actors out there who'd kill for a part in one of Sir Jeremy Chalmers's shows. But as far as I can see, all you've got is a random pile of different-colored bricks."

"I can still build a prison from them, if only I had a few more."

"If you build it, they will come."

Banks laughed.

"Seriously, Alan, after what you've told me, my money's on the college crowd and the possible drug connection."

"Why?"

"Because it sounds like a nasty business that went down there, and it's something you know about, with a number of definable suspects. And because methamphetamine, coke, heroin and the like are dangerous and very profitable substances. People who make their money from those sorts of things wouldn't think twice about chucking someone off a bridge if they thought he was going to start competing with them or rat them out to us. The Kyle kid was in jail, fair enough, but dealers have people they work for, or who work for them, and what Miller did might have annoyed someone at a very high level, someone McClusky worked for. Just theorizing."

"But four years had gone by, Ken. Why wait so long?"

"You could say the same about forty years. More so. Something obviously happened to trigger events, either way. Once you find that trigger, you'll be on the home stretch."

10

GERRY MASTERSON PULLED UP OUTSIDE THE MODERN
semi in Stockton around the time Banks was leaving Armley
Jail to meet Ken Blackstone. It had taken her all day on the phone and
the Internet to track down Judy Sallis, who had agreed to talk to her
about what she could remember of her days as an English student at
the University of Essex, from 1971 to 1974.

The gray sky threatened more rain, but it had held off so far. The
waterlogged garden had seen better days, and the front door needed a
new coat of paint, but other than that, the house, both inside and out,
was well maintained and sparkling clean. The furnishings in the living
room appeared to be new, though they weren't quite to Gerry's taste.
The maroon three-piece suite looked as if it came from that dreadful
place they kept advertising on ITV just when you were just settling
into a good detective drama. Gerry sat on the sofa, as directed, and
made herself comfortable. Tea wasn't long in coming, along with a
plate of digestive biscuits and custard creams. Bad for her figure and
her complexion, she knew, but she took one anyway, just to be polite.

Judy Sallis was a stout woman of about sixty, with a rather long
nose and a recent perm. She kept her head constantly thrust forward,
henlike, as if she were always on the verge of saying something of
import, or offering encouragement. Solicitous, some people would
call it. Unnerving, more like, Gerry thought. From her research, she

knew that Judy Sallis was a retired schoolteacher, had been retired for five years now, divorced for eight; she had lived in Stockton most of her life after university. She had two children, both far away, with families of their own to raise.

"What can I do for you, love?" she said, sitting down opposite Gerry in an armchair and smoothing her skirt. "Only you were a bit vague on the telephone."

"Sorry," said Gerry. "Force of habit, I suppose. It's just that when the police come calling, people often don't want to get involved."

"Well, my conscience is clean. And to be honest, I could do with a bit of excitement in my life."

Gerry smiled. "I'm sorry to let you down, but what I want to talk to you about is hardly exciting."

"You'd be surprised what passes for excitement for me these days, love. You mentioned the university days, my old residence. Rayleigh Tower. That's enough to make my day, for a start. I haven't thought of that place in ages."

"Good times?"

"Oh, yes. Mostly. Some hard work, too."

"Well, I've been trying to find people who lived there at the time you did, and you're about the first person I've been able to trace who was willing or able to talk to me."

"Depends what you want to know. What they said about the sixties applies to the early seventies, too, you know. If you can remember it, you weren't there."

"But not as much, surely?"

"Oh, I wouldn't be too sure about that."

Gerry opened her notebook. "I was wondering if you remembered anyone from those days, two people in particular?"

"Try me."

"Ronnie Bellamy and Gavin Miller."

"I knew them both," said Judy. "Not very well. But it wasn't a large university at the time. And Gavin was in English, like me. We were even in the same tutorial group that first year. I read about what happened to him in the paper. It's terrible. Poor Gavin. Suspicious death, they said. Does that mean murder?"

"Or manslaughter," said Gerry. "We think so."

"You don't think Ronnie Bellamy did it, do you?"

"No," said Gerry, with more conviction than she felt. "It's just that we're finding out as much about his university background as we can, and her name came up from those days."

"Yes, it would. Ronnie was around. She's someone else now, of course, isn't she? A famous writer."

"That's right," said Gerry. "Charlotte Summers. She lives in East-vale."

"I like her books. I went to one of her book signings at Waterstones a few years ago. She didn't remember me. But then she always was a bit aloof, despite the leftist politics and all. Or maybe because of them. Of course, she's a real Lady now, too. There was an article about her in the *D&S* a couple of years ago. Or was it the *Northern Echo*?"

There had been profiles of Lady Chalmers/Charlotte Summers in the *Guardian,* the *Sunday Times,* and the *Independent* recently, according to Gerry's research, but she gathered that, up here in Stockton, you haven't really made it until you are written up in the *Darlington and Stockton Times* or the *Northern Echo.* "Ronnie Bellamy was involved in campus politics back then, wasn't she?"

"Yes. More than just campus politics. Ronnie was *very* political. Dyed-in-the-wool communist. Demos and sit-ins and up the revolution and all that. All over the place, too. London. Manchester. Birmingham. She wanted to change the world. She was some sort of bigwig in the Marxist Society, I recollect. I know that sounds odd, that they're all supposed to be equal and all that, but it really didn't work that way. The strong, devious and ambitious will always rise to the top in any political system, won't they? It's only whether they trample on the masses or try to help them once they've climbed up the greasy pole that makes any difference. Look at the unions. Who did they ever want to help or protect except their own members? Not that you can blame them, mind you. Nobody else was going to do it for them."

"Was Ronnie Bellamy strong, devious and ambitious?"

"Probably. I mean, look where she is now. Married a lord, didn't she?"

Not quite, Gerry thought, but there was no point correcting Judy Sallis on the point. "And you? Were you in the Marxist Society?"

"Me? Good lord, no. As you can probably guess, I've no time for politics or politicians. Hadn't then, and I haven't now. You have to remember, though, those were very stormy days. The Heath government. Strikes. The three-day workweek. People thought the country was coming apart at the seams. We even had striking miners all over campus. Chaos it was. But exciting, too."

"I would imagine so." Gerry took another custard cream, just to be sociable. "How well did you know Ronnie Bellamy?"

"I knew who she was, saw her around the place. Not socially, like, she was in with a different crowd, but I heard her speak at rallies a couple of times. I just went out of curiosity, really, and for something to do. Rabble-rousing stuff about the workers' revolution, mostly. She was a bit of a personality."

"Do you remember anything about the crowd she went about with, her friends, boyfriends, that sort of thing?"

"Oh, she wasn't short of boyfriends. She was quite beautiful, I remember, even as a revolutionary. No peasant skirts and hairy legs for her. A Gucci socialist all the way. Designer jeans before designer jeans were invented. Usually flared, with fancy embroidery on the bum, if I remember right. Of course, we all wore them. It was the fashion at the time. But hers always seemed more expensive, more elegant." Judy paused. "Maybe it was just her bum," she added wistfully. "She was a bit like that woman popular in films at the time. Her in *Straw Dogs*. Susan George."

Gerry had never heard of *Straw Dogs* or Susan George, so she remained in the dark on the matter of Veronica Bellamy's looks, except from the pictures she had come across in her research. "Were there any boyfriends in particular?"

"No, none that come to mind. It's funny, though, you should mention Gavin. I knew him. We had a few lectures together, and sometimes a group of us would get together for a coffee, or maybe even go to the union bar for a few drinks on an evening. Gavin was often around. He was quite a fit lad, but a bit shy, a bit bookish, a bit introverted. Wrote poetry, as I remember."

"Did Gavin have anything to do with the Marxist Society?"

"Gavin? No. He was with the other lot. The dopers."

"What do you mean? He took drugs?"

"Well, yes. Of course. This was the early seventies, after all, love. Not much different from the late sixties. There were very distinctive groups at university, especially back then. There were the straights, of course, who went to all the lectures and wrote their essays, or whatever, and had nothing to do with the world around them. There were the politicos, usually left wing, who abhorred bourgeois individualism, personal emotion and, of course, anything like the sort of navel gazing you got from acid trips or smoking some really good Afghani black or Moroccan red. Those were the dopers. They were too into mysticism, the occult and Eastern religion to give a damn about the workers or the revolution. Poets and dreamers, all of them. Some of them were so introspective they disappeared up their own arseholes. They'd sit around in someone's flat and smoke joints and listen to the Grateful Dead, Pink Floyd or Stockhausen and make cryptic comments about life, the universe and everything. They could listen to John Cage's four minutes and thirty-three seconds of silence for hours on end and not get bored."

Gerry laughed, though she had never heard of John Cage. "This was Gavin's crowd?"

"Very much so. Partly mine, too, sometimes, though I never felt I fully belonged. Funny when you think back on it all, isn't it? But you wouldn't know, would you? Gavin was a dreamer. A thinker. A poet. Not a doer. Which is where Ronnie Bellamy comes in."

"How?" asked Gerry, sensing the excitement of possible revelation.

"He was in love with her, wasn't he?"

"Was he?"

"Oh, yes."

"Were his feelings requited?"

Judy thought for a moment. "Hard to say. They went out together for a while in the first term and into the second."

Gerry felt a tremor of excitement. "And then?"

"It ended."

"How?"

"I have no idea. But I can tell you something: it wasn't Gavin's idea. Like a lovesick puppy he was, trying to get back with her, until he obviously realized it was no use. It had just been a casual affair to her, a fling, but she was a doer, and he was a dreamer. Besides, she was posh, too, whatever politics she adopted. Gavin was just your ordinary middle-class boy. It could never work."

"Did they remain friends?"

"No. They both moved on after a while."

"How did Gavin handle the rejection?"

"Not well, really. But, you know, I think he sort of enjoyed it in a way, the misery of unrequited love. I mean in a Leonard Cohen sort of way. At least he was feeling *something,* even if it was the pain of rejection." She glanced up rather sheepishly at Gerry. "I slept with him once, you know, after he and Ronnie split up. Mostly because I felt sorry for him. He was very tender and poetic." She patted her hair. "I wasn't such a bad looker myself, back in the day."

Gerry smiled. Far be it for her to comment on Judy's activities back in the day, though she did wonder what a poetic lover might be like. Someone who quoted Keats and Wordsworth in bed? She hadn't done too badly in English herself at school, an A in her A-levels, at any rate, and she thought perhaps Byron and Marvell might be more appropriate. Maybe John Donne, too. The one about the stiff compasses. Or maybe it meant that he moved in certain poetic rhythms, iambic pentameter shagging, *da-dum-da-dum-da-dum-da-dum-da-dum.* And played Leonard Cohen records, too, because this, she reminded herself, was an age before CDs, and she hadn't been born. Banks would be much better at having this conversation. At least he would have a stronger grasp of what Judy Sallis was talking about, like who Susan George was, for example, and John Cage. She put such flippant thoughts out of her mind and got back to business. "What happened to Gavin?"

"He got a girlfriend he liked. Not as passionately as his great love, Ronnie, of course. But they went out together for the rest of that first year, at least. Nancy Winterson was her name. Nice girl. Good for Gavin, I thought. Sensitive, thoughtful, pretty in a pale, fragile, poetic sort of way. Bit of a Pre-Raphaelite look about her, not unlike you, love, if you don't mind me saying so."

Gerry was sure she blushed. She was also not convinced that being seen as pale, fragile and poetic was necessarily such a good thing, especially in a detective constable. "Did Gavin continue to take drugs?"

Judy looked at Gerry. "How old are you, love?"

"Twenty-six."

"Twenty-six. Christ. Well, you were born into a different world, where drugs are nothing but evil. When you ask if he kept on taking drugs, it sounds, forgive me, like a typical police question. One didn't really *take* drugs or *keep on taking* them, unless they were prescriptions for some illness or other, or maybe if you were a heroin addict. Gavin smoked dope. I smoked dope. We all smoked dope."

"Except the Marxists?"

"Oh, you'd be surprised. Even some of them smoked dope. Ronnie Bellamy certainly dabbled from time to time, especially when she and Gavin were an item. It wasn't all work and no play. But the point was that it wasn't some sort of bad thing you did, or crime you committed. We didn't see it as that much different from having a drink or smoking a cigarette. It was a part of life. So to ask if he kept on taking drugs is sort of meaningless, do you see, like asking if he kept on breathing. Or like a religion. Do you see what I mean?"

"Like Rastas?"

"Exactly. That's why they admired the Rasta culture so much, and some of the Eastern mystic sects who used mind-altering substances. Or the Mexicans with their peyote. Carlos Castaneda and all that desert magic stuff."

Gerry had never heard of Carlos Castaneda, either. There was a whole world back there waiting to be explored, but she doubted she would ever get around to it. "What about the other drugs? LSD?"

"We took LSD a bit more seriously, though I knew a couple of kids who ate it like Smarties. We knew it could be dangerous, but we also knew it had been legal until not too long ago, and that it was a seriously mind-altering substance. That was what we wanted to do, had we been the least bit articulate about it—alter our minds. The Marxists wanted to alter society from the outside, and we wanted to alter the people in it from the inside."

"Did Veronica ever take LSD?"

"That I can't tell you for certain, but I should imagine so, while she was with Gavin. It's a sort of initiation, and he took it quite regularly then."

While Gerry was amazed at this casual abuse of Class A drugs, she was determined not to let it show. It was, indeed, another age. These days it was ecstasy, bubble and bath salts. "So your crowd didn't get along with the Marxists?"

"We got along just fine mostly, though we didn't mix that much, except at concerts and in the bar and stuff. They were all right, most of them. It was just that they were always trying to convince you they were right, like the Jehovah's Witnesses or someone. It got a bit boring, sometimes, listening to the same arguments over and over again."

"And Ronnie?"

"She was all right, too, I suppose. But she was . . . I can't . . . wait . . . do you know what those American prom queens are like, the ones you see in movies like *Carrie*? Beautiful, rich, privileged, bitchy, aloof, always get the best-looking guys. What was it, the quarterback?"

Gerry nodded. "I've seen the films."

"Well, Ronnie was like that. Prom queen of the Marxist Society."

"Why do you think it ended between her and Gavin?"

"I reckon it just fizzled out. She probably got bored with him and all that sitting around smoking dope and navel gazing. She wanted to be out there on the barricades. But something definitely happened. Don't ask me what, because I don't know. One day he was mooning, the next he was walking around with a face like a slapped arse."

"Do you have any ideas why, any guesses?"

"My guess is as good as yours, love. It was just like it was on one day and off the next. If you ask me he got too serious, maybe told her he loved her or something. That would have been just like Gavin. Whatever it was, he seemed to pull himself together pretty soon, after a couple of weeks of Leonard Cohen records, and then he hooked up with Nancy."

"Do you know where Nancy is now?"

"No idea, love. We weren't that close."

"No matter," said Gerry. They had a name; they could always find her if they wanted to. "When was all this? When Gavin and Veronica split up?"

"Not long after new year, I think. Maybe late January, early February. 1972. You won't remember, you weren't born then, but it seemed like everyone was on strike. The miners were doing those flying pickets, you know, when a whole group of extra picketers can turn up almost anywhere at short notice. During the strike, the whole country had revolving power cuts, and I used to love it on an evening when the electricity went off. As long as you had a shilling for the gas meter, you could keep warm, and we all used to congregate in Brian Kelly's or Sue Harper's flat and smoke dope. You couldn't play records, of course, because the electricity was off, but someone always had a guitar, and a tambourine, maybe even a flute or a recorder, and we had some good old singsongs."

Gerry made notes. "So there was a marked change in Gavin's behavior around that time? Early February 1972, right?"

"Yes. About then."

"And Ronnie's?"

"No. She carried on as much as ever. In her element. Prom queen of the Marxist Society. For a while longer at least. Like I said, I think it was a one-sided relationship, such as it was. A bit of fun for her, and a bit too serious for him. Come April or thereabouts, she seemed to fade into the background a bit more."

"Any reason?"

"Not as far as I know. I mean, we weren't close enough that we'd discuss such things. Just got tired of épater-ing la bourgeoisie, I suppose. And there were exams to think about. I mean, when it came right down to it, she was pretty bourgeois herself underneath all that party-line rubbish. Another cuppa?"

"No, thanks," said Gerry, putting away her notebook and looking at her watch. "Is that the time? I'd better be getting back to the station, or they'll be wondering what happened to me."

"Well, it's been nice talking to you," said Judy. "It's funny, opening the floodgates like that. I'll probably start remembering all kinds of things after you've gone." She sounded rather sad that Gerry was leaving.

Gerry gave her a card. "This is my mobile," she said. "Ring me whenever you like if you remember something, even if it doesn't seem important to you."

"Will do."

"There is just one thing you might be able to help me with," Gerry said, stopping with her hand on the door handle.

"If I can."

"I could probably track down a list of Marxist Society members from back then, but is there anyone you remember who you think I could get in touch with? Someone who might be helpful?"

"Well, there's Mandy Parsons, I suppose. She only comes to mind because I've seen her on telly recently. She teaches political science or something like that in Leeds."

"The uni?"

"I think so. Anyway, she was sounding off about the abuse of female asylum seekers and the horrors of female circumcision in the *Guardian* women's section and on the local TV news not more than a month or so ago, and I remembered her from back then. She was no prom queen, but she had her ideology sorted, did Mandy. Gone feminist now, of course, but there's probably still a bit of the old lefty in her. Marxist Feminist, perhaps."

Gerry thanked Judy Sallis and walked towards her car, confused in political ideology and lost in thought.

FOR THE second time that day, Winsome approached the house where Lisa Gray had her flat. She had been doing a lot of thinking since her earlier visit with Annie, and she had come to one or two conclusions she wanted to test out. She intended to find out once and for all what part Eastvale College played in Gavin Miller's murder, if any, and to get the truth out of Lisa, whatever the cost. She thought she could do it with kindness, that Lisa might be ready to unburden herself, but if she had to take her down to the station and put her in a cell for twenty-four hours, browbeat her the way Annie had, then she would do it.

It was early evening, dark, the wet leaves muffling her footsteps as she approached the tall, narrow house, and when she first rang the bell, Winsome thought that Lisa was probably out. Then a small weary voice came over the intercom. "Hello?"

"Lisa, it's me. Winsome. DS Jackman."

There was a long pause, and Winsome could almost feel Lisa thinking, hear the cogs turning. She knew what the visit was about. Finally, she said, "You'd better come up," and the intercom buzzed.

Once she was in the flat, Winsome accepted the offer of chamomile tea and found its warmth and scent a great comfort as she settled into the armchair.

"I suppose you've come back because you want me to tell you everything, haven't you?"

"It would help."

"What makes you think I haven't?"

"I don't know," said Winsome. "Too many gaps in the story, maybe? Too many bits and pieces that don't add up. I started thinking there might be good reasons for your erratic and self-destructive behavior, for Lomax thinking you so completely unreliable, for your withdrawal from college life." There was also something Annie had passed on about Banks's interview with Kyle McClusky. Kyle had said that someone must have complained to Gavin Miller about his selling drugs, and that it was probably a woman who had been a victim of roofies and rape.

"I'm glad you came by yourself this time. I didn't like your friend. Sorry."

"Annie's an acquired taste."

"That's one way of putting it. I didn't do anything wrong, you know. Where do you want me to begin?"

"Where do you *think* it all began?"

The flames cast shadows in the hollows of Lisa's pale elfin features, glimmered orange and red in her big eyes. She took out a pouch of Drum tobacco and rolled a cigarette. "It's all right," she said. "Only tobacco."

"What's all right about tobacco?"

"You don't . . . ? Oh, bloody hell. Do you want me to . . . ?"

"It's all right," said Winsome. "I wouldn't dream of trying to stop someone from doing what they want in their own home."

The firelight caught the shape of a smile on Lisa's face. "As long as it's not illegal."

"That's right."

"Good. Because this is about the only place I can do it these days." Lisa lit the cigarette, pulled a shred of tobacco from her lower lip and settled down cross-legged by the hearth. "Are we sitting comfortably? Then I'll begin."

Winsome nodded and leaned back in her chair, cradling her mug of tea. She knew that she ought to be taking notes but thought if she took out her notebook it would ruin the mood, the rapport. If anything of value came up, she was sure that she would be able to get Lisa to make an official statement later. But this was delicate, fragile, she suspected, if even half of what she had suspected were true. It might not even be directly relevant to the case.

"It was over four years ago. February. Not too cold or wet. Not like Februaries these days. A mild night. I was nineteen. I thought I was a sophisticated Goth, really I did. I had the black gear, black lipstick and kohl, the chunky crosses, rings and amulets, the music. Bauhaus, PJ Harvey, Sisters of Mercy, the Cure, Joy Division."

Of these, Winsome had heard only of Joy Division, and even then she couldn't remember where she had heard of them. Banks, perhaps? Though she didn't think he was into Goth music. One of them had died, she thought.

"I'd been to a concert at the college. Wendy House. I was in my final year. There was a group of us. We'd been drinking a bit, but not a lot, and nothing more, you know, no drugs or anything. There was a boy who seemed interested in me. He wasn't at the college, and he said he'd come up from Bradford to see the band. I didn't know him, but he was fit, so we let him hang out with us in the bar later. When we all split up and went our own ways, he said he'd walk me home. I wasn't drunk, and he seemed nice enough, so I didn't mind, I wasn't nervous or anything. We were just chatting like mates about the concert, music and stuff. Like I said, it was a mild night. I lived closer to the heart of the campus then, but it was an old house, much like this one. I had a bottle of cheap wine at home, and I offered him some, poured some for myself and went to the toilet. When I got back and started drinking it, after a while things started to get hazy. The next thing I knew it was morning, and I had a splitting headache, a dry mouth and . . . I . . . I felt terribly sore, you know, between my legs. I felt down there, and I was all sticky. I was also naked, and I didn't remember getting undressed. I wasn't a virgin, so it didn't take me long to figure out what had happened. But it hadn't happened with my consent. At least, I didn't think so. I honestly couldn't remember. The last thing I could bring to mind was walking back in the room from going to the loo and drinking my wine. I think there was some Wilco on the stereo. I just knew I hadn't invited it, unless asking a boy in for a nightcap was asking for it, the way some people would have you believe. Maybe if he'd kissed me, I'd have let him. But no more. I wasn't promiscuous. I didn't even have a boyfriend at the time. We might have gone out together a few times and after a while, if we really liked each other, then we might have made love. But not like this. I didn't have a chance for any of that. He raped me, and I didn't remember a thing."

"I'm sorry, Lisa," Winsome said. "I mean it. What did you do?"

The shadows flickered over Lisa's face. She sucked on her cigarette, and the tip burned brighter. "I got myself together. It took a while. The first day I just didn't want to get out of the bath. I still hurt, and there was some blood. When I was able to, I talked to a few people who I knew had been with us that night, but nobody remembered who he was. I thought he must have come with someone, that someone must have invited him, but I got nowhere. I honestly don't think people were covering for him. There was no way they could have known what he did. Maybe he came up with some mates and got separated, hung with us? There was only one odd thing I remembered from the bar earlier on the night it happened."

"Kyle McClusky," said Winsome.

"Yes." Lisa peered at Winsome from under her ragged fringe. The hollows around her eyes were exaggeratedly dark, as if she had reverted to her Goth days and applied a heavy coating of kohl. "I distinctly remember the boy—I can't remember his name, if I ever knew it, or what he looks like—talking to Kyle by the entrance to the toilets. I'd seen Kyle before at some of the same lectures I went to, but I didn't really know him, or that he sold drugs."

"So you approached Kyle?"

"Yes. Naturally, he laughed it off, denied the whole thing, said he'd no idea what I was talking about, and if I repeated any of it to anyone, I'd be in trouble. But I knew he was lying. And I talked to others. People who knew he sold crystal meth and roofies. It didn't take me long to work out what had happened."

"So you went to Gavin Miller."

"I went to the only person I knew who I thought could help. Maybe now you can understand why I didn't go to the police? Imagine what a fine witness I would have made on the stand, not remembering a thing, stumbling over the answer to every question, being made to seem like a slut. Even a sudden glimpse of my own shadow made me jump for weeks after. Everyone knows that roofies are what nice college boys give to half-pissed slappers to get them into bed."

Winsome didn't like to tell Lisa, but she was probably right. She wouldn't even have got as far as court with the flimsy story she had to tell. And even if she had, only about 6.5 percent of rape prosecutions are successful. The odds are that her rapist would have walked free. No wonder about 95 percent of rapes went unreported.

"Did you tell Gavin Miller what happened to you?"

"No. I didn't tell anyone that. I just told him about Kyle selling the drugs and all. But I think he might have guessed. If he did, he was gentleman enough not to say anything. He told me he'd deal with Kyle."

So Kyle had been wrong in that Lisa hadn't told Gavin Miller, but his assumption had been close enough to the truth. "But you didn't know Kyle was connected with Beth and Kayleigh?"

"No. They weren't part of my scene. When I did find out, later, after the hearing and all, it still didn't seem relevant until I settled down to think about it, the way you thought about our earlier conversation."

"What did you do after the rape?"

"At first I was incapable of doing anything. I couldn't even think straight, let alone help anyone. I didn't deal with it well at all, especially not for the first few weeks. I drank too much, cut up wild. Life and soul of the party. That was me. But I didn't sleep around. I couldn't bear the idea of anybody touching me. Nobody could touch me. Not in any way. I felt dirty. Soiled. And worthless. It was a very strange time, like I was spinning wildly around something I couldn't quite make out, a huge dark ugly mass at the center of myself, a dark star that was trying to drag the rest of me, all the good bits, if there were any left, into itself, and it took all the energy I had to struggle against it and just keep spinning. There were nights I didn't dare go to sleep in case it sucked me in during the night. Even when I could, I always left the lights on. I still do. Anyway, after a while, a few weeks after Mr. Miller's dismissal, I realized what must have happened, what the girls must have done. I racked my brains for what to do. I felt responsible, like it was my fault Mr. Miller had got fired, that it happened because he helped me. I was sure those girls had set him up, but there was no way of proving it. I only knew they were pally with Kyle, because I saw the three of them at a party once, giggling in the corner, like I said. But that's hardly evidence, is it? I wasn't even sure how long ago it had happened then, but I knew it had been a while. Not that long, maybe, because I think it had all happened in March and it wasn't the end of the year yet. It was April when I . . . I couldn't deal with it. I just let things go, my studies, my appearance—not that I'd ever cared about it much, except, you know, the Goth look—my friends."

"What about your family?"

Lisa stiffened. "I didn't tell them anything. They wouldn't have been interested, anyway. My dad bailed years ago, and the string of useless, idle buggers my mother took in after that would've only laughed in my face and then grabbed my tits."

Winsome nodded. Not a point to pursue, then. "So you were alone with your feelings?"

"I got used to it. Am used to it. It's amazing what you can get used to when you have to. Things are different now, in a lot of ways, but I still feel alone. When it comes right down to it, we're born alone and we die alone, and pretty much all the time in between we're alone, too. Mr. Miller was right about that."

"You talked about things like that?"

"Life, philosophy, being, religion? Sure."

"What did you do in the end?"

"You already know what I did, don't you? That's why you're here."

"One reason. But I'd like you to tell me the whole truth."

"Why? So you can repeat it in court?"

"Lisa, that's not where this is going, and you know it."

"Yeah . . . well. OK, so I went and told Mr. Lomax that I'd overheard Beth and Kayleigh talking in the bogs about how they'd set up Mr. Miller because of what he did to Kyle, and how easy it was to fool everybody."

"But you hadn't heard anything of the kind, had you?"

Lisa looked away, sideways at the wall, the one with the Doors poster. Winsome followed her gaze. That young Door was certainly mesmerizing, she thought. "No," said Lisa. "I made it up about overhearing them."

Winsome didn't ask why; she had no reason to. Clearly Lisa had thought she could somehow mitigate her guilt at getting Miller involved in the Kyle McClusky business in the first place, and consequently losing him his job, by speaking up in Gavin Miller's favor, even if it meant lying. But it had been too little, too late, and by then she had gone off the rails and had gained a reputation for unreliability in all things. "What made you think they'd invented the story in the first place?" Winsome asked. "Couldn't Gavin Miller have actually been guilty of sexual misconduct?"

"No. I couldn't believe that. I knew Mr. Miller, and I didn't think he'd do something like that. I know all men are bastards, but Mr. Miller was . . . he was different, even then, when he was still teaching. Haunted. Deep. Sad. But not in a pathetic way."

"Were you in love with him?"

"God, no! I mean, not in that way. Not at all. It never even entered my mind. I admired him, liked him, enjoyed his company, and I felt guilty for getting him into trouble. But love? No. He was just a sort of mentor, I suppose. He encouraged me to think for myself."

"OK," said Winsome, holding up her hands. "Just checking. Affairs of the heart aren't my specialty."

Lisa tilted her head and gave a small smile. "So I gather."

"What happened in April? What set you on the road to clarity?"

"What almost sent me over the edge, you mean. Surely you know that, too?"

"I have some thoughts, but I can only hope I'm wrong."

Lisa rolled another cigarette. Her hands were shaking slightly. "Well, you're not." She looked Winsome in the eye. "You're probably thinking AIDS or pregnancy, right?"

"Something along those lines, yes."

"Well, I found out I was pregnant."

Only the hissing and crackling of the fire broke the silence of the next few seconds, which seemed to stretch out into even deeper unexplored terrain. Winsome didn't quite know how to respond. In a way, it was none of her business, not relevant to the case. But in another way, she had insinuated herself into Lisa's life, beyond the mere facts, the truth and the lies, and she felt put on the spot. She could respond like a cop or respond like a friend, an older sister, whatever. Or she could not respond at all. Her choice.

Lisa broke the silence and the discomfort by asking Winsome if she wanted another cup of tea. She said yes gratefully and gazed back at the poster of the beautiful half-naked man while Lisa put the kettle on.

"Mr. Miller gave that poster to me. Beautiful, isn't he?"

Winsome hadn't noticed Lisa come back. She nodded. "Who is it?"

Lisa's eyes widened. "You've never heard of Jim Morrison?"

"That's Jim Morrison?"

"Lead singer from the Doors." Lisa put another log on the fire. "He died on the third of July, 1971."

"I know the name," said Winsome, "but I didn't know what he looked like. I'm afraid I don't pay much attention to those sorts of things. He died young, didn't he?"

"He was twenty-seven years old."

"Drugs?"

"Heart failure."

"Caused by drugs?"

"Probably. He was a notorious user and boozer. He's buried in Père

Lachaise cemetery in Paris. I've been there. To his grave. Most of us who were there weren't even born when he died."

"You like his music?"

"I like his words. His poetry. He was a tortured soul. A true poet."

Neither spoke for a moment. Lisa just stared at the Doors poster in some sort of reverence, or so Winsome thought. She guessed that Jim Morrison was probably a bad boy, and not at all the kind of person her parents would have wanted her to meet. But sometimes . . . there was something in her that longed for such an adventure, throwing away all the maps and all the stop signs. Caution to the wind. The moment passed.

"I had an abortion, of course," Lisa said. "I don't suppose you approve of that, do you?"

"I believe that a woman has the right to choose, but I think it should be a considered choice."

"Oh, it was. Remember what shape I was in at the time? I wouldn't have made a good mother at all. Certainly not with my own mother as an example."

"You don't know that," Winsome said. "You can't."

"Maybe not," Lisa said slowly. "Call it a pretty good intuition, like the one about Beth and Kayleigh. But I wasn't thinking about becoming a mother at the time. I just wanted rid of it. That's what it was, an 'it,' a cancerous growth inside me. I wanted it cut out."

"And after that?"

"After that, it was the end of term, end of the year, end of my academic career. I failed, naturally. I left England, took all my savings and got the Eurostar to Paris. That's when I visited Père Lachaise. After that, I wandered around Europe doing odd jobs, menial jobs, working as a waitress or an office cleaner. Drinking myself to sleep at night from cheap bottles of wine I'd sneaked into my cheap hostel beds. There were boys, friendships, even, but still no sex. I still couldn't . . . I suppose it was a sort of healing process. I was just like, frozen, as far as all that went. At a certain point, I'd just seize up and that was it. There were times when life started to seem worthwhile again. Looking at great works of art in the Louvre, the Rijksmuseum or the Prado, or in tiny out-of-the-way churches in sleepy Italian villages. It didn't convert me to religion or anything, but it did bolster my spirits. I felt sort of like the Frankenstein monster must have done when the electric current traveled through its being, as if all my different bits and pieces were someone else's and were suddenly melding together into one, coming to life, becoming me. It was a slow process. A rebirth. I was away more than two years. Drifting. Mostly in France and Spain. There was a boy, towards the end. Things went all right, for a while. And now." She held out her arms. "Tra-la! I'm back."

"Have you ever thought of getting a proper job?"

Lisa pulled a face. "Don't push it."

"Why not? You're clearly an intelligent woman. There must be lots of things you can do. You could even go back to college or uni and finish your degree."

"I might not have a lot of money, or a career path to follow, but I'm happy doing what I'm doing for the moment, being who I am. Believe me, it's a rare experience in my life, so don't knock it."

"I didn't mean to. Am I preaching at you again?"

"No, not really." She held her thumb and forefinger a short distance apart. "Well, maybe just a little bit. You just expect everyone to follow the same sort of tried and tested path you followed. I don't mean to be insulting, but it's not very exciting, is it?"

"Being a detective? I don't know. It has its moments."

"Yes. The Bull. That dropkick."

"It wasn't a dropkick!"

"OK. OK. Whatever." She blew on the top of her tea. "But you know what I mean."

"My options were limited, too," said Winsome. "But maybe not for the same reasons as yours. And my dad was a cop, back in a little hill town above Montego Bay. He's retired now. He was my hero. Lucky he lived that long. I don't suppose I was very imaginative in my choice of a career, but I like it."

"You came here by yourself?"

"Yes. With my family's blessing. They wanted a better life for me. A life they couldn't have. I did well in school back home and came here to go to university."

"What did you study?"

"Psychology."

"I'm sorry. I didn't mean to be critical. I can be a bit overdefensive at times." Lisa paused. "So what's going to happen to me now? I didn't see you taking any notes, so I assume I can deny everything I said? Your word against mine."

"If you like," said Winsome.

"It depends. Are you going to arrest me?"

"Why would I do that?"

"I must have done something wrong somewhere in all that I've told you."

"Being raped isn't illegal, having an abortion isn't illegal, traveling around Europe isn't illegal. Maybe you're not as much of a criminal as you like to think you are."

"What about lying to the police?"

"Well, that's another matter. In general, lying isn't an arrestable offense. We'd have to put the whole world in jail if we could arrest people for lying. But you've slowed us down and misdirected us. We have many ways of dealing with that. Mostly it's up to the individual officer's discretion. And remember, you can always just deny everything you told me."

"I'm not like that."

"I didn't think so. As far as I can see, you're the victim in this, not the perpetrator."

"I'm not a perp! Well, that's a relief."

Winsome smiled. "Did you ever tell anyone at all about what happened to you? The rape? The pregnancy? The abortion?"

Lisa shook her head. "Nope. You're the first."

"Don't you think you ought to seek professional help after what you've been through?"

"A shrink?"

"Not necessarily. A counselor of some sort."

"Maybe that's what I needed four years ago, but I think I have my life together the way I like it now."

"Why did you tell me about it?"

"I don't know. It just seemed . . . right. I must say, though, it seems a long way from Mr. Miller's murder. I don't see how it helps you."

"Maybe it doesn't, but we don't work in quite as linear a way as that, however straight you think we are. I add bits to the overall picture, then—"

"What bits?" Lisa sounded concerned.

"Relevant bits. Not about a young girl getting raped, then finding out she's pregnant and having an abortion."

"I don't want anyone else knowing what happened to me. I don't want to be treated like a victim."

"Don't worry, you won't be." Winsome shifted in her armchair, put her mug down on the table and leaned forward. "But let's just examine one possibility that comes out of what you've told me tonight. You told me that you suspected Gavin Miller knew what had happened to you, about the roofies and the rape?"

"Yes. I can't really say why. It was just the way he looked at me. Maybe I'm imagining it. He'd probably have said something if he'd known, made me go see someone, like you suggested, or go to the police."

"Perhaps. But let's say, for the sake of argument, that he did suspect something of the sort. You don't know who the boy was. You can't even describe him. You say you didn't really pursue it, didn't try to find out."

"What good would it have done?"

"But what if Gavin Miller did try to find out? What if he succeeded? You like to think he cared about you, so maybe that was his way of doing something to help. He got Kyle McClusky off the campus, but maybe he got more. The name of the boy who bought the drug and gave it to you."

"That took him four and a half years?"

"These things happen. Maybe he was too devastated to try to find out at first, after he was dismissed. Maybe he didn't even pick up the trail until you two reconnected a few months ago. Maybe he bumped into one of your old friends who was at the concert and in the bar with you that night. He or she might have remembered what the boy looked like, or what his name was. You never even asked them. Who knows?"

"But if that were the case, wouldn't it have been the boy who did it to me who got hurt, not Mr. Miller?"

"I know it sounds far-fetched, but sometimes even police officers have to let our imaginations run free. Perhaps Gavin Miller arranged to meet him. On the railway bridge near his home, say. The boy went along, perhaps expecting blackmail, whatever. Gavin Miller confronted him. There was a fight. As you know, Mr. Miller wasn't in such good shape towards the end. He was malnourished and emaciated. I doubt he could have put up much of a fight against a younger and stronger opponent."

"Christ," said Lisa. "Are you saying I got him killed now? That it was because of me?"

"It's not all about you. If it did happen that way, it was about Gavin Miller. What he needed. Besides, all I'm doing is putting things together, making connections, stretching the facts a bit to do it. Half the time we make up stories from what we know, then test them out."

"But Mr. Miller didn't say anything about it when we met for coffee earlier this year. We never talked about the past at all, except like, way back, when he was a hippie and all that."

"But you didn't say anything to anyone about it. At least not until tonight, to me. Maybe Gavin Miller did work it out and kept it to himself for reasons of his own. Especially if he intended to harm the boy in revenge for what he'd done to you. Anyway, I'm only giving you a hypothetical example of how some of the things you've told me might affect the investigation. It's only speculation. There are some things I'll have to share with my boss—crimes have been committed, not by you, but against you—but I promise none of what you told me will go any further than that and I'll keep what I can to myself. What you told me is . . . well . . . it's . . ."

"In confidence?" suggested Lisa.

"Yes."

"Like between friends?"

Winsome reached for her mug. "Yes."

Lisa smiled. "All right, then."

"SO WHAT brings you here at this time of night?" Banks asked when he answered the insistent knocking at his door.

"You know damn well what," said Annie, walking in and slam-
ming the door behind her.

"No, I don't." He hated it when people said that and he didn't
know damn well what. His mother used to say it, without the swear-
ing, if ever he asked what he was supposed to have done wrong: "You
know quite well." It always made him feel like a naughty boy.

"Come off it, Alan. You've been playing us for fools, Winsome and
me, running two investigations and sending us out on the dummy
one. You've been using us as cover. You don't believe for a moment
that Gavin Miller's death has anything to do with his getting dismissed from Eastvale College. With Beth Gallagher or Kayleigh
Vernon or Trevor Lomax or Jim Cooper and that crowd. You think
it's all about what happened forty years ago at the University of Essex.
That's why you've had little Miss Masterson running around doing
your private research and God knows what else for you while you send
us off to waste our bloody time!"

They were standing in what used to be Banks's living room and
was now a sort of office-cum-den. "Stop pacing and sit down," Banks
said. "Catch your breath. Drink? Shall we go through to the back and
have a—"

"No, I don't want a bloody drink. And I don't want to go through
to the back. I won't be stopping." Annie remained on her feet while
Banks sat. "Of all the shitty tricks you've ever pulled, Alan, this one
has to be . . ."

"That's not true," Banks argued. "Both lines of inquiry are still
equally important. Essential. We have no idea why Gavin Miller was
killed. We can't afford to overlook Lomax and Cooper and the rest."

"But you lean towards Lady Chalmers, don't you, even though
you've been warned off?"

"So what if I do? It's not *your* job on the line. Do I think she killed
him? No, I don't. Do I think she's closely connected somehow with
what happened? Damn right, I do. But it could equally as well have
been Trevor Lomax, Jim Cooper or Dayle Snider."

"Yet you haven't let Winsome or me in on any of this. It's just been
you and your pretty little—"

"That's not true, and you know it. Hold on a minute, Annie. Are you sure this isn't just you being jealous? Because there's nothing to be jealous of. There's nothing between me and Gerry."

"Oh come off it, Alan. Just look at the sweet simpering little thing. She practically wets her knickers every time she gets near you."

"That's not true, and it's bloody rude of you to say it," came another voice from the hall, shortly followed by Gerry Masterson herself, striding through from the conservatory. Her face was red, and she was breathing hard. "If anyone's jealous, it's you, you miserable bitch. Jealous that DCI Banks has trusted me with the job and not you."

"Don't be so stupid. And don't—"

"I'm not stupid. You march in here and practically call me a tart, accuse me of sleeping with my boss, and you expect me to just stand there and take it. You can't talk about me like that, even if you do outrank me. Yes, ma'am, no ma'am. Is that what you expect? Well, I'm doing my job as professionally as I can under difficult circumstances, and I suggest you try and do the same instead of playing the jealous girlfriend. As far as I can see, you're the only one in this room who *has* slept with the boss."

"Why, you pissy little bitch!" Annie flew at her.

"Annie! Gerry!" cried Banks, getting between them before things went any further. "Stop it. Both of you. Let's all sit down, take a deep breath and have a drink. I don't know about you two, but I bloody need one." He managed to shepherd them both, stiff shouldered, still bristling with rage, through the connecting door into the entertainment room. It seemed the safest bet, and the closest. There were comfortable chairs and dim, relaxing lighting, and a disc of Chopin's Nocturnes was playing. There was also a cocktail cabinet and a small wine rack beside a row of glasses. Banks reached for a bottle of Layers. Thank God it was screw-top, he thought. His hands were shaking too much to handle a corkscrew. As he poured, he said, "Let's all just try and calm down and get this sorted. There's no need for fighting."

"She can't talk about me like that just because she's my boss," said Gerry.

"Gerry, sit down." Banks handed her a glass. Her hand was shaking, too, he noticed.

Annie was still breathing fire and stalking the room. "Annie." Banks held out the glass.

For a moment Annie just glared at him, then she took the glass and flopped down in the nearest armchair, slopping a little wine down her front. Luckily, she was wearing a burgundy top. She ran her free hand through her mass of curly brown hair.

Gerry also sat, about as far away from Annie as she could get, Banks noticed, and took a demure sip of wine.

"Right," said Banks. "Let's all put our ranks aside for the moment. What's this all about, Annie?"

"I've seen her notes. The phone calls. The research."

"You've been going through my desk while I was out, haven't you? Prying into my affairs," said Gerry. "Poking around my desk. I suppose you've been into my computer, too?"

Annie looked away. "Oh, don't get your knickers in a knot."

Banks took it that she was guilty as charged. "That's not on, Annie," he said. "You know that."

"Why not? I have a right to know what's going on. She works under me. I'm deputy investigating officer, or don't you remember? I'm her superior officer, and I have a right to know what the people under me are up to."

"Superior? That's a laugh. I do my assigned work, my duty," said Gerry. "HOLMES Two is up to date. You find fault with my data handling if you can."

"It's not your fault," said Banks, speaking to both of them. "None of this. It's mine. I've handled it badly. I should have come clean."

"A bit late for that now, isn't it?" said Annie.

Banks took a slug of wine. All they needed now was to get drunk and fall into some sort of *Who's Afraid of Virginia Woolf?* drunken row. But that was two married couples, he remembered. Still, he would keep his intake to a low level. "It's a very delicate situation," Banks said, choosing his words carefully. "A balancing act. As everyone knows, I got a hell of a bollocking from the AC *and* the ACC the other day, and I was told in no uncertain terms to lay off the Lady Chalmers angle. But as I'm sure everyone also knows—and you, in particular, Annie—I don't take kindly to being given orders simply because someone plays golf with the chief constable and passes on a complaint. What neither of you know is that Lady Chalmers phoned me the other night and apologized, said it wasn't down to her that it happened. It was her brother-in-law, Anthony Litton, who was present when you and I talked to her last Thursday, Annie. So you can't say I didn't include you in that, can you, in addition to telling you and Winsome my thoughts on Lady Chalmers the other day. And who got the bollocking? It wasn't you."

"Oh, so she's off the hook now, is she, because she phoned and made up?" said Annie. "I suppose you had a nice old nostalgic chat about how good the sixties were, didn't you? Fancy her as well, do you?"

"Cut it out, Annie. What I'm trying to say is that it made me even more suspicious in some ways. What Gerry's been doing—what I've been asking her to do—is vital to any investigation of what role Lady Chalmers may have played in the events. And in case you don't realize it, Gerry also happens to be the best researcher we have. She's also the one taking the risks by doing that research. If you were to think about it all clearly, I've been protecting you ever since I got the bollocking last Thursday."

"Oh, come off it, Alan. You can't get away with that. It's *me* you're talking to. Annie Cabbot. Remember? Your 'partner.'" She glared at Gerry Masterson. "And I mean that in a professional sense. When have I ever made you think I don't have the stomach to do what it takes to get the job done?"

"Never. But this is different."

"Bollocks, it's different."

"I'm sorry, Annie, but—"

"Well, at least you're sorry. That's a start." Annie drank some more wine. She seemed to be calming down a little, Banks thought. He would have to play this very carefully if he wanted to pull the team together rather than push them apart.

"Is it true that I'm so easily expendable?" Gerry asked quietly. "That you've been using me as some sort of cover to protect your favorites, DI Cabbot and DS Jackman? Because if that's true—"

"Of course it isn't true," said Banks, not quite used to getting it from both barrels like this. "I told you. You're the best researcher we have. That's why I asked you to do it."

"Anybody could have done what I've done. I was a fool, wasn't I? You never let me in on any of the important interviews. You used me. I've never even *met* Lady Chalmers. You'd either go by yourself, or take DI Cabbot here, while I slaved over the computer and the phone just waiting for AC Gervaise to walk in and catch me."

"Don't be silly, Gerry," said Banks. "The work you've been doing is essential. That's just my way. If anything happened, I'd take the flak for you. You must know that. Annie? You, too. Tell her."

Annie glanced from one to the other, obviously considering her options. Finally, she said, "He's right. He might be a stubborn and devious bastard, but he's there for the team when the chips are down. He'll always take one for the team. Which is why it pisses me off so much that he didn't let me and Winsome in on his little game." She reached for the bottle and refilled her glass.

"We were spread too thin, Annie. Someone had to deal with Lomax and the college crowd."

"Muggins here."

"There's no muggins about it. It's still odds on that one of them did it. We have, however, made quite a bit of progress today."

Annie raised her eyebrows. "Oh? Well, I can hardly say that I have. All I've done is hit a brick wall with Lisa Gray. And I'm sick to bloody death of that college and everyone in it."

"But Winsome went back to talk to Lisa again," Banks said. "And before you start flying off the handle about her doing things behind your back, she told me she did it because she felt she had a rapport with Lisa, and she also felt that Lisa was on the verge of opening up. She judged there was a better chance if she went by herself, and she was right."

Annie snorted. "So maybe I was a bit hard on the Gray girl. But you know how Winsome likes to take on lame ducks."

"You're one to talk, with that Polish girl you took home with you a few months ago."

Annie's lips tightened to a straight white line, but she took a deep breath and another sip of wine, and relaxed. "OK, so I'm the one behind in this game, the one who's not coming up with the goods.

You've made that obvious enough. So go on, bring me up to speed."

Banks let the sarcasm drip off him. He was used to that. It meant Annie was on the mend. "Sometimes we do get involved," he said. "We know we shouldn't, but we do. And you know what? Sometimes it helps. Lisa Gray was a victim of rape, a rape that occurred after a boy slipped her a dose of Rohypnol he bought from Kyle McClusky. That's why she went to Gavin Miller instead of the police. Because she was ashamed and afraid, and because he wouldn't ask her all kinds of personal and probing questions. We do our best with rape victims, as you both know, but it's a difficult business, a balancing act at best, soft lights and music or no. These girls have been terribly violated. I can't begin to know how they feel." He looked at Annie who, he was fully aware, knew very well how it felt.

Annie glared back at him. "So what happened?" she asked.

"When she made the link between Kyle and Beth and Kayleigh, she made up a story about hearing the girls crow over the stunt they'd pulled on Gavin Miller."

"So she lied about overhearing them in the toilets?"

"Yes. She'd seen them at a party. That's how she knew they were friends."

"Dammit, I *thought* so. I thought it was rather a long time after the events themselves to be talking about them like that. So Winsome got it out of her? Good for her."

"Lisa was going through a bad time. Guilt, shame, feeling dirty. She was drinking a lot, trying to block out what she knew had happened, even though her memories of it were fragmentary. She also felt responsible for what the girls did to Miller, when she managed to put it all together in her fogged-up brain. It was the best she could do. At least she tried."

"What about the rapist?" Gerry asked.

"Lisa said he was just someone she met at a concert and went to the bar with later. She doesn't remember his name or what he looks like. She said he seemed like a nice bloke. Thinks he came from Bradford."

"So he got away with it?"

"So it would appear. But Kyle McClusky is in jail, admittedly for something else, but he is in jail."

"A lot of good that'll do him," Annie said. "I could think of a few better punishments for rapists, or for scum like him who facilitate rape. So? Result?"

"The college crowd is still very much in the picture. They've all lied or held things back. Many things could have happened over the four years that passed to bring events to a head at that railway bridge, most of them centering around Gavin Miller finding out about all the behind-the-scenes stuff nobody told him at the time."

"But we've no evidence that he did find out."

"That's the problem. And that's what we're still digging for. There were plenty of dangerous secrets around, and don't forget Gavin Miller was desperately short of money. I think it's possible that blackmail may have been involved somewhere along the line. We know he didn't get a loan or win it on the lottery. Drugs are still a possibility. Miller might have thought them a way to turn a quick profit, and he could easily have stepped on the wrong toes."

"The toes of people who throw people from bridges?" said Annie.

"Exactly. We're not ruling it out, so Winsome will liaise again with the drugs squad and see if they can turn anything up."

Annie topped up her wine. Banks was about to tell her she should slow down, that she was driving, but if push came to shove, she could take his spare room. It had happened before, during her convalescence after the shooting. Gerry was fine, still nursing her first glass, about three-quarters full. Banks didn't care himself. He wasn't going anywhere. He took the bottle after Annie and finished with it. There was only about a mouthful left.

"So where do we go now?" Annie asked.

"Wherever we go," Banks said, "we go as a team. The Chalmers line of inquiry is still open and thriving, as far as I'm concerned, and everything any of us gets will be shared with all. As I understand it, Gerry's got a line on one of the members of the Marxist Society who was around at the same time as Veronica Bellamy. Gerry?"

Gerry still seemed a bit agitated, and still resentful of Annie, but she began a hesitant, though thorough, account of her talk with Judy Sallis that evening, and the lead that it had given her to Dr. Mandy Parsons. When she had finished, there was a pause, then Annie said, "Good work. The finding *and* the questioning."

A ghost of a smile flickered across Gerry's face at the compliment.

"But don't get cocky about it," Annie added. She glanced at Banks. "And tomorrow?"

"Business as usual. I'll be talking to Veronica Chalmers again, first thing, and I don't care who knows about it. She lied about not knowing Miller at university, and I want to know why."

"She was only shagging him," Annie said. "That's why."

"There has to be more to it than that."

"Maybe not. It's probably something she was ashamed of, if she knew what he'd become. I can think of a few old boyfriends I wouldn't want to admit to. Besides, Miller's been murdered. Nobody wants to admit to being involved with a murder victim, even if it was forty years ago."

Banks gave her an inquiring glance. Annie countered it with an enigmatic smile. "It could have even been more recent than that. We don't know."

"Lady Veronica Chalmers and the decrepit Gavin Miller having an affair?" said Banks. "Give us a break."

"These things happen."

"In your dreams."

"And if AC Gervaise finds out what I've been digging up about Veronica's past," said Gerry, "then we're all in for it."

"Yes," said Banks. "Then it'll be time for your 'I am Spartacus' impersonations." Annie managed a little snigger at that, though the reference seemed lost on Gerry. "Seriously, though," Banks went on. "Are we OK with this?"

Annie and Gerry looked at one another and nodded. "It's a pity Winsome isn't here," Annie said.

"Winsome's on side. I've spoken with her on the phone," said Banks. "It wasn't quite the same as the little discussion we've had here tonight, but she's up for whatever happens."

"And what does happen?"

"That depends very much on what I get from Veronica and what Gerry gets from our Marxist Society lady tomorrow. It might not be a bad idea," Banks added, "if you or Winsome went with her to Leeds. And before anyone takes umbrage at that, it's neither a measure of any shortcomings on Gerry's part, nor my appeasement of Annie's hurt feelings. It's the way we should have played it all along. We complement one another; we don't compete. And two of us makes it official. With notes."

"But you're keeping Lady Chalmers to yourself?" Annie commented.

"Oh, yes. I think so. For the moment. And again, I think it's because I'm far more likely to get something out of her if there's just the two of us."

"You've got nothing but a bunch of lies so far," Annie said.

"I'm aware of that. It might be very fragile, but I think there's at least a bit of rapport between us. And I think she's heading for a fall. She's scared. Like Winsome said about Lisa Gray, she's going to get tired of all the lies and evasions and open up about her fears to someone. Me, I hope. You might take the piss out of us both being of that same generation, the sixties and all, but things like that can be damn useful, having stuff in common. We're both Van Morrison fans, too."

"Fair enough. I've got nothing against Van Morrison. Quite like 'Have I Told You Lately,' as a matter of fact." Then she glanced at Gerry. "I'll go to Leeds with you."

Gerry swallowed and nodded uncertainly. Then she stood up. "I'd better go now. I think we've finished, haven't we? Finished our business?"

Banks stood up, too. "Yes. And thanks, Gerry." He looked at Annie, who hadn't moved. "Annie, you shouldn't be driving."

In the brief silence that followed, Banks worried that there might be an explosion coming, but Annie said simply, "I know. You're probably right. What do you suggest? A taxi? It's a long way."

"I can give you a lift home, if you like," Gerry volunteered.

Annie stared at her for a few moments, then got to her feet. "Fine," she said. "Excellent. Harkside's a bit out of your way, mind."

"That's all right." She gestured to the half-full wineglass she had set on the table.

When they had left, Banks closed the door with a sigh of relief and leaned back on it until he heard the car drive away. Annie had drunk the best part of the bottle of wine, so he picked another from the rack, then he put it back and decided tonight's shenanigans called for a large

Laphroaig. Then he rummaged through his CD collection to find something that suited his mood. He stopped at *Bitches Brew,* thinking that might be a good choice in the light of the evening's entertainment, but he quickly suppressed the politically incorrect thought. On second thought, he realized, he wasn't the one who had used the "b" word, and he rather felt like a bit of late-sixties Miles Davis funky experimentation, so he put it on anyway. Loud.

11

BANKS WASN'T HAPPY ABOUT VISITING LADY CHALMERS at her house again on Tuesday morning, but needs must. He would have much preferred an interview room, or his office, to the grand mansion, where he always felt intimidated by the ostentatious display of wealth. But he hadn't wanted to let her know he was coming this time, and he knew there was no way she would agree to come down to the station, or go anywhere else with him, for that matter, without Ralph Nathan or Anthony Litton in tow. Besides, at least this way, there was a chance that AC Gervaise wouldn't find out so quickly, not if Lady Chalmers or Oriana didn't tell her. He had made sure before turning into the drive that there were no signs of the media in the area.

Oriana seemed marginally more pleased to see him this time than when he had called by with Annie the other day. At least she greeted him with a smile, and it seemed genuinely warm. If she thought he was her ally in trying to plumb the depths of Lady Chalmers's anxiety and depression, then she was right, in a way, though it was not perhaps for the same reasons.

When Oriana came back from consulting with Lady Chalmers, Banks found himself led towards a different room this time. Before he went in, Oriana touched his arm gently. He tried to ignore the electric tingle that her touch sent through him. When he looked at her, he could tell that she was both imploring him to be kind and encouraging him to uncover the reasons for her employer's troubles. Banks hoped he could, but he had a sneaking feeling that the discussion would be more fractious than that. He gave Oriana an encouraging smile and went into the room.

It had the same view of the town center, castle and river as its neighbor, but was much smaller, and most of the walls were covered by bookcases, many of them filled with copies of Charlotte Summers books in a variety of languages. A heavy mahogany desk stood under the window, and Lady Chalmers sat there in jeans and a white cashmere jumper, her desk littered with papers weighted down by a mug with "The trouble with being a famous writer is that sometimes you have to write" written on it. There was also a large computer screen, the kind that didn't need anything but a wireless keyboard and a mouse. She offered Banks the only other chair in the room and swiveled around so that she faced him. Mozart's Clarinet Quintet was playing from speakers concealed somewhere in the room, or perhaps from the computer itself.

"I like to listen to Mozart while I'm working," said Lady Chalmers. "It seems to help channel the creativity."

"He'd certainly be good for that," said Banks. "I'm sorry to interrupt your work."

"That's all right. I'm not having a particularly fruitful day. I can't seem to concentrate. As a matter of fact, I'm glad for the interruption. It gives me an excuse to take a break for a while. I'd also like to apologize about our last meeting, or its aftermath. And for that rather silly telephone call." She blushed. "As you probably guessed, I was a little drunk. It doesn't happen very often."

"I'm glad to hear it," said Banks. He was beginning to feel as if he were the one who had been summoned here. Behind Lady Chalmers's shoulder, the computer screen saver went through a random cycle of photographs. Exotic places—perhaps a Greek island, an ancient amphitheater, the Champs-Élysées, an Asian street market, the Amalfi coast. There were also some family shots of the children, Angelina and Samantha, at various ages. Oriana in a bikini, which was a sight to behold, smiling, her sunglasses up on her forehead. Lady Chalmers

and her husband, Banks assumed, standing on a yacht beside Anthony
Litton, and a woman Banks took to be his late wife, Veronica's sister,
Francesca. He noticed a strong resemblance between the sisters. Oliver
Litton came up, too, and he had some of his mother's looks, though
there was nothing feminine about him. With his handsome, chiseled
features, bald head and broad shoulders, he looked more like a football
player than a potential home secretary. The photographs were dis-
tracting, but Banks didn't want Lady Chalmers to turn them off. He
also hoped that Oriana in a bikini would come around again before he
left. Naturally, there was no sign of Gavin Miller in any of the photos.
None of them seemed older than ten or fifteen years, as far as he could
judge.

"How can I help you this time?" Lady Chalmers asked.

"It's a bit delicate," said Banks, "but first I'd like to ask you if there's
anything you're worried about, afraid of, that sort of thing?"

Her answer came too fast and lacked conviction. "No. Why? Should
I be?"

"Not at all. It's just . . . maybe an impression . . . your phone call
and everything . . . that something may be troubling you."

"Then you have the wrong impression."

But Banks could tell by the signs of strain in her expression, and the
discoloration under her eyes, as well as the haunted look in them, that
this was far from the case. She was looking closer to her true age
today. She was also very subdued, but he could sense something powerful within, barely suppressed. What was she hiding? And why? It
was obviously a great burden on her, yet she seemed determined to the
point of self-sacrifice to bear it.

Could she possibly suspect someone close to her? Banks wondered.
Were the three women lying about their alibi to protect one of their
number? Oriana. Veronica. Angelina. Was one of them a killer? No,
Banks couldn't accept that. It didn't make sense. It was a violent crime.
Someone had beaten Gavin Miller, then literally picked him up and
thrown him over the edge of the railway bridge like a sack of rubbish.
Banks couldn't see any of the three women doing that. But there was
definitely something that felt wrong, something out of kilter in the
household, and he was determined to get to the bottom of it. He de-

cided to try a direct approach. "We now know that you knew Gavin Miller at university," he said. "That's what I really wanted to talk to you about. Why you denied it."

Lady Chalmers slumped a little in her chair. A head and shoulders of her standing with her nephew Oliver rose and faded on the screen, followed by the two of them standing in front of a cherry tree in blossom. It could have been taken in Tokyo, for all Banks knew. "I don't know what you mean," she said. "It was such a long time ago. If I knew him, it could only have been in passing."

"You went out with him for three or four months in late 1971 and perhaps a month or so more in early 1972."

"That's ridiculous."

She wasn't a good liar, and Banks could tell easily that she was simply denying by rote now. The game was already becoming tiresome to her. "Why are you lying to me about something I already know to be true, Lady Chalmers? Perhaps if you told me the truth, it would help clear this mess up, and you could get on with your life, get back to normal."

She gave him a pitying look, as if such a thing were never to be. "Normal? What's the truth, anyway? Why does everyone rate it so highly? Do you think it really sets you free?"

"Sometimes," said Banks. "But let's stick to the facts for now. Were you sleeping with Gavin Miller at university in the early seventies?"

"If you think you already know the answer, why ask me? I slept with lots of boys at university. Does that shock you?" When Banks didn't appear shocked, she went on. "You can't expect me to remember their names after all this time."

"This was different," Banks said. "He was in love with you."

"Oh, Mr. Banks. How naïve you are. They were all in love with me. At least to hear them speak. For a week or two, at any rate."

"You didn't return his feelings."

"Am I supposed to feel guilty about that, or something? Do you think that's why I killed him? Because he was in love with me forty years ago, and I didn't love him back? I expect it was just a bit of fun, like all the rest. I was young. Impulsive. Capricious."

"So you do admit that you went out with him?"

"How quaint that sounds. Went out. Perhaps. I'm just saying he was nothing special, and I don't really remember anything about him."

"Would he have remembered you?"

"I'd like to think so, but I doubt it. Tell me, Mr. Banks, in all honesty, would you remember or recognize all or any of the girls you slept with when you were a student? If you were ever a student, that is."

Banks ignored the implied jibe at his education. "There weren't that many," he said.

"You're implying that I'm a slut?"

"Nothing of the kind. You're the one who said you slept with a lot of boys at university. I'm only asking about your relationship with Gavin Miller."

"Relationship? Would you really call it that?"

This was like trying to catch smoke between your fingers, Banks was beginning to feel. Then, when he looked again at Lady Chalmers's eyes, he saw they were not only haunted but a little glazed, which indicated that she may have been drinking, or perhaps was on some sort of medication. He guessed the latter, as it was still morning, and he could neither smell nor see any signs of alcohol. Valium or something, then. To take the edge off, muffle the anxiety and make talking to her like trying to grasp smoke. There was nothing to do but persevere. "I wouldn't know what to call it. I'm assuming it's true that you did go out with Gavin Miller back then. Why not? After all, he was a handsome enough boy, and he probably flattered you. Wrote poems about you, perhaps? What I'd like you to tell me is why you denied this in all our conversations."

"Because I don't remember," said Lady Chalmers. "I'm not saying I didn't sleep with him, I just don't remember it, that's all."

"Why did you stop seeing him?"

"I obviously got bored. Or I found a better lay."

"You don't need to be crude. It doesn't suit you."

"How do you know? How can you presume to know anything about me?"

"I stand corrected. Let's say you got bored with him, then, and you had a better opportunity waiting in the wings. When he rang you a couple of weeks ago asking for donations to the alumni society, did you know who he was?"

"No. Of course not. It was over forty years ago. I wouldn't have known him if I'd passed him in the street, let alone by just his voice. I certainly didn't recognize him from that picture you showed me."

Banks took the older photograph from his briefcase, the one they thought had been taken in the early eighties. "What about this?" he asked, holding it in front of her.

"Perhaps," she said, her eyes shutting slowly.

Banks put the photo away. "He didn't mention your shared past when he phoned?"

"Of course he did. But it meant nothing to me. You make it sound like some grand affair, for crying out loud. It was just a fuck."

"So you moved on to someone else?"

"I suppose so. It wasn't all to do with men, you know. I was also busy studying."

"And there was the Marxist Society, too, I believe?"

"For a while."

"I hear you were keen, quite a firebrand."

"Are you trying to embarrass me with my youthful politics now, Mr. Banks? What does that have to do with anything? Are you going to arrest me for being a communist forty years ago? Yes, I admit it, officer, I was a member of the Marxist Society. It was a long time ago. I was young and idealistic. Weren't you ever young and idealistic? I thought communism would solve all the world's problems. I still believe in equality, whatever you may think of me. Maybe you'd call me a champagne socialist. Isn't that the term today for rich people like me who spout on and on about inequality and social injustice? *Guardian* readers? I think everyone should have Veuve Clicquot rather than Freixenet, if that's what they want."

"Or a decent single-malt whisky," said Banks. "I couldn't agree more. Though I doubt the distillers and the winemakers would agree."

Lady Chalmers smiled. "Capitalist pigs." She took a deep breath and let it out slowly. "What can I say? We were young, naïve, privileged intellectuals. There were people around then with the real will and power to do things, to change things, to do it violently, if necessary, through social upheaval. I was a bit too queasy for that. They could cause serious political and social unrest. We were intellectuals, theorists and ideologists. They were activists. The front line."

"The unions?"

"Yes, for the most part. As you might remember, they were very militant back then. There was the romantic idea of the true revolutionary hero, the proud worker standing on the barricades brandishing the red flag, not the bloke you see by the roadside leaning on his shovel and having a cup of tea every time you pass by some roadworks. Establishing the true workers' state. It was a very powerful idea. Very real."

"Mostly I remember the power *cuts*," said Banks. "Why did Gavin Miller telephone you after all this time?"

Lady Chalmers let out another breath and said, "He wanted to touch me for some money, for old times' sake. A few hundred pounds, just to get him on his feet. Apparently he'd fallen on hard times."

"What did you tell him?"

"No, of course."

"And how did he react?"

"Well, there wasn't very much he could do, really, was there? He tried to bring up old times, how 'fantastic' we were together, and he actually got a bit weepy. That did it for me. I think he was drunk or on drugs or something. In the end, I just told him quite firmly not to ring me again and put the phone down."

Banks leaned back in his chair. "I don't really understand any need for secrecy about all this. Why didn't you tell me right from the start and have done with it? You could have saved us both a lot of trouble."

"Because I didn't want to get involved, all right?" said Lady Chalmers. "If you must know the truth, I was ashamed. I know that sounds like a cliché, but I had nothing whatsoever to do with Gavin Miller's death, and I didn't see why I had to answer all sorts of prying questions about my past and my personal life and open myself up to suspicion by admitting I knew him, even if it was years ago."

"But you opened yourself up to more suspicion by lying."

Lady Chalmers gave Banks a brave smile. "I know that now. I really believed that you'd simply give up and go away. I thought I could hide behind . . . who I am, what I am, my title, my status in the community." She gave a harsh laugh. "What a betrayal of those youthful ideals, don't you think?"

"If we all remained true to the dreams of our youth," said Banks, "it would be a very strange world indeed."

"But a better one, perhaps," Lady Chalmers whispered, almost to herself.

Banks sometimes wished he had followed Schiller's advice, himself. He had let some of those dreams go far too easily. But this was no time to get maudlin. "Had you ever seen him around town? Did you know he was living here in Eastvale?"

"I wouldn't have recognized him if I had seen him. Look, Mr. Banks, we slept together for a few weeks a long time ago. I'm sure it was very nice, but I don't remember it. We were kids. We were stoned most of the time. I don't even remember seeing him around during the rest of my time at Essex, to tell the truth. Why would I know him here forty years later? It's not as if we moved in the same circles, and I don't mean to sound snobbish by saying that, but it's true. And I certainly had nothing to do with his death."

Banks imagined she might be telling the truth, or something close to it. By the time Ronnie Bellamy and Gavin Miller had ended up in Eastvale, they had both changed a great deal, and both had moved on. Ronnie Bellamy even had a new name, two if you counted her pseudonym. She was no longer the lovely young activist, Ronnie Bellamy, but Lady Chalmers, wife of a multimillionaire Broadway and West End producer. Perhaps Gavin Miller had seen her about town and recognized her. It was possible. He was the one who had been in love, after all, and the unrequited lover has an entirely different perspective on the affair. But he certainly hadn't had the courage or desire to approach her, and she had probably not recognized him, as she claimed, even if she had seen him. Perhaps that was the end of the story, if only Banks's scar weren't itching and he weren't convinced there was something he was missing.

Though Banks had told the truth about not sleeping with a lot of girls at college, there were still old girlfriends he wouldn't recognize if he saw them in the street. So why did he find it so hard to accept that

Lady Chalmers and Gavin Miller had managed to live in the same
town for three years or so without one knowing of the other's existence? Miller's grand passion had been a young man's infatuation, no
doubt quickly burned out once he had been rejected. Gerry had told
him that even Judy Sallis had said Gavin had moved on to someone
else fairly quickly. And Lady Chalmers hadn't given a thought to the
whole thing since. Why should she? She never had any shortage of
suitors. Miller had simply been one in a long list of conquests.

So let it go, he told himself. You have your answers.

But he couldn't. Because if Gavin Miller's phone call was as innocent as Lady Chalmers made it out to be, why had she been so troubled for the whole of the following week, as Oriana had said she was?
And why did she also appear to be frightened of something *after* Gavin
Miller had been murdered? Because when he looked at her, even now,
with the Valium, or whatever it was, dulling her anxieties, he could
still see that she was troubled, and he realized that whatever she had
told him, however much it had cost her pride, it was all calculated to
get rid of him as soon as possible. She had really told him nothing he
didn't already know. "What are you frightened of, Ronnie?" he asked,
staring into her cloudy green eyes.

She held his gaze for several moments, holding her head high, but
obviously with difficulty. "Nothing," she said finally, turning away.
"Now, I think you should go. I've told you everything you need to
know. As far as I'm concerned, this whole business is over. I won't say
anything about this conversation to anyone. I'm sure you know what I
mean. But if you keep pestering me, things might be different."

Banks nodded. Dismissed, then. Behind her, on the screen, Oriana
in a bikini came around again, but the real Oriana wasn't around to
show him to the door.

Just as Banks was about to get into his car, a silver E Type Jaguar
pulled into the drive and blocked his way. A man got out and walked
towards him. Even without the clue of the customized JEM 1 number
plate, Banks knew who he was. He got that sinking feeling. *Shit.* Still,
he supposed, he would have to talk to him sometime.

"Are you Banks?" Sir Jeremy said.

Banks reached for his warrant card.

"No need for that. Are you Banks?"

"Yes."

Sir Jeremy gestured with his thumb to the passenger side of his car. "Get in."

ANNIE AND Gerry Masterson didn't talk much on the way to Leeds. Gerry kept her attention on the road, especially when they got close to the city itself, and they half listened to talk shows on local radio. Annie said it was a relief not to have to suffer Banks's musical tastes for a change. Gerry admitted that she didn't understand half the pop culture references he made. Annie said it was an age thing.

They had settled their differences the previous evening, when Gerry had given Annie a lift home from Newhope Cottage, both of them ending up laughing over what they imagined Banks's reaction would be when they'd left. A sigh of relief, no doubt, Annie had guessed, probably followed by a large Laphroaig and some loud atonal music. Annie had apologized for getting too steamed up over the Lady Chalmers investigation, and the things she had said, and Gerry had apologized for losing her temper and getting personal. Secretly, Annie had been glad to see a spark of fire in Gerry, whom she had thought rather insipid until then, but she wasn't going to tell her that. She was also dismayed to find out that the whole station knew about her and Banks, but she realized she should have expected that, given that the place had more grapevines than a vineyard.

Gerry drove through Otley, then on through Bramhope and Lawnswood towards Headingley. It was difficult finding somewhere to park near the university, but she managed to find a spot just large enough to squeeze the Ford Focus into on a side street of dark old brick houses with basements and dormers, all converted into student bedsits. They would have lunch in Leeds before going back, Annie said. Somewhere nice like that little Italian restaurant she remembered from a previous visit with Banks. Or even a nice country pub on the way home. That was one of the perks of a day out in the field. They might not be able to recoup expenses for it, but what the hell.

Annie had visited the University of Leeds campus before, though she couldn't profess to know her way around. They walked down Woodhouse Lane and entered beside the broad steps of the Parkinson Building, below the tall white tower of the Brotherton Library. It was a very open campus, Annie had always thought, built on split levels, with a great deal of outdoor space, trees, little patches of green, a mix of old brick buildings and houses and sixties concrete and glass buildings in the style of Le Corbusier.

She stopped and asked directions from a passing student, who told her that the Social Sciences Building was the modern one just a little further ahead, on their left. After that, it was easy enough to find Dr. Mandy Parsons's office, a pleasant enough space, though cluttered, like most academic offices Annie had ever seen. It wasn't quite as messy as Trevor Lomax's, Annie thought, but she still had to clear a pile of student essays from the third chair before they could all sit down. The office smelled vaguely of cigar smoke under the veneer of air freshener.

Annie's patience was wearing thin after her dealings with Lomax and Cooper, and the prospects of sitting in yet another messy office listening to erudite witticisms didn't appeal to her at all. These academics seemed to live in a rarefied world that she didn't quite understand. Annie was no philistine, and she had done well in university herself, but she also believed that unless you got out there and really got your hands dirty, you couldn't have much of an idea what life was all about. That was what all the best artists did, anyway; they stared at the world, took it apart, and rearranged it just for the sake of it, or to understand it better, to make some sort of statement about what it was, could be or should be. Most academics only dreamed of somebody else rearranging it for them. Maybe Dr. Mandy Parsons would turn out to be different, with her feminist and Marxist beliefs, but Annie doubted it. Anyway, she felt prickly even before the questions began. She would have to watch herself, let Gerry do most of the asking. After all, it was Gerry who had tracked her down.

"Thanks for agreeing to see us at such short notice," said Gerry, proffering her hand.

"It was you who called?"

"Yes. This is my colleague, DI Annie Cabbot."

Annie and Dr. Parsons shook hands. "I'd hardly have thought it would take two of you to handle me," Dr. Parsons joked. "What am I supposed to have done?"

"You?" said Annie. "Nothing, as far as we know."

"Oh, that's a pity. I do still try so hard to be a fly in the ointment."

"And I'm sure you are," Annie said. Mandy Parsons was tall and slim, with almost no hips or bust. She wore dark trousers and a plain pink shirt, and her cropped hair was shot through with gray. Black-rimmed glasses perched on the bridge of her slightly hooked nose.

"Tell me," Dr. Parsons said, tapping her pen against the desk. "It must still be difficult for a woman to get on in the police force, even today. After all, it's still very much a male domain, isn't it?"

"Very much so," said Annie. "But we've made a few inroads, as you can see. There are two of us right here in your office as proof. Our area commander is a woman, too."

"Then there's Winsome," Gerry reminded her.

"Yes. There's a black woman we work with, too. A detective sergeant. She's very good. So that's gold stars all round on the gender and race employment stats. In fact, I sometimes feel sorry for poor old DCI Alan Banks. But we've got him trained, haven't we, Gerry? He's well outnumbered. Only got young Harry Potter for solidarity."

Dr. Parsons seemed puzzled, and perhaps annoyed, but all she said was "I take it that a DCI is higher in rank than a DI? So there's still a long way to go?"

"There's always still a long way to go, isn't there?" Annie said.

"But what about the sexist attitudes? I mean, don't you come in for a lot of crude sexist jokes, the sort of thing that's demeaning to women? There must still be a lot of policemen around who don't think a woman's place is in the police force at all."

"More than a few," said Annie, thinking back to the time she was raped by a colleague she had thought she could trust. "But we're managing to whittle their numbers down slowly. We don't want to take up too much of your time, but my colleague and I would like to have a chat with you about your years at the University of Essex, if that's all right?"

Dr. Parsons leaned back in her chair, put her pen down and linked her hands on the desk in front of her. She had large knuckles and long fingers, adorned with a few chunky rings, Annie noticed. "Perfectly fine with me."

Gerry picked up the questioning. "Your name was given to us by another alumni, Judy Sallis."

Dr. Parsons frowned. "I don't remember knowing anyone by that name."

"It doesn't matter. You probably didn't know her. But she remembered you. Something in the papers jogged her memory recently. Something about female asylum seekers."

"Ah, yes, a hobbyhorse of mine, I'm afraid. The problem of female circumcision is—"

"And she said you were head of the Marxist Society at Essex in the early seventies. Something like that."

Dr. Parsons paused, perhaps deciding whether to be annoyed by Gerry's riding roughshod over her comment, then said, "Well, we didn't exactly have a *head,* as such. That would be leaning far too close to the cult of the leader. I did a lot of the organization, though, from writing to printing out pamphlets and manifestos—I think we had an old spirit duplicator back then, a Banda. You made a 'spirit master' first, which I always found a slightly mystical and disturbing term, like something out of a horror novel. They came out purple. Remember that smell of spirit alcohol, the wet sheets? No, of course you wouldn't. You're too young. Anyway, we shared tasks at all levels. It seemed the only nondiscriminating way to go about it."

"But weren't some people better at doing some things than others?" Gerry asked.

Dr. Parsons gave her a long-suffering look. "Of course. But anybody can run off a few copies, hand them out on the street, sweep a floor, wash the dishes, can't they, and there's no reason why everybody shouldn't have to do menial work like that, is there?"

"I suppose not. Unless their time could be better spent doing something more valuable that nobody else could do as well."

"I can see you need a bit of reeducation."

"Did you know a woman called Ronnie Bellamy?"

Dr. Parsons clapped her hands together. "Ronnie Bellamy? Of

course I did. She was one of our most capable members. Why do you ask?"

"When did she join?"

"Shortly after she started at the university," said Dr. Parsons. "Perhaps November, December 1971. She was in her first year. Couldn't wait to get cracking. I was already in my second year then, so I'd been around a while. I was able to show her the ropes and all."

"How to use the spirit duplicator?"

Dr. Parsons laughed. "Yes. That as well. But Ronnie's real skill was being able to write a coherent pamphlet, get across our ideas and persuade people to believe. It must have been all that expensive schooling, but her way with language was almost magical. She was a good speaker, too, and she had a lot of energy, but I must say that I often thought her looks rather got in the way of her delivery."

"I understand she was a very attractive young woman," Gerry said. "Nicely dressed, too."

"The kind of student casual elegance that costs a packet, yes. You see far more of it today then you did then, of course. Most of us were hardly walking adverts for the fashion industry. But you're right. It could sometimes be a bit of a distraction for the male members of the society, or the men who attended our meetings in general."

"What? Beauty a distraction from Marxist ideology?" Annie butted in. "Well, slap me around the head with a copy of *Das Kapital*." She knew she shouldn't have interrupted but she couldn't help herself.

Dr. Parsons laughed, but it sounded hollow. "I take your point, DI Cabbot," she said. Then she leaned forward and clasped her hands again, elbows on the desk. "But this was a time of great struggle, and we were very sincere and very serious about what we were doing. We wanted a fairer society, and we believed that meant a socialist society. We thought that by getting rid of the capitalist system, we could bring about the end of famine, of war, unemployment, pollution. You name it. All the evils of the world. Marx and Marxism seemed to offer an essential analysis of the capitalist society we lived in, and until we understood it, we could hardly go about dismantling it and changing it. Remember, we were students, young, full of idealism and vigor. We were also academics in training. Lenin said, 'Without revolutionary theory there can be no revolutionary action.' We believed him." She turned thoughtful for a moment. "Mind you, he also said, 'Anyone who knows anything of history knows that great social changes are impossible without feminine upheaval. Social progress can be measured exactly by the social position of the fair sex, the ugly ones included.'"

Gerry laughed. "But what about Stalin?" she asked. "Where does he come in? How do you explain him?"

Dr. Parsons smiled indulgently, as if she had been asked this question many times before. "We didn't have to explain Stalin. He was an aberration. It wasn't about the cult of the leader for us. Or even about the expansion of the Soviet empire. If anything, we were against colonialism. We had enough of that in our past. It was the workers' revolution that interested us. Yes, we wanted to spread the socialist doctrine, and hopefully the socialist system, to all corners of the world, but we were starting out in our little corner. That was all that counted. Overthrowing the capitalist system for a fairer, more equal one. The overthrow of the ruling class and the ascent of the workers to power. A true workers' state."

"But wouldn't it require some rather drastic measures?"

"It would mean a rebuilding not only of the state as we knew it, but of the human social being. It wouldn't be a time for the personal and the sensual, that's for certain."

"Do you still believe in it?"

"Unfashionable as it is today, I do, to some extent."

"You said Ronnie Bellamy was a good propagandist."

Dr. Parsons narrowed her eyes. "I don't recollect using the word 'propagandist.' That's a capitalist euphemism for anything they don't want to hear. But yes. She was good with language, and she was an efficient mobilizer of people, a very persuasive dialectician."

"In what way?"

"You have to consider the times," Dr. Parsons went on. "It was a period of great social upheaval here. All over Europe, in fact. Remember, the Paris student demos and the Prague Spring weren't so far in the past, and the Americans still had Nixon and Vietnam. And Watergate not so far in the future. At the time we're talking about, though, late 1971 and early 1972, the miners' strike was the biggest issue for us. It almost brought down the government. I don't know if you know much about it, but one of the tactics the miners used was flying pickets. Groups of workers that could be transported quickly to bolster picket lines and blockade ports and power stations and such all over the country."

"It sounds like war," said Gerry.

"It was. Class war. Them against us. Anyway, the point is, or one point is, that by late January 1972, we had over a thousand South Yorkshire miners allocated to help with flying pickets in East Anglia. Essex was a pretty volatile place politically at the time. We had Marxists, Trotskyists and International Socialists all over the place, and we agreed to offer accommodation in campus residences to as many miners as we could. Solidarity was important to us. The unity of theory and practice, ideology and action. We got away with it for a while, too, until the bloody university authorities threatened to take out a High Court injunction."

"And Ronnie Bellamy was involved in all this?" said Gerry. "It's hard to believe."

"Not at all. She was one of the powers behind the accommodation movement, almost got herself kicked out over it. And she was also one of the ones who got first dibs, you could say, though that hardly sounds very egalitarian, does it?"

"What do you mean, first dibs?" Gerry asked.

"The miners, dear. Hunks. Right?"

Annie was confused. She had never thought of miners as hunks. Drunks, more like. She had assumed they were all rather grimy and coarse and mostly drunk when they weren't underground. Not that she had ever met one. A distant great-uncle on her mother's side had been a miner, but he had died before she was born. She didn't think he was a hunk, though.

"Oh, I see," Gerry said, blushing. "Do you mean there was . . . er . . . ?"

"Fraternization?"

"Yes."

"And fornication?"

"Er . . . well . . . yes."

Dr Parsons smiled at her discomfort. "Shagging like minks, dearie. Shagging like minks. I tell you, it was like a D. H. Lawrence novel come to life. Even Arthur Scargill admitted he had a devil of a time getting his men back home when the time came to go. Having too good a time of it, they were. Even a revolutionary has to get his leg over every now and then."

"And who was Ronnie Bellamy in all this?" Gerry asked. "Lady Chatterley?"

"Ha! Very good. I was thinking more of the miners in *Sons and Lovers,* actually, but you've got a point there. Very ladylike was our Ronnie, even back then. Very regal. I read a profile of her not so long ago in the *Guardian.* I understand she's actually a *real* Lady now?"

"Indeed."

"So why are you investigating her?"

It was a shrewd question, Annie thought, and she hoped that Gerry was too smart to answer it.

"As a matter of fact, we're not. It's just a lead-in to our investigation into the death of Gavin Miller. Apparently they knew one another back then, and we're trying to find out as much about him as we can. You must excuse me, I'm quite new to all this, and I sometimes get sidetracked, just out of pure interest in something. You can learn so much on this job. It's quite fascinating, I think, about the students putting up the miners."

Very good, Annie thought. Nicely done.

"Well, we had the ideology. We'd read our Marx, and we could go through all the arguments. Some of the miners were in the movement and knew their Marx, but many of them had only the raw revolutionary spirit. Not to mention the brawn. It was a highly charged combination. And don't forget, many of these miners *were educated men.* Up to a point. It was true that most of them had been denied a formal education by the corrupt capitalist education system, but they were far from stupid, and were easily able to grasp the basic tenets of Marxist dialectic and communism in general. A number of them were already members of the Communist Party. Arthur Scargill said during the 1984 miners' strike that his father still read the dictionary every day because he felt a mastery of words was vital. It's far too easy to dismiss the intellectual grasp and capacities of workingmen simply because they haven't been exposed to literature—all those dead white male poets—and philosophy, and because they work with their hands rather than their minds. But you'd be surprised."

"I'm sure I would," said Gerry. "Was there any one who stands out in particular?"

"For Ronnie? You're telling me. Only the hunkiest."

"Was this . . . I mean, was it very public?"

"Not really. It was all a bit undercover, in more ways than one. I'd say everyone was fairly discreet. I knew, of course, because I was helping to organize the accommodation, too, but I'd hardly say it was public knowledge. I remember things got a bit fraught once when her boyfriend walked in and caught them in flagrante."

"Gavin Miller?"

"One and the same. He was one of the dopers, though I saw him at one of our meetings once. He came to impress Ronnie, I think. He had one of those superior cynical grins on his face the whole time. Stoned, most likely. Anyway, that would have taken the grin off his face. Caught them at it, shagging away, right there on the carpet in one of the residence flats."

"Were you there, too?"

"No, Ronnie told me about it later."

"What did he do?"

"Gavin? Do?"

"Yes."

"Like most of the dopers, he didn't do anything. Probably wrote a poem later about how bad it made him feel. And nor would you have done anything if you'd seen Joe Jarvis back then. Muscles on his arms like twisted steel cables. Pecs you wouldn't believe. And what I believe they call a six-pack these days. But a gentle enough soul when you got to know him. A keen, hard intelligence, though, but unnurtured back then, or should I say unpolluted by any capitalist education indoctrination system."

"Do you still talk like that?"

Dr. Parsons laughed. "We never did, really. Most of us, anyway. We just put it on for outsiders because they expect it."

Gerry laughed. "Did Gavin Miller have anything to do with the Marxist Society?"

"Other than attending that one meeting? No."

"What about you? With the miners?"

Dr. Parsons gave a tight smile. "Thank you for thinking of me, my dear, but I'm afraid my persuasion was the same then as it is today." She paused, relishing her own words. "Their obvious charms were lost on me, but I still know a hunk when I see one."

"So let me get this clear," Annie cut in. "Ronnie Bellamy helped the Marxist Society by arranging accommodation for striking miners, somewhere they could stay and shag their brains out before blockading ports and power stations so the rest of the country could freeze in their homes?"

Dr. Parsons tilted her head and narrowed her eyes. "Well, I suppose you could put it that way. You can't make an omelette without breaking eggs, as they say. But you must have been rather young to remember all that, mustn't you?"

"I don't remember it at all. I was brought up in an artists' colony in St. Ives. A commune, if you like. My father's an artist. We didn't have electricity, at least not for quite a while, when I was really little. We were all bourgeois individualists with perhaps just a hint of socialism in the mix. At least, they had a kitty for the food and stuff—pay what you can—and we all took the household duties in turn."

"Admirable."

"Yes. When the lights went out all over the country, we all sat around the campfire singing Bob Dylan songs like we did most evenings. I think 'The Times They Are A-Changin'' was probably the first song I ever heard. Anyway, to get back to the point. Ronnie Bellamy had a stormy affair with Joe Jarvis?"

"Yes. She did seem rather struck with him, at least for the time they were together."

"And after Gavin Miller walked in on them, was that was the end for them?" Annie asked. "I mean for Ronnie and Gavin?"

"Well, I'd think so, wouldn't you, dearie?" said Dr. Parsons, with arched brows. "Though as I recollect it, she'd finished with him some time before that, but he just didn't want to let go. I can't say I blame him. The one time Ronnie and I . . . well, never mind that."

"Are we talking about *the* Joe Jarvis?"

"We are, indeed. But this was before his meteoric rise to fame."

"And fall from grace," Annie added. She glanced at Gerry to let her know that all would be revealed later, and Gerry indicated that she was going to pick up the thread of the interview again.

"You said Gavin Miller just walked away when he found Ronnie with another man. Were there any repercussions?"

"Do you mean did Ronnie appear with a black eye or something? No. None that I know of. I can't say I ever heard or saw much of Gavin Miller after that."

Judy Sallis had already filled in part of that story. Gavin had taken up with Nancy Winterson, and he had no further contact with Ronnie Bellamy, as far as they knew. "What about Ronnie and this Joe Jarvis? Did they continue to see one another through this time?"

"The miners weren't with us for very long, but I think they did, yes. For a couple of weeks at least. Ronnie used to go out on the pickets, too, when she was allowed. It wasn't quite legal. She wasn't in the union."

"And after the strike?"

"I shouldn't think so," said Dr. Parsons. "I would guess that Joe Jarvis went back to his pit in Mexborough, and Ronnie moved on to her next conquest. You don't expect me to remember them all, do you?"

"No. It's really only the dynamics of her relationships with Gavin Miller and Joe Jarvis we're interested in. But it always helps to get as complete a sense of someone's character as we can."

"Well, Ronnie always was a complex lady, that's for sure. But Gavin Miller was just . . . I don't know . . . a bit aimless. Wishy-washy. I didn't know him well, of course, but I wasn't averse to the odd toke myself now and then, and he or his friends usually had some of the best hash on campus. They also had some very lovely girls in their crowd, and they weren't averse to being a bit experimental when the fumes got to them, so to speak. Oh, don't look so disapproving, dear," said Dr. Parsons, as if she could read Gerry's thoughts on her face. "It just lowers the inhibitions, that's all. It doesn't cause unconsciousness or make anybody do what they don't want to do. It's not like roofies or anything."

"I'm glad to hear it," said Gerry. "Did you stay in touch with Ronnie and Gavin for the rest of your studies?"

"No. As I said, Gavin sort of disappeared from the scene after his split with Ronnie, and I never got invited to their little soirees anymore. As for Ronnie, I've never seen her so exhilarated as those weeks during the strike. There were many other battles to fight, too, ideological as well as practical, but the miners got what they wanted and went back to work, and Ronnie seemed to lose heart with the whole movement. She sort of withdrew from the scene before the end of the year. By her second year, which was my final, I hardly saw her at all. She said she was still committed, and she appeared at meetings occasionally, gave the odd speech, but she had a lot of time constraints. And I must confess that I had a lot of neglected work to catch up on, too, if I wanted a good degree, which I did. Even then, I wanted to teach. I thought it would be the best way I could contribute to the revolution. So I scaled down my own practical political activities, too. It's always a good idea to give way to new blood, anyway, don't you think?"

Gerry looked at Annie, who made a winding-up motion.

"Thanks for your time," Gerry said, putting away her notebook.

"I hope I've been helpful."

"I don't suppose you remember anyone who might have wanted to harm Gavin Miller, do you?" Gerry asked. She realized what a stupid question it must sound as soon as it came out.

"What? From forty-odd years ago? No, I can't think of anyone. What sort of thing are you talking about? Blood feud? Mafia vendetta, or something?"

"No, of course not. Just thought I'd ask."

"Sorry I can't help you."

When they got out into the open air, Annie took a deep breath. "That was good, Gerry," she said. "Very good."

"It was fascinating," Gerry said. "But has it really got us anywhere? I get the feeling I asked all the wrong questions."

They headed back up Woodhouse Lane to the car. "Not at all," said Annie. "Not at all. In fact, I think it's got us quite a long way. Now, let me tell you what I know about Joe Jarvis, and you can fill in the gaps later with your research."

SIR JEREMY Chalmers gave Banks a sidelong glance. "Don't worry. Your car will be quite safe at Brierley until we get back."

They were heading out of town, along the dale towards Helmthorpe, but Sir Jeremy turned off to the left on an unfenced road which meandered through a couple of sleepy hamlets up to the vast moors above. Banks thought the landscape looked more like a bog than the usual wilderness of gorse and heather, cut with steep, shallow ravines and peppered with rocky outcrops, all dark tones and lowering skies. He would have bet there were quicksand and mires, like the Dartmoor of *The Hound of the Baskervilles*. It wasn't raining at the moment, but there had been so much of the wet stuff lately that, even up here, the ground was waterlogged for days after the last actual shower. Luckily, the cambered road surface was fine, apart from where it was full of potholes. Sir Jeremy splashed through them without even appearing to notice. They reached a passing place, and Sir Jeremy pulled in and turned off the engine. He took a couple of deep breaths, still holding the wheel, then got out. Banks followed suit. It had been a mostly silent journey so far.

Though the clouds were low, the view was staggering in all directions. Distant hilltops floated above the mist like disembodied monoliths, water trickled in a nearby gully, and a lone curlew cried above them. The peewits were silent, though; they had already moved down to the lower meadow for the winter.

Banks had the absurd idea at first that Sir Jeremy was going to hit him, but he did nothing.

"I love it up here," Sir Jeremy said finally. "Far from the madding crowd. A man can think up here." He rested the backs of his thighs against the bonnet of the car and squinted at Banks. "You've been causing my family a lot of grief lately."

"It's not my intention, believe me."

"I know. I suppose you'll say you're only doing your job."

"A man has been brutally murdered, Sir Jeremy. A man your wife knew, and whom she talked to on the telephone a week before he died."

"She knew him? This Miller person?"

Banks was surprised at the reaction. Sir Jeremy clearly didn't know that. Had Lady Chalmers not told her husband about the phone call?

"Yes," he said. "I'm sorry. I assumed you would have known. They went out together for a while at university."

"Oh, that's all," he said, clearly relieved. "I should imagine Ronnie went out with lots of boys at university. She was quite a beauty. I've never asked for a list of her conquests, and she's never asked for a list of mine. You surely don't think I believe I'm the first one?" He paused. "You don't—surely you don't think I killed this Miller person out of jealousy?"

Though the thought had crossed Banks's mind, it sounded absurd out in the open like that. "It's not a matter of that," he said. "It's the evasions. At first she denied knowing him, then, when we faced her with concrete evidence, she admitted that she did."

"So she lied. She didn't want to get involved. Would you?"

Banks had realized many times before, when he had been asked this question, that he probably wouldn't. But he could live with contradiction, and he certainly wasn't going to admit as much to a witness or possible suspect. "People lie to us all the time in my business," he said.

Sir Jeremy gave a quiet laugh. "I wouldn't, by any means, say it was restricted to your business."

"Perhaps not. But it happens enough to be an occupational hazard."

"I suppose it also makes you suspicious of everyone. You begin to think that people are going to lie before they even open their mouths."

"Sometimes. But I try to get over it." Banks sighed. "Look, we're people, too. I don't go about my job to cause anyone trouble. Except criminals. I happen to like Lady Chalmers. It would sadden me to hurt her. But if she had only explained from the beginning her connection with Gavin Miller, instead of weaving a tissue of lies, then I'd have an easier time believing what she says now. As it is at the moment, yes, I think I would treat any further utterance from her with suspicion."

Sir Jeremy seemed to contemplate that for a moment, then he nodded. "Fair enough." He next surprised Banks by taking a packet of Marlboros from his top pocket and lighting one. He offered Banks the packet, and for one terrible instant, the urge coursed through him again and almost overwhelmed him. "No, thanks," he said, brushing it aside. Ninety-nine percent of the time he never thought about smoking, or the idea of it repulsed him, but that other one percent in him just longed to return to being a smoker again, to being a member of that happy, carefree fraternity, now drawn even closer together, as they were fellow outlaws, pariahs, in the eyes of most people. "I understand my brother-in-law Tony caused you a few problems?" Sir Jeremy said.

"He did."

"I'm sorry about that, but you must realize that we're a close-knit family. He thought he was only protecting Ronnie. I'm very protective of my wife. I was too far away to be of any help, or I'd have done the same. It was a natural instinct."

"To pull strings, peddle influence?"

"It's one of the things I do well. It's why I'm so successful at my business. Do you have any idea what it's like to put together a multimillion-dollar Broadway musical?"

"No. Do you have any idea what it's like to catch a particularly slippery murderer?"

"Touché, Mr. Banks."

"What about Lady Chalmers's circle? Oriana Serroni, for example?" Banks asked.

Sir Jeremy frowned. "What about her?"

"Do you think she might have anything to do with this business?"

"I can't imagine what. I've known Oriana more or less all her life, and as far as I'm concerned she's above reproach." He gave Banks a curious glance. "She likes you."

"What makes you think that?"

"The way she defended you when Tony jumped in, or so Ronnie told me." Sir Jeremy paused. "And I believe she had lunch with you recently?"

So Oriana had told Sir Jeremy and, no doubt, Lady Chalmers, about the lunch. In a way, that pleased him. She had been adamant about not telling Nathan and Anthony Litton, which was what he cared about most. Banks remembered Oriana's frostiness on the day he and Annie had confronted Lady Chalmers surrounded by her lawyer and brother-in-law. How easily we can misread or misinterpret events, he thought. Perhaps she was more disturbed by the lawyer's presence than by Banks's and Annie's arrival.

A breeze sprang up and ruffled Sir Jeremy's longish gray hair. He was wearing jeans and a zip-up leather jacket over a checked shirt, and he seemed warm enough in them. Banks was only wearing his best M&S suit, the one he always wore to go and talk to people who lived in big houses, the same one he'd been wearing all week, and he felt the chill.

"I'm still surprised you didn't know about your wife and Gavin Miller," Banks went on. "One thing I've been trying to clear up is whether they were in contact at all over the previous twenty-five years or so that you've lived in Eastvale. He actually taught at the college here for three years or so not long ago."

"I think I would have known about it if they had," said Sir Jeremy. "I'm not always out of the country, and contrary to what you think, my wife is not a duplicitous woman. Besides, from what Tony tells me, he was a college lecturer who got dismissed for sexual misconduct and let himself go to seed. He was desperate for money, and I think he tried to play on old times to trick my wife out of some."

"That's one way of looking at it," Banks agreed.

"You mean there's another?"

"Gavin Miller was unjustly accused and dismissed for something he didn't do, in revenge for something he had done to a friend of one of the girls. Something that actually benefited the community." He knew that this was going too far, giving out such information to Sir Jeremy, but he felt that a certain level of frankness was called for.

"You're saying he was some kind of saint? You know this for a fact?"

"We think we know what happened and why, yes. But I'm not saying he was a saint. Yes, he had let himself go to seed, and yes, he was desperate for money. His personal hygiene sucked, too. He may even have tried to con your wife out of some money. But he was still a human being, and he was badly abused."

Sir Jeremy took it all in and said, "He still doesn't sound like the kind of person Ronnie would hang about with."

"I agree," said Banks. "So you'd say that she's had nothing to do with him since her university days?"

"I would. I can't prove it beyond any shadow of a doubt—I haven't been with her every minute of every day—but that's what I believe. I can certainly swear to you that, if she did, I had no knowledge of it. We all have people from our pasts we leave by the wayside. Sometimes they come back to haunt us. That's what happened with this man. He thought an old girlfriend might be a soft touch. That he got murdered around the same time he tried to con my wife out of a few quid is mere coincidence. Do you really think Ronnie would murder someone for such a paltry amount? Or that I would? She's not a violent person, I assure you. Her nature is actually very kindly, and about the only thing that really surprises me is that she *didn't* give him what he asked for. She's a sucker for street people and the like, always handing out money."

"Maybe if he'd asked her nicely?" Banks said.

Sir Jeremy trod out his cigarette. "Yes. Maybe."

"Or maybe he did. Maybe she gave him some money, then someone who knew he had it on him murdered him. But he couldn't get it. He heard someone coming, so he ran off. But the problem with that theory is that nobody could have walked along that railway track and not seen Gavin Miller's body, yet it wasn't discovered or reported until the following morning. Someone else who didn't want to get involved, perhaps? Someone up to no good who couldn't afford to be associated with a recently deceased loser?"

"Hm," said Sir Jeremy. "I can see you have a few more problems that need solving, but I honestly don't think any of them are to do with Ronnie. She specifically says that she didn't give Miller any money, and I believe her, just as I believe the three women spent the evening at Brierley as they say they did. The memories his telephone call triggered were probably not good ones for Ronnie, or they may have left her completely unmoved. He might have taken a hectoring tone, something I can tell you would be guaranteed to put her off, or maybe he said something she doesn't want to tell me, or you, about. But I believe her."

Banks was starting to get cold, wishing they could just get in the car again and drive away, but Sir Jeremy seemed especially communicative out here on the moors, and he didn't want to break the spell. "Did you ever meet Gavin Miller?" Banks asked.

"Me? No. I thought I'd already made that clear. I'd never even heard of him until Ronnie told me you'd been around asking about him, then I read about his death in the papers."

"So she didn't tell you about his phone call at the time he made it?"

"No. I don't suppose she thought it was important." Sir Jeremy hesitated.

"What is it?" Banks asked.

Sir Jeremy pulled out another cigarette and lit it. After inhaling deeply and letting the plume of smoke disperse on the wind, he said, "It's been a horrendously busy time for me. As you know, I've been over in New York trying to put this damn show together, then I had some difficult meetings in London about the UK production. Quite honestly, it's all been a bit of a nightmare, and I've probably neglected Ronnie to some extent. Too much on my plate. I haven't been there for her. She's used to that, of course, but I might have missed a few signals this time."

"What do you mean?" Banks asked.

"Well, now I think about it, she seemed generally worried and distracted when I got back from New York. She never said why, and as she hadn't told me about the phone call, I couldn't make any sense of her behavior. But I also had too much going on in my life to take the time and really talk to her, as I should have done, to try to find out what was happening. We do talk, you know. Ronnie isn't secretive with me, and she does like to get things out in the open, problems and stuff. But I never asked her what was bothering her, and then I just wasn't around. The phone's not the same, especially when you're calling from thousands of miles away. To be honest, it was easier to blame you for all Ronnie's distress, but when I think about it, I have to admit that it started *before* you first talked to her."

Oriana had told Banks much the same thing, but he wasn't going to rat her out to Sir Jeremy. "And since the murder?"

"Well, obviously, she's been even more upset. But again, I put that down to you and your persistent questions and insinuations. Perhaps she thought more of this Miller than I realized, or than she realized. The whole thing must have brought back some powerful memories. Perhaps she felt guilty. You know, maybe if she had given him money, he wouldn't have died. That sort of thing. This was one time I really had no idea what was bothering her. Who knows how the human mind works, what tortuous and labyrinthine paths we lead ourselves down?"

"How was she before the phone call?"

"Fine. As far as I know. Happy, healthy, productive. She's always had problems with her nerves now and then. Just episodes. Nothing serious. It's just her nature. Highly strung. She's an idealist and a perfectionist, and that's tough to keep up in this world. Easier perhaps when you're young, but a damn sight harder as you get older. But she was fine. Since the phone call, it's like the nerves have come back."

He was being very open and forthright, Banks thought, wondering if there was a reason behind it. "And since the murder?"

Sir Jeremy gave Banks a direct look. "Again, I thought it was your fault. But I've found her crying for no reason, jumping at shadows. She's been taking Valium again. I'm only grateful that Angelina and Oriana have been around to help keep her together. The strain is showing."

"What do you think it's all about?"

"I have absolutely no idea, but what bothers me most is that I think she's scared of something. I'm worried that she might be in danger. I think we need your help, Mr. Banks, and you can rely on me not to interfere at higher levels, if you take my meaning. But I don't know what it is you're supposed to do." Sir Jeremy checked his watch and pulled his jacket collar tight to keep out the chill. "Come on," he said, with a forced grin. "I've got a meeting in Edinburgh this evening. Let's get back to that lovely Porsche of yours."

THE RAIN had started up again with a vengeance, a broad band of it all the way from the Midlands to the Scottish Borders. A brisk wind lashed it against the conservatory windows and it swirled in dark, glistening patterns over the glass roof.

Banks sat listening to Rahsaan Roland Kirk's *Does Your House Have Lions*. When you got beyond the showmanship, playing three saxes at once, for example, the man could really play. After polishing off the remains of some takeaway pad Thai noodles that were fast approaching their chuck-out date, Banks had spent much of the early evening on the telephone and computer. It was partly work, partly family, including a long chat with Tracy in Newcastle and an e-mail to his parents, who were still on the Southeast Asia cruise. Brian was in Lyon, and most likely onstage, so Banks just left a brief message on his mobile.

Now he had just finished reading through the thick file on Joe Jarvis that Annie and Gerry had quickly put together for him after their visit to Dr. Mandy Parsons. Banks already knew a fair bit about Jarvis—one of his father's heroes—as did most people who followed the news with any level of interest, but there were always surprises. He hadn't known that Jarvis was a devoted Shostakovich fan, for example, or that his favorite reading included Jane Austen, Anton Chekhov and Émile Zola, none of whom Banks had ever read, though he had seen various versions of *Pride and Prejudice* and *Emma* on TV and had watched a few episodes of *The Paradise*. He had always wanted to read *Germinal* and Chekhov's short stories, and perhaps now was a good time. The secondhand copies he had bought years ago were still on his bookshelf.

There were plenty of photographs of Jarvis at various stages in his career in the file, and he had certainly been a ruggedly handsome young man in the early seventies, when Ronnie had known him. As time went on and his career path took him further and further from the pit, he had come to look more distinguished. He was certainly a familiar figure, at any rate, which was hardly surprising considering the number of times he'd been splashed over the media.

As the rain poured down and Roland Kirk played on, Banks closed the folder on his knee. The basic facts were simple enough. Joe Jarvis was born in Mexborough, South Yorkshire, in 1947, into a mining family going back three generations. He had started working down the pit at the age of sixteen, and at the time of the 1972 miners' strike, he was a twenty-five-year-old coal face worker, just a few years older than Ronnie Bellamy and from another universe entirely.

It was after the '72 strike that things had started to get interesting, and complicated, in Jarvis's career. He joined the Communist Party in

1973, quickly became a pit delegate, and after that, it seemed there was no stopping him. A keen supporter of education through the Workers' Education Association, he took a part-time course in economics and international politics at Sheffield University in the late seventies. He had also become more active in the National Union of Miners, and over the years he rose steadily through the ranks, or climbed higher up the greasy pole, depending on your point of view: shop steward, member of the branch committee, branch delegate, and from there he moved on to paid, full-time union positions, leaving the coal face behind forever in 1982, though he never became president of the NUM. That position went to Arthur Scargill.

A vehement opponent of Margaret Thatcher, Jarvis often appeared on TV during the 1984 miners' strike, and he was also pictured holding banners and linking arms at pickets. He had been one of the loudest protestors of the practice of bringing in extra police from the Met to bolster containment of the picketers. These were the men who were "up for it," Banks remembered, ready to crack a few northern heads, the ones his father always brought up when the matter of Banks's career arose, the ones who had waved their rolls of five-pound notes, overtime pay, at the starving miners, and used it to woo the local girls, some of whom were only too willing to be wooed. At least they didn't rape and pillage, as the Russians had in Berlin after the war.

In turn vilified and lauded, Jarvis proved an able leader of men and a tricky opponent of the National Coal Board negotiators. Loyalty and solidarity were his keywords. He would have given his life for his fellow miners. Some said he was the man behind Scargill, others that he always played second fiddle. Whatever the truth was—and he never commented on his position himself—he was always right there, up at the front line when the going got tough, as it had over the last two or three years.

Some official papers found in a Moscow basement and finally released showed that Arthur Scargill had begged the Russians for money to support the 1984 strike and asked that its source be kept secret. Of course, Scargill bore the brunt of this publicly, and did so very well, but the shadowy figure of Jarvis, though retired by then, had plenty of his own explaining to do. He had been a key figure in the negotiations and had made frequent trips to Moscow during the time he was employed by the NUM. There were also accusations of financial ties with Colonel Gaddafi's government in Libya.

During the Cold War, of course, the Russians were interested in doing all they could to wreck the capitalist system and foment uprising all over the world, and the Libyans had no great love for England, either. Jarvis was eloquent in his own defense, but a lot of mud was slung in the media, and some of it stuck. Jarvis had always been proud to tell people he was a member of the Communist Party, even when it was unfashionable, and when leaving it and joining the Labour Party, as Scargill had done, would have furthered his career. There were rumors of MI5 investigations and hints of espionage accusations, yet even his greatest detractors would have had to admit that Jarvis didn't have access to any information the Russians would have been interested in. What he could do, though, was stir up unrest, help to bring about the ideal conditions for a workers' revolution—work as an agent provocateur—and the climate in the miners' strikes had been ideal for that. But no slush fund was found, and there was no secret Moscow money stashed away in numbered Swiss bank accounts. At least, not that HMG's best could find.

Though it was well known that Jarvis strongly disagreed with Scargill's policy of calling the 1984 strike without taking a ballot of members, he never publicly denounced his friend and mentor, even when the latter went so far as to defend Stalin and attack the Polish Solidarity movement, or when he later sued the NUM for kicking him out and claimed expenses from the union for his expensive Barbican flat.

No charges were ever brought against Jarvis, and when the hue and cry died down, he returned to his retirement and his silence, apparently spending most of his time on his allotment in Mexborough, reading his beloved Chekhov and growing vegetables. He didn't have an expensive flat in London, but a modest terrace in Mexborough, not too far from where he had grown up.

His address had been easy enough to find; it was in the telephone directory.

The music had come to an end, and Banks had to go through to the entertainment room to change the disc. He could have made life easier by buying an automatic CD changer that held five or ten discs, but he found that the more complicated a piece of equipment was, the more likely it was to go wrong. Besides, he never knew what he wanted to listen to next, let alone three or four discs ahead. In the end he went for something a little more relaxing than Roland Kirk, as it was getting close to bedtime—*See You on the Ice* by Carice van Houten—and poured himself a small nightcap of Laphroaig.

The rain was still hammering down. It was like living under a waterfall. Banks supposed it would end one day soon, then they would have snow and ice to look forward to. He remembered the Arizona desert and the balmy heat and unique light of Los Angeles—Santa Monica, the Hollywood Hills, Laurel Canyon, Mulholland Drive—the breathtaking beauty of the California coast all the way up to San Francisco. He also remembered Sophia, whose ghost he had been trying to let lay through his travels. The sun had shone all the time he was there, though one evening, while he was enjoying dinner in Tiburon, on the other side of the bay, with a charming divorcée he had met at the hotel, the cityscape across the water suddenly disappeared so completely that everyone in the restaurant gasped and thought the power had gone off. It was fog, though, which had rolled in so quickly under the Golden Gate Bridge that nobody had noticed it was coming, and most of it had dispersed when it was time to go back to the hotel. Perhaps it was time for another big trip, he thought, if he could afford it. India, perhaps. Or China, Vietnam, Brazil? There was no shortage of possibilities. There was no one he needed to forget this time, but why should one even need an excuse to go on a long journey? He glanced at a few tour itineraries on his tablet, then decided it was about time for bed.

The whisky in his glass was just about finished when his phone rang. He checked his watch. After midnight. Thinking it might be Brian returning his call after the concert, he picked up his mobile. He didn't recognize the number, but he answered it anyway.

"I'm sorry to be calling you so late," the familiar voice said, "but you did give me your card and said to call anytime if I had something to tell you. I hope I didn't wake you."

"You didn't," said Banks, almost adding that it was nice to hear Oriana's voice again, perhaps because Carice van Houten was singing "You.Me.Bed.Now." at the time. But something in her tone warned him this was not a social call, as if it ever could be. "Is something wrong?"

"Yes," said Oriana. "Something is very wrong. It's Ronnie. There's been an accident."

12

THE LITTLE COFFEE SHOP ON MARKET STREET WASN'T part of a chain, and Banks had always enjoyed the care and dedication the owners put into the brews and blends they made. He arrived a little early on Wednesday morning, and as he had been at the office already for an hour and a half reviewing the paperwork on the Miller case, drinking coffee from the machine, he decided on green tea instead.

He had gathered from Oriana the previous evening that Lady Chalmers had been driving home from Anthony Litton's house, near Buxton. It was Oliver's birthday. Ronnie knew he was spending it with his father on his way back to London from some meetings in Manchester, and she had decided to go and pay him a surprise birthday visit. Everyone told her she shouldn't have been driving. The weather was terrible. Apparently, Anthony Litton had told her she should stop over, but she wanted to come home. She was driving back through the Peaks when her car went through a fence and off the road beside a swollen, fast-flowing river. She would have been washed away if the car wheels hadn't got stuck in the deep mud on the riverbank.

Paramedics had attended her at the scene, and then she had been examined briefly at the nearest hospital. Her injuries weren't serious, Oriana had said, just a few cuts and bruises, but mostly shock. She had insisted on going home. The doctors had no objection, and the local police all loved Oliver Litton, so it wasn't hard to find a volunteer to drive her. The car would be towed back later.

Banks was sipping the slightly bitter but aromatic tea when the bell pinged over the door and Oriana walked in. She looked frazzled and drawn, which was only to be expected, given that she had probably had little or no sleep. The owner's wife, Sandy, came over to ask if she wanted anything, and she ordered a latte. The place wasn't too busy, and they had Classic FM playing quietly in the background.

Once Oriana had sat down and removed her tan jacket, she seemed to be a little shy and uncomfortable to find herself alone with Banks in a café, even though they had already had lunch together. She was casually but stylishly dressed in jeans and russet-colored top, with a dark green silk scarf around her neck. Banks could hear Sandy making the latte, the violent grinding of the espresso machine and the hissing of the steamer heating the milk. It all sounded rather like someone sucking the dregs of a soft drink through a straw. "How is Lady Chalmers?" he asked.

Oriana kept her eyes down and stared at the tablecloth the whole time she talked. "She's fine. Well, you know . . . still a bit dazed, but that's mostly from the sedative. The doctor's been, and he says she'll have a few nasty bruises but no permanent disfigurement or anything like that. He says she had a lucky escape. It was also fortunate that she wasn't driving too fast, she was wearing a seat belt, and the fence slowed her down even more. A little more momentum, and that would have been it."

"It's not that often you can call crashing through a fence and getting stuck in the mud lucky."

Oriana glanced up at him and smiled. "No," she said. "I'm sorry about phoning you so late last night. It's just so . . . embarrassing. I panicked. I didn't know where to turn. What can I say?"

"You don't have to apologize," Banks told her. "I'm just glad to hear that she's on the mend. Sir Jeremy got back all right?"

"About half past one, yes. He's exhausted, too."

"I'm not surprised." Sandy delivered Oriana's latte. "You were clearly worried about more than just Lady Chalmers's immediate injuries last night. You said she was frightened?"

Oriana nodded. "That's what worried me the most."

"You've said this before, that since Gavin Miller's murder she's been edgy and nervous."

"Yes. It's true."

"But she hasn't told you why?"

"No. I've asked her once or twice. Indirectly, I suppose, you know, if anything was bothering her, but she always said no. One time she just smiled and said nothing I should worry about. That was as far as I could get with her."

It was about as far as Sir Jeremy had got, too, Banks remembered. "Does she usually confide in you? I mean, are you close friends?"

"I like to think so, yes. I know there's an age difference, but I think of her more as a big sister than a mother figure. Believe me, if you met my mother, you'd soon realize how little I need a mother figure."

"And your father?"

Oriana blushed. "My father's a sweet man. I adore him."

"Tell me about what happened last night."

"I already told you. It was just as I said on the telephone. Ronnie rang me from the hospital, told me she'd had an accident, but assured me she was all right and the police were bringing her home."

"What time was this?"

"About half past nine."

"So she wasn't stopping at her brother-in-law's for very long?"

"No. She drove down about four o'clock. They were to have an early dinner, just Ronnie, Tony and Oliver. Oliver's wife and children were in London, and Fran, Tony's wife, died a couple of years ago."

"Yes, I know," said Banks.

Oriana raised an eyebrow, then went on. "After dinner, Oliver had to leave for London immediately. His driver was waiting. It was dark, of course, and raining very hard. I don't know if you know that part of the country, but there are a lot of minor roads, many unlit. It's also quite hilly. It can be very treacherous."

"I know a little about the Peak District," Banks said. "I've been there once or twice for days out, many years ago."

"With your wife and children? Brian and . . . ?"

"Tracy. Yes. Have you ever been there, to Anthony Litton's house?"

"Once or twice. Yes."

"But not last night?"

"No."

"Why not? Boyfriend? Hot date, instead, perhaps?"

Oriana smiled. "I should say that's an impertinent question and refuse to answer it, but I did ask you about your wife. It's simple really. I just stayed in, read for a while, then Angelina and I watched a movie. If you want to know—"

"I don't need to know what movie you watched. I'm not treating you as a suspect in anything. I don't need an alibi."

Oriana made a mock pout. "Oh. How disappointing."

Banks laughed. "It's not often I get that response. Besides, it's not as if you really have one, is it? An alibi, I mean." He drank some more green tea, and went on. "And the thing I didn't tell you when you asked about my wife was that we've been divorced for more than ten years now." Banks paused. "You seemed to indicate last night that Lady Chalmers thought she was in some kind of danger. Can you tell me any more about that?"

"I think perhaps I overreacted. She was in shock, as you said. Perhaps a little panic spread to me."

"Was she driving the MG?"

"Yes. She loves it, even in bad weather, when it would be much more sensible to drive the Rav 4."

"'Who Drove the Red Sports Car?'" Banks said.

"I'm sorry?"

"Oh, nothing. Just a song. Van Morrison. Lady Chalmers would know it. Where's the car now? Was it badly damaged?"

"Apparently not. They're supposed to be towing it back up today or tomorrow."

"Oriana," said Banks quietly, "can you please keep what we've talked about, even that we met, to yourself for the time being? Give me a couple of days. I'll see what I can dig up. Keep a close eye on Lady Chalmers. If possible, don't let her go out alone."

"Is she really in danger?"

"It's possible."

"But why?"

"That," said Banks, "is what I would like to try and find out."

"WHY DID you want to have lunch with me?" Winsome asked Lisa as they took their seats in the Maharaja, an old pub recently converted into an Indian restaurant. The smells of cumin and coriander permeated the air. The decor was pure upmarket-Indian-restaurant-in-a-box, with dark wood paneling, brass or carved wooden statues of elephants and many-armed gods, paintings of women in saris with red dots on their foreheads, lots of gilt edging and deep velvety red curtains, wall hangings and banquettes. Even the waiter had an Indian accent. He probably *was* Indian.

"Do I have to have a reason?" Lisa was certainly dressed for the occasion, though the Maharaja was casual as far as dress code went. She wore a navy skirt and a matching tailored jacket over her cream blouse. She was even wearing tights and seemed to have applied a little makeup. Winsome thought she looked as if she were going to a job interview. They didn't attract anywhere near as many glances as they had in the coffee shop a few days earlier.

"Not at all," Winsome said. "I'm just surprised, you know. I mean what you've just been through, reliving your past, it can't have been easy. Often in things like that, most people, well, they tend to blame the one who pushed them a bit."

"Well, I'm not most people."

"I can see that. You scrub up nicely, by the way."

Lisa blushed, and they ordered rogan josh, chicken tikka, aloo gobi, and raita and naan to accompany the meal. Winsome liked to eat Indian food using her bread as a scoop for pieces of meat drenched in sauce. Lisa ordered a bottle of Stella, but Winsome was sticking to Diet Coke. And plenty of water. "I don't suppose you can tell me anything about how the case is going, can you?" Lisa asked.

"I can't. Not even if I knew anything. But as far as I know, there are no new developments."

"Do you think you'll ever find out who did it?"

"We'll do our best, Lisa. That's all I can say. Now, how are you?"

"I'm fine, I suppose."

"Was there any particular reason you wanted to see me?"

"It must have been quite difficult for you, too, the other night, when I unburdened myself on you. I don't usually do that. It was like opening a floodgate. I don't know how you did it."

"I didn't do anything," Winsome said. "The time was right for you. It must have been a terrible experience, the period you described, and this business brought it all back. If it's worth anything, I think you've done a remarkable job of coming through it."

"Hardly," said Lisa. "But thank you for saying so. I'm still half paralyzed with fear and self-loathing most of the time."

"What are you dressed up for, anyway? Are you after a job or something?"

"Would you employ me?"

"Not up to me, but I can't see why anybody wouldn't. You're bright and enthusiastic, even presentable at the moment."

"Hey!"

Winsome smiled. "Sorry."

"As a matter of fact I'm trying for a job in that pub over the road from your police station."

"The Queen's Arms?"

"That's the one. A 'proper job' as you called it. I haven't had a lot of experience, but they're advertising, and I know someone who used to work there. She'll put in a good word for me. It's a start. I'll continue with my writing, of course. That's my real passion. Do you think they'll . . . you know . . ." She touched her piercings.

"It might be a good idea to remove some of them, if you can. Temporarily, of course."

Lisa nodded. "I thought so. OK."

"It's not that they're prejudiced or anything, I've seen girls working there with piercings, but people who deal with the public on a daily basis tend to be just a little bit on the conservative side when it comes to body art."

"I understand. It's all right. I'm getting a bit bored with them, anyway, to tell you the truth." She fingered her eyebrow ring. "And that one even hurts a bit."

Winsome laughed. "Then it would be a good place to start." She paused. "I can put in a good word for you, too, if you'd like me to?"

"You would?"

"Of course. I'm not saying my word would count for a lot there, but they know me. There is one thing, though."

"Oh?"

"The drugs."

"Don't worry, I won't toke up on the job."

"That's not what I . . ." Winsome laughed. "Oh, never mind."

Their food arrived, delivered by the small Indian waiter in the white suit, who smiled and bowed before them and said, "Happy eating." Winsome tore a naan in half and scooped out a mouthful of rogan josh. Delicious.

They both ate in silence for a while, nothing but the quiet hum of conversations and the distant sound of sitar and tablas. "Is there something you wanted to tell me?" Winsome asked after a while.

Lisa looked her in the eye. "I think you know there is. That's what I like about you. You don't push it, do you? But you know things. You make people want to tell you things of their own free will. It's different."

"I'm still a policewoman at heart, Lisa, so be careful."

"You mean, don't tell you anything that might incriminate me?"

"Something like that."

"Don't worry. You've had plenty of chances to arrest me, and you haven't done it yet." Lisa paused, and they both carried on eating for a while. "I didn't tell you everything," she said finally.

"I don't imagine you did."

"Do you know what I'm going to say?"

"I have a good idea, but I'd still rather hear it from you."

"Then you can say you knew it all along?"

Winsome regarded her in all seriousness, then she spooned up some chicken tikka in the ragged remains of her naan. "I wouldn't do that unless it was true."

Lisa contemplated her for a moment. "No," she said. "You wouldn't. As you might have guessed, it's something else that doesn't reflect too well on me."

"You're too hard on yourself."

"Hear me out first."

"I'm listening."

"I lied to you when I told you I didn't find the boy who did it. Is that what you suspected?"

"I'm all ears," said Winsome. "You did seem to brush over that part
of the story rather too quickly. I'd like to know the full story. Unless
you murdered him and dumped his body in the River Aire, of course.
Then you might be better off keeping your own counsel."

"It wasn't anything like that. Mick, one of the blokes who was with
us at the concert that night, knew him. His name was Rob, and he
was up from Bradford, as I said. I made out to Mick that I was interested in Rob, you know, said a few flattering things, but I didn't know
how to get in touch with him. Mick told me. This would have been
about a week after it happened, before I knew I was pregnant. Not
that it would have made any difference."

"So what did you do?"

"I went to Bradford and located him. It wasn't hard. He was a student at the uni there, and he lived in a bedsit on one of those streets off
Great Horton Road, opposite the main campus."

"What happened when you found him?"

"I watched him. I got a bed-and-breakfast nearby, and I watched
him. I must have spent hours waiting for him to set off to classes. I followed him, watched where he went, who he talked to, what he did.
The student pub at night, pictures with a girl, all that sort of thing.
And do you know what?"

"What?"

"The thing that surprised me most, even in the fragile and angry
state that I was in, was just how fucking ordinary he was, how he'd
done something momentous and horribly destructive to me, yet he
just went about his life chatting, laughing, watching movies, going to
classes, as if nothing had ever happened. I mean, I expected a monster,
right? Remember, all I really knew was what had been done to me,
and I wasn't even certain about that. But the more I watched him, the
more ordinary I saw he was."

"What had you been planning to do?"

"Planning? I don't know. I assumed something would occur to me
when the time came."

"And did it?"

"I suppose so, but hardly what I expected. I thought at one time I
might even kill him, or at least chop his balls off and shove them down

his throat. You know, stick a dildo up his arse and tattoo I AM A RAPIST PIG or something on his chest. But I'm not Lisbeth Salander. Sorry if I'm shocking you. Do you know that book?"

"I've seen the film," said Winsome. "The one with Daniel Craig." She remembered how much it had made her squirm. She certainly wouldn't go and see any of the others in the trilogy, or read them.

"It was mostly him being so ordinary that got to me. I had a knife with me. Is that illegal?"

"Probably."

"But I never used it. I was just going to knock on his door one night, force him at knifepoint to take me up to his flat, then do all that stuff to him."

Winsome wiped her hands on a crisp linen serviette. "Few people could really do that, Lisa. You do realize that, don't you? Most of us aren't violent by nature; we shy away from it. I gather you changed your mind?"

"It didn't seem like that. I mean, I was improvising. Not even sure my mind was made up. I can only say that with hindsight, you know, that I wanted to hurt him the same way he'd hurt me. An eye for an eye. Maybe I watched him for too long. Maybe it was like that Stockholm syndrome thing, and I became too fond of him. I don't think so, but you know what I mean. I spent so long watching him that he became human and ordinary, no longer a rapist monster."

"Lisa, you should have gone to the police."

She showed a flash of anger. "Yes? And what would he have said? He'd have denied it, that's what, then he might have beaten me up or something, and got away with that, too. And what proof did I have? His word against mine. What do you think *you* would have done if I'd walked into your office and told you what I'm telling you now?"

"Calm down," said Winsome. "I'm sorry. I know we seem . . . ineffective . . . sometimes, but our hands are tied. All I'm saying is we would have tried. *I* would have tried."

"It wouldn't have made any difference, anyway. I don't think I could have stood up in court and gone through it all, with the prosecution making out I was a slut and that I asked for it and all that."

"It might not have been that way."

"Tell me about it."

They sat silently for a while. Winsome had lost her appetite, and she left the remains of the lunch. Lisa didn't seem interested in eating any more, either. The waiter asked their permission and cleared away the mess. Lisa ordered another Stella. Winsome could see how hard this was for her, and felt for her. She determined to make no more judgments, no more comments about what she thought Lisa *ought* to have done. "I'm sorry, Lisa. I just have a copper's nature, that's all. I know where you're coming from, believe me. I know why you didn't report it. Most victims don't, and that just makes our job a million times harder. But I don't blame you. I do want to know what you actually did."

Lisa studied her and nodded. "After about a week in Bradford, watching him and following him, plotting in my imagination in bed at night what I was going to do to him, I finally approached him. It was in a square, by the university. He was by himself, but there were plenty of people around. I went up to him and called him by his name. At first, I could tell he didn't recognize me, then it dawned on him. I could sense it, that he was getting ready to scarper. 'Before you run away,' I said, 'I just want you to know that I know you drugged me and raped me, and it was a cowardly cruel and vicious thing to do, and I hope you rot in hell for it.' It wasn't as effective as it might have been because I was scared and angry and I had a hell of a job holding back the tears."

"How did he react?"

"He turned pale, then he just started shaking his head in horror and backing away. Finally, he turned tail and ran."

"And you?"

"I went back to Eastvale and got pissed. I bottled it. Don't you see? I had my chance, and I bottled it."

THE ALLOTMENTS were bordered on one side by a railway line on a raised embankment beside a canal, and on the other three by an old estate of weathered redbrick terraces and semis. Though it had originally been a council estate, most of the houses, at least the best of them, had been privately owned since Thatcher put them up for grabs in 1980. Whether Joe Jarvis believed in private property and owned one, Banks didn't know. He probably thought it made more sense than the local council owning it.

As Banks approached via a ginnel between the ends of two terraces, a diesel train rattled along the railway track. Banks could see the passengers looking up from their newspapers and books as they passed by. He saw the little parcels of land in front of him and noticed that most of them were waterlogged. Here, on their small patches of earth, the locals grew root vegetables, the occasional herb bush, even tomatoes and marrows, but there were none in sight at the moment. Nothing seemed to be growing. The place seemed blighted and barren, as if suffering the effects of some biblical curse. Rain was all well and good for growing things, Banks thought, but not this deluge. Surely Noah was somewhere around shepherding pairs of animals onto his ark. Still, Banks thought as he followed the path Mrs. Jarvis had said would take him to her husband's allotment, it wasn't raining today, and for small mercies like that he must be grateful.

Even the cindered path between the allotments was muddy, and Banks wished he had put on his wellies instead of his slip-ons. He approached the small hut, where he became aware of a shadowy, still figure sitting on a chair in the open doorway. "Mr. Jarvis?" he said, approaching.

"Who wants to know?"

Banks held out his warrant card. The man examined it and grunted. "I should've known."

"Can I talk to you?"

"What about?"

"Ronnie Bellamy."

The man's expression didn't change, but Banks could sense a flurry of confusing emotions running through him. He was frail, hollow chested, his skin like paper, face furrowed with wrinkles, his dark eyes sunk deep in their sockets, the whites a grayish yellow color, with a wide gap between the bottom of the iris and the lower eyelid. *Sanpaku.* Banks remembered the term from an old John Lennon song. He'd had to look it up. It was Japanese for "three whites" and rumored in some branches of alternative medicine to indicate serious illness in a person. "Now there's a blast from the past," Jarvis whispered. "She's all right, isn't she? Nothing's happened to her? You haven't come to bring me bad news?"

"She's fine," said Banks. "Well, more or less. May I sit down?"

Jarvis contemplated him for a moment, then he grunted, got up unsteadily and disappeared into the small shed. When he came out he was carrying a blue-and-white-striped fold-up chair, which he handed to Banks. There wasn't room for the two of them in the doorway, and Jarvis clearly wasn't budging from his spot, so Banks set up opposite him, careful to avoid sinking the legs in the mud. The last thing he wanted was to go arse over heel in the middle of an interview, unofficial as it was. Sometimes he thought he had a career death wish, breaking all the rules in the book. If Jarvis came out with anything important, anything usable in court, the CPS would be down on Banks like a ton of bricks for not conducting the interview under the prescribed conditions. Not to mention AC Gervaise and ACC McLaughlin.

"Why do you want to talk to me about Ronnie?" Jarvis asked once they were settled. He pulled an unfiltered Senior Service from a battered packet of ten and lit it with a match. The first drag set him off coughing, but he soon recovered. "And before you ask," he said, "I've been diagnosed with terminal cancer. I stopped smoking for nigh on twenty years, but I always vowed I'd start again if it didn't matter anymore. Now it doesn't. Death's not far away. I can smell it coming."

"I'm sorry to hear that," said Banks.

"Oh, I don't want your pity. I've made my peace, what there was to make, and I regret nothing. I'm not afraid. I just want you to know you're talking to a dying man. There's nothing you lot can do to me anymore."

"I don't want to do anything to you," said Banks, "except talk."

"Then you must excuse me. My past experience with the police has been quite different."

"So I understand," said Banks. "If it's of any interest to you, my father tried his damnedest to argue me out of joining the force. You're a hero of his. He was a sheet metal worker, but he never forgot the miners' strikes of the seventies and eighties, and the way the police taunted the pickets, flashing their overtime pay."

Banks could have sworn a little smile crossed Jarvis's features, but it was gone as soon as it started. "Have you ever been down a mine, Mr. Banks?"

"I took the kids to the National Coal Mining Museum in Wakefield once. We had a tour."

Jarvis waved his cigarette dismissively. "If you had, you'd wonder why we fought so bloody hard to keep the infernal places open. Awful dark dangerous frightening holes, they are. Every time that lift gate closed on me, I felt panic, a constriction in my throat, a tightness in my chest." He tapped his chest and coughed again. "Then the heat, the darkness, the smell, the coal dust, the noise. But they were the lifeblood of the community. That's why we fought to keep them open. The men who worked there were heroes. And they'd die for each other. To the private owners, then to the NCB after nationalization, we were nothing but slaves. Worthless menials. Poor pay, no pithead facilities, no proper ventilation, dangerous working conditions. I ask you, Mr. Banks, is that any way to treat your heroes? It was like what happens to some of those young men coming back from Iraq or Afghanistan after enduring the most dreadful and dangerous conditions for their country. They're shunned. It's as if people are suddenly ashamed or afraid of them. Of what they've done. Of what they've had to do to defend their country. Our communities were closed down. Our members lost their jobs, their livelihoods. And nobody cared. What could we do but fight for them, fight for ourselves and our communities? We gave everything." He trod out his cigarette. "My grandfather used to come home from his shift, or from the pub, and he was so exhausted it was all he could do to sit at the table, drink his John Smith's Magnet Ale, and chain-smoke Woodbines. I don't remember him ever saying a word to me. He could never get rid of the coal dust from the lines in his face and hands. Never get it from under his nails or out of his hair. He was untouchable. He was remote. He was a miner. He was a hero. Dead at fifty-nine from silicosis. And you have to understand all that to understand why it was something that we fought so hard for, as hard and dangerous a living as it was, as filthy, like living in hell. But it was all we had."

Banks paused through another coughing fit. He wanted to bring the topic around to Veronica Chalmers, but he felt it best to let Jarvis get the vitriol out of his system, if he ever could. Perhaps it was the years of public speaking and stirring up the mob, but Jarvis did seem both eloquent and long-winded, as if he were constantly addressing an audience. "I understand what you're saying, Mr. Jarvis. It's not a life I could ever have lived. But I'd like to talk about the early days, the '72 strike. The University of Essex."

"Oh, I know you don't want to hear it," Jarvis said. His eyes twinkled for a moment. "But nobody gets away without the lecture. It's my stock in trade. Essex, you say? It was Essex that politicized me, and a lot of that was down to Ronnie, believe it or not. Before then, I was just a hungry, angry miner after better pay and better working conditions. Afterwards, I was committed to the creation of a workers' state. We used to take the piss out of students all the time, and believe me, most of them deserved it. They were an idle bunch of drug-taking long-haired wastrels with their heads up their arses. But some of them . . . well, some of them knew what they were talking about, and they did it with a passion and commitment that couldn't fail to move you."

"And Ronnie Bellamy was one of those?"

"Ronnie was . . . oh, aye," he said. "But it was more than that. Can you understand what it was like for me, a young lad from the South Yorkshire mines with little education worth speaking of, and there I was, with all those young brainy sods, who not only seemed to understand and sympathize with our plight, but could put it in a broader context. The thing was, they hadn't a clue what to do about it. It was us who showed them how to organize. The flying pickets, the tactics, and all the rest. They got an inside view of what the strategy of a strike was about, and I like to think it changed their way of thinking a bit. Not about the cause, mind you, but what to do about it."

"And you? The strike changed you?"

"Oh, aye. I realized the value of education, for a start, and I took practical steps, took courses, read books. History, politics, economics, poetry, novels, the lot. Books opened up a whole new world for me. I'm still no intellectual, but I can hold my head up in any academic gathering. I'm not afraid of the intellectuals anymore. There's a price, mind you."

"Oh?"

"Aye. Have you ever read Tony Harrison?"

"No."

"He's a poet from Leeds. Read him. He understands it best. When someone like me, coming from where I come from, gets educated, he loses touch with his roots, he gets educated out of his class, and he leaves his culture behind. Abandons it for another, you might say, and he ends up in a kind of limbo. He can't go back to what he left behind, and he isn't accepted anywhere else."

"That happened to you?"

"To some extent, aye. I fought against it, but even after Essex, when the process had barely begun, going home just wasn't the same again. It felt like a wrench. I was restless, eager for more. Not money, but knowledge. And the more I got, the less I had in common with most of the people around me, the people I grew up with. Read Tony Harrison. You're the son of a sheet metal worker, yourself, but you seem educated. You should understand."

Banks did understand. Certainly being a policeman separated him from the rest of society, but even before that, his college diploma and experience of the academic life in the London of the late sixties and early seventies had also singled him out as different. It always felt jarring when he went back home to Peterborough and found his old friends doing the same things they had done before, stuck in the same old dead-end jobs, saving up for the new house, another baby on the way, a new car. Most of them would never move more than a mile from where they were born. Oh, they would travel; there would be exotic holidays—Costa del Sol, Crete, Tunisia, Sharm el-Sheikh, even Goa, Acapulco and Orlando, but their minds would never move far from the semi in Peterborough. They took the piss out of him mercilessly for the clothes he wore, the way he talked and the thoughts and ideas he expressed. It had all happened to him, too, later, of course— wife, family, mortgage, car—and no matter how badly that had ended, he wouldn't have had it any different for the world. But he had never stopped learning, and he knew what Joe Jarvis meant when he said education cuts you off from your class and from your roots. Perhaps it makes you free, too, but freedom can be a frightening and dangerous thing when you feel so alone. Another diesel rattled by, this one almost empty. "About Ronnie Bellamy," he said again.

Jarvis smiled, showing uneven but healthy teeth. "You must forgive me. I do tend to ramble sometimes. I see it as an old man's prerogative. Especially one who doesn't have long left."

"Old?"

"I'm sixty-five. And dying, remember?"

"You had a fling with Ronnie Bellamy at Essex during the time they put you up there in the student residence, didn't you?"

"How did you find out about that?"

"That doesn't matter. Is it true?"

Jarvis stared at him, then he got up and disappeared in the shed, returning with a half bottle of Famous Grouse and two tea mugs. "You'll join me?"

Banks thought it wise to agree. Besides, he liked Famous Grouse.

Jarvis poured them each a generous measure and sat down again. "I don't know what you'd call it. A fling? Maybe. A brief romance, perhaps? Whatever it was, it was all new to me. The excitement of the strike, the travel, these students with their generosity and their idealistic notions. New to them, too. They'd never seen the likes of us before. We were the reality. The true face of the working class they'd just talked about in their meetings. We swore, we farted, we sang rugby songs. We smoked, we drank, we fought. We thought Les Dawson and Bernard Manning were funny. We were what it was all about, what they'd been reading about, and here we were, in with them, ready to give the ruling classes a good working over. Suddenly the revolution was *real,* the workers' state a real possibility."

"And Ronnie was a part of that?"

"For me, yes. Ronnie was special. I felt some sort of spark with her the first time we met. I loved her passion, commitment and fierce intelligence, and her grasp of ideology, her ability to explain it, even to a thickie like me. I'd never even thought about most of the things we discussed. Class war, means of production, and all the rest of the Marxist dialectic. She taught me to *think.* And she was just a lost little rich girl trying to find herself in the world. Way out of my league, of course, but somehow that didn't seem to matter very much. She was posh, but she never talked down. And she was a proper bobby dazzler, as they used to say. That sweet smile, those big green eyes. Believe it or not, I was a handsome, strapping young lad back then. I suppose I was a bit of rough trade for her, and she was a taste of caviar and champagne for me. Yes, we did have a passionate romance. A fling, I suppose you'd have to call it, really. I don't know if there was much real love involved, but there was certainly a powerful infatuation. Nature took its course, and for a while I was living in another world. The colliery didn't exist. The pit. South Yorkshire didn't exist. My life was in that bedroom, or out on the picket line, or just sitting talking in the student pub. With Ronnie. A far cry from Mexborough, I can tell you. I suppose I was dazzled by it all."

"I'm not here to judge your action, Mr. Jarvis," Banks said.

"Then why are you here, if you're not after something and Ronnie is fine?"

"It's a difficult case. Sensitive. A man called Gavin Miller was found dead near Eastvale, where I work. He's been murdered."

"Surely Ronnie isn't a suspect? Believe me, she couldn't harm anyone."

"Not even in the service of the revolution?"

"We're not all heartless murderers, Mr. Banks."

"No. I'm sorry. We discovered that she knew him when they were both at the University of Essex in the period we're talking about, and that they'd also been in contact recently. Were you and Ronnie inseparable during your time at Essex?"

"Yes. Pretty much. Two weeks it lasted. Two weeks, and I can remember it all as if it were yesterday. Have you talked to her lately? Have you seen her? How does she look? I've seen photos in the paper, of course, I know she's famous now, but . . ."

"She's still beautiful, Mr. Jarvis. You'd swear she wasn't a day over forty."

He nodded. "I knew she would be. That sort of beauty never fades." He paused, lost in memories. "She'd have a hell of a shock if she could see me now, wouldn't she?" He coughed again. Banks watched a barge passing slowly by on the canal and wondered if it was carrying coal.

"How many people knew about the relationship?" Banks asked.

Jarvis cleared his throat. "Nobody. Well, there's Ronnie and me, of course, and maybe one or two of the other MS, Marxist Society, members. It's impossible to keep something like that a complete secret, but we were discreet for the most part. And it's not as if we were the only ones who'd paired up. It was happening all over the campus."

"What about her boyfriend, Gavin Miller?"

"That's the one who got killed?"

"Yes."

"I didn't know his name, but he obviously knew. I mean, we were stark bollock naked when he barged in once. There's not much mistaking what's happening in a situation like that, is there?"

Banks couldn't help but smile. "I suppose not. Was anything ever said about it?"

"No. He buggered off as soon as he saw what was what. No heroics. Ronnie told me she was finished with him, anyway. He was just still mooning after her, writing poems and whatnot. I got the impression he was becoming a bit of a nuisance, but we never really mentioned him again. I can't believe he'd still be getting in touch with her after all these years."

"We think it's possible that somebody, maybe Miller, might have been blackmailing Ronnie, and that it could have been over her affair with you. However discreet you were, it's pretty obvious that Gavin Miller knew about it, and he'd have been easily able to follow your career over the years."

"But what interest would that possibly hold for anyone?"

"She's Lady Chalmers now."

"I know. But they're not going to take that away from her just because she had a fling with a striking miner forty years ago, are they?"

"Well," said Banks, "think about it. She was a rich girl, and you, as you say, were a striking miner. It makes an interesting story. And with her nephew Oliver Litton about to become home secretary, or so the pundits would have us believe, and your history of Russian connections, communism, backroom deals, trips to Moscow and the like, any journalist worth his salt could easily make something out of it."

"That gives your future home secretary a motive perhaps, but not Ronnie."

"Except Oliver Litton doesn't know anything about it. At least, I'm assuming he doesn't, if neither you nor Ronnie told anyone. Her immediate family doesn't even know."

"I didn't, and I doubt that she did." Jarvis started coughing again. When he had finished, he said, "I don't know how I can help you. I don't really understand what any of this means."

"Me, neither," said Banks, smiling. "That's why I'm asking the questions."

"If you think this Gavin Miller was blackmailing Ronnie over her fling with me," Jarvis said, "and that it had any importance for her, that he was a threat of any kind, then it seems to me as if you're saying it gives her a pretty strong motive for killing him."

"Not necessarily. We know she couldn't have done it."

"Hired someone, then."

"It's possible," Banks said. "But if Miller was blackmailing Lady Chalmers, there may have been others, victims we don't know about, and one of them might have killed him. He was desperately short of money when he was killed, and who's to know to what lengths he might have gone, who he might have antagonized?"

"Well, I didn't do it," said Jarvis.

Banks smiled. "No," he said. He heard a low-flying aircraft pass overhead on its way to some regional airport. It was late afternoon, and already getting dark.

"You think I might have hired a Russian hit man? I'm sorry to disappoint you, but I don't have those contacts anymore. Everything's changed over there. They're not interested in the revolution anymore. The communists used to take over countries with tanks, now if they want another country, the Russian Mafia just buys one."

"I did have a theory that both Ronnie and Gavin Miller might have been recruited by the Russians back in the day."

Jarvis laughed. "Them? Recruited? That's a good one."

"But they were active, weren't they, the Russians? In 1972. With money, with helping spread chaos and set the scene for a communist revolution?"

"They were buzzing around, yes, but it was the union leaders they were interested in, not students standing on the sidelines, like Ronnie and Miller. Oh, they had a few agitators there, people who could turn a peaceful demonstration into a riot. But the Russians had no use for intellectuals. No more than Pol Pot did. And when it comes right down to it, I really didn't have a lot of time for the Russians. I didn't like them, and I never trusted them. We used each other. It was a convenience." He looked around the allotment and said, "Believe it or not, I love this place. I love this country. I'm proud of my homeland. It's where I belong. It's where I'll die. Now if only we could get rid of the bastards in power and change the system, make it a fairer and more egalitarian place to live, I'd die a happy man."

"I'm not sure Lady Chalmers would want to change it now."

"Well, she wouldn't, would she? I must say, you disappoint me, Mr. Banks. Russian sleepers? Your ideas are getting very far-fetched."

Banks scratched his chin. "I disappoint myself sometimes," he said. "Too much imagination, I suppose. You can't help me any further, then?"

"I don't see how I can, do you? I've got nothing to hide. Yes, we had a fling; yes, I've had a soft spot for her in my heart ever since, and I've followed her career. But from a distance. Vicariously. The closest I've got is reading a Charlotte Summers book." He smiled. "And what drivel that was. We've never met, written or spoken in all the intervening years, though I have thought of it many times, and I haven't told anyone about the affair. Including my wife and family, though I didn't marry until two years after Essex. And I'd very much appreciate it if you'd respect that and give me the same courtesy. It's not as if you'll have to hold your tongue for very long."

"It's not in my plans to spread the word, Mr. Jarvis, believe me. What happened with your own family? Did you have children?"

"Aye. A girl and a boy."

"Did the lad become a miner?"

"Shit, no! Do you think I'd encourage them to do that after what you've heard me say here today? No." His expression turned sad. "Though it might have been better in some ways if he had."

"Why's that?"

"Oh, Eddie's turned out all right, I suppose. He's a lathe operator, but you know what the manufacturing sector's been like these past three decades or so. Thatcherland. She gutted the north. He's been in and out of work like a yo-yo most of his life. It takes its toll. He drinks. Got divorced last year, lost custody of the kids. And my daughter Stef married an idle sod who doesn't know the meaning of the word 'work.' Never done a day's hard graft in his life, like his father before him. All he does is go to the pub and back and provide her with more mouths to feed. I warned her. I told them. But do they listen?" He shook his head. "For all my ideals and my beliefs, Mr. Banks, I can't exactly say I've brought up a family to be proud of."

"You shouldn't be so hard on yourself."

"Easy for you to say, with a son in a successful rock band."

Banks couldn't mask his surprise. "How . . . ?"

"I read the papers, Mr. Banks, and I watch telly. I might be old and dying, but I'm not square. There aren't that many coppers with sons in the charts. Now, I'm more of a Shostakovich man myself." Jarvis reached for another cigarette.

"About Shostakovich," said Banks. "I'm very fond of him, myself. I think the whole question of where he stood in relation to Stalin is fascinating. Any insights into that?"

13

THE RED SPORTS CAR WAS PARKED IN ITS USUAL PLACE
on the gravel drive outside Brierley House. Clearly, Lady Chalmers's local garage hadn't got around to taking it in for repairs yet.
When he got out of the Porsche, he walked over to the MG to check
out the damage. It wasn't too bad, he thought. The front headlamp
was smashed, the tire ripped, the fender and passenger door gouged
and dented by the crash through the fence. But all that could be easily
fixed. What interested Banks were the scratches and dents on the
driver's side. They could hardly have been caused by the fence.

Neither Oriana nor Lady Chalmers was in immediate evidence,
and it was a disheveled Sir Jeremy who opened the door. Wearing a
baggy gray sweater and faded jeans, he was unshaven and looked as if
he hadn't slept in days. The telltale tufts of hair sculpted into whorls
and flattened areas by a pillow showed that he had at least tried to
catch a nap.

"Banks, it's you," he said, clearly distraught. "Have you seen it? We
were expecting it back yesterday, but it didn't get here until this
morning, just before you arrived. Come in. I want to talk to you."

He led Banks into a study, or office, that was clearly his, with theatrical posters on the walls, the iconic *Les Mis* and *Cats,* along with
some for his own productions: *The Power and the Glory, Carmilla* and
On the Beach. There were a number of trophies and awards of various

shapes, sizes and materials on the bookcases, slotted between rows of theater books and bound scripts. The wainscoting was dark and the wallpaper above it not much lighter. This room didn't have the panoramic view of the town, but instead looked out on the house next door across the separating lawn. Banks guessed that Sir Jeremy probably didn't spend a lot of time here, as he had offices in London and spent a great deal of time traveling.

"Sit down. Sit down." It sounded more like a command than a request. Banks sat. Sir Jeremy flopped into his leather swivel chair. "You saw it?"

"I take it you mean the damage to Lady Chalmers's car?" he said.

"Well, of course. What do you think? What do you make of it?"

"She was lucky it was a barbed-wire fence she drove through," said Banks. "A drystone wall would have been a lot more serious, even if she hadn't gone into the river."

"Yes, yes," said Sir Jeremy, "but I mean the *other* side. The *driver's* side."

"What did Lady Chalmers say?"

"She was still very groggy from the sedative when I spoke to her, but she said she doesn't know how it happened. Perhaps someone ran into the car while it was parked somewhere."

"Have you seen the marks before?"

"No, but I've been away, and I must admit I've been so busy it's been a long time since I actually paid any attention to Ronnie's car."

"Wouldn't she have had the damage fixed rather than leave it for so long?"

"Hmm," said Sir Jeremy. "I'm not so sure. Ronnie can be remarkably blasé about material things. She's been known to procrastinate. If it were left to Ronnie, it would probably sit in the drive for a week or two first. Usually I organize things like that, or Oriana might if I'm away."

"The damage seems fresh to me."

"Me, too. That's just it. Now she's drawn in on herself. Put the shutters up. She says she just wants to be left alone for a while, that she's fine and needs a bit of peace and a little space to regroup. Fair enough. But I'm worried, Banks."

"What do you think happened?"

"I think it's more than likely that someone deliberately ran her into that fence, no doubt with the thought that she would land in the river and drown."

"You think it was attempted murder?"

"Well, what does it look like to you, man?"

"Who could have done that?"

"No idea. Someone must have followed her, seized the opportunity."

"Why?"

"How should I know? That's your job. But if you ask me, it was probably something to do with whoever killed this Gavin Miller."

"What did the Derbyshire police say?"

"Nothing."

"Have they started an investigation?"

"I don't know. I don't think so. According to Oriana, the officers who brought Ronnie home just wanted to make sure she was all right. They were very polite. They didn't ask any questions. I think she had already told them what happened."

"And she hadn't mentioned any other car being involved?"

"Apparently not. Is that what it is, though? What I thought when I saw the damage? What I just told you?"

"There could be other explanations," said Banks. "We shouldn't jump to conclusions."

"What other explanation?"

"You said yourself that it might be older damage she hadn't got around to getting repaired." But even as he spoke, Banks doubted this explanation. He had visited Brierley House a few times, and had on at least one occasion admired the old red MG parked there. He didn't remember seeing any damage at all; the car had always seemed superbly well cared for, in the way you often find with antique motors. "Or it could have been an accident," he went on.

"But Ronnie didn't mention another car. That's just it. She said she went off the road, and the damage on the driver's side is old. Is she lying to me?"

Banks wasn't going to tell him that he suspected Lady Chalmers had been doing a lot of lying lately. "The weather conditions were dreadful," he said. "Perhaps Lady Chalmers didn't even notice that another car glanced into her side?"

"Oh, come on. You're grasping at straws."

"So you're convinced that someone gave her a nudge towards that river?"

"What else could it be? The scratches, the way she seemed so frightened, so shocked."

"That could all have been due to the accident," Banks said. "But I take your point seriously. Any idea who might have done such a thing?"

"None at all."

"Do you mind if we take the car in for forensic examination? That should tell us a great deal about how the damage occurred, and it might even give us a way of identifying the other car involved if there was one."

"Be my guest."

"And there's one more thing."

"Yes?"

"Do I have your permission to talk to Lady Chalmers again? Alone."

IT WAS a fine late afternoon, the rain holding at bay for the second day in a row, with even a little weak sunshine breaking through the cloud cover, and temperatures in the mid-teens. Warm enough, at any rate, to go without an overcoat. It had taken Gerry a good part of the day to fill in the gaps Banks needed filling in before paying his next visit to Lady Chalmers, but thanks to her determination and resourcefulness, he thought he had what he needed now.

Lady Chalmers was sitting in the garden, a dark blue knitted shawl wrapped around her shoulders, her flaxen hair resting on it straight and damp, as if fresh from the shower. From that angle, Banks could even see a little gray in it. When he came beside her to take the other wicker chair, she turned and looked up at him. He saw some of the beauty that Joe Jarvis must have seen in her forty years ago: the eyes, the porcelain complexion. Then she smiled sadly at him, and he saw the beauty of that, too. He also saw the bruise on her left temple and the cut and swollen lower lip, but those were the only visible results of her accident.

"I thought you'd come," she said. It wasn't an accusation or a complaint, just a weary statement of fact.

Banks sat down. "Will you tell me what happened?"

Lady Chalmers gazed at the view below, the cobbled market square, the castle on its hill, the formal gardens leading down to the river, the old church in the foreground, the constant background noise of the terraced falls. The shadows, where there were any, were lengthening as the winter sun was setting fast. "I'd like to tell you," she said. "It's tearing me apart. I feel if I don't tell someone soon, I'll . . . I don't know what. But it's so hard. You see, I've never told anyone. Not Jem, not Francesca, not Sam or Angelina, not Oriana. Not anyone."

"Not even Joe Jarvis?"

She looked at Banks, just a hint of surprise in her expression. "Not even Joe. You've talked to him?"

"Yes."

"I should have known you'd find out about him. How is he?"

"Not so good." Banks stopped short of going into detail. "He's very ill, in fact."

It was as if a cloud passed over her face. "I'm sorry to hear that. I haven't seen or heard from him in over forty years, but I'm still sorry to hear that." She put her hand over her heart. "Do you understand that?"

"I think so."

"I love my family, Mr. Banks. I'd do anything to protect them. I think you know that, too."

"That's not always possible, but if it's me you're worried about, you needn't be. All I want is the person who killed Gavin Miller. I'm not in the business of spilling family secrets."

"That would be inevitable, I think," she said. "If I'm right. But I think you may also suspect that much already."

"I still need to hear it from you. If it helps, you're right, I do think I know most of it already."

"A reward for your persistence?"

"A ghost to be laid to rest. A festering wound to be cleansed."

"If only." She stared out at the view again.

"I'm still only guessing at this point, but I think Oliver Litton is your son. Am I right?"

Lady Chalmers said nothing for a long time. Banks saw a muscle tic beside her jaw. In the end, she inclined her head in the slightest of nods. "How do you know?"

"I said it was a guess, and it was. Mostly. I spotted a resemblance when I examined some old photos of Joe Jarvis, back in his political firebrand days. It was just a little thing, hardly realized consciously, but it stuck in my mind. There were the photos of you and Oliver together on your screen saver, as well, the last time we talked. There wasn't such a strong resemblance—he takes mostly after his father—but you and your sister were alike, and there was definitely something in his looks that made me think of her. Or you. And there was definitely something about the way you looked standing together that felt like more than just aunt and nephew. It just sort of snagged in my memory." Banks remembered a similar photograph of his mother and his late brother, Roy, that had that same indefinable quality of mother and son. Pride, definitely, a sort of "I made this" expression.

"Then, I did the maths," Banks went on. "When I heard that you went down to Buxton for Oliver's birthday on such a miserable night, I wondered why, and when I found out that Oliver was indeed born in November 1972, which meant that he was conceived in January or February, I became even more convinced that I might be on to something. That was when Joe Jarvis and the South Yorkshire miners were in residence at Rayleigh. And when my colleague then discovered that you didn't return to the University of Essex for your second year until two months into the first term, in December, that did it for me. It could be easily proven, of course, by DNA tests."

"There's no need for that," Lady Chalmers said.

"What happened? How did Gavin Miller find out?"

"Mostly doing the maths, I should imagine. But he had a lot more than you to go on just to start with. I think he always knew, or suspected. Don't forget: he was there. He walked in on me and Joe once."

"I know about that."

"Well, Gavin was a bit of a pest, to be honest, following me about and such. We did go out for a while, but I broke it off with him at the end of the first term, before Christmas. He just didn't want to take no for an answer. Nothing violent or anything, just a constant, irritating presence. He may well have followed me to Buxton and spied on me over the summer. I thought I saw him on the one or two rare occasions I ventured into town."

"That was while you were pregnant?"

"Yes, but before I was showing. I was lucky, I suppose, in that my 'baby bump,' as they call them these days, was easy to cover up with loose clothing for quite a long time into the pregnancy. As you have probably guessed, I didn't want the baby, but the idea of abortion was abhorrent to me. I knew that Tony and Fran had been trying for a baby for ages without any success, so it seemed the perfect solution. Fran and I were very close. When I got pregnant, I ran crying to her and told her everything. But I didn't want anyone else to know, not my parents, not anyone except the three of us."

"And that was how it stayed?"

"That was how it stayed. I finished out the first year, then I went to stay at Buxton for the 'confinement.' And, believe me, it was a confinement. We couldn't go through official channels, of course, but Tony was a practicing gynecologist. He took care of everything. He so wanted a son. We simply made out that my sister was pregnant, and that I was there to be with her. Everyone knew we were close. Neither of us went out much at all during that last month or two. It was hot, too, but no bikinis in the garden. I certainly didn't leave the house, and if Fran ever did, she shoved a cushion down her front. It was so funny. She was terrified someone would ask if they could touch her tummy and feel the baby move. But people didn't do that so much back then, at least not in our circles. It would have been considered vulgar."

"It seems like a complicated way to go about things, hiding one pregnancy and faking another. If they wanted a baby so much, what about IVF, or straightforward official adoption?"

"IVF wasn't available then. That didn't come in until the late sev-

enties. Tony actually worked on it in the early days, but they decided
once they had Oliver that it wasn't for them. Oliver was enough, and
they certainly didn't want the risk of triplets or quadruplets. And as for
official adoption, that would have involved the authorities. None of us
wanted that. I didn't want my parents to know I'd had a baby, for a
start."

"But why not?"

"You don't understand. You didn't know them. I'd caused them
enough—they'd have disowned me. I didn't want that. I was very
confused."

"OK," said Banks.

"And Tony and Fran didn't want even the slightest risk of losing the
child. Fran also loved the idea of the baby being mine, family. It was
the next best thing to having her own. And you know as well as I do
that things can easily go wrong once you bring the social services into
anything."

"So you brought it off."

"With ease. Oliver went to full term and I went back to Essex in
December. By then, of course, Fran and Tony were already the proud
parents of a fine baby boy. And that's how it stayed."

"Why did Gavin Miller leave it so long to approach you?"

Lady Chalmers adjusted the shawl around her shoulders. Banks
looked down on the square and saw the local bus bouncing its way
over the cobbles. "You have to understand, Mr. Banks, that Gavin
Miller wasn't a bad person. Not by his nature. He did what he did
because he was desperate. He wasn't a habitual criminal, and he clearly
wasn't very good at it. He told me that he had always suspected from
the evidence at the time, because he paid such close scrutiny to me.
He could probably even tell when I came back in December, when
term had already begun, that I'd had a baby, because, as you said, the
timing was right, and what possible reason could I have for missing
the first two months of my second year? I also didn't have my usual
slim figure back by then, of course, so I still wore loose clothing. That
wasn't so odd in itself. Most people were neither interested nor particularly suspicious—lots of girls wore loose clothing and it meant
nothing—but Gavin was still something of a stalker, though we didn't

call them that back then. But the real reason Gavin called when he did is a simple one. Oliver is tipped to be the next home secretary in the forthcoming cabinet reshuffle, as you know. And even if he doesn't get the position this time around, everyone knows he's set for great things in the future. He has the perfect image, him and his lovely wife, Tania, their two beautiful children, Miles and Primrose. Imagine how it would go down if it suddenly came out that he was the bastard son of a spoiled little Marxist rich girl and a striking coal miner, with connections to the Communist Party, once suspected of being a Russian spy? You see, I've followed Joe's career closely."

"I still don't see how it's worthy of blackmail," said Banks. "Surely nobody would care about Joe Jarvis's politics these days? He's hardly a force to be reckoned with. Those communist connections came later, anyway, after you had parted. And none of it is Oliver's fault. There's no wrongdoing on his part in any of this."

"What do they say? No smoke without fire. Dirt sticks. All the clichés apply. It's not so much the politics, not in isolation. You must know even better than I do what sort of spin an unscrupulous journalist would put on a story like that. And let's not forget that Fran and Tony broke the law in passing Oliver off as their own son without going through the proper adoption process. Me, too, perhaps, by letting them. I didn't want anyone to know I'd had a baby, and they wanted the world to think they had. And imagine the effect on poor Oliver, himself, after all this time." She shook her head. "I couldn't let it happen. I'd never forgive myself. Perhaps Tony and I are the only ones left who know the secret, but Tony never showed that he realized how much Oliver meant to me. I was his mother. I took as much pride as Tony and Fran in his achievements. I loved him every bit as much as they did, only I could never say so, never show it. Not to him. Not to anyone." She sniffed and rummaged for a handkerchief somewhere inside her shawl. "I'm sorry."

"No need to be. I know you love Oliver. What I need to know is who killed Gavin? Was it the same person who tried to run you into the river?"

"You think it was me, don't you? That I hired someone. That maybe I drove myself into the river."

"The thought crossed my mind, and now you've just given me a motive."

"Gavin rang out of the blue. The phone call you came to ask me about. He told me he knew about Oliver and that DNA would prove it, as you said. He asked for five thousand pounds to keep quiet. He promised me that would be the only payment. He was almost apologetic, not like a hardened blackmailer at all, though I have no experience of such people. A desperate man, a man at the end of his tether. Even so, the call shook me to my roots. We arranged to meet on the bridge in a week's time."

"You'd been there before?"

"Never. But I knew where he meant. I'd driven through Coverton a few times on the way to Barnard Castle."

"But you didn't turn up at the meeting."

"No."

"What happened?"

She paused, as if she were having difficulty getting the words out. "This is really hard, even after all that's happened."

"Take your time."

Lady Chalmers shot him a glance. "As if that would help." She took a deep breath. A couple of crows set up squawking in one of the trees below the bottom of the garden. "All right. As soon as I'd finished talking to Gavin, I phoned Tony. He was livid. He had so much more to lose than I did. Or so he thought. His son—or apparent son—about to become home secretary, brought down by some sordid scandal. He couldn't face something like that. He asked me the details and said to forget about it and leave it to him. Tony was always capable of handling things, the way he did when Oliver was born. I couldn't forget, of course. The phone call was always on my mind. The proposed meeting gnawed away at me all week. People must have noticed. I'm sure Oriana did. Anyway, the next thing I heard was that Gavin had been found dead under the bridge, and then you turned up."

"What did you think?"

She clutched the shawl around her neck. "I didn't know what to think at first."

"Did you talk to Tony again?"

"Yes. Several times. Especially after you came around. He was interested in how the investigation was progressing."

"I'll bet he was. Did he say anything?"

"I asked him what happened, naturally, and he told me that Gavin
said this was only the first payment, that there would be more, and
when Tony objected, Gavin became upset, then angry, demanding
more money right there on the spot. Tony said he acted like he was on
drugs or something. He grabbed Tony and tried to snatch his wallet
from his inside pocket. They struggled. There was a scuffle, and Gavin
fell off the bridge. Tony said he simply panicked and ran off and drove
home."

Banks knew that it couldn't have happened as easily as that. The
side of the bridge was too high for Gavin Miller simply to fall over it.
He had to have been at least partially lifted off his feet and bundled
over. Tony Litton was powerful enough to do that. There was nothing
to be gained from telling Lady Chalmers this, though. She could
hardly handle the fact that Tony had killed Gavin Miller accidentally,
let alone that he had deliberately murdered him, and tried to murder
her.

"So you believed that Gavin Miller's death was a tragic accident?"

"Yes. Of course. At the time. Tony told me that there was no
reason to do or say anything. If I just sat it out, he said, stuck to the
story, then everything would blow over and we'd all be fine. Naturally, I didn't want him to go to trial, or to jail. But it worried me.
And you kept coming back, kept asking questions, uncovering fragments of my past, getting closer to the truth. That's why he tried to
have you taken off the case. He said he would be able to handle the
police."

"Why did you phone me from London?"

Lady Chalmers looked away. "I was a bit drunk. Things weren't sitting easily with me. Jem was back, but I couldn't talk to him. I was
confused, worried. I thought maybe if we made a personal connection, then you'd realize it wasn't me and go away."

"So what happened next?"

"When I went down for Oliver's birthday, Oliver left for London
immediately after dinner. He hadn't seen his wife and children for

some days. He had a driver waiting. Tony could see what a state I was in, and he was worried I was on the verge of telling all. I think I was pretty close to the breaking point. He wanted me to stay the night in the guest bedroom, but I think I was scared that he might do something. I don't know what, but the whole setup was making me nervous. I don't suppose I was entirely convinced that what happened to Gavin was a complete accident. There was always something about Tony. Something a bit cold and calculating. Pragmatic. There were only the two of us, and we were the only ones in the world who knew. I was scared. Of my own brother-in-law. So I insisted on going home. I've always been a good driver. The MG's a bit leaky perhaps, but it holds the road well. I wasn't too worried about driving home."

"Do you think it was Anthony Litton who nudged you into the river?"

"I was on a narrow country lane beside the river. It was dark, no streetlights, just the car's headlamps, and the rain was coming down in buckets. The windscreen wipers couldn't keep up with it. Everything was blurred. I was slowing down, thinking of stopping for a while until it eased off. I didn't see the car. I felt a bump, and then I was losing control, crashing through the fence. I didn't see the car."

"But ever since then, you've been terrified because you think it was Tony, don't you, and it's been eating away at you?"

"I couldn't accept it at first. I told myself that even if there had been another car, and it wasn't just my imagination, me losing control in the rain, then it was still an accident, just some stranger who was having trouble staying on the road, too. Admittedly, he shouldn't have been overtaking under such conditions, but . . . well, you know what some drivers are like."

"Indeed. What changed your mind?"

"When I was lying there, in hospital, while they checked me out, I realized that it had to be him, that it was no accident. We were the only two left who knew. We'd argued, after Oliver left. I said Tony should tell you the truth, if it had all been an accident. He said he couldn't. I don't think he trusted me to keep quiet anymore. He was afraid of what any kind of trouble with the police would do to Oliver's career prospects. I was worried about Oliver, too, of course, and it was just tearing me apart. But Tony had staked his whole life on Oliver, and he couldn't bear the thought of it all unraveling, even at the expense of his sister-in-law, the true mother of his child. Can you imagine what it's like, *knowing* that your own brother-in-law is trying to kill you?"

"No, I can't," said Banks.

"Before that realization came to me, I never would have said a thing, no matter what I suspected about Gavin's death. That's the irony, Mr. Banks. If Tony hadn't tried to kill me, he could have still kept everything he wanted. I would have kept his secret, even if it destroyed my sanity. Now . . . What are you going to do?"

"I don't know," said Banks. "A detailed forensic examination of your car should be able to link it with the car that nudged you off the road, and tell us whether it was Anthony Litton's. That's not enough evidence in itself, though. A good lawyer could argue that you'd been in the same place together all evening, that you could have easily bumped into his car on your way out, for example. And it's certainly not enough evidence to convict him of Gavin Miller's murder." Even taking into consideration the height of the bridge's side, Banks thought, this same good lawyer could still make a strong case for accidental death, manslaughter, at the most. But if any of that happened, as Lady Chalmers had said, there was every chance that Oliver Litton's promising future would be ruined, through no fault of his own. Litton was a rare politician in that he was popular with the people and most of his peers. He stood a little to the right of his party, and even the police welcomed some of the reforms he had promised to bring in if he was given the job.

"Will I go to jail?"

Banks looked out over Eastvale, in all its beauty spread out below him under the gray sky, his mind working furiously. A cool breeze shook the tops of the trees, and the crows flew off noisily. "What for?" he said. "I'd be a liar if I promised I could predict how this is all going to turn out in court, if it ever gets there." Then he turned to Lady Chalmers. "There is one thing I can promise you, though. I will do my best to see that you don't go to prison." Banks thought of his visit to Kyle McClusky and the sound of heavy doors being locked, weighed it against Veronica's deceptions and prevarications. "I certainly don't want to see you there. You've been very foolish, protecting a killer, even if he was your brother-in-law, but it's understandable why, and I think you'd have any jury on your side. I don't think you could have foreseen Gavin's murder. You also protected your brother-in-law, even after you came to suspect him of murder, but that would also be very hard to prove in court. Even if it could be proven, there would no doubt be a great deal of jury sympathy for you. I don't have anything to arrest you for. Maybe we could make a case out for obstructing the police in their inquiries, wasting police time, failing to register the birth of a child, even aiding and abetting, which is a lot more serious, but . . . Anthony and Oliver Litton have powerful friends. You and Sir Jeremy have powerful friends. Who knows what sort of influence could be brought to bear? I'm sure that as a politician, Oliver is also bound to have enemies and rivals, even in his own party, who will be sniffing around for anything that can be used against him. I can't promise to keep this from the press or the courts, but it's not my intention to make it public."

"But do *you* have to tell anyone?"

"I have to tell my boss. She'll determine what's to be done then. And what I want you to do is to tell your husband and your children. Oriana, too. They deserve to know. It won't be easy, but they're your family. You told me you'd do anything to protect them, and it may seem like this would do just the opposite, but believe me, it won't. They'll stand by you. In the end, it will bring you closer and make you stronger."

"And Tony? What about him?"

"I think you'd better leave Mr. Litton to me," said Banks.

14

I T WAS WELL AFTER DARK THAT THURSDAY EVENING, and the fog was thickening fast when Banks arrived at Anthony Litton's Derbyshire manor house, which was as out of the way as it could be, in that strange no-man's-land between Buxton and Macclesfield. Though certainly as large and impressive as Brierley, and surrounded by a high wall, the house was older and altogether more heavy and gloomy in its aspect, the dark stone, the brooding gables and squat solidity of its symmetry. Lights were showing in two of the downstairs windows, which meant Banks was probably in luck. He wasn't entirely certain how to approach Litton, though he had been trying to work out a strategy on the drive down, amply aided by Shostakovich's Fifth Symphony playing loudly on the Porsche's music system.

Banks pulled up where the drive ended, in front of the door. There was another car parked to his right, a dark Mercedes, in front of the closed garage doors. When he got out and examined it, he noticed that there were deep scratches and a dent on the passenger side. Was Litton so arrogant that he couldn't even be bothered to put it in the garage, out of sight? Did he have that much confidence in Lady Chalmers's silence?

Banks rang the bell and waited, surprised when Litton himself answered. He had been expecting a butler or a maid in a house like that. "It's you, isn't it?" Litton welcomed him. "That detective who was browbeating Ronnie up at Brierley the other day. What are you doing here? What do you want now?"

"I'd like to talk to you," Banks said.

Litton glowered and stood his ground, a stocky, angry figure, then he seemed to relent. He looked over Banks's shoulder, then right and left. "Are you alone?"

"Yes."

"I thought you lot always traveled in packs."

"Only when we're hunting dangerous animals." Banks had considered bringing Annie or Winsome with him, but had decided he needed discretion more than company at this point.

"I suppose that ought to reassure me. Come in. You've got ten minutes." He led Banks into a sitting room that probably had a beautiful view of the surrounding hills in daylight. Now the large picture windows were covered by heavy red velvet curtains. A log fire blazed in the large hearth, though it wasn't a particularly cold evening, and its flames glinted on the oil paintings that hung on the walls, outlining their relief. Litton sat on a sofa, perching at the edge like a man with little time to spare, and offered nothing in the way of refreshments. That suited Banks just fine. "Out with it, man," Litton urged.

Banks determined not to be goaded or wound up by Litton's demeanor. He had the upper hand here, he kept reminding himself. "I notice your car has some damage on the passenger side," he began.

"Some of those bloody drystone walls bulge out way too far," Litton answered. "You know what it's like. You must have the same problem up in North Yorkshire."

"I also know that Lady Veronica Chalmers was forced off the road shortly after she left here in the rain the other night."

"Forced? As I understood it, no other car was involved."

"That's not exactly true," Banks said. "There's also damage to the driver's side of her car."

"And you think I'm responsible?"

"Well, it wouldn't be too difficult to match the paint chips."

"You've got a nerve. And what if you did? Ronnie bumped my car on her way out. I distinctly remember it. She was in a hurry because of the worsening weather. There you are. And where's your motive?"

"You killed Gavin Miller, and Lady Chalmers knew about it. You thought you'd convinced her it was an accident, but she still harbored some doubts. After what happened the other night, she has none at all."

"Who? That old drunk who fell off the bridge? The one you were harassing Ronnie about?"

"He wasn't old. And if he was drunk, you're the only one who knows it."

"Don't come your clever tricks with me. Why on earth would I kill someone I didn't even know?"

"It's complicated," Banks said. "But Lady Chalmers now feels certain you did, and that it was you who tried to kill her. That was your mistake, Mr. Litton. You went too far."

"Ronnie would never testify against me. We're family."

"I wouldn't be too sure of that. You've made her life a misery lately. I think you pushed her beyond the breaking point."

Litton folded his arms. "No. She would never do that to Oliver."

Banks paused to give his words added weight. "Because Oliver is her son?"

At first, Litton gaped, then he got to his feet, walked over to the drinks cabinet and poured himself a large whisky, neat, from a cut-glass decanter. When he sat down again, he sank back in the chair, no longer a man in a hurry. "So what makes you think that?"

"Never mind. The point is that a simple DNA test would prove it. I assume you know who the father is, too? Joe Jarvis. She might not have opened up to you about what happened, but she would have opened up to her sister."

"What are you going to do about it?"

"That's what everybody keeps asking me. Why don't you tell me what happened first." Banks spread his hands. "Don't worry. I'm not wired for sound."

Litton narrowed his eyes and glared at Banks for a while, then he said, "It was an accident. Gavin Miller. All right, Ronnie phoned me in some distress and said he'd been in touch, and he wanted money to keep quiet. As you know, Oliver has a bright future ahead of him, and this Miller character had read about him. He remembered some things from the old student days with Veronica—how she 'disappeared' for a while, how she was late back for her second year, how she looked when she did come back. Eventually he put it all together." Litton glanced at Banks. "And like you, all he had to do was threaten her with the possibility of exposure, and we were sunk, Oliver's career along with us. I know that nobody could force her to take a DNA test, but Ronnie thought that if the media kept on demanding it, not doing so would be tantamount to an admission of guilt. She didn't know what to do."

"So you offered to take care of things for her, to meet Miller in her place?"

"Yes. It was a paltry enough sum. Five thousand pounds. Showed very little imagination, I thought."

"You paid him."

"Yes. You know I did. And I made sure the bills wouldn't be traced and that you wouldn't find my fingerprints on them."

"Why did you do that?"

"What do you mean?"

"What would be the point in going to all that trouble over the bills if you were simply giving the money to Gavin Miller? I could understand it if you were planning on getting rid of him or something, making sure there was no forensic evidence to link you to the payment, but you said it was an accident, not premeditated murder."

Litton narrowed his eyes. "You think you're a real clever bastard, don't you, Banks?"

"So why did you kill him?"

Litton hammered his fist on his knee. "I told you. It was an accident."

"How did it happen?"

"He just wouldn't give up. I told you, the man was drunk, on drugs, whatever. He was practically incoherent. He kept going on about how he remembered Ronnie, saying intimate things about her, how she had betrayed him, but how he still thought they should be together again. It was disgusting, sick. I tried to just walk away, but he grabbed my lapels. I could tell then that he'd been drinking whisky along with whatever else he'd been taking. He breathed the fumes in

my face. He said he realized he hadn't asked for enough and he'd be
back for more. We grappled, struggled. He was going for my wallet,
wanted more right then and there. I struggled back, and the next
thing I knew he was gone. I looked over the bridge and saw him lying
there at an awkward angle. I didn't know he was dead, but I knew I
had to get away from there before anyone came."

"So you left the money?"

"Yes. I panicked. It was too risky to go down there."

"The side of the bridge was quite high," Banks said. "A simple push
wouldn't have sent him over. He had to have been lifted off his feet."

"He was light as a feather, Banks. I had no idea. I shook him the
way you do, tried to get him off me, lifted him and thrust him into
the side of the bridge, or so I thought, just to knock the breath out of
him, and he went over. Simple as that. OK, so I lost my temper. But I
didn't kill him deliberately. You have to believe that."

Banks digested what he had just heard, still not certain whether to
believe Litton. He was a bullish man, and strong, so his story would
probably hold some credibility with a court, should the case ever get
to one. But there was an alternative explanation. "When you asked
him what evidence he had," Banks asked, "what did he tell you?"

"He was just like you," Litton sneered. "A few wild suppositions
that couldn't be substantiated, and the threat of DNA. I knew we
couldn't survive that."

"But he hadn't actually carried out any DNA tests?"

"No. How could he? He'd have had to have something of Ronnie's,
Oliver's and Jarvis's. What was he going to do, sort through their rubbish? Break in and steal a toothbrush or a hairbrush?"

And pay for the test, too, Banks thought. "He might have managed
it, eventually," he said. "But the point is that he hadn't. All he had was
a theory and the *possibility* of proof. DNA."

"I don't understand."

"Gavin Miller wasn't a particularly good blackmailer," Banks said.
"Probably because he'd never done it before, and it was in many ways
against his nature. He wasn't a natural criminal, just a man who'd lost
his moral compass because he'd been ill treated and found himself in
dire circumstances. From his point of view, his life had been nothing

but a series of betrayals. Lady Chalmers betrayed him, his wife betrayed him, the college betrayed him, his most recent girlfriend betrayed him. Even Trevor Lomax, his close friend, betrayed him, though I don't think he knew the full extent of Lomax's treachery, thankfully. He was desperate and confused. Blackmail must have seemed his easiest option. Miller was an oddball, an eccentric, true, but apart from a bit of recreational drug use, not a habitual criminal. What blackmailer would admit to his victim that he actually has nothing substantial to bargain with? You didn't have to talk to Gavin Miller for very long to realize that other than this foolish and greedy drunken man standing before you, there was nothing else to betray your secret and ruin Oliver's career. Since your wife's death, the only people who knew were you and Lady Chalmers, and she certainly wasn't going to tell. Oliver is her son, and she is every bit as proud of him and protective of him as you are, if not more so. But you pushed her too hard, Tony. Everyone has their breaking point, and that moment on the road, when she realized who it was who had tried to send her to her death, was hers. What were you going to do, try again?"

"This is absurd, Banks. Even if it did come out that Oliver was the son of my sister-in-law and a dyed-in-the-wool communist union agitator, it was hardly his doing, was it? It could hardly reflect badly on him."

"Don't pretend to be so naïve," said Banks. "You know damn well it would mean the end for Oliver Litton and all his political ambitions, and the sad thing is that you're right—it would be through no fault of his own. In fact, he seems to have led an exemplary life and career so far. Even if the link between Oliver and Joe Jarvis wasn't enough to sink his career, the subterfuge of his birth and the illegalities involved in passing off Lady Chalmers's child as your own would be. In this day and age, a politician has to be spotless, and that sometimes involves being spotless in matters beyond his control."

Litton got up to refill his glass. "I asked you before," Banks heard him say as the whisky gurgled into the glass. "What are you going to do about it? If you arrest me, I'll deny it all, of course, but you'll still destroy Oliver. Ronnie, too, and her family. Is that what you want?

That's just what Miller would have done. Do you want to complete the blackmailer's work for him?"

"I don't—" Banks began, but before he could finish he felt a heavy blow to the back of his head that sent stars flashing through his brain and seemed to put so much pressure on his eyeballs from the inside that he thought they would burst from their sockets. It was over in a second, or less, and he let the welcome darkness flood into his veins as he slid to the floor.

IT COULD have been hours or days since he fell unconscious, Banks felt, as he struggled to sit up, his head a mass of raging pain, the bile rising in his gorge. He was immediately sick on the carpet and slid down to the floor again. This time he lay there, trying to take slow, deep breaths, aware of his heart pounding and the blood rushing in his ears. He didn't know if any permanent damage had been done, but there seemed to be quite a bit of blood. It had soaked through his collar and into the carpet around where his head had lain. Beside the stain he saw the cut-glass decanter. So that was what Litton had hit him with. Christ, he thought, it could have killed him.

When he felt able, he struggled to a sitting position in the armchair and lay his head against the back. Bugger Litton's lace antimacassars. He still felt sick, and his head and his thoughts throbbed and swirled. His vision was blurred and the back of his head burned. After spending a while sitting there, he risked a glance at his watch, and slowly, the face and hands came into focus. It was going on for midnight. That was at least two hours since he had arrived. If Litton had made a run for it he had a hell of a start. Banks listened as best he could with the pounding in his head, but he could hear no other sounds in the house.

The next Herculean task was to get to the bathroom and clean up. The stairway looked as if it stretched about as high as the one in the Led Zeppelin song. Banks's first attempt to get to his feet failed miserably, his legs like rubber, and it wasn't until about ten minutes later that he felt up to trying again, gripping the sides of the armchair and pushing with all his might. The world swam, and his head hammered; he felt so dizzy that he thought he might fall over again, but he made it. He stood swaying a while until he thought he had regained a modicum of his balance and made a few hesitant steps towards the staircase.

He found the bathroom easily enough and set the taps running in the sink. When the temperature was right and he leaned forward to stick his head under the water, he felt a wave of nausea and dizziness and almost slid to the floor. But he held on to the sink and let the water flow across his head like a tropical downpour.

Afterwards, he touched the back of his head and felt a lump the size of a bird's egg, but the bleeding seemed to have stopped, and most of the blood had washed away. He grabbed a large fluffy white towel, which he used to dry his head, carefully patting the area around the wound. The towel came away a bit pink with blood, but Banks thought it was just the residue. His vision had cleared, his balance seemed restored, and all that remained was the throbbing pain. He ransacked the bathroom cabinet and found a bottle of prescription painkillers plastered with warnings. He palmed two of them and put the bottle in his pocket, then tottered downstairs and poured himself a whisky and soda to wash them down with. A few minutes later, he was ready for his first small steps into the world outside.

Litton's car was gone, but the Porsche stood exactly where it had been. Fog swirled around the grounds like a Hammer movie set. He had no idea what Litton was up to now, though the only explanation he could come up with was flight. He had realized the game was up and was making his escape. But Banks also realized that so much of what Litton had done, so much of what made him tick, was tied up with Oliver and Lady Chalmers, that there was a chance he had flown to one or the other seeking sanctuary and support. Given that Oliver didn't know the secret of his own birth, Lady Chalmers would probably be the better choice. She was a woman, Litton would figure, and though she may have betrayed him to Banks, he would imagine that with a little charm, fake humility and a plea for family loyalty—especially for Oliver's sake—he could perhaps win back her trust and head the trouble off at the pass. He had an injured police officer to cope with, of course, but no doubt he could explain that, too. And perhaps with the Litton and Chalmers spheres of influence combined, he could get enough people who counted to swallow it all.

Banks got in his car, and fearing that Litton had removed some essential engine part, stuck the key in the ignition and gritted his teeth as he turned it. The engine started first time, as it always did. Wherever Litton was going, Banks realized, north or south, there was only one road to get there. It branched north and south a few miles to the east, but up to that point, the only other way you could go was east. That part of the Peak District wasn't exactly crisscrossed by north-south routes.

Banks knew that he probably shouldn't be driving, especially with the painkillers he had taken, but he felt fit enough to do it, and he was damned if he was going to spend the night either at Litton's house or in a local hospital. The fog didn't help, though visibility wasn't anywhere near as bad as it could have been.

Not more than three miles along the road, he saw flashing lights, blurred in the mist, ahead of him, and a vague shape in the middle of the road, which was blocked by patrol cars. It was a uniformed police officer, waving his torch around in circles. Banks pulled gently to a halt and rolled down his window to see a young patrol constable.

"What's the problem, officer?" he asked.

"I'm sorry, sir. This road is closed due to an accident. I'm afraid you'll have to turn back."

Banks could just make out, beyond the roadblock, a part of the drystone wall knocked down, but he couldn't see beyond that. Not certain whether it was worth the risk or not, Banks let his curiosity get the better of him and pulled out his warrant card. "Anything I can help you with?" he said, flashing the card.

The officer seemed to come to attention immediately. "No, sir. We've got everything under control."

"What happened?"

"Car went through the wall and into the river."

"The driver?"

"We haven't found a body yet, only the car, half-submerged. It looks as if the driver might have got out through his window, but the current's pretty strong. It's doubtful anyone survived. If he had, it would be a first."

"Anything on the car?"

"Registered to Mr. Anthony Litton, sir. He's the father of Oliver Litton. You've heard of him?"

"Indeed I have."

The constable shook his head. "And just the other night, not more than two miles away, his sister-in-law ran through a fence. Luckily, she came out of it all right."

"Well, if I can't help, I'll be on my way," said Banks, thankful that the young constable hadn't asked him what he was doing on a minor road so far off his patch. He also realized that he probably looked a bit of a mess, and he was glad the constable hadn't shone his torch on him. "I'm afraid I don't know the roads around here very well," Banks said. "And I don't have satnav. How do I get north?"

The constable scratched his head. "Well, sir, you can't really get there from here, if you catch my drift. Not with this road out of commission. I'd say your best bet is to turn back, keep going till you see the signposts to Stockport and Manchester Airport, then it's a hop, skip and a jump to the M62. That'll be your quickest way."

"Thank you," Banks said, then backed up to a lay-by to make his turn, as the road was quite narrow. He was aware of the young constable watching him as he went. Perhaps he had smelled the whisky on his breath or noticed the blood on his collar. He could also feel the painkillers kicking in, the throbbing in his head receding to a distant hammering, like someone fixing a fence in the far distance, and a pleasant, heavy warmth filled his head and his arms. He thought some loud music might help him stay awake, but his brain rejected every choice. He needed to think, no matter how difficult it was. In the end, he settled for silence. It would have to be enough.

THE SUMMONS, when it came, arrived at the ungodly hour of seven o'clock on Friday morning—ungodly most of all because Banks hadn't crawled into bed until almost three. He seemed to remember his mother saying years ago that you're not supposed to go to sleep with a suspected concussion, but he had been able to stay awake no longer. When he woke to the gentle blues riff of his mobile and heard the clipped voice of AC Gervaise telling him, "Now. My office," he struggled to sit up, then rolled out of bed towards the shower. He noticed there was blood on his pillow, but not much. And he had awoken from his sleep, so all was well. Almost. He had a moment of panic when he worried, too late, that Anthony Litton might have faked the car accident and gone after Lady Chalmers. He should have phoned her last night when he got home, he thought. But if Litton killed Lady Chalmers, that would be the end for him, and he didn't seem to Banks like the kind of man who would throw away what he wanted so much. He would also have had a difficult time getting to Eastvale without a car.

Taking a few minutes extra to make himself a cup of instant coffee and swallow more painkillers and a slice of buttered toast, Banks skipped the shave and hurried out to the Porsche. It was a damp, chilly morning, the tops of the dalesides obscured by clouds, and a mist settled low in the valley, so the tower of Helmthorpe church resembled a ship's mast in the ocean.

Banks had had neither the time nor the inclination to think very much since his hazy journey back from the Litton house. On his way to the station, he decided on the approach that he thought would cause him the least grief. The coffee worked a little magic during the drive, and when he pulled up at the back of Eastvale Police HQ, he was feeling at least 80 percent human again. His head still spun and throbbed, though, despite the painkillers he had taken.

AC Gervaise was waiting behind her desk and, as expected, ACC McLaughlin was in his usual comfortable chair. The CC himself wouldn't come out of his hole even for something of this obvious magnitude. What did rather knock the wind out of Banks, though, was the presence of a gray, nondescript man sitting beside the window.

"I understand you have already met, Mr. Browne, DCI Banks?" said Gervaise.

"Mr. Browne," said Banks. "With an 'e.' Yes, indeed."

Browne inclined his head briefly in greeting, his expression inscrutable as ever. They had met once before during a particularly politically sensitive case, and all Banks really knew about him was that he was someone big in MI5. He had had a serious run-in with them during that case, and now it appeared that he was due for another. How many run-ins with MI5 could the average police career survive? he wondered.

"You look awful," Gervaise said.

Banks rubbed the back of his head gently. Even that hurt. He winced. "I've had better days."

"And nights, so we've heard," said McLaughlin. "According to the Derbyshire police, that is."

So the patrol constable had spotted something odd, seen blood or smelled whisky, and made inquiries, Banks thought. Well, good for him; he'd go far. "Yes, sir."

"Tell us what you think you were doing going off half-cocked, alone, to interview Anthony Litton," said Gervaise.

"I had nothing definite to go on," said Banks. "Suspicions, a confirmation of sorts from Lady Chalmers that, should she change her mind, wouldn't be worth the breath it was spoken with. I was also aware of the sensitive nature of the case. The last thing I wanted to do was rush in there with the heavy brigade 'half-cocked,' as you put it, and slap the cuffs on Anthony Litton. I wanted to know what was going on before I decided what to do about it."

"And you think that's your place, to make decisions like that?"

"I was the only one who knew all the details. But I was planning on laying out what I knew in front of you, ma'am."

"But first you went and broke all the rules in the book?" said McLaughlin.

"One or two, perhaps." Banks held his thumb and forefinger slightly apart. "Just little ones."

McLaughlin glowered. "The most important of which was interviewing a potential murder suspect alone."

"I talk to people a lot by myself," said Banks. "I find I get more out of them that way."

"It's not a matter of getting more out of them, Alan," said Gervaise. "It's a matter of following the correct procedure, of obtaining evidence that can be used in court. Your recent exploits have got us nothing of the kind."

"Well, that should suit everyone well enough, shouldn't it?"

Banks noticed Browne's mouth curl at one edge in a little smile.

"What on earth made you dash off to Derbyshire?" Gervaise asked.

"Someone had run Lady Chalmers off the road," Banks answered. "She'd just left her brother-in-law's house. I thought he might know something. When I arrived, I noticed scratches and dents on the passenger side of his car. I wanted to know how he got them, so I asked him."

"And did he tell you?"

"He said they must have happened when she drove away from his house in a hurry. But he was lying."

"You know this for a fact?"

"It's the only thing that makes any sense. Besides, unless he'd moved it for some reason after Veronica's crash, Litton's car was parked to the right of the house, in front of the garage doors."

"So?"

"Well, I'm assuming that Lady Chalmers pulled up in front of the house, as I did. That's where the drive leads, naturally, at any rate, and there's no room on the other side of the car."

"I still don't get it," said Gervaise.

"No matter how Lady Chalmers left the house, by backing out, doing a three-point turn, whatever, if she'd hit Litton's car, she would have hit it on the driver's side, and the damage was on the passenger side, consistent with his overtaking and forcing another car off the road."

"It's hardly evidence, is it, though?" said Gervaise. "More like sheer speculation."

"It makes sense of the facts."

"Why on earth would Anthony Litton want to harm his own sister-in-law?" Gervaise asked.

"Because she knew he killed Gavin Miller, though he had convinced her it was an accident, and he felt she was becoming unstable. He knew she'd been talking to me, for example, and he was starting to feel it would only be a matter of time before she snapped." Banks looked at Gervaise and McLaughlin. "He first complained to you about me, remember, hoping to nip it in the bud. I think he realized he couldn't, that she'd blurt it all out sooner or later, and that more drastic action was required."

"How do you know he killed Gavin Miller?"

"He admitted to it. He said it was an accident, too, that they struggled, and Miller fell off the bridge."

"And you think he's lying again?"

"Pretty much."

"You'll have to explain a bit better than that, Alan."

"It's simple, really," said Banks. "Gavin Miller and Veronica Bellamy, as she then was, were at the University of Essex together. From what I could gather, they had gone out together for a few months in their first year. Miller must have thought there was money in it, so he contacted Lady Chalmers and asked her for money to keep quiet."

"About what?" asked McLaughlin.

"Their relationship? Some other indiscretion? Some crime they had committed? Drugs use, most likely? I don't know exactly what. But it doesn't matter. It wouldn't have taken much."

"But why so long after?" asked Gervaise. "That must have been forty years ago."

"Because Miller was in desperate straits. Apparently, he had some woolly-headed notion about opening a record shop, and he wanted funding. He was also unraveling mentally, I think. A mix of drink and drugs and a deepening depression. And because Oliver Litton was all over the news. That was the trigger. Miller thought that if he caused the family trouble at a time like this, something that was bound to be splashed over all the tabloid front pages, given that Sir Jeremy and Lady Chalmers are celebrities of a kind, it might be worth a few thousand quid to them just to shut him up. And you all know what reporters are like. They'll make a sow's ear out of a silk purse in no time. It was potentially a very vulnerable time for Oliver Litton, especially with the opposition, and even contenders from his own party, searching for anything they could smear him with, however remote or spurious."

"Fair enough," said Gervaise. "But why was it necessary to kill Miller? Couldn't his death have been an accident, as Litton said?"

"It could have been, but it wasn't," said Banks. "Lady Chalmers called her brother-in-law and asked for his help when Miller first got in touch with her, and he said he would deal with the problem, so he went to the arranged meeting with Miller instead of her. Her husband was abroad, and I doubt that she wanted him to know any sordid truths about her past, anyway. He knew nothing about Miller, and he accepted the story that he had phoned to con money out of her, posing as a member of the alumni society. According to Anthony Litton, Miller was drunk, or stoned, or both, when they met, and he became aggressive, demanding more money, physically attacking Mr. Litton, and saying vile things about Lady Chalmers and the things they'd done all those years ago. There was a struggle, and Miller was so emaciated he ended up over the side and Litton scarpered. At the most, Litton said, it was manslaughter. And that was probably what it would have come to in court. But I think he set out to kill Miller, to put an end to his blackmail, once and for all. We all know that blackmailers always come back for more. He couldn't risk that, not with his son's career at stake."

"That's it?"

"Yes. Whoever killed Miller must have physically lifted him off the ground to drop him over that bridge. It's my opinion that it would have been very unlikely to happen by accident, and Stefan Nowak and Dr. Glendenning concur. There were also antemortem wounds indicating a struggle of some sort."

"And now Anthony Litton's dead, too?"

"As you no doubt know," Banks said. "I approached the accident scene on my way home. They hadn't found the body when I drove up, and they turned me back, but I'm sure it didn't take them long, and I'm equally sure they told you all about it."

"It was Anthony Litton," said Browne, speaking up for the first time. "The police found his body several yards downstream. Drowned. It seems he'd managed to get out of the car and was trying to swim for safety, but the current was too strong, and he wasn't much of a swimmer. It was an accident black spot, according to the police at the scene." He paused and put his finger to his chin. "Though you might be forgiven for thinking that someone who lived in the neighborhood would be aware of that fact and would consequently drive more carefully." Browne shrugged. "According to the accident investigator, he must have been doing about sixty. No matter. It was a bad night. Fog and all. The thing is, as soon as we heard what had happened, we—that is, some colleagues of mine—paid a hasty visit to Mr. Litton's home in search of any, well, *sensitive* material, and they found . . . well, perhaps you can tell me what they found, DCI Banks?"

There was no point lying about that, Banks thought. "I think Mr. Litton panicked when I got the truth out of him. He took me by surprise, hit me over the head with a cut-glass decanter." He turned to show them all the bump. "It bled quite a lot, and I lost consciousness for some time. When I came to, he was gone. I cleaned myself up and went out to try and find him. All I found was the accident scene."

"We were able to clean up the mess before any questions were asked," said Browne. "You see, none of us have the depth of understanding of this case that you have, Mr. Banks, especially after the extensive inquiries you and your team have been making into Lady Chalmers's past, but I'm sure it's all quite irrelevant now." He stared blankly at Banks.

"Quite irrelevant," Banks said.

Browne nodded slowly. "Yes. You see, as I'm sure you are also aware, we, and our sister organization the police force, of course, have a very strong interest in wanting Oliver Litton to become the new home secretary, though we are aware it's still not a foregone conclusion. It would be a tragedy if anything were to jeopardize his chances at this stage. For the first time in a long time, we would have a sympathetic and understanding home secretary, and perhaps some of these dreadful enforced budget cuts we've all been undergoing might be somewhat eased. Perhaps. At least the prospect is far, far better than any of the alternatives, even if nothing changes."

"Well," said Banks, spreading his hands, "the last thing I wanted was for the press to get hold of the story and distort it out of all proportion."

"Admirable, Mr. Banks," said Browne, a glint in his eye. "Of course, the young Mr. Litton will be the recipient of a great deal of sympathy over the loss of his father at a time when it certainly can't do his future career any harm. Perhaps a few days of personal time, for grieving, you understand, the funeral, then back into the fray with renewed vigor. After all, it was a tragic accident. A terrible night, a notorious black spot. What can one say?"

"Indeed," said Banks. Why did he always feel he was entering into a John le Carré novel every time he talked to Mr. Browne? Well, this was only the second time, to be strictly fair, but he felt that it could never be otherwise. "And the murder of Gavin Miller?" he said.

"Hardly murder, wouldn't you think?" said Browne. "A bit of a puzzle, still, but one that will fade very quickly. Nobody much cares about Gavin Miller."

"But what about my team?"

"What about them? Do they know anything?"

"Just some background. They've put in a lot of work."

"Then there's no need to worry, is there, if all they know is a little background. You were getting nowhere, the investigation is being scaled down. Soon, everyone will have forgotten about it."

"Are there any other promising leads?" asked McLaughlin.

"No," said Banks. "We were looking into drugs, and connections with Eastvale College, but we kept hitting a brick wall."

"There you are," said Browne. "People will assume it was probably a criminal gang who does something like that. Such killers are notoriously difficult to bring to justice."

"Then I don't really think we can justify the cost of an ongoing investigation, can we?" McLaughlin said. "I think we can safely put it on the back burner."

"What about Lady Chalmers?" Banks asked. "He tried to kill her."

"We've had a brief word," said Browne. "Naturally, she is also grief stricken. I understand that she and her sister were very close, and since her sister's death, her brother-in-law and her nephew have been even closer to her. She's bearing up well. I'd say she'll be right as rain, given a little time."

"And me?" said Banks.

"Just a little bump on the head," said Browne. "You'll recover."

"I didn't mean that. Should I be looking over my shoulder for the rest of my days?"

Browne raised an eyebrow. "No need to be melodramatic. Oh, we'll keep an eye on you. The way we always do. I heard rumors of a promotion." He glanced towards ACC McLaughlin. "That should be nice."

Banks turned to Gervaise and McLaughlin. Neither of them seemed very happy. "Well," said Banks, "I'm not sure I've behaved myself well enough for that."

"Oh, nonsense," said Browne, standing to leave. "You did exactly the right thing. Discreet inquiries. No sending for the cavalry. A plausible conclusion to a relatively simple case. As it happens, you've done us all a favor this time, whether you intended to or not. Do much better, and the next thing you know we'll be asking you to join us."

"I'm not sure whether to take that as a compliment or an insult," Banks said.

Browne chuckled and left the office, waving farewell without turning around as he went.

ACC McLaughlin set off in thinly disguised pursuit, leaving Banks only with a pointed frown that lingered like the Cheshire cat's smile.

"Coffee, Alan?" asked Gervaise.

"Please, ma'am."

Gervaise poured excellent, strong coffee from her machine. Banks popped another couple of painkillers. Of course, he knew he'd given them all the pack of lies they had wanted, but it was a plausible pack of lies. And why not? he told himself.

Gervaise fixed him with a penetrating gaze as she handed him the coffee. "Do you know the truth about what happened, Alan?"

"Yes. I think so."

"Is there anything more that needs to be done?"

As far as Banks was concerned, Anthony Litton had murdered Gavin Miller to ensure his continuing silence over Oliver's true parentage. But it could have been manslaughter. Anthony Litton, Banks also suspected very strongly, had committed suicide. But it could have been an accident. Banks had no proof of any of his suspicions, except what people had said to him in private, and he certainly wasn't going to attempt to force a DNA test on Lady Chalmers, Joe Jarvis and Oliver Litton. Anthony Litton was dead, and Lady Chalmers was free of her blackmailer. It was true that she had known what was going on, but she couldn't believe that her brother-in-law was a cold-blooded killer until he tried to murder her. Why should Oliver Litton's career suffer because of it all? He was the only true innocent in the whole business, insofar as any politician could be called innocent, except for Lady Chalmers's immediate family, Sir Jeremy, Angelina, Samantha, the daughter he hadn't met, and Oriana, of course.

There was the remote possibility that Veronica Chalmers was a great actress and that she had masterminded the whole thing, manipulated Anthony Litton into getting rid of Miller for her, even that the whole lot of them were in it together, that she had deliberately bumped Litton's car on her way out of his gates and run herself through the fence to the edge of the river, but Banks considered that highly unlikely, not being drawn to wide-ranging conspiracy theories. The more links in the chain of a conspiracy, the more likely one is to break. Anthony Litton had, after all, confessed to him that he had killed Miller, though he maintained it was an accident. There had been no sense that he had done so under instruction, and he didn't seem the kind of man to be easily manipulated. Banks could live with that.

"No," he said, and finished his coffee.

Gervaise opened her laptop computer and prepared to start typing. First, she glanced up at Banks and almost smiled at him. "Now for Christ's sake, Alan, go and get your head seen to."

15

I T WAS FOLK NIGHT AT THE DOG AND GUN. BANKS HAD a brief chat with Penny Cartwright, who was the main attraction tonight, then took his pint down to the garden wall, rested it on the stone and looked out over the meandering river and water meadows, still saturated here and there, the water right at the upper level of its banks. Back in the pub someone was singing "The Water Is Wide." A three-quarter moon shone down on it all, dripping silver on the swirling currents and casting shadows in the overhanging trees. It was one of those magical nights in late November, Indian summer perhaps, when for a short while you can forget the chills, the rain, the fogs, and that winter with its snow and freezing rain is so close. His head also felt much better, though the spot where Litton had clobbered him was still tender.

An even bigger headache had been keeping what transpired in Gervaise's office from his team, especially those closest to him: Annie, Winsome, Gerry Masterson. Fortunately, they were running out of leads. Nothing new had come up, and apart from a few further visits to the college, a chat with Miller's post-Veronica girlfriend Nancy Winterson, and a little alibi checking, there was nothing left to be done. It wasn't as if this had never happened before. Not all cases were solved quickly, and this was one that looked like it was drifting naturally towards the cold case files. Perhaps, Banks thought, at some time in the distant future, a retired detective would pick up the file and put the pieces together. By then, most likely, Oliver Litton would be long gone, and Banks and Lady Chalmers would be in their graves.

Of course, Annie, Winsome and Gerry weren't stupid, and Banks could tell they had formed their own theories about what might have happened. Gerry, in particular, having done so much research—including discovering that Lady Chalmers had been two months late back for her second year—was in a strong position to work things out, and Banks was convinced that she had perhaps guessed at least part of the truth. But whether out of caution or lack of interest, nobody had said anything about it, and the matter of Gavin Miller's death had drifted away from them, obscured by a haze of crime statistics, post office robberies and sexual assaults.

But Banks was still feeling a little sad. Though he had been able to rationalize and compartmentalize almost everything else that had happened over the past week or so, one thing that stuck in his mind was how much he had enjoyed his afternoon at the allotment with Joe Jarvis. Far from being a left-wing firebrand, the bagman, rumored to be in league with the Russians, he had been a sick man with a headful of memories and, perhaps, still some traces of revolutionary zeal, and of passion for a girl from another world he had known centuries ago. The image of the frail man, not much older than Banks himself, shrunken in on himself, lined and pinched, skin pale and dry as parchment, had haunted him for days. Their discussion about Shostakovich had ranged far and wide, and Banks had come away feeling he had learned far more than he had imparted. He had also felt a strong connection with Jarvis because their working-class roots were similar, though both were educated, or employed, out of their class.

He was also aware that there was something to be resolved that actually could be resolved, though he couldn't predict the outcome. He had a good idea how it would go, but no absolute certainty, and that was why he had postponed taking any action. Because if he was wrong, the resulting furor could destroy the very lives he wanted to protect.

Quite simply, he had wanted to tell Joe Jarvis that Ronnie Bellamy had borne him a son, and that this son was quite likely to be appointed the next home secretary. He could hardly imagine the expression on the dying miner's face when he told him, but he knew that the irony wouldn't be lost on him. There he was, a South Yorkshire miner, thorn in the side of government all his life, commie filth to many, and *his son* was going to be home secretary. Of course, it would have validated so many of Jarvis's, and Banks's, ideas about class, opportunities, the right schools and colleges, knowing the right people and all the rest, as being the only way to the top. Would Oliver Jarvis, son of a Mexborough miner, have had the same opportunities as Oliver Litton, son of a Harley Street specialist, gynecologist to the gentry, to become home secretary? Of course he wouldn't. No more than Banks had, himself. His parents had known nobody of influence, had not had the money to send him to the best schools. Besides, even if they had, he wouldn't have spoken with the right accent to be accepted there.

In protecting the wealthy and privileged, in this case Lady Chalmers and her family, Banks had denied Joe Jarvis the knowledge of his son and his achievements. For, in the end, he hadn't told him. There wasn't a day had gone by since that morning in Gervaise's office when Banks hadn't been on the verge of getting into his car and driving down to Mexborough. In the end, it was only the news that Joe Jarvis had been taken into hospital in a coma from which he was not expected to recover that stopped him. Even then, he had fantasized about turning up at Jarvis's bedside and whispering the revelation to him, imagining a slight twitch at the corner of the miner's lips, that might be an unconscious tic or the image of a smile.

But he hadn't gone.

Would the risk have been worth it? Banks didn't know. If Jarvis had been alive and kicking, in one last burst of political spirit and outrage, he might well have spilled the beans to the media and not only ruined the career of a decent, innocent man, but of a man who the lords and masters of the security services and the emergency services all wanted to see at the helm. Someone who understood their goals and their plight. So had Banks done the right thing in procrastinating? He would never know. Would Oliver Litton ever discover who his mother was? That was out of his hands, too.

For some reason, sipping his pint and gazing out over the moonlit river thinking ~~such thoughts made him~~ crave a cigarette. But the craving soon passed. Just as he glanced at his watch to check the time, a figure appeared beside him. She was wearing jeans and a dark green turtleneck jumper and carrying a brown leather shoulder bag and a glass of red wine. Banks turned to face her. "You've come," he said. He had offered to go and pick her up, but she had declined, saying she would make her own way there, and Banks had taken that as an omen that she wanted the option to change her mind.

Oriana smiled and dipped her head shyly. "Of course. I told you I would. I keep my word." She put her glass down beside his and joined him looking out over the river. "It's beautiful here," she said.

"Yes. It's a fine night. Is everything all right at Brierley House?"

"Things are OK. Everyone's still a bit down in the dumps over Tony, of course, but we're doing all right. Oliver's been up to visit."

"What did Lady Chalmers tell you?"

"About what? The accident? Nothing more than she did at first. Why?"

"No reason." Banks had wondered whether Lady Chalmers had followed his advice and told her family about Oliver's true origins. Apparently not. She might not have told Oriana, of course, but Oriana would have sensed the change in the atmosphere around the house if the secret was out. Perhaps she would get around to it in her own time, in her own way. It really wasn't his business. No more than informing Oliver Litton that his late father had tried to kill his birth mother. Though his job largely involved searching for the truth, Banks had also learned over the years that some things were better left hidden. "So you like English folk music?" he asked.

"Very much. My grandfather learned many songs in the POW camp and working in the fields. Opera was his first love, of course—he was a proud Italian, after all—but he learned many English folk songs. He taught them to me when I was young. I haven't got much of a singing voice, mind you. But I love the old songs, even if some of them are so very sad."

"Yes. There's a lot of wisdom in them, though. Like 'The Water Is Wide.' Someone was singing it just before you arrived. 'Love grows old, and waxes cold, and fades away like the morning dew.'"

Oriana gave him a curious look. "But would you really not even bother to attempt doing something because it won't last forever? Would you avoid doing something because you were afraid that it might not work out, or that you would fail? That's no life."

"Like what?"

Oriana sipped some wine and laughed. "Oh, I don't know. Like falling in love or something? Isn't that what most of the folk songs are about?"

"That or murder." Banks drank some beer. "I probably have done, on occasion."

"What, fallen in love or murdered?"

"Fallen in love. But I meant avoid something because it would inevitably end. Or probably more for fear of rejection than fear for its future, or lack of one."

"But all things end. Isn't it far better to seize the moment?"

"Probably."

"Even if it is only a moment?"

"Sometimes." Banks looked at her. She returned his gaze. Her eyes shone in the silver light. "You really are very beautiful, you know," he said.

She didn't seem to react to his words. Banks didn't know what to say, but he felt as if he were on a fulcrum. He could let the moment pass, and perhaps never find it again, or he could go the other way and seize it, despite everything, the fears, the pitfalls, the folly. He drew her to him and kissed her. She didn't resist, which was the best he could say at first, then she began to respond, to give herself up to it. Afterwards, she asked, "What did you do that for?"

"It felt like the right thing to do."

"To seize the moment?"

"Yes." Banks kissed her again. It was even better the second time.

When they drew apart, Oriana picked up her glass, took a sip and leaned her elbow on the wall, half turning to face him.

"And that one?"

"Because I wanted to."

She laughed, then her expression turned serious, and she stared into the shadows beyond the wide water. "I go away a lot."

"I know. I don't get much time off."

"And I don't really approve of the job you do."

"I don't approve of it myself, half the time."

"And you think I'm too young for you."

"I do."

"But I find most men my age far too shallow."

The music started up again inside the pub, an instrumental introduction, followed by Penny's richly textured voice singing "Queen of Hearts" to a hearty round of applause.

Oriana picked up her glass, turned and made to walk over the lawn, glancing briefly over her shoulder. "We'd better go inside," she said. "Come on. They're playing our song."

Banks remained by the wall. Then he saw her stretch out her hand behind her, as one might, perhaps, for a wayward child, and he laughed, took a step forward and grasped it. All the way to the pub he felt as if he were walking on air.

Acknowledgments

I WOULD LIKE TO THANK ALL THE PEOPLE WHO HELPED me with this book. My first reader was Sheila Halladay, who sent me back to the word processor with a few pages of notes. I think that meant a lot less work for everyone else!

At Hodder, I'd like to thank Carolyn Mays and Katy Rouse for their careful editing, and Justine Taylor for copyediting. At Morrow, thanks to Carolyn Marino and Amanda Bergeron for editing, and to Greg Villepique and Andrea Molitor for copyediting. At McClelland and Stewart, thanks to Ellen Seligman and Kendra Ward for a thorough editing job.

I would also like to thank the publicity teams—Kerry Hood and Poppy North at Hodder, Laurie Connors at Morrow, Shona Cook and Ashley Dunn at McClelland & Stewart, and Debby de Groot in Toronto.

Thanks also to my "special" agents Dominick Abel and David Grossman.

In addition, I would like to thank Nick Reckert for the interesting walks that seem to suggest so many possible crime scenes.

Finally, thanks to all the sales teams who make the deals and set up the special promotions, and to the reps who get out there on the road and sell the book.

BOOKS BY PETER ROBINSON

IN THE DARK PLACES
Hardcover, Large Print, and eBook

CHILDREN OF THE REVOLUTION
Trade Paperback, Large Print, and eBook

WATCHING THE DARK
Trade Paperback, Large Print, and eBook

BEFORE THE POISON
Trade Paperback, Large Print, and eBook

BAD BOY
Trade Paperback, Large Print, and eBook

THE PRICE OF LOVE AND OTHER STORIES
Trade Paperback and eBook

ALL THE COLORS OF DARKNESS
Trade Paperback, Large Print, and eBook

FRIEND OF THE DEVIL
Trade Paperback and eBook

PIECE OF MY HEART
Mass Market and eBook

STRANGE AFFAIR
Mass Market, Large Print, Audio CD, and eBook

PLAYING WITH FIRE
Trade Paperback, Large Print, and eBook

THE FIRST CUT
Trade Paperback and eBook

CLOSE TO HOME
Mass Market and eBook

AFTERMATH
Trade Paperback and eBook

COLD IS THE GRAVE
Mass Market and eBook

IN A DRY SEASON
Mass Market and eBook

BLOOD AT THE ROOT
Mass Market and eBook

INNOCENT GRAVES
Mass Market and eBook

BLOOD AT THE ROOT
Mass Market and eBook

INNOCENT GRAVES
Mass Market and eBook

FINAL ACCOUNT
Mass Market and eBook

WEDNESDAY'S CHILD
Mass Market

PAST REASON HATED
Mass Market

THE HANGING VALLEY
Mass Market

A NECESSARY END
Mass Market

A DEDICATED MAN
Mass Market

GALLOWS VIEW
Mass Market

Available wherever books are sold.